CROOKED SHADOW

ANDY MASLEN

TYTON PRESS

Three Kingdoms

Ivory Nation

Other Fiction:

Blood Loss – A Vampire Story

You're Always With Me (coming soon)

For Aoife and Baird McKinney

If you stand straight, do not fear a crooked shadow.
    — Chinese proverb

1

ALDEBURGH, SUFFOLK, ENGLAND

Gabriel Wolfe checked his rear-view mirror and tried to ignore the dead woman with long copper-red hair blowing around her face like flames.

He swallowed and screwed his eyes tight shut. When he opened them again, she was gone. His heart was racing.

It had been happening more and more recently. Britta Falskog, who'd lost her life just a few hundred yards away, on the stony beach, was back.

Why? It didn't make any sense. Eli, his fiancée, had shot the assassin dead on the spot. They'd attended the funeral in Sweden. Gabriel had travelled to Russia to find and kill the people behind the hit.

The tragedy was another in a long line that dotted his life like dark clouds in a summer sky. But it was over. He'd moved on. Eli had asked him to marry her – typical of their relationship that it should have been this way round – and he'd agreed. Readily. No thought of anyone but her.

He'd thought his PTSD was a thing of the past, too. In remission, if not actually cured. He didn't concern himself with the diagnostic niceties. But the flashbacks had gone. So, too, the waking nightmares when a dead comrade, Michael 'Smudge' Smith, would appear in the most unexpected places, jaw hanging off, or missing altogether.

So why the hell was Britta Falskog back in his life? What was she telling him?

Britta had got close to him. And she'd paid with her life. Now Eli was embarking on the same course of action. And he was terrified the same fate would befall her.

No. He wouldn't let it. He couldn't. Mustn't. He shook his head violently. Pushed the thoughts down.

He inhaled deeply and sighed the breath out again. He gripped Lucille's fat-rimmed steering wheel and turned the key. The Camaro's engine turned over with a slow, purposeful cough.

He backed out of the narrow drive, inching past the white-painted gate post. He reflected, not for the first time, that owning a car designed for the spacious driveways, suburban avenues and six-lane freeways of America came with drawbacks. Most notably when confronted with Britain's narrower, twistier and altogether less-forgiving roads.

But the car was a gift from the widow of a friend. And, for that reason, hard to let go.

Gabriel reversed across the narrow strip of Tarmac that separated his house from the car park at the end of Slaughden Road. He waved to the owner of the boatyard that neighboured his property and then stuck the transmission into Drive and pulled away.

Aldeburgh was busy this particular Friday morning. Holidaymakers ambled along the pavements licking ice creams and peering in the windows of the artsy gift shops that flourished in this chi-chi town on the Suffolk coast.

Gabriel nodded to a couple of people he knew coming the other way down the High Street and then, when he reached the outskirts of the town, gave the Camaro its head.

The speed limit was sixty, but he felt no compunction in flouting the law. As a Department operative, he had a plastic card in his wallet that functioned as a literal Get Out Of Jail Free Card. But that wasn't why he took the big black muscle car up to eighty, and then ninety as the road straightened out.

If he was pulled over, he'd take the points on his licence, and the fine, on the chin. But there was something inside him, some compulsion, that drove him, whip and spur, to take himself to the limits. Behind the wheel or with a knife or a pistol in his hand, it was the same feeling.

He'd sometimes wondered whether it was a death wish of a kind. But he'd dismissed it. After meeting, and then becoming engaged to Eli, he'd rediscovered such a zest for life that the thought of dying, in action or even in bed, had become truly abhorrent to him. In fact, for the first time in his adult life, the fear of death had crept into his consciousness.

He'd talked to Eli about it. She'd tried to reassure him. Said it was normal for people in their occupation. Hell, it was normal, full stop. And who, or what, did he think he was? Superman?

They were just human beings. Men and women. Everybody felt scared from time to time. Had he told her about the visions of Britta? No. He had not. It wasn't fair to load that onto her as well.

Now she was far away, somewhere in South America. A Department op. Total dark.

He'd never been a religious man. He'd seen too much evil to believe in the idea of an all-good, all-knowing, all-powerful God. Eli did. With reservations. Being Jewish, the Holocaust tested her belief to the absolute limits. Somehow, though, she had retained her faith.

But religious or not, he wanted so desperately for her to return to him in one piece – one alive piece – that he'd found himself praying for her safety, night after night.

He didn't imagine a particular end for himself. Though he had a wide and varied mental library of possibilities, none of them involving soft, line-dried sheets smelling of the sea and the meadow flowers in his back garden.

It was more a vague sense of unease. A feeling that, after so many years facing down dangers of almost unimaginable intensity, he'd become aware of his own mortality.

Where once he'd thought only of the mission, or the people alongside whom he was fighting, now he thought of himself, too. And his future.

He tried to channel the feeling into greater preparedness. Checking kit even more thoroughly. Assessing new situations with even greater attention to tiny details. Reading and re-reading briefing notes until the small hours. Striving, always, to identify flaws others might have missed that could compromise the mission and put his life in danger.

Because despite its outwardly devil-may-care image within the security apparatus, The Department was run, ultimately, by bureaucrats. People without skin in the game. Even Don Webster, Gabriel's former CO in the SAS and now boss of his new outfit, was little more than an office-bound paper-pusher these days.

Don had complained about it himself. Nearer seventy than sixty, his rifle-wielding days were long behind him. But still the old warhorse – friends and rivals alike called him 'Dobbin' – yearned for the harness. The weight of armour. The clash of steel and the whine of bullets.

Now that belonged to the operatives. People like Gabriel and Eli. Others, too, though The Department operated on a decentralised basis and teams were kept separate for security reasons. No regimental dinners, annual parades or even casual meals at discreet restaurants for them.

Where had this sudden anxiety about death come from? He thought he knew. Partly, his forthcoming marriage to Eli. An event he'd once thought was for other people. Then, after proposing to Britta and, ultimately, being rejected, as something out of his reach.

Eli had made a play for him early on in their relationship, which until then he'd seen as purely professional. But after Britta's murder, their partnership had deepened into intimacy and then love. And now they were on the cusp of a life together, as man and wife. Or, given that Eli had proposed to Gabriel, as woman and husband.

Either way, Gabriel had something he cared desperately about for the first time in his life since his brother's death.

So, there was Eli. And another woman who had entered his life in an unexpected way. Wei Mei, his sister. Christened Tara Wolfe and kidnapped as a six-month-old baby and lost to the family for good, everybody assumed. She'd been working in Hong Kong as a bodyguard to a now-dead triad leader. Now she ran the triad herself and was gradually moving its considerable funds into legitimate businesses.

He dabbed the brake to scrub a little speed off as he approached a sweeping left-hand curve in the road. Beneath him, he felt the mass of the car shift on the suspension as it settled into the bend at a steady fifty-five.

Some engineer in Detroit had done a good job of setting up the Camaro's steering, and he could feel every undulation and patch of loose grit on the road surface through his fingertips. He smiled as the nearside wheels flirted with the edge of the Tarmac at the apex of the bend.

He glanced up at the rear-view mirror and his stomach jumped. Had he just seen her again? A flash of copper in the hedgerow? He looked again. But she'd gone. Maybe it had just been sun striking some reddish foliage. He forced himself to smile. *Just enjoy the drive, Wolfe.*

A white car with orange lights flashing on its roof and grille filled the windscreen. Its horn blared.

He reared back in his seat. Gripped the wheel tighter.

Behind the car trundled a huge low-loader. It carried a bright green-and-yellow combine harvester. The unwieldy combo took up three-quarters of the entire width of the road.

His stomach plunged. Adrenaline surged though his bloodstream, recalibrating his systems. Fast.

His heart rate doubled. His pulse dilated. His palms became slick with sweat. Time slowed down. Another effect of the adrenaline.

The car driver was leaning on the horn. Gabriel had time to register the open-mouthed look of horror on his face.

Swerving left, the car hit the soft verge, slewed sideways and rolled over, smashing through the hedge bordering the road.

Pieces of plastic trim flew up in the air, arcing left and right.

The driver of the low-loader had no such option. The massive vehicle and its unwieldy load must have weighed twenty tonnes or more. Its inertia dictated it would stay on course.

Gabriel swerved right, close enough to the low-loader's cab to see the screaming face of the driver and ploughed through the same hedge that the escort car had ripped through. Fifty yards further on, he skidded to a halt in a wheat field.

Mercifully, his passage through the hedge had not triggered the Camaro's air bags. Gabriel sat with his hands still clamped to the steering wheel, chest heaving.

Reality seemed heightened. The wheat outside his window gleamed gold. The trees on the far side of the field glowed with vivid greens. He wrenched open his door and climbed out, wincing as he knocked an already bruised shin on the door frame. He ran back to where the car was lying on its side.

He leaned down to look into the cabin. The driver was unconscious, hanging in his seat belt. Gabriel smelled petrol. He searched for the source. And found it. Beneath the car, fuel spewed from the ruptured tank, staining the tawny earth a dark oxblood.

Gabriel climbed up onto the side of the car and pulled the door open. The stink of petrol was stronger in here. But the engine was off, so he was confident the vapour wouldn't ignite.

He slithered inside, past the driver, and unclipped his seatbelt. The unconscious man slumped sideways and Gabriel lowered him onto the inner side of the passenger door.

There was no way he could lift the guy out of the driver's door above their heads. He needed to get the car onto its wheels again, then drag the man free.

Gabriel hoisted himself up, using the centre console as a step. He pushed his way out of the door and swung down over the side of the car. The door above him slammed shut with a bang.

He heard a shout. Turning, he saw two men running across the field towards him.

'Get back!' he yelled. 'Fuel leak!'

They ran on for a few more steps, then stopped. He turned away, back to the car. He ran round to the roof side and started rocking it forwards and backwards, allowing the momentum to build a little with each pendulum-like swing.

This was the big risk. As he pushed the car down onto its wheels, a metal part could scrape against another and produce a spark. And then?

Game over.

Nobody would survive the fireball. He'd seen enough roadside IEDs go off to know what a burnt-out car did to its occupants. And he felt it again. That momentary flash of fear. What if? it said. What if it *does* blow up? He pushed it away. He wasn't going to leave a man to die.

He kept pushing.

The car reached the balance point.

He let it swing back towards him one more time, then, as the car began its final traverse away from him, he pushed harder and, as his muscles screamed, felt it reach, then overtake, the tipping point.

With a thump and a crack as the windscreen crazed and sagged inwards, the car fell through ninety degrees and came to rest on its wheels.

Gabriel raced round and dragged the passenger door open. The driver flopped halfway through the aperture. Face bloody. Eyes closed. Still out cold.

He grabbed the man under his arms and heaved him free, hoping he'd no broken bones, especially a rib that could puncture a lung.

As the guy's feet hit the earth, Gabriel leaned backwards and propelled himself away from the car with his heels. After going ten feet, he yelled out.

'Help me!'

The two others ran forward. He heard their boots thumping on the hard earth, and the swish of the wheat stalks.

'You, his waist. You, his ankles,' Gabriel said, shifting his grip under the man's armpits.

They took a few staggering steps, finding their rhythm. Gabriel breathed a sigh of relief.

Behind them, the petrol vapour ignited with a *whoomp*.

'Faster!' Gabriel urged.

They took a few more staggering steps, then the petrol tank exploded.

The blast threw them all to the ground. The orange fireball boiled up into the air above their heads. Gabriel felt the intense heat sear his skin.

Something hit him in the back. Left side. High up. He reached over his shoulder and his questing fingertips closed on a jagged piece of glass. Not in too deep. He'd have known. The adrenaline meant no pain. For now.

His ears ringing, Gabriel picked himself up. The two men from the low-loader were getting to their knees. Wide, white eyes stared from blackened faces. Their mouths were hanging open. They seemed stunned.

He'd seen it before. Battlefield shock. Civilians caught up in a firefight. Blast victims sitting in lakes of blood – theirs and other people's – after a suicide bombing on a London bus.

He grabbed the nearest man by his shoulders and brought their faces to within inches of each other.

'We have to get him to safety. He's badly hurt.'

Nodding, but otherwise expressionless, the man got to his feet. Together with Gabriel, he pulled his colleague upright.

Together, they carried the driver well away from the car and laid him on his back near the edge of the field.

Gabriel began methodically checking the unconscious man for injuries. He found a pulse beneath his jaw, weak, but steady.

As gently as he could, he ran his palms over the arms then legs. No major breaks. He bent his ear to the man's nose and listened to his breathing. It was slow and deep, but he could hear no rasping or bubbling that might indicate a punctured lung.

'The ambulance is on its way,' the taller of the two men. He glared down at Gabriel. 'And the police.'

'Good,' Gabriel said. He felt a flash of pain from his left shoulder blade and half-turned away. 'What've I got stuck in my back?'

The man peered down.

'Looks like a wing mirror.'

2

It could have been worse. That's what Gabriel was thinking as he left Ipswich Magistrates Court on Elm Street. It could have been a complete nightmare. Three points on his licence and a three hundred pound fine, he could cope with. His lawyer had pleaded extenuating circumstances and pointed out that Gabriel had saved a man's life.

Shaking his head, he crossed the road to the carpark and found his hire car: a Toyota Yaris hatchback. Compared to the Camaro's overpowered V8, the little car's motor was comically tinny. Grinning despite himself, he pulled out, carefully, into the mid-morning traffic.

Yes. It could have been a lot worse. The car driver could have died, burnt to a crisp inside his car. The low-loader could have overturned, dumping God knew how many tens of thousands of pounds' worth of high-end agricultural machinery into the ditch.

A new thought struck him. *He* could have been killed. He dismissed it. Never would have happened. Hadn't he avoided the collision? So he'd had to drive through a hedge and into a wheat field? That was what reactions were for.

In fact, now he thought about it, the real problem wasn't his driving at all. He'd been well inside the speed limit. The problem was the Camaro. Too heavy, too wide, too *American* for British roads. In something lighter and nimbler, he'd have been able to squeeze round both the escort car and the low-loader.

Reaching the scenic route that led due east towards the coast, he negotiated the twisting bends with a level of care he felt sure the magistrates would have approved of. Definitely due care and attention.

So, if not the Camaro, which he could easily put into storage, what then? He thought back fondly to his deep-blue Maserati GT. He'd loved that car, right up to the point a contract killer called Sasha Beck blew it up with an anti-tank weapon.

She'd been driving an Aston Martin that day. Maybe that was the way to go. Buy British. He nodded. After an Italian thoroughbred and a 'Yank Tank', he should go down the patriotic route.

An Aston like Sasha's? He could afford it. The money in the Swiss bank account lay untouched. And he had other accounts in the UK he hardly used. But it was too obvious, and, in his line of work, he could just imagine Don's laconic response if he turned up in one. *Very nice, Old Sport. Thinking of changing our name to Bond, are we?* No, Astons were out.

He glanced sideways. Two chestnut horses were racing around a paddock, kicking out their hind legs and shaking their manes. Prancing for the sheer joy of it. When was the last time *he'd* done anything for sheer joy?

Getting engaged to Eli counted. For sure. But it was a moment in time. A heart-burstingly happy punctuation mark in a long, dark sentence of increasingly bloody events, from Iran to Siberia, Hong Kong to South Africa.

He shook his head and looked back at the road ahead. Forced himself to return to the business of choosing a car. British, but not built by some multinational. Something small, quick and agile. A McLaren, maybe. Or a Lotus.

When he got back to the house he called the garage repairing the Camaro. The conversation was brief, but highly informative.

He'd managed to trash the whole front end, gouge the sides in spectacular fashion and do various bits of expensive damage to the alloy wheels and suspension.

'How much?' he asked when the garage guy had finished.

'All in, including the virtually total respray you need, I'm afraid it's at least ten thou. The Camaro's a nice car, but your insurers might want to write it off.'

Gabriel had foreseen this. He had no intention of claiming. He'd already agreed with the other driver's insurance company to pay for a replacement car in cash. And no way was he going to permit some clerk in an insurance office to write off Vinnie Calder's pride and joy.

'Do the work, please,' he said. 'I'll be happy to pay whatever it takes.'

'You're the boss.'

The call ended, Gabriel made a pot of tea and took everything out to the garden on a tray. He chose a spot where he could look out over the flat, marshy land sitting between his house and the River Alde.

His phone rang. He looked down and sighed.

'Hi, Don.'

'Hello, Old Sport. How did it go this morning?'

'You knew about that, did you?'

'I make it my business to know what my people get up to in their own time. Up to and including having their collars felt for what we might loosely call minor motoring offences.'

Gabriel scratched the back of his head. Trust Don to have feelers that stretched even as far as Ipswich Magistrates Court.

'Three points and three hundred to Her Maj,' he said.

'Don't be flippant, Gabriel. It wasn't clever. At all. That driver's lucky to be alive.'

Gabriel felt his pulse tick up. 'I know. Because I saved his life. The magistrate made a point of mentioning it.'

'*My* point,' Don said, steel entering his voice, 'is that *you* were lucky, too. Lucky you didn't cause a man's death. And your own, I hasten to add. Not sure how Eli would have taken that news when she returned home.'

'I'm sorry. It was a one-in-a-million chance. You should have seen the size of the truck. I—'

'I *did* see the size of it. I also saw the photographs of the burnt-out car in the field, an unconscious driver with concussion, and the piece of crap sticking out of your left shoulder blade like a bloody angel's wing coming in.'

Gabriel heard real anger in Don's voice now. Why was he reacting so strongly? Surely other Department operatives got into scrapes worse than this without having their ears chewed off.

'Boss, I'm really sorry. What do you want me to say?'

Don was making the humming sound he produced when he was thinking. Breathing in and out through his nose: 'Hmm, mm-hmm.' Finally, he spoke.

'It's not what I want you to say, or not to me, at any rate. It's what I want you to do.'

'Which is?'

'When was the last time you went to see Fariyah?'

Ah. Now he understood. It was true, Gabriel hadn't been to see his psychiatrist for a while. He thought back. A year? More? He couldn't remember.

'I can't remember exactly. But I'm fine in that area, boss. Really.'

'I want you to see her anyway. If you're right as rain, good. She can let me know without breaking any confidences and life goes on as normal.'

'What are you saying?'

'I'm saying, Old Sport, that I don't like it when my people become noticeable. Bad for business. You're one of my top operators, but I need to know you're reliable.'

'It was a road accident, boss, that's all. I didn't go crazy in Ipswich town centre with a M16.'

'Please don't fight me on this,' Don said. He sounded weary, now, rather than angry. 'Talk to Fariyah. Maybe the accident was just bad luck. It happens, Lord knows I've had a few near-misses in the old Jensen before now,' he said. 'But she has her methods, as you know. It'll be a chance for you to get a professional opinion. Think of it as a check-up. Nothing more. I'm not about to bench you or ask for your badge and gun.'

Gabriel realised he'd run out of road, and agreed. After a few more pleasantries, Don ended the call, pleading a meeting.

3

Fariyah told him she was booked solid for a week. 'Even for old friends like you, Gabriel,' she added, presumably in an attempt to soften the blow.

Gabriel didn't mind. He felt he'd been sent rather than volunteering, so the delay didn't bother him.

The appointment was at her home in Hampstead. He'd visited her in the leafy north London enclave once before and parked the Toyota outside the grand Victorian house with five minutes to spare.

Feelingly suddenly nervous and not knowing why, he climbed the stone steps up to the front door and rang the bell. He straightened his jacket and fiddled with his shirt collar, which was rubbing his neck.

The door opened. Fariyah smiled, her deep-brown eyes crinkling at the corners. Today her hijab was in a soft gold, shot through with strands of bright pink.

'Gabriel, come in,' she said, standing aside and holding the wide front door open for him.

A strong smell of burnt toast his assailed his nostrils. 'Someone nuke their breakfast?'

She laughed. 'That would be Juno. Brains of a Nobel prize winner, practical skills of a wombat.'

Gabriel accepted her offer of a coffee and then followed her from the kitchen to her consulting room, a conservatory built onto the back of the house, giving onto a large, rambling garden.

She motioned for him to take a low armchair upholstered in a nubbly cream fabric. He placed his mug on a side table, noting, as he always did, the box of tissues placed strategically near the client's chair.

Fariyah gathered up a pen and notebook and placed both on a black leather folder on her lap. Since he'd last seen her she had gained some weight, though he thought it suited her, rounding out her curves rather than making her look fat.

He rubbed the back of his head and scratched at his right ear, which had suddenly started itching furiously. Then he caught her watching him and snatched his hand away. That felt like a giveaway so he went back to running his fingers through his hair. He tried for a smile but it felt tight, forced. He abandoned the attempt.

Why wouldn't she say something? Bloody head-shrinkers. It was like being observed by a zoo keeper. What did that make him, then? A captive animal? Caged? Under observation? Well, of course it did! That was the whole point of being here, wasn't it?

He cracked.

'Long time, no see,' he said, picking up his coffee and taking a sip.

It really was very good. Under different circumstances he'd have really enjoyed the flavour.

'How have you been?' she asked.

He was relieved to see her soft, plump hands stayed resting in her lap. No attempt to pick up the pen and start scribbling.

'Me? Good! Yeah, really good.'

He stopped. Had he really just said that out loud? How was that for the phoniest ever statement made by a patient to a psychiatrist?

She nodded. 'Oh, good. Well, in that case, I suppose we're done here. You can go and I'll let Don know you're as right as rain.'

The trouble was, she made no attempt to rise from her own

chair. Gabriel knew she wouldn't, either. She was simply waiting for him to start being truthful. And why was he finding it so hard this time? He'd shared his most painful memories with this softly spoken woman over the previous five years or so and she'd never been anything other than understanding, non-judgemental and, above all, compassionate.

He sighed out a breath.

'Sorry.'

She raised her thick, curved eyebrows.

'For what, exactly?'

'For lying. The truth is, I'm not fine at all. Not by a long chalk.'

'Tell me, then. What brought you to my door this time?'

He looked at her and wondered where to begin. With the accident? The proximate cause of his making an appointment? Or with the disturbing flashes of his dead ex-fiancée. A memory flickered into life like a slide projector firing up in a darkened room. A village so far out in the Chinese hinterland it was closer to Kazakhstan than Beijing.

He'd been sitting under a tree chatting to a lorry driver nicknamed Little Dog. They'd been sharing a few details of their personal lives and Gabriel had told him about Eli.

'Have you got a photo?' he'd asked, and Gabriel had to admit he did not.

Frowning, Little Dog produced a folded but clearly much-treasured colour photo of his own fiancée, a schoolteacher. Gabriel sent the memory packing.

'I'm engaged,' he said.

Fariyah's face broke into a smile. 'Congratulations! Tell me all about her. It is a "her", I assume?'

He smiled. 'Very open-minded of you, even though you knew about Britta. Yes, she is a she. Her name's Eli Schochat. She's Israeli. We met through work.'

'Well, apart from being extremely good to hear, I think it says a great deal about your psychological state if you felt ready to commit to a lifelong partnership with a person, rather than just the job.'

'You knew about Britta, though.'

'I did, yes. But, and please don't think I am speaking ill of the dead, especially since I never met her, but your proposal to Britta always seemed hasty to me. As if you were trying to strap yourself into a life you weren't ready for.'

He shook his head. 'I think you're probably right. But the thing is, I don't carry a photo of Eli in my wallet.'

She frowned, a quick expression, little more than a couple of fine lines on her forehead, then they were gone.

'That doesn't mean anything. I'm sure you have plenty on your phone.'

'No. None. What does that mean, do you think?'

Fariyah finished her coffee and set the mug down on the table between them before answering.

'What do you think it means?'

He frowned. He supposed he shouldn't have expected Fariyah to tell him what things meant. Her job was to help him arrive at the meanings of things himself, steering him here, nudging him like a reluctant horse when he strayed away from the path.

'I don't know. It could mean I've been too busy to take a photo of her.'

'Really,' Fariyah said flatly, not even bothering to disguise her opinion by framing it as a question.

'OK, not that. I just …' He scratched at the top of his head furiously, 'what if something happens to her? Because of me? I'll be left like one of those sad-sack blokes who never clear out their wife's clothes after they've died. Just clutching a, a *fucking* photo because that's all they have left.'

His pulse was racing. Oh. So they'd got to that point in the conversation already, had they?

'Does Eli have pictures of you?' Fariyah asked.

'Yes. Loads. She's always taking them. Selfies. The two of us, I mean. Or just me on my own, when I'm not looking.'

'What do you think Eli would do if something happened to you? And I'm assuming, given your line of work, we're talking about being killed,' she added.

Gabriel puffed out his cheeks. 'I don't know. She'd grieve, I suppose. She's Jewish so she'd probably sit *shiva*. And then she'd go back to work and pick up the pieces of her life and find a way to live with it.'

'That sounds about right. You know, people get married all the time and they never think their spouse is going to die,' she said. 'But everybody dies, Gabriel. In the end. Not because they're shot or blown up either. Just illness, or an accident or just old age. Death is *part* of life. It's no reason to avoid other parts of life, like marriage or having children.'

He reared back in the soft chair and bumped his head on the wall behind him.

'We're not having kids!'

'No?'

'Of course not!'

She smiled. 'Why "of course"?'

'Fariyah, come on. You know what we do for a living. Can you really see Eli sitting at home changing nappies while I'm off taking out the country's enemies?'

'Never having met her, I don't know. So you wouldn't consider taking on those responsibilities yourself?'

Was that a mischievous twinkle in her eye? Gabriel thought it must be. He grinned. 'You're playing me. Very clever.'

She shook her head. 'Not at all. But let's tease what you said apart a little, shall we? Obviously being an operative for The Department would preclude also being an active parent. But there are plenty of people who work for HMG in the armed forces and the security services who are also married and have children.'

'Yeah, of course. But not when both are field agents.'

'Not both parents, no. But you seem very sure that Eli would want to stay in harness rather than become a mother.'

'That's a bit sexist, isn't it?'

'Well unless you know something I don't, at the very least, the woman has to take time off work to give birth. Let's not go too far down this rabbit hole. It doesn't sound like you've discussed it with Eli, in any case, so it's moot.'

'Agreed,' Gabriel said, relieved that Fariyah would stop pushing him on the subject of becoming a father.

'So no photos,' Fariyah said. 'I wonder why?'

'It could be a security thing.'

'It could. Have you photos of her at home?'

Gabriel bit his lip. 'No.'

Fariyah offered him a searching gaze. He hated it when she did this. Not speaking, just looking at him. It always made him feel the same way: that she was seeing his thoughts projected onto a screen.

He felt suddenly uncomfortable and got up from the chair and crossed to the window. The mid-October sun was slanting across the garden, rendering the red leaves of a tall Japanese maple translucent. Other trees were losing their leaves altogether, and the lawn was scattered with brown, yellow and orange pyramids.

'Is there something you're not telling me?' Fariyah asked from her chair.

Gabriel turned. She was twisted round and still scrutinising him.

He returned to sit facing her. Found his pulse had returned to normal. Maybe it was because he'd decided to be honest. Might as well tell her and get it over with.

He scratched his left cheekbone, running his fingertips over the thin scar there, noticing the lack of feeling on that narrow strip of skin.

'I've started seeing Britta again.' He noticed the flicker of incomprehension on Fariyah's face. 'Like before. Her ghost. You'd probably call it a visual hallucination. But it's her.'

Now Fariyah did pick up her notebook; she jotted down a couple of sentences. She returned her questioning gaze to Gabriel.

'How often has she been appearing to you?'

'Every few days.'

'Any particular circumstances? Anything you feel might be triggering her to appear?'

'You make it sound like she's making the decision to appear. Like she's real.'

Fariyah nodded. 'We can call her "it" if you'd prefer, but we both know that Britta meant a great deal to you. Just because a person dies, their influence on us doesn't disappear. Hallucinations, ghosts if you prefer, can be our way of holding onto a person. What do you think she's trying to tell you?'

'I was hoping you'd tell me.'

'Indulge me, Gabriel,' Fariyah said with a gentle smile.

Gabriel closed his eyes and rubbed hard on the lids: orange blobs split and coalesced on his retinas. He thought back to the last day he'd spent with Britta.

They'd walked on the beach: she, him and Eli. Laughing, bantering, enjoying a few carefree moments between missions. Then she stumbled and the hitman sent by Russian gangsters to annihilate Gabriel shot her dead by mistake. He'd paid with his life, Eli had seen to that. But Britta died instantly.

'Britta took a bullet meant for me. She's telling me that I can't protect people. Eli, I mean.' He opened his eyes. 'Does that sound plausible?'

'It sounds entirely plausible: you take Britta's appearance as a reminder that you aren't strong enough to protect those you love. And that, therefore, you shouldn't become close to anyone in case they die,' she said. 'But it's equally possible that she's simply reminding you of a fact of life. We are born. We live. We die. Perhaps Britta is telling you to pay more attention to the middle part of the story.'

She may have been right. The trouble was, Gabriel could understand what she was saying on a purely rational basis. It was just, he didn't accept it on the emotional level. Time for another confession.

'After I saw her the last time, I almost killed myself, and another man. I was driving and I took a bend too fast,' he said. 'I avoided a collision but we both went through a hedge and his car turned over. He was trapped. I got him out before his car exploded, but it was close. It's like I have a death wish.'

Fariyah's brow furrowed.

'Did you see her then, as well?'

'No. I don't think so. Just me.'

'I'd be very careful thinking in terms of death wishes. You had a car accident. So do thousands of people every day. Millions, if we open it out to the world,' she said. 'Not everyone who almost kills themselves behind the wheel has a death wish. Sometimes it's just plain old bad luck. Or carelessness, if you prefer.'

'Look, Fariyah, we could go on talking about this all day. But what I need is something practical. Don sent me because he thinks I'm out of control. So what can I do about it? I don't want it all to start up again.'

He didn't have to say what he meant. Fariyah had treated him for his PTSD for several years, and, together, they'd beaten it. Or at least, beaten it back into a deep, dark hole from where it couldn't reach up to Gabriel's conscious mind to hurt him.

She smiled. 'Ever the practical man. OK, let's talk about strategies. When did Britta start reappearing to you?'

Gabriel shrugged. 'I don't know. Six months ago? A year?'

'And has anything else happened during that time that might have disturbed you emotionally?'

Gabriel snorted. 'You *do* know what my day job is like, don't you?'

Fariyah inclined her head. 'Aside from the high-stakes operations Don sends you on.'

He saw it then. And wondered why he hadn't mentioned it to Fariyah right at the beginning. He told her now.

'I located my sister. She was kidnapped when she was a baby. She lives in Hong Kong.'

Once more, Fariyah's eyebrows lifted. 'A fiancée *and* a sister! How old is she?'

'Mei's thirty-eight.'

'And you hadn't seen her in all that time?'

'No.'

'How was it, meeting a long-lost sister?'

'It was amazing. Like we'd always known each other. I mean, we're still filling in all the gaps – basically our whole lives are gaps – but there's a connection.'

'Which is fantastic. And even more of a reason to focus on the life you're living, rather than the deaths you're fearing. You said she was kidnapped.'

'Yes, by low-level triad members. They were tipped off by a police officer. He was Special Branch, assigned to protect my parents. And their children.'

'Was he ever caught?'

'No. No, he wasn't.'

'Perhaps you should start there, then. You see, Gabriel, your family life, right from infancy, was marred by tragedy. You're about to get married, and, whether you like it or not, I am sure Eli will at least be thinking about children. That is not sexist, by the way,' she added, 'just biology. I think your fears about being unable to protect Eli are actually projections from your childhood, when your parents were unable to protect you or your siblings. You worry about Eli, which is natural, up to a point, And you reacted quite strongly when I suggested you might yourself become a parent. Perhaps you need to resolve those feelings of guilt by finding the man who kidnapped your sister.'

'And then what? Killing him? That's not part of your advice, is it? I'm sure there's something in the code of practice about suggesting assassinations.'

Fariyah smiled. 'Perhaps you could step outside your normal *modus operandi* and have him arrested.'

Gabriel nodded. 'Maybe I could, at that.'

4

The burly man with a livid scar bisecting his face approached his boss. He was nervous, despite having found and detained the suspect.

The boss had a violent and unpredictable temper. Smiling and joking, sharing out the sweet, nutty pastries he'd bought at the baker's one minute; the next, barking out the foulest insults and smacking people around with his fists.

'Ratko, I found him,' the burly man said, shoving his captive forwards with a hard push between his shoulder blades that sent him stumbling into the boss's office.

Popović looked up from that day's *International Herald Tribune* and smiled at his subordinate. Who found his expression – glittering blue eyes and a flash of pointed white teeth – anything but reassuring.

'Well done, Miro. I knew I could trust you.' He pointed to a corner of the office. 'Stand there. In case I need you.'

Miroslav did as he was told. In truth, if the boss had told him to remove one of his fingers with the razor-sharp knife he kept perpetually on his belt, he would have asked which one.

The boss inspired that kind of compliance. He called it respect. Most of those who worked for him, apart from the psychos, saw it more in the way of the old joke. What do you call a gorilla with a machine gun? Whatever it wants you to.

Popović turned his attention to the man Miroslav had brought back from the financial district. He was an international treasury manager with Erste Bank Serbia. His name was Erich Kanstner and he had relocated to Novi Sad from Frankfurt three years earlier.

Miroslav had found it childishly easy to detain Kanstner. He'd simply waited at a pavement cafe opposite the bank headquarters on Bulevar Mihajla Pupina.

When his mark appeared, as he did every day, at 12.30 p.m. to walk the hundred metres to a Turkish restaurant, Miroslav closed in. He approached him from behind and to the left and tapped him on the shoulder. Kanstner turned to find the point of Miroslav's pigsticker denting the left-hand side of his shirt, just over the soft place above his belt.

Miroslav suggested, in a friendly but urgent tone, that perhaps Kanstner would like to climb into Miroslav's Skoda and take a trip out to the country.

And now the German banker, who had become literally fat on the money the boss was paying him, had crossed a line. Miroslav felt kind of sorry for Kanstner. He was trembling: the movement so violent it was actually shaking his pallid jowls. Miroslav shrugged off the fleeting wave of sympathy. Kanstner had brought it on himself.

The boss had once explained to Miroslav how the money laundering business worked. He followed it about as far as the boss getting money from some heavyweight oligarch in Russia and then transferring it into other businesses in other, what did he call them? Jurisdictions? Maybe.

Anyway, somehow, you put the money into a bank and the guys on the inside did some kind of financial magic and lo! and behold, the money came out the other side clean as a baby's arse with a fresh diaper.

To be honest, a lot of the financial details went straight over

Miroslav's head. But the one thing he remembered was when the boss said you had to expect the bankers to skim off the top.

Five percent was the accepted amount. The boss called it 'shrinkage'. It made a kind of sense to Miroslav. The cash pile sent from Moscow did shrink as it passed through each new pair of hands.

The boss took his cut for washing the cash. The bankers took theirs. And, he supposed, there were others somewhere up or down the chain who also feathered their nests. But when the amounts ran into the tens of millions every year, it didn't seem to matter.

So why was Kanstner standing before the boss in his wood-panelled office looking like he was about to shit his pants, or faint, or both?

The oldest reason. Miroslav smirked. Not quite. Because the oldest was pussy, wasn't it? OK, the second oldest. Greed. Yes, unfortunately for him, Erich Kanstner had let greed get the better of him.

The boss had stopped smiling. His craggy features had returned to his usual expression. Like he wanted to hurt somebody. His silvery moustache and beard, cropped close below his hollow cheekbones, glinted in the light spearing in through the windows.

'You know, Erich,' he said, 'my grandmother had a favourite saying. Do you want to hear it?'

Kanstner puts his hands out. 'Ratko, please, I can explain.'

The boss pooched his lips out and shook his head, holding up a hand for silence.

'And you'll have your chance. In a moment. But first, humour me. Would you like to hear my *baka*'s proverb?'

'Yes, then.'

'Good. It goes like this.' The boss cleared his throat. '"It is better to make money in the straw market than to lose it in the money market." Now, what do you suppose that means?'

Kanstner's lower lip was trembling. Miroslav looked on with feelings of disgust. The banker ought to show more spine.

'I don't know, Ratko. Please, let me—'

'You see, *I* think it means honest work is better than speculation.'

Then he shot out a hard-edged laugh that made Kanstner flinch. 'Probably just a load of old shit! Who knows.' He lowered his voice so Kanstner had to lean forward. 'The thing is, Erich, when those I work for entrust me with their business, they have certain *expectations*. I, too, have expectations. One of these expectations is that I am not going to lose my business partners' cash in the money market. Or by no more than what everyone agrees is a reasonable percentage for expenses, risk-mitigation and so on. Tell me, do I compensate you adequately for the work you do for me?'

'Yes, Ratko. Of course. I'm sorry. I can explain.'

The boss frowned, grooving deep lines into his forehead.

'Yes, so you keep saying. The problem is that your explanation won't bring the money back. Or will it? Can you repay the—' He looked over at Miroslav. 'What did I say the amount was, Miro?'

Glad to have something to contribute, Miroslav stood straighter. 'Fourteen-point-seven-five million US.'

The boss smiled. This time the expression looked genuine enough. Miroslav relaxed. A little.

'Thanks, Miro. Yes, Erich, you have stolen the thick end of fifteen million dollars from me and, indirectly, the people I work for. Over and above the five percent you've been skimming. And the generous monthly payment I make to your Swiss bank account. Am I missing something? Were the terms of our initial agreement insufficiently attractive?'

'No. But, Ratko, I can get it. I can repay you.'

'When?'

'Not now, obviously, but soon.'

'How soon?'

'Well, I don't know. These things take time. I'll have to figure out a way to move some of the bank's own funds around.'

The boss shook his head. Then he scratched his silvery beard. In the silence of the sound-proofed office, Miroslav could hear the boss's fingernails raking through the tough, wiry bristles.

'There you are, you see. You *can't* pay it back. Which is awkward for me, because I have to report to my partners tomorrow, do you see? Tomorrow, Erich,' he said. 'And if they see a fifteen-million-dollar-shaped hole in the accounts, well, let's just say they won't be best pleased. Fortunately for me, I can cover the loss with a temporary financial manoeuvre of my own.'

Miroslav watched the German relax. Bad mistake.

'How long can you give me, Ratko?' Kanstner asked.

The boss's boomerang-shaped eyebrows shot up. 'What? No, I'm sorry, Erich, you've got hold of the wrong end of the stick. You and I? We're done.' He looked over at Miroslav.

'Take him out the back.'

Miroslav strode forward and gripped Kanstner's right bicep and led him out of the office, down the hallway and through a narrow door into the yard at the back of the boss's country house. House! Ha! That was a laugh. It was a castle. A real one. Left over from the days of the Hapsburg Empire, apparently. Anyway, a stone-built fortress high in the hills with turrets, a crenelated wall around the outside and only one steep pathway in.

A large corrugated-iron barn occupied the concrete yard's southern side. Inside, stolen cars – high-end German models, mostly – waited to be ringed before shipping on to Bosnia, Croatia, Montenegro and Kosovo.

In the centre of the yard stood a hay rick. The boss had Miroslav and a couple of the boys building it at first light, using a trailer-load of straw he'd bought from his nearest neighbour. They'd built the rick according to an illustration the boss had shown them in an art book from the house. Like a circular hut with a pointy roof. Once they'd finished, he instructed them to dig out a hollow in the centre.

Miroslav stood beside Kanstner and waited for the boss to emerge from the house. Which he did a few moments later, a pistol in his left hand.

He marched up to Kanstner and shot him through the right knee. Kanstner collapsed sideways, his screams bouncing off the undulating metal sides of the barn.

Miroslav jumped back, but not quick enough to prevent the banker's blood spattering his jeans. The boss stood over Kanstner and shot him again, through the other knee. Twice more he fired, the elbows this time. Kanstner's screams were the worst Miroslav had ever heard, and he'd heard plenty. Mostly during the war in Bosnia, but afterwards, too.

The blood was going everywhere as Kanstner rolled in the dirt.

The boss pointed at the hay rick.

'Put him in,' he said, sticking the pistol into the back of his waistband.

Miroslav bent and hoisted the banker up, carrying him like a bride into a new life. Only this threshold marked the border between life and death. He ignored his ravings – an incoherent stream of pleas for mercy that bounced off his eardrums – and the blood.

He dumped him into the hollow they'd created earlier and turned to the boss. Who nodded.

Miroslav gathered up armfuls of loose straw and started packing it in round Kanstner's lower legs, working steadily until only his head was visible. The boss walked over to the rick and leant in to speak to Kanstner, whose eyes were rolling in his head. From shock, Miroslav supposed.

'My neighbour made money in the straw market, Erich. While I lost it in the money market. Goodbye.'

He pulled a gleaming chrome Zippo from his trouser pocket, flipped up the lid and thumbed the little wheel with a rasp of steel on flint. Crouching, he touched the tip of the orange flame to the straw, which crackled into life. As Kanstner screamed, Popović straightened, wincing and rubbing a spot in the small of his back before walking away.

Miroslav could see Kanstner's head through the flames. It shook wildly from side to side, then went still. The hair blazed briefly in a yellow wreath then all that was left was blackened skin that wavered through the heat haze.

The heat intensified and Miroslav stepped back, the boss at his side.

They stood together for another ten minutes until the bulk of the rick was gone and whitish strands of ashy straw spiralled up in the column of superheated air.

'When it's cooled down, take whatever's left and leave it outside the bank,' the boss said. '*Pour encourager les autres.*'

'Sorry, boss, what?'

The boss tutted. 'It's French. It means to encourage the others.'

Miroslav smiled. 'I get it. To stay in line, you mean?'

'In one. Coffee?'

Miroslav nodded. He'd done well. He could feel it. And that was good. Always good to be on the right side of the boss.

Miroslav was right to feel safe for a while. Because Ratko Popović was an extremely dangerous man to cross. As the unfortunate German banker had so recently discovered.

5

The North Sea was uncharacteristically calm for October. Gabriel had risen early, made a soldier's fry-up – eggs, bacon, sausage, baked beans, fried bread – then taken the boat out.

On the ocean, a couple of miles from shore, he had space to think. With a couple of gulls wheeling and crying above the mast, he stared across the greyish water.

The boat, which he'd inherited from his father, was christened Lin, for his mother. She'd stepped off the side one day after finding her husband dead of a heart attack. Drowned herself in shame after failing to save him because she was passed out, drunk, below deck.

Nobody knew for sure that was how it happened. But the police and coroner's investigations had reached the same conclusion. Gerald Wolfe's death was verified by a Home Office-approved pathologist as having been the direct result of a massive heart attack. Lin Wolfe's blood alcohol level was measured at four times the legal limit for driving and would most likely have produced unconsciousness.

She'd left a brief scrawled note, in lipstick, on the side of the cabin. 'I killed him,' it read. That was all.

The investigators interpreted it to mean that she'd committed suicide out of guilt for her husband's death.

But in later life, after Gabriel had finally discovered the truth about the death of his younger brother, Michael, he'd reached a different conclusion. That Lin Wolfe bore the additional burden of having been passed out drunk when Michael jumped into Victoria Harbour in Hong Kong and drowned.

And why was she drunk? Because a few years earlier, she'd lost her daughter to a kidnapper.

Gabriel slammed his fist against the wheel. It had all started with the greed of a corrupt British policeman. Sure, the triad 49ers, low-level operators on the fringes of the colony's gang culture, had entered the property and taken Tara. But without the intelligence supplied by Steve Ponting, they would have had nothing.

A kidnapped sister. A dead brother. An alcoholic mother. And what of Gabriel himself? His life hadn't exactly been filled with unalloyed pleasure, had it? Total memory loss of the time Michael had been alive until Fariyah had patiently led him to discover the truth about his childhood. PTSD lurking like a crocodile beneath the surface of a muddy African river until a betrayed SAS op lifted it to the surface. Whereupon it had snapped its jaws shut around him and sunk its teeth deep into his soul.

Even now, with the prospect of a normal life with Eli dangled in front of him, he still felt unsure. As if a capricious god could reach down and snatch it all away from him.

The wind had gusted up and he heeled the boat over, finding 'the slot' where the competing forces of wind in the sails and water on the keel met and balanced each other in perfect equilibrium. The yacht surged forward, Gabriel leaning at thirty degrees to the angle of the deck in order to remain vertical.

A plan began to take shape in his mind. The objective was a simple one. Find Steve Ponting.

Fariyah had suggested Gabriel effect an arrest of some kind. And, yes, that was certainly a possibility. But what were the prospects of a conviction after so many years had elapsed?

He realised he had no idea whether crimes like kidnapping had any sort of statute of limitations. Or was that only an American thing? Or just something they put in the movies? It would be easy enough to find out.

But the only hard evidence, a bloodstained fabric sample, pointed at a now-dead triad boss. Everything else was hearsay. And the key piece of witness evidence had been delivered by a man now in the British witness protection system and harder to find than Ponting himself.

Gabriel's jaw clenched. Ponting ought to die for what he'd done. For the damage he'd wreaked on the Wolfe family. He'd find him and explain to him why he had to die, and then Gabriel would put a bullet in him and end, finally, the family's agonies.

He sighed out a breath into the wind buffeting him head-on as he tacked to port. Was this the foundation for a happy married life? Exacting bloody retribution on a man who must be in his late sixties or older? Mei was alive, after all. She and Gabriel were the survivors. Could he not just stop the killing?

An odd question for a professional assassin to ask himself. But the work for The Department fell into a different category. Removing Britain's enemies from the board was a job. An operational task with a clear strategic rationale. One that tapped into Gabriel's patriotism. Pursuing vendettas against the people who'd crossed him had taken him to some very dark places.

Now he was considering taking up another, against the man who'd done so much to shape the trajectory of Gabriel's life.

Even his decision to join the army was a reaction against his father's expectation that Gabriel would follow him into the diplomatic service. And why had the young man been so adamant he wouldn't take the route laid out for him by his father? Because he'd been full of anger, whipped on by a vengeful spirit even before he truly knew why.

The sea had roughened while he'd been thinking about Ponting. The waves were three or four-feet high. Not enough to cause serious worry, but hard enough to negotiate that turning for shore was the only practical option.

With spray whipping from the wave-tips and spattering his face with salt, Gabriel hauled the wheel over and made the necessary changes to the sails to point the prow towards Aldeburgh.

The effort required to pilot the small boat safely to harbour drove all thoughts of Ponting out of Gabriel's mind. By the time he reached safe haven, every muscle was aching and his hair was standing up in spikes. Freezing sweat had run down the inside of his jacket, chilling him to the bone so he shuddered with cold as he stepped off the boat.

Ten minutes later, he was standing under a scalding shower, eyes closed, letting the heat spread through his tissues, deep into his muscles. He leaned against the wall, fingers spread on the tiles as the water sluiced over his back.

To find Ponting, he'd need help. In support, and also on the ground. Normally he'd ask Eli but she was out of touch. But he had someone else in mind. Someone who, like him, had skin in the game. Wei Mei.

It was she who'd killed Fang Jian, the triad boss formerly known as Ricky Fang and then 'Snake'. He'd been one of the two kidnappers who'd stolen the infant Tara Wolfe from her home in the diplomatic compound.

As for support, Gabriel had at his disposal a network of skilled investigators, former special ops members and serving cops. They worked together as and when they needed each other, in a system of mutual aid.

Then there were the characters he'd met over the years who didn't fit into so neat a category as the others but who were nevertheless powerful, influential and connected people.

Gabriel stepped out of the shower and grabbed a towel. He had work to do.

6

Gabriel sat at his desk, a freshly made mug of coffee by his right elbow. He called a retired police officer named Jack Yates. Yates had worked with Ponting in the Royal Hong Kong Police – the RHKP – in the eighties. Like a lot of coppers, Jack was divorced. He lived on his own to the south of London, gardening, going on golfing weekends with a few old buddies from the force, and dreaming of owning a boat.

'Jack? It's Gabriel Wolfe.'

Jack sounded genuinely pleased to hear from him.

'Hello, dear boy. How's life treating you? Taken up golf yet?'

Gabriel smiled. 'No, not yet. Too busy. Listen, you told me last time we met that you liked sailing. I don't suppose I could tempt you up to Aldeburgh to come out on the boat with me? I've plenty of room here, so you could stay.'

Jack paused before answering. Gabriel feared he might refuse the offer. Maybe he'd never really been serious about sailing at all. Just liked subscribing to the magazines.

'That sounds like fun,' Jack said finally. 'Haven't really got out of Carshalton for ages. When were you thinking of?'

'Whenever you can make it. I'm at home just now. Between jobs.'

'No time like the present, then, is there? How about tomorrow? Is that any good? I could make it later, if that's inconvenient.'

'No, tomorrow's good. Just call me when you arrive. It's a small town. Wherever I am, I can be home in ten minutes.'

Next Gabriel called a Zurich number and asked to speak to Amos Peled.

Amos was a Nazi-hunter, in deep cover as a banker. And even though the men and women he tracked down were mostly dead now of disease or old age, there were others his paymasters in Jerusalem wanted tabs kept on.

The pleasantries out of the way, Amos spoke first.

'How can I help you, Gabriel? I assume this isn't a social call.'

Gabriel smiled. 'Sorry, Amos. You're right.'

'That's perfectly fine. It's what keeps me getting up each morning and going into the office. Tell me.'

'I'm looking for a man named Steve Ponting. An ex-Special Branch officer from the UK.'

Amos was all business.

'Age? Roughly?'

'Mid-to late sixties. He was on duty in Hong Kong in the mid-eighties. That was a young man's game, but he had a serious job, protecting my family. So he probably wasn't a rookie. Say he was thirty then. That would make him sixty-six now.'

'Description?'

'All I know is he was tall and well built. He used to box for the police.'

'He might have some scars or boxing injuries. Broken nose. Those fat ears, what do they call them, cauliflowers? Let me know if you get a better description. Last known movements?'

'He left Hong Kong in 1984. That's all I know at the moment. But I'm thinking thirty was too young to retire. What do ex-coppers do? They go into security work.'

'So could he be working with a big corporation?'

'Somehow I doubt it. I think he would have gone freelance.'

'Tell me, what did this man do in 1984 that has you on his trail? Remember, I am a hunter. I can spot another.'

'He betrayed us. My family, I mean. He arranged the kidnap of my baby sister.'

'OK. I understand. Did your parents get her back?'

'No.'

'The kidnappers killed her?'

'No. They messed up. She was taken to the mainland. But I found her by chance a couple of years ago.'

'She is well? Thriving?'

'She is.'

'Then we can be thankful for something good to have come out of it all. Listen, Gabriel, I will do what I can to help you. I have contacts throughout the banking world,' he said. 'Maybe this Ponting character moved further from the law. If he is involved in organised crime, that usually leads to banks, I'm sorry to say. I'll let you know the moment I hear of anything.'

'Thanks, Amos. I'm really grateful.'

'So, tell me. Are you still seeing that lovely Israeli girl? Eli, wasn't it?'

Gabriel smiled. 'Yes. We're engaged.'

'Oh, then *mazeltov*! When?'

'Not sure. We haven't set the date yet. Soon, I hope.' Gabriel hesitated, then, 'Amos, would you come?'

'To your wedding? It would be my pleasure! Just let me know when and where.'

Gabriel put his phone down on the desk. Amos's questions had made him realise just how little he knew about Steve Ponting. He dragged over a notepad and started listing the issues he needed to tackle.

A photo would be a good start. It would be old, but Gabriel knew a couple of people he could approach who might be able to digitally age it. The Met would be his best source.

Ponting's personnel file might have been computerised. The mid-eighties were early in the days of PCs, but law enforcement agencies were just starting to get mainframe computers. An outside bet would be a paper folder, lodged in some storage facility in the suburbs or deep in the bowels of Scotland Yard.

Then, the big question. What did Ponting do after leaving the police? He was corrupt. Gabriel doubted the kidnap was his first foray into criminality. Too big a jump to make from being a clean cop. So he'd already embarked on a parallel path.

Ponting would have needed to make a living. His share of the ransom would only have been nine thousand pounds. Hardly enough to retire on. Once a bent cop, always a bent cop. He wouldn't have gone into corporate security. And, somehow, Gabriel couldn't see him opening a pub or a sporting equipment shop.

No, a man like Ponting would have made the transition all the way. He'd have gone into full-blown law-breaking. And Amos was right. He wouldn't have bothered with low-level stuff, burglary and bugging. He'd have wanted to play for bigger stakes. Banks, fraud, extortion – maybe he'd stuck with kidnapping. Plenty of big companies and rich families preferred to pay ransoms rather than involve the police.

All of which screamed, 'organised crime', just as Amos had said. Which was good news. Because organised crime groups had bigger footprints than sole traders. They left more of a trail. And Gabriel Wolfe was good at following trails.

* * *

Gabriel was queuing in the bakery the next morning. It was just after ten. Jack Yates had phoned to say he expected to arrive at around midday, so Gabriel had plenty of time.

The shop was filled with the smell of freshly baked bread. They baked everything on the premises, and a vent at the back of the building piped smells ranging from crusty white loaves to fruity, spicy hot cross buns.

From behind him, he heard female voices.

'Go on, ask him. I dare you.'

'Shut up, for God's sake! He'll hear us.'

He turned, smiling.

'Ask me what?'

The two women were in their forties. One blonde, the other brunette. Clearly wealthy, with gold and precious jewels at their throats and dangling from their ear lobes.

The blonde wore a waxed jacket over a white shirt with the collar turned up, jeans tucked into riding boots. Her friend wore rainbow-patterned yoga pants and Nike trainers. Her top half was swathed in a soft-looking woollen jumper in an ashy grey. Cashmere, probably.

The brunette was grinning, but also blushing.

'My *friend* wants me to ask you something,' she said, glaring at the blonde woman, who was smiling roguishly. 'I've got this painting at home and, well, we think it's you.'

Now he understood. He felt a blush creeping over his cheeks. Determined to fight his corner, he smiled back.

'Oh, really. What's it of?'

'We-ell. It's a soldier. An old-fashioned one. Greek, I imagine. You know, with a shield, and a big sword.'

Her friend cackled at this. '*Very* big.'

'Is it by Bev Watchett?'

Bev was a local artist Gabriel and Eli had got to know well. She'd asked Gabriel to sit for her. Though 'sitting' had meant lying. Naked. With replica weapons. She'd recreated a famous statue for the painting. *The Fallen Warrior*. At the time he'd not stopped to consider that Bev might sell it. Now he knew who'd bought it.

'She's a friend of ours,' the blonde said. 'Liz and I buy a lot of her work. Paul wasn't too happy though, was he Liz?'

The brunette smiled at Gabriel, the blush gone, though Gabriel's remained as a hot presence on his cheeks.

'I think it makes him feel inadequate,' she said. Then she and her friend burst out laughing.

Gabriel opened his mouth, then realised he had nothing to say.

'Yes, sir?' The girl behind the counter called out to him. Thanking her inwardly, he turned gratefully and placed his order.

He accepted the carrier bag of a farmhouse loaf and baguettes and moved aside so the two women behind him could approach the counter. As he opened the door he heard the blonde's voice carry clear across the shop.

'Nice arse!'

Then a surge of giggling.

He left, the brass bell ringing gaily on its cold steel spring above the door. Bloody Bev Watchett!

Gabriel spent the rest of the morning online, trying, and failing, to find any information on Steve Ponting. He'd found dozens of men with that name on social media, but none appeared to be the former Special Branch officer. He wasn't really surprised.

He thought of a small flat on Ko Shing Street in Hong Kong. A room crammed with computers in varying states of repair, but dominated by a desk on which several fully functional and highly specced machines glowed at all hours of the day and night. Proprietor: *Wūshī* – the Wizard. A hacker with the gelled, spiked-up hair and slender jaw of a K-Pop boy-band singer and a taste for infiltrating official databases. Especially those deemed uncrackable by their guardians.

Gabriel sent a six-word email.

I have a job for you.

The reply appeared in his inbox just a few seconds later. Gabriel checked his watch. 11.55 a.m. – so 6.55 p.m. in Hong Kong. It was half the length of Gabriel's but carried plenty of meaning.

brief in person

Gabriel answered, thinking automatically of flight times to the island.

K

His phone rang. He glanced at the screen.

'Hi, Jack. Where are you?'

'Just arrived in Aldeburgh. Don't worry, I'm on hands-free.'

'I'll put the kettle on. Fancy a brew?'

'Top fella. I'm parched.'

Gabriel saw a metallic-grey Audi A4 pull off the road onto his drive five minutes later. He went to the front door and opened it, stepping out into the teeth of a gale that had blown up while he'd been researching Ponting.

Jack climbed out of the car, waved at Gabriel, then retrieved a blue leather holdall from the boot.

Once inside, with Jack's bag stowed in the guest bedroom, Gabriel poured tea into two oversized mugs. He led Jack into the sitting room, which faced the road, the carpark beyond, and, finally, the sea, iron-grey now, with white caps shedding spume as they crashed in over the stones.

'Thanks for coming up, Jack.'

'Thanks for inviting me.' Jack nodded towards the window. 'Though I have to say, I'm not sure I'm sailor enough to go out in that lot. Filthy bloody day, isn't it?'

Gabriel nodded as he blew on his tea. 'It's been better.'

Jack took a sip of his tea and winced. 'Bloody hell, that's hot! What did you do, make it with boiling water?'

Gabriel smiled. Jack's sense of humour was straight down the middle, but he liked him for it. Here was a man with no side. He'd actually welled up when Gabriel had admitted his true identity after arriving at his home using a false name.

'Listen, Gabriel. I know this isn't about sailing. Or not all, anyway. That's fine. A boat of my own's probably more of a pipe dream than anything else. But I know you've got something on your mind and you think I can help,' he said. 'That's good. I've got bugger all else to occupy myself these days so if you need me, I'm in, whatever it is. And I'm going to make a wild guess. Is it something to do with Tara?'

Gabriel nodded. Sure, now, he'd made the right call by inviting Jack to help him.

'It is. And thanks for agreeing to come, despite me not being straight with you. I should have been. I'm sorry.'

Jack shook his head. 'No need. And I do expect you to take me out if it calms down a bit. So, what's up? Is it Ponting?'

'It is. I want to find him. I'm working on the assumption he left the RHKP and went into crime as the day job. Probably highish-level stuff. So I also assume organised.'

Jack nodded and surprised Gabriel by pulling out a notebook and opening it to a clean page. He jotted down a note.

'That's what I always thought, too. He was bent, Gabriel. One thing honest cops hate even more than the people we arrest are the bad apples,' he said. 'Give us all a bad name. If you're after Ponting, that's all I need to know. But there's something *you* need to know.'

'What's that?'

'The chances of getting him charged by the CPS are nil, I would say. It's not that there's a statue of limitations. Kidnapping's an indictable offence, so it stays open. But there's not going to be enough evidence. Didn't you say the DNA came from someone else?'

'I did. He's dead now in any case.'

'Well, good riddance. What I'm saying is, you won't get Ponting into a courtroom. Although—'

'What?'

'Maybe that's not the way your mind's working.'

Gabriel looked into Jack's eyes, searching for a glimmer of complicity. A flicker of insight into what would be the likely outcome of his hunt for Ponting.

'At this point, I'm just trying to find him. I haven't really thought about how I was going to get justice.'

Jack slurped some more of his tea. 'Course you haven't.' Then he winked. There it was. The sign Gabriel had been waiting for. He had a partner he could trust. 'I'll do whatever I can to help you find him. After that, I'm out. I'll leave the justice part up to you. Word to the wise, though?'

'What's that?'

'There's no statute of limitations on murder either, so be careful.'

7

After the previous day's squally weather, the bright sunshine and steady wind from the south came as a welcome relief. The two men breakfasted early and were out on the water by 8.00 a.m.

Gabriel offered the helm to Jack and enjoyed the ride as he took the boat on a north-easterly heading that would, if they stayed true, take them all the way to Oslo.

They sailed for an hour, talking little, simply acting as parts of a larger system comprising them, the boat, the sea and the wind. At just after nine, Jack gave the command to heave to and began a slow tack into the wind.

As the boat slowed, Gabriel loosened the main sail to the leeward side, and backed the jib. Jack lashed the wheel hard over to starboard. The forces from the wind on her sails and the water on her rudder equalised. Forward progress rendered impossible, *Lin* slowly wiggled sideways, at, Gabriel estimated, just a knot or two, leaving a slick to the starboard side that smoothed out the incoming waves.

Gabriel went below and brewed tea. He took two mugs, and a packet of chocolate biscuits, up on deck and joined Jack on the benches padded with white-vinyl cushions that lined the stern.

'Thanks, skipper,' Jack said, accepting the mug and snagging a couple of the biscuits.

'I've got a guy I know who's going to help me track Ponting down,' Gabriel said. 'But from an ex-copper's perspective, where do you think he'd go after leaving Hong Kong?'

Jack nodded and swallowed the mouthful of biscuit he'd been chewing ruminatively.

'Ever hear of the Costa del Crime?'

'No. What is it?'

Jack leaned back against the rail. 'Back in the late seventies, '78 I think it was, the extradition agreement between Spain and the UK collapsed. A whole bunch of British villains moved down to the Costas and started buying up property,' he said. 'Fuengirola, Marbella, Estepona, all the way down to the Rock, basically. They were there, flashing their wealth, livin' it large, as we used to say.'

'You think he could have headed that way?'

'I don't know. But we had more bent coppers in those days than we should have done. I know personally of a few who joined the villains they'd been taking wodges of cash from. Might be a place to start.'

Gabriel envisioned a fifty-mile stretch of Spain's Mediterranean coastline. 'I know you've been out of the force for a while, Jack, but is there anywhere you'd start if you were me?' he asked. 'Even a town would be a start. Help me narrow the search parameters a little.'

Jack finished his tea, emptying the last few drops over the side. 'All the big-hitters, yes? The guys who were in the Sunday papers? They tended to go for Marbella, or maybe Fuengirola. But the second-tier guys, they kept a lower profile,' he said. 'They didn't have so much money for one thing. This one cop I knew, he was Drug Squad working out of West End Central back then. Nasty piece of work named Roy McAllister. He bought a bar in San Luis de Sabinillas. I think a few others made their homes there. Birds of a feather and all that, you know?'

Gabriel did.

'I'll start there,' he said.

He finished his own tea and took the mugs down to the galley. Five minutes later, with the sails re-rigged for forward progress and the helm unlashed, they were moving swiftly through the water. They reached shore at just after midday.

Gabriel suggested fish and chips on the beach as the weather was so warm. They were early enough to beat the tourist crowd and only had to queue outside the Aldeburgh Fish & Chip Shop for five minutes. As they moved closer to the shop doorway and then the hallowed ground of the interior, the smell of hot oil, chips and vinegar enveloped them, making Gabriel's mouth fill with saliva.

'Smells good,' Jack said with a smile.

They ordered cod, chips and two takeaway cups of tea and took the food down Aldeburgh Court, a short pedestrianised road along King Street and then onto the shingle beach itself.

The fish was perfect: firm, opaque white flakes surrounded by crunchy, bronze-gold batter and smothered in salt and vinegar. As he chewed, Gabriel looked out at the North Sea. Always cold, even in summer, and though well-behaved now, the iron-grey water was capable of putting the frighteners on mariners of many years' experience, let alone casual weekend 'yachties' up from London.

He didn't know what sort of predators inhabited the warm, tranquil waters of the Med. But from what Jack had told him out on the boat, he was forming an impression of a place where strolling around ex-pat bars asking questions would lead very quickly to the wrong sort of attention.

What Jack said next confirmed it.

'A word to the wise, Gabriel. Tread very carefully if you're going down there. The media love to paint them as a bunch of washed-up, East End hard men with orange tans and beer bellies, but that was from years back,' he said. 'Even then, you didn't want to get on the wrong side of them. But there's all sorts down there now and they don't muck about. Russians, Pakistanis, Armenians, Serbs, Yemenis: it's like the United Nations, only with machetes and nine-mils instead of ID cards and voting buttons.'

'Noted.'

* * *

Jack left after breakfast the next morning with a promise to keep in touch and a repeat of the advice he'd offered the day before about the denizens of the Costa del Crime.

Gabriel's final question was about Ponting's tenure in Hong Kong. Jack scratched his head in an almost cartoonish impression of 'man trying to remember a long-ago date' then looked directly at Gabriel, eyes wide, a grin on his face.

'He arrived on 10 July 1982. I remember because the World Cup final was the next day. We all went into town to watch it. Italy beat West Germany three-one.'

After waving him off, Gabriel went for a walk up the coast. He wanted some space to consider his options. With an onshore breeze filling his lungs with clean sea air smelling of ozone, he covered a couple of miles walking along the grassy strip of land between the marshes and the pebbly beach without even realising.

What were his options? He could head to Hong Kong and meet up with Wūshī. If Ponting had any sort of digital footprint at all, however faded by time, Wūshī would find it. It was a long way to go if the end result was learning that Steve Ponting – correction, the Steve Ponting Gabriel wanted – didn't exist.

Of course, Wei Mei was out there and they could spend some time together. But she was running a business and wouldn't be able to drop everything just because her big brother decided to drop in.

Or he could try his luck in southern Spain. But then what? Drive down to Luis de Sabinillas, sashay into the likeliest-looking British pub and say, 'I say, you chaps, does anyone know a former bent copper by the name of Roy McAllister? I believe he owns a bar hereabouts'?

Yes, because that would work, wouldn't it? They'd all shake their heads while staring into their pints of bitter and then, as soon as he left, call McAllister and tell him some nosy bastard from home was asking after him.

Gabriel looked up. He'd reached the final manmade landmark on the narrow spit of land extending south from Aldeburgh: a

Martello tower. The nineteenth-century coastal fort had been built to defend the British Isles against Napoleon's armies. Now an enterprising couple had transformed it into a B&B.

He walked once around its four-leaf-clover-shaped outside, dipping down in the moat that the defenders had dug on the landward side, then rounding the tower on the beach side before heading back towards home.

With the stones on the beach crunching beneath his feet, he made a decision. Hong Kong first. He had contacts there: on both sides of the law. And one, an investigator for a law firm, who sometimes straddled the boundary line between the two.

Back home again, he made some tea and took his mug upstairs to the small bedroom at the back of the house he used as an office. He called Mei, checking the time as he did so. It was 11.05 a.m. in England, so 6.05 p.m. in Hong Kong.

Mei picked up after two rings.

'Hey, BB! How are you?'

Her nickname for him had nothing to do with the great blues singer. It stood, simply, for Big Brother. He smiled as he heard the happiness in her voice. Was it for him? Was life really that simple? You rang your little sister and she was pleased to hear from you?

'Hey. I'm good. How are you? Can you talk?' he asked, dropping into Cantonese.

'Yeah, yeah. All good. I've moved seventy-five percent of our assets into regular companies. Negotiating with the Chinese is harder than fighting other triads, though. God, they're hard bargainers!'

'If there's anything I can do, just tell me, OK?'

Mei laughed. 'For sure. But what are you going to do? Fly out here and shoot another high-ranking official?'

Gabriel ran his fingers through his hair. Killing Comrade Liu hadn't been part of his plan the last time he'd been in HK. But then, the body counts on his ops often ended up higher than planned.

'Whatever you need, Sis,' he said. 'Actually, I'm flying out in the next couple of days, as soon as I can get a flight.'

'Yeah? That's great! We can hang out. What's the occasion?'

Over the next few minutes, Gabriel filled Mei in on his plans to track down Ponting. She told him that Wūshī was still working, and still the best hacker in Hong Kong. They agreed to meet once Gabriel had landed and got settled in the house he still owned on the wooded hills overlooking Victoria Harbour.

8

NOVI SAD

Miroslav's grandfather had been one of the Yugoslav partisans who'd kicked the Nazis out of Novi Sad in '44. Miro had sat on his *Deda*'s knee as a small boy and lapped up stories of bloodcurdling combat, despite the tutting from his mother who thought such tales would give her son nightmares.

Then, Novi Sad had been little more than a rural town serving a dispersed community of farmers and those they traded with, from grain merchants to meat wholesalers.

Now, it had risen through the era of Communism and out the other side to become Serbia's second city, with thriving manufacturing and financial centres. It was to the second of these commercial hubs that Miro was driving this particular morning. For the journey, he'd opted for a black Ford Transit with blacked-out side windows. The plates were fakes, naturally, unscrewed from a similar van about to go into the compactor at a scrapyard owned by Ratko's outfit.

Beside him, Andrej, Ratko's younger son, sat, checking his social media. Only eighteen, Andrej was keen to prove himself. It was one of the things Miro admired about Ratko. How he didn't give his sons a free pass. They wanted in? OK, good. Then let them show they had the spine for the work.

'Hey, put that away, we're nearly there,' Miro said.

Exercising the caution that had earned him the nickname 'Mouse', he slowed the van as he approached the huge, multi-lane junction where Bulevar Jaše Tomića crossed Bulevar Oslobodenja. Maybe the citizens of Novi Sad had once been good drivers, under the iron boot of the Commies, but now their driving and lane discipline was as free as the markets that allowed people like Ratko to prosper.

Belching black smoke, a blue-and-white city bus lurched out from Bulevar Oslobodenja, narrowly avoiding a gleaming white BMW. Miroslav waited, enjoying the looks of fury on the car driver's face as he reflected how close he'd just come to meeting his Maker.

Seeing his chance, he accelerated across the road and made the turn. Ahead, the tinted-glass sides of the Erste Bank headquarters loomed up, its royal-blue sign a spot of bright colour amongst the drab concrete and stone everywhere else.

It pained him that he had to draw attention to himself by driving onto the pavement. But Ratko had been quite specific about where exactly they were to deposit Kanstner's body.

He braked to a stop and pulled the balaclava down over his face. Turning to Andrej, who was doing the same, he nodded.

'Ready?'

Andrej nodded.

In a coordinated move they'd practised with a shop dummy, they jumped out and marched to the rear doors. Miro pulled them open as Andrej clambered inside. With the boy on the head end and Miro at the feet, they lifted the blackened, stinking … thing … off the thick polythene sheet and carried it up the steps to the smart terrace in front of the bank's main doors. The final touch was Kanstner's laminated bank ID card on a blue-and-red lanyard, which Andrej dropped onto the chest.

Miro kept looking around as they dumped the corpse. He saw a young woman pushing a baby in a stroller. She screamed as they dropped Kanstner outside his former workplace. They were back inside the van just a couple of seconds later and roaring off in a screech of rubber that left black curves on the pavement.

He was pleased. He thought having a witness would add to the story that would inevitably find its way into the pages and website of the local paper. He thought *Diary* was a pretty good name for a newspaper. Dear Diary. Today I saw a corrupt banker's burnt remains dumped like so much household trash outside his own bank.

The idea made him laugh.

'What's so funny?' Andrej asked, looking up from his phone.

'Nothing. Go back to your Instagram.'

'It's TikTok.'

'Whatever. Look, you did good back there. Not many kids would have the stomach for the work.'

'Thanks, Miro. Make sure you tell my dad, OK?'

'Don't worry. He'll hear all about it.'

* * *

In his quiet, wood-panelled office 789 miles east of Erste Bank's Serbian headquarters, Amos Peled was leafing through the salmon-pink pages of that day's *Financial Times*. A news article at the bottom of the second page caught his eye. Specifically, the headline.

Banker's burnt body dumped outside bank

For Amos, the phrase 'burnt body' carried unpleasant memories. He read on. Erich Kanstner, a specialist in foreign exchange, had been seconded from Frankfurt to Novi Sad, Serbia. Two days ago, a black transit van had pulled up outside the bank's headquarters. According to a witness, a young woman, two masked men had jumped out and carried his charred corpse up to the steps and left it there in broad daylight.

Something about the story piqued his curiosity. Then he remembered. In his younger days, he'd personally captured a former Nazi officer named Franz Kanstner. He wondered whether the banker was a relative. After spending half an hour on some fairly basic background research on Kanstner, he made a call to an Israeli number. After introducing himself and providing a codeword, he was put straight through to the deputy director of Mossad, an old friend.

After exchanging pleasantries, Amos got to the point.

'I need a check run on a German banker. One Erich Kanstner.' He spelled out both names. 'He's just been murdered and his burnt body dumped outside his bank's Serbian HQ. Can you have someone run that surname through the Nazi database for me?'

'You think it could be connected to your work?'

'He was young, so not directly.'

'But something's making your antennae twitch?'

'I don't know. Maybe.'

'Pretty brutal way to kill a banker.'

'That's partly it. I haven't been able to find out whether he was burnt to death or killed first,' he said, 'but it's a bit extreme, wouldn't you say? Like someone was sending a message.'

'Let me do some digging. I'll put an analyst onto Erste Bank. But you have the banking contacts; what's your opinion?'

'They're clean as far as the Nazis went. But who knows in that part of the world? It could be to do with the Bosnian war: someone settling an old score.'

Amos hung up and returned to the paper. But he couldn't settle. He called his secretary and asked her to arrange some coffee and cake. He stared at the backs of his hands. The skin was so thin that where it wasn't marred by the ever-spreading liver spots, he could see the blue veins meandering beneath the surface like rivers.

He was old. And his work was nearly done. Soon there would be no Nazis left, or not from the original gang. Those remaining were all in their late nineties now.

He'd helped secure a conviction for over 5,000 counts of accessory murder against a former camp guard the previous year.

Tried as a minor because he'd been seventeen at the time he served in the SS, the man received a two-year suspended sentence. Scant justice. But the work was what kept him going. Maybe God was giving him one final trail to follow. Or two, counting the enquiry from Gabriel Wolfe.

9

The cops gathered in the autopsy suite at the Clinical Centre of Vojvodina, Novi Sad's main hospital. Each bore a variation of the same facial expression. Lips tight or twisted in disgust. Nose wrinkled. Skin around the eyes taut. The skin directly beneath their nostrils glistened with a waxy paste that smelled of mint and disinfectant. They all used it, almost as a religious ritual, despite knowing they'd be struggling for days to rid themselves of the revolting stink of burnt human flesh.

In contrast to their rumpled dark suits and scuffed leather jackets, the pathologist's electric-blue scrubs cut an almost festive dash. He drew the navy cotton sheet covering the corpse down to the feet and handed it to the mortician.

There was a chorus of indrawn breaths. The men were experienced members of Novi Sad's murder squad, but somehow the sight of a crispy critter never failed to arouse profound feelings.

The boss, Detective Sergeant Pacariz, held his emotions in check. He just stared at the face, or what was left of it. The eyes were gone, and only the teeth, bared in a dramatic grin from a black, lipless orifice seemed untouched by the fire.

He pointed to the corpse's upraised fists.

'See that?' he said to Stan, the new kid on the squad.

Stan nodded. He'd turned a pale green. Pacariz hoped for the kid's sake he didn't throw up. The older guys could be merciless with rookies.

'It's called the pugilistic attitude,' Pacariz continued, hoping he could distract the kid with a fresh piece of knowledge he could store away in that encyclopaedic brain of his. 'Happens when the muscles contract in the heat.'

Stan nodded and made a note. Pacariz was pleased to see a glimmer of normal pink enter his cheeks.

'We know what killed him,' he said to the pathologist. 'Anything out of the ordinary strike you?'

'First of all, no we *don't* know what killed him,' the pathologist snapped.

Pacariz smiled. Old man Sekulić was like a grumpy old sow with too many piglets on the teat until he'd had his third coffee of the day. Pacariz reckoned he'd only had one so far.

'For all we know he could have been stabbed, shot, poisoned, drowned and run through with a sword. All we know at the moment is the corpse before us has been almost entirely burnt.'

'Sorry, Doc. But on the *assumption*,' he raised his hands to ward off another retort, unconsciously mirroring the dead man's pose, 'that he was burnt alive, is there anything that strikes your experienced eye we might focus on?'

The sliver of flattery was finely judged. Too obvious and Sekulić would respond with sarcasm or worse. He cleared his throat and picked up a scalpel. He pointed it at the left upper canine tooth.

'See anything?'

'No.'

'Look closer!'

Pacariz bent over the head, holding his breath. Sekulić tapped the tooth, making an unpleasant metallic ticking sound with the scalpel.

'Something's stuck between the canine and the first pre-molar.'

Pacariz saw it, then. The circular end of what might be a fine black twig.

'What is that, charcoal? Something from the fire?'

'I don't know! I'm a doctor not a fucking x-ray machine,' Sekulić barked. 'We'll have to look, won't we?'

Unceremoniously, he grabbed the lower jaw and jerked his wrist downwards. The carbonised muscles and ligaments sheared with a loud, dry crackle. Stan groaned and turned away. He made it as far as a bucket, strategically placed well away from the dissection table.

Bizarrely, the inside of the corpse's mouth was pink, in stark contrast to the blackened flesh surrounding it.

'Well, well, and what's this?' Sekulić asked, reaching for a pair of tweezers from the tray of gleaming stainless-steel instruments.

He extracted a three-centimetre length of pale straw, from the unburnt end of which dangled a seed-head bearing fine hairs. He dropped it into a dish preferred by the mortician.

'Since you ventured into my area of expertise with your ill-judged comment on cause of death, I'll return the favour and *assume*,' heavy and sarcastic emphasis, 'that your victim was burnt on a pile of straw. In his death agonies, he either partially inhaled or simply bit off one of the stalks.'

Pacariz nodded. 'Thanks, Doc.'

He meant it. Maybe if they could identify the species of grass they'd find out where it was grown.

Later, he contacted Interpol and, through them, the Metropolitan Police and, through *them*, a particular forensic botanist. Andrew Glover was based in the UK. Pacariz knew of him because he'd worked with the ICTY matching corpses retrieved from the massacre at Srebrenica to the original mass graves. Glover had used pollen grains and other plant materials to secure the chain of evidence.

Glover agreed to take the case, but pleaded pressure of work saying it would be a week or so before he could analyse the specimen.

10

HONG KONG

Gabriel texted Mei as soon as he reached the terminal building at Hong Kong International Airport. Her reply arrived as he was waiting by the carousel for his luggage.

In Singapore for two days. I'll call you.

Although they'd spent as much time as they both could manage together since reuniting in Fang Jian's office, he didn't feel the emotional gravity of a family relationship when he thought of Mei. It was more like a journey of rediscovery than reunion.

So he wasn't saddened that he'd have to wait for a couple of days before meeting up with his sister. He could acclimatise and get over the jet lag, which he'd noticed had become worse in the last couple of years. Jesus! Was age catching up with him?

He spotted his cases tumbling from the top of the conveyor and onto the carousel. He loaded them onto his trolley and made his way to the taxi rank out front.

Half an hour later he was letting himself into the hillside house and inhaling its familiar scent of sandalwood incense. He employed a cleaner while he wasn't in residence and supposed it was she who lit the joss sticks. He never saw any ash or black-tipped sticks lying around, so she was fastidious in tidying away the evidence.

The incense made him think of Eli. She used a special soap she had sent over from Israel in cartons the size of shoe boxes. Her mother bought them for her from a local shop that made the lemon and sandalwood blocks out back in a tiny workshop.

He tried not to worry about Eli. Wherever she was she'd be doing what she did best, supported by The Department just as he was. But it was harder now they were engaged. He pushed the thought down. He'd continue his new habit of praying for her. But later. Not now.

The next morning, after calling ahead to make sure Wūshī was up, Gabriel made his way to Ko Shing Street. The streets were just as he remembered them, alive with the slap-slap-slap of people's sandalled feet on the hot pavements, the shouts and whistles of builders working high overhead on the thick bamboo scaffolding that always surrounded a percentage of the city's high-rises, the toots of car horns, calls of street-food vendors and the Babel of voices from a hundred different countries.

He passed a stinky tofu restaurant and gagged at the smell: a rank odour combining smelly socks with blue cheese. He liked to think of himself as an unfussy eater, and Lord knew he'd survived on all kinds of weird foodstuffs over the years, but he drew the line at stinky tofu.

There was only one other dish he'd ever struggled with. A few years earlier he'd been in Cambodia and his host, a journalist named Lina Ly, had introduced him to a local delicacy: deep-fried tarantula.

He thought that describing his relationship with spiders as a phobia would be like saying MI6 didn't always see eye-to-eye with the FSB. Actually, scrap that. He had it on unimpeachable authority that relations between the two foreign intelligence organisations were rather more cordial than his had ever been with eight-legged monsters.

He'd never let it interfere with his work. It was more by way of background radiation for workers in nuclear plants. Something to be known about, understood – and ignored. But putting a fried one into his mouth and actually chewing? That had taken all his reserves of combat-hardened mental resolve. The results had been worth it, as he'd enjoyed a couple of days, and nights, in Lina's company.

That was another thing he supposed was all in the past now. The flirting, the no-names-no-pack-drill, tension-releasing encounters wherever he happened to find himself working. He didn't mind. Was pleased to be giving them all up, in fact. Eli was what mattered now.

He reached Wūshī's apartment building and texted to let him know he'd arrived. The door buzzed and he pushed through. Inside was as humid as out, only now with an added layer of fast-food smells contributing to the humidity's clammy embrace.

Gabriel took the elevator to Wūshī's floor, walked down the corridor and knocked on the door.

'It's open, man,' came the answering call.

Gabriel went in, smiling at Wūshī's continuing preference for a mid-Atlantic accent that made him sound like an eighties DJ.

Still only in his twenties, Wūshī had accumulated over a decade of experience at the pinnacle of hacking. He had clients on both sides of what he called 'the Great Divide, man' by which he meant the line separating those who made their money legitimately from those who did not. Since he operated at a level of secrecy that would have shamed many intelligence agencies, and maintained strict firewalls between accounts, it didn't seem to harm his business.

'I'm in the kitchen,' Wūshī called.

That was a first. Every previous time Gabriel had visited, which admittedly wasn't more than he could count on the fingers of one hand, Wūshī had been in his 'data-cave'.

That room might have been designed by the Devil, if the Devil had been seeking to tempt teenage boys with all the toys they could imagine. Matte-black or chromed computers, bathed in purple or turquoise backlight. A bank of huge flat-screen monitors. Exotic electric guitars. And a collection of vinyl action figures, mostly female, and displaying impressively pneumatic physiques.

In total contrast, the kitchen was a temple to cutting-edge design. Stainless-steel surfaces gleamed under LED downlighters. A magnetic wall-rack held an array of sleek chef's knives ranging in size from a tiny paring knife just a few inches long to something akin to a machete. And, grouped at one end of a surface punctuated by a white ceramic double-sink, more stainless steel: what appeared to be a fryer, a mixer, a food-processor and a high-end coffee machine.

Wūshī, tall, skinny, almost androgynous good looks, wore a black cotton apron, tied at the front. His hands were floury and, instead of shaking, he offered Gabriel a small, precise bow. A lock of his black hair, of which the tips were bleached blond, flopped over one made-up eye.

Gabriel returned the bow and glanced past Wūshī's left shoulder to the ball of dough sitting in a skim of flour on the work surface.

'What are you making?'

'Bao buns. You hungry?'

'For home-made bao buns? Always.'

He watched Wūshī working the dough, kneading it for a few more minutes then shaping it into flattened balls and finally thin circles.

As the younger man's slender fingers wrapped balls of pork and coriander filling into neat little parcels with twisted tops, Gabriel remembered watching Master Zhao performing the same sequence of neat, repetitive actions in the kitchen that now belonged to him.

He sighed. The old man had been dead for a few years now, more collateral damage from the life Gabriel had chosen.

'You OK, man?'

'Yeah. Fine. Just remembering an old friend.'

Wūshī talked as he worked, rolling, enfolding, twisting and repeating.

'So, you want to tell me about the job?'

Gabriel explained what he wanted. Everything and anything on Steve Ponting, formerly of the RHKP.

'Got a starting point for me? Apart from the name, I mean.'

'Not yet. I've got some more people to call on while I'm out here. I'm hoping one of them might know more about what he did after he left.'

'Was he fired or did he quit?'

'I think he quit. He managed to hide his corruption.' A thought occurred to him. 'Follow the money!'

'You mean the ransom money?' Wūshī asked, while placing four of the little white parcels into a bamboo steamer and setting it above a copper saucepan of boiling water.

'No. That would have been all cash. No trail. No point. I mean the official money. Maybe he'd served long enough to get a police pension.'

'Good idea. If they were paying him a pension, he'd have given them a bank account. Maybe different to the one for his pay. Even if he changed his name, he'd still have needed an account.' Wūshī rolled his eyes. 'Greed. It gets them every time.'

Once Wūshī had finished steaming the buns, he served them onto two black plates and poured green tea into matching cups.

Gabriel took a bite. His mouth flooded with flavours, from the softly seasoned pork, shot through with a hint of liquorice from star anise, to the fresh, aromatic coriander and, right at the end, a kick of chilli.

'Good?' Wūshī asked round a mouthful.

'Very. If the hacking work ever dries up I know a few chefs in town who'd hire you for these alone.'

Wūshī laughed. 'Man, if the hacking business goes south, we're all in trouble. I've never been busier. You want to talk money?'

'Are you going to stiff me?'

'No.'

'Then no, let's not. You get me what I need and I'll pay you what you want.'

'Deal,' Wūshī said, wiping his hand on his apron and extending it across the table.

11

Halfway through Gabriel's third day in Hong Kong, Mei called to say she was back.

'When can we meet?' he asked.

'How about now?'

'Where are you?'

'I'm at my office.'

'At the Golden Dragon?'

'No. I sold it. That was the old life, BB. I'm a CEO now,' she said, and he could hear the amusement in her voice. 'My office is downtown. Thirtieth floor of The Center on Queen's Road Central.'

Gabriel checked his watch, a rose-gold Bremont. It was a replacement for the Breitling his father had given him. It had come off and sunk in a sea of skull-studded red mud in a Cambodian killing field, where it had been joined by a CIA agent sent to kill him.

'I can be there by one.'

'OK. We're called Lang Investments.'

Gabriel smiled. He had no need to make a note. Years ago he'd used the same name as an alias. It was a little in-joke that brother and sister had found irresistible. *Láng* in Cantonese meant 'Wolf'.

Half an hour later, he approached the security desk at The Center. The young woman on reception, beautifully made up and with her sleek dark hair swept up in a sophisticated style smiled at him.

'Yes, sir?'

'I have an appointment to see—'

He realised he didn't know what Mei was calling herself these days. Had she reverted to her given name, Tara Wolfe? Or chosen a completely new one to signal a definitive break with her triad past?

'Excuse me for just a second,' he said with a smile.

Turning away from her and strolling over to a group of grey leather armchairs, he called Mei.

'Are you here?'

'Yeah, but this is ridiculous. I don't know your name.'

'Oh, yeah. I should have told you. Sorry, I forgot. It's Alice Lang.'

Five minutes later, Gabriel was making small-talk with a suited assistant, a young man of Western appearance, as they travelled up in the lift to the thirtieth floor.

'This way, please,' he said, gesturing with an open arm for Gabriel to follow him.

As he walked down the carpeted corridor, admiring the modern art prints on the walls, Gabriel felt a fizz of excitement ignite in his belly. Not nerves, definitely not that. But just that indefinable pleasure of being with a living – correction, the *only* living – member of his family again.

As the assistant closed the wide double doors behind him, Gabriel grinned as he saw Mei. She rushed round the aircraft carrier-sized glass and aluminium desk and threw her arms round him.

'Hey, it's good to see you, BB,' she whispered into his ear before releasing him from a grip he suspected had crushed other men to death.

'You too, Sis. How was your trip to Singapore?'

She flapped a hand. 'Oh, you know, business deals. So boring. Just a bunch of fat old men in cheap suits who think they can outwit me 'cause I'm a woman.'

She motioned for him to sit in one of the white leather and chrome armchairs grouped by a picture window looking out over the harbour.

'I'm guessing they got more than they bargained for?'

She laughed. 'Less!'

'You look good,' he said.

It was true. At thirty-eight, she looked ten years younger, with unlined skin and a light tan that softened the sharp lines of her cheekbones and pointy chin. She was wearing a white trouser suit, the tailored lines of which emphasised the athletic physique she'd built up in her years acting as one of Fang's bodyguards, his fabled 'Lotus Blossoms'. Their uniform had always been white leather: the colour suited her.

She smiled. 'I like being legal. Definitely less stressful. Are you OK? You look tired.'

He rubbed a hand over his face. 'I haven't been sleeping very well. The jet lag hit me hard this time.'

Her forehead creased. 'Why aren't you sleeping well? Do you still meditate? Do your yoga?'

'Yes, but it's not helping. It's why I'm here, really. I mean apart from to see you. You remember I told you about Britta.'

'Your ex-fiancée, yes. She took a bullet meant for you.'

Gabriel jerked back at the bluntness of Mei's words. Maybe a sister he'd grown up with, a sister who'd known more about him would have softened the sentence, but, he reflected, that wasn't Mei, was it? And it wasn't her fault, either.

'Yeah, well I used to think I saw her,' he said quietly, 'you know, in the distance. Sometimes up close, like we were talking. It wasn't healthy. I had a lot of therapy and she disappeared.'

'But now she's back?'

Gabriel nodded. 'But now she's back.'

'Why?'

Gabriel scratched at his scalp. 'I honestly don't know, but I'm going after the guy who set up the kidnapping. I think everything goes back to that moment in our lives. Yours, mine, even hers. I feel like I'm stuck in this loop, always returning to the same point. You know I have PTSD, right?'

Mei nodded. 'You said it was fixed.'

'And it was. Or fixed enough that it wasn't screwing me up anymore. At first I thought it was caused by losing someone when I was in uniform,' he said. 'Then it looked like that just released my deep-seated guilt over Michael's death. But now I think it goes all the way back to that night when Fang and his accomplice took you from Mum and Dad's house.'

Mei frowned. 'How? I don't understand.'

Gabriel leaned forward, clasping his hands and letting them dangle between his knees.

'Ponting arranged for Fang and this guy called Ronald Bao Dai to kidnap you. When Mum and Dad couldn't get you back, Mum started drinking heavily. When Michael and I were playing rugby in the park down at Victoria Harbour, Mum was drunk. She passed out, so by the time Michael went in after the ball she couldn't help me. He drowned.

'Dad wrote me this letter. I only saw it a year or so back. He wrote it for me to read after his death. Mum became a full-blown alcoholic. I was just trouble from then on. They couldn't handle me so I went to live with Master Zhao.

'At the end, they were out on the boat and Dad had a heart attack. Mum was dead to the world and Dad,' Gabriel swallowed hard, trying to speak past the lump in his throat, 'Dad was just dead. They found her body in the water. The coroner thought she'd killed herself out of grief.'

He rubbed at his eyes, which were wet with tears.

Mei came round the low table separating them and put her arms around him.

'Don't cry, BB.' She patted his back.

'Can you see now, Sis? Ponting cast a shadow over our lives. The crooked bastard blighted them all. Mine, yours, Dad's, Mum's. Even Master Zhao died because of it.'

Holding him tighter, Mei whispered by his ear.

'You can't let him get to you anymore. You've got to get to him instead.'

Gabriel nodded. 'That's the plan.'

Mei stood and held out her hands, grasping his and pulling him to his feet.

'Let's eat. Then we can discuss what we're going to do about Ponting.'

'We?'

She smiled. But it was a deadly smile: the sort of expression a cobra would make before striking, if it could.

'He attacked our family. We're all that's left. So we're going to make him pay.' She headed for the door, then turned and smiled. 'Come on, I'll take you to the best Vietnamese restaurant in Hong Kong.'

On the street, Mei threaded her arm through Gabriel's and led him away from the financial district. As they travelled east, the streets lost some of their sheen, and, little by little, the smart version of Hong Kong, the designer shops and German-engineered automobiles, gave away to something grittier.

The shopfronts got smaller, displaying racks of brightly coloured fruit and vegetables. Walking down an alley, Gabriel saw an old woman squatting over a drain, her multiple skirts drawn up around her hips to keep them out of the filth. She caught his eye and grinned, toothless gums shining pink from the grime of her face.

Then, shouting and the deep pop of tear-gas launchers.

From a side street, three young people rushed into the alley. In all-black outfits, their faces covered by bandanas, they resembled comic-book bandits. Each wore goggles but Gabriel could still discern the wide-eyed look, half-fear, half-exhilaration, that came from fighting running battles. White smoke drifted up behind them.

'We should go,' he said to Mei.

But it was too late. Round the corner came four police in full riot gear: helmets, body armour, shin guards and heavy boots. One carried a short, fat-barrelled gun, the other three long, black, shiny batons.

Mei stepped to one side as the cops arrived but then half-turned as if to walk away and stuck her right foot out, tripping the leading cop. He cried out as his helmeted skull smacked against the cobbles.

The other three stopped in their pursuit and turned to attack Mei. Gabriel didn't think. Thinking was too slow. It was time to act.

Gabriel stepped in and swept a foot in a scything motion, taking one of the cop's feet out from under him.

As he fell, Gabriel pivoted, straight-arming a second cop in the centre of his chest. He grabbed the baton and twisted it free in a vicious back and forth movement that dislocated the guy's shoulder with a loud pop.

Over his scream, Gabriel jabbed the end of the baton hard into the visor of the cop who Mai had tripped. He'd just got to his knees and was pulling a pistol. The thrust snapped his head back and Gabriel followed it up with a sharp blow with the side of the stick that smashed the visor. A third strike smashed the cop's wrist.

He dropped the pistol and Gabriel kicked it into a pile of rubbish against a slimy-looking wall. As the cop scrabbled to raise his visor, Gabriel grabbed him by both shoulders, raised him a couple of feet off the ground and then slammed him down onto the cobbles. The helmet cracked and the cop went limp.

A cop swung his baton at Mei's head. She ducked under and shot out a blade hand, catching him in the one unprotected part of his anatomy: a thin strip of skin under his helmet's chin-guard. He emitted a squawking cough and clutched his throat. A kick sent his head clattering sideways into the wall where he slumped, unmoving.

Gabriel readied himself to attack one of the two remaining riot cops when he felt the hard and unmistakeable presence of a pistol barrel pressed into the back of his skull.

He tensed, expecting a bullet. Then he heard running footsteps, a loud hissing and a shout of confusion and the pressure vanished.

He spun round. The bandits were back. Students, he assumed, or democracy activists. One held an aerosol can. The cop who just seconds earlier had been about to blow Gabriel's head off was flailing around, the clear plastic visor of his riot helmet now obscured with black spray paint that dripped and spattered as he shook his head.

Another protestor performed the same action on the another cop. Mei and Gabriel, moving in synchrony, disarmed him and his colleague. A chop to the wrist in Mei's case, and a wrench of the shoulder in Gabriel's.

Gabriel used a discarded baton to knock out his man, driving its end, with ferocious force, into a spot at the base of his neck. The nerves beneath the skin controlling consciousness shorted out under the onslaught.

Mei delivered a combination of kicks to the last man standing, taking him in the solar plexus and then, as he doubled over, his wind driven from him, slamming his helmeted head down onto the cobbles.

'Thank you,' one of the bandits said, before all three sprinted away, chucking their spray cans into the trash pile.

The last he saw of them, as they turned the corner into the wider street at the end of the alley, was of them pulling off their masks and goggles, stuffing them into knapsacks and slowing from a run to a sauntering gait. Not bad for students.

Panting, he turned to Mei. Astonishingly, her white trouser suit bore no signs of the fight at all. She'd stayed on her feet the whole time. She tucked a stray strand of hair behind her ear.

'Come on,' she said. 'Before they wake up.'

Taking the same route as the students, they left the noisome alley and its four latest occupants, merging into the midday crowds in the heavily populated shopping street beyond.

12

Once the adrenaline from the action in the alley had dissipated, Gabriel was consumed by hunger. They walked down the street, both keeping a discreet eye out for police.

'That was a massive risk back there,' he said after a minute of casual but alert progress among the lunchtime shoppers.

'I hate them,' Mei said, simply. 'The CCP is turning Hong Kong into a prison. Those guys were probably just school kids. They see their freedoms being stolen and they're angry. I am too. No way I was going to let those thugs take them in for a beating, or worse.'

'I'm with you on that. But how does it square with you going legit? Those cops will have you in a report by this afternoon.'

She shook her head.

'No they won't. They'll be too ashamed. Taken out by two civilians and a couple of kids with spray cans? They'd get their arses kicked from here to Beijing for incompetence.'

'But what if they see you in the street again?' he asked. 'I'll probably be all right. All Westerners look the same to them.'

It was a lame attempt at humour, but it was the best Gabriel could do, and he was genuinely worried for Mei's safety.

'I'll be fine. Though I'd probably better get rid of the suit. Pity, it's my favourite Valentino.'

Taking a roundabout route, during which they saw no cops of any kind, riot or otherwise, Mei led him to the restaurant. It was a tiny place called *Bầy Sói*, squeezed in between a cheque-cashing joint and a shoe-repair shop.

A middle-aged woman in a floral smock and black trousers emerged from behind a curtain of multi-coloured plastic stripes at the back of the dining room, which was just big enough for six small tables.

'*Em Alice!*' she exclaimed.

She came up to Mei and gave her a hug, while speaking in rapid-fire Vietnamese. Then she looked at Gabriel, smiled, turned back to Mei and asked a question.

Mei laughed and answered in Vietnamese. Gabriel was impressed. Mastering languages must have been a family trait. She turned to him.

'Anh Thanh asked if you were my boyfriend. I told her you were my brother. And then she asked if you were married.'

The restaurateur looked at him and batted her eyelashes theatrically. Gabriel smiled, stumped, for once, as Vietnamese was not one of the many tongues he'd mastered.

'Tell her I'm spoken for,' he said with a grin, 'but if I was a free man, I'd be asking what time she got off work.'

Mei related his flirtatious suggestion, and at this the restaurateur shrieked with laughter and reached out to slap Gabriel on the chest. She showed them to a table and brought them two stubby green bottles of Bia Saigon beer.

'On the house,' she said to Gabriel in English.

Once she'd left them, disappearing behind the rattling plastic steps, Gabriel turned to Mei.

'Have you got an assistant?'

'Of course.'

'Call them, then. Get them to bring you a change of clothes.'

She nodded and pulled out her phone. She issued a couple of instructions, then put it away again.

'No need to order,' Mei said, picking up her beer and clinking the neck against Gabriel's. 'Anh Thanh will bring us the best.'

The thought of four pissed-off Chinese riot police simply giving Mei a free pass out of humiliation was comforting, but it didn't feel secure enough. Yes, she had the chops – literally – to defeat individual enemies, or even a pack of them. But getting into it with the CCP? That was a whole other level of conflict.

'Why don't you come back to England with me for a while? Just until the trouble with those cops blows over.'

'It's fine, BB. I told you, don't worry,' she said with a sly smile. 'If it gets sticky, I have people on the payroll still. The kind that keep the authorities out of our hair.'

'I'm sure you do. But come anyway. I have some business here, then I'm flying out,' he said. 'I've been thinking I might even sell the house.'

As he said it, he realised he meant it, even though the idea seemed to come from nowhere. Something about Master Zhao's house wasn't right any longer. Every moment he spent there felt like a moment when the past reached up from the depths of his subconscious and tried to pull him back. Back to places he no longer wanted to go.

'Really? I thought you loved it. You said it reminded you of Master Zhao.'

'It does. But I think that might not be healthy for me anymore. Anyway, things are changing here. Those riot cops were just one of the symptoms,' he said. 'Please come. I can take you to see Mum and Dad's grave. I showed you Michael's before. You can meet the whole family.'

He'd meant it as a joke, but, as he said it, tears pricked behind his eyes. He hid it with a long pull on his beer. Then Anh Thanh arrived with two little plates of translucent pancake rolls through whose delicate pastry he could see the curled pink forms of king prawns and the feathery leaves of coriander.

They were delicious, so fresh-tasting he imagined the prawns must have been swimming in the deep waters beyond the bay that same day.

Mei finished a mouthful, then dabbed her lips with a paper napkin she pulled from a stainless-steel dispenser on the table.

'It'll take me a few days to arrange things. The deal I was negotiating in Singapore needs a lot of attention. But in a few days, yes. OK. Let's go.'

Gabriel smiled, feeling the tension that had accompanied him all the way from the fight in the alley ease off. Just a little.

They were finishing their pudding: a sweet-sour fruit salad with mango sorbet when a young Hong Konger arrived bearing a glossy yellow shopping bag on twisted rope handles. It bore the swirling black logo of one of the high-end department stores. He squeezed his way through the other diners and placed the bag at Mei's feet.

'I hope you like it, Ms Lang,' he said with an anxious smile.

She smiled up at him. 'I'm sure it'll be fine. Dark, yes?'

He nodded. 'French navy linen with satin trim. Very understated. Very you.'

'Thank you, Paul,' she said.

Nodding, he turned on the heel of his expensive-looking shoes and left. Mei got to her feet. 'Won't be a minute,' she said, then picked up the bag and slipped through the plastic curtain.

While Gabriel waited, he considered what action he should take to disappear from the police radar for the remainder of his time in Hong Kong.

Although he'd made a joke of it with Mei, he was reasonably sure that in the confusion of the fight, the riot cops wouldn't have been able to fix his appearance in their minds. Just another *gwáiló* in a dark suit. Even his height, which at five-ten, was less than the average for his generation of Brits, and his build, athletic but not bulky, worked in his favour.

Had he been a six foot four, two hundred and fifty pound, blonde-haired monster, they'd have no trouble locating him on CCTV. But the physique that had enabled him to operate so effectively in the SAS, offering stamina, agility and speed, was identical to hundreds of thousands of locals.

Nonetheless, he decided that he'd buy a baseball cap from the first stallholder he came to and, after leaving Mei at her office building, get a cab back to his house. From there, he could set up meetings and then travel incognito after dark.

With a light rattle of the plastic strips separating the dining room from the kitchen, Mei reappeared. Smiling, she held her arms out from her body.

'Well, how do I look?'

The suit was a perfect fit. He assumed her assistant had her measurements in his phone. Neither of them had looked as though the request was a first.

He nodded. 'Like an anonymous business lady.'

'Good. I paid Anh Thanh. We can go.'

They took a similarly discreet route back to her building and after embracing by the doors, Gabriel left her with a promise to speak on the phone about the trip to England.

He hailed a passing red and white Toyota Crown taxi and was locking the front door behind him twenty minutes later.

With a cup of tea in front of him on the desk in the office facing the garden, Gabriel called his Hong Kong lawyer, John Chang. John was a partner in the law firm that Gabriel's father had used when he was working in the colony.

After introducing himself, he got straight to the point.

'John, I need to ask you a favour. Can I borrow Peter again? I'm trying to track down an ex-RHKP officer. I'm more than happy to pay for his time. I don't think you owe me any more freebies.'

Peter Nesbitt was an investigator for Chang, Greaves, Luan and Whitney. Like a lot of law firms, they retained a former copper for those aspects of their work that called for a capable man, or occasionally woman, with contacts in high – and low – places.

'You hadn't heard, then?' Chang sighed. 'Why would you have? I am afraid Peter died earlier this year. It was testicular cancer. It was too advanced by the time he visited his doctor.'

Gabriel leaned back and rubbed a hand over his eyes. He felt, not grief. Not exactly. But a weight. It settled over him like a coat too heavy for the weather, pinning him to the chair. He'd grown to like Nesbitt in the brief time they'd spent together when he'd last been in Hong Kong. And now, he, too, was gone.

'Did he suffer much?' he asked.

'No. His doctors were very good. He had excellent palliative care. And Rosemary was with him at the end.'

Gabriel didn't know what else to say. He asked Chang to pass on his condolences to the widow and ended the call.

Feeling the need to shake off the grey mood that had enveloped him, he changed into a much-washed kung fu outfit and went downstairs to the dojo. He fought the mechanised training aid he called 'the octopus' for half an hour, dodging inside its eight whirling wooden arms, then showered and lay on his bed, eyes closed.

The physical exertion had cleared his mind and metabolised whatever hormones and chemicals in his brain were depressing him. He could feel a clarity now, and, as he lay there, breathing slowly, he repeated a simple calming mantra taught to him by Master Zhao.

A reverberating bang jerked him into full alertness. Heart racing, he sprang off the bed and rushed to the window, expecting to see riot police swarming across the moss lawn.

Imprinted on the glass was the ghostly impression of a bird: from head to tail to outstretched wings, every spread feather as clear as if drawn by an artist. He opened the casement, looking down into the garden. Lying on the stone flags beneath him, its wings folded neatly by its sides, was a dead bird. He saw electric-blue wing flashes popping from its cinnamon-coloured plumage: a jay.

Gabriel went downstairs and picked up the dead bird. Lying in his cupped hands, it weighed practically nothing, an odd sensation given its size. He could feel the fading heat given off by its body beneath the silky feathers, though its eyes had glazed over, all spark of life departed.

Cradling its still-warm body, he took it to a flower bed and laid it on the soft, moist earth. He fetched a trowel from a small wooden shed behind a screen of black-stemmed bamboo and returned to scoop out a grave. He laid the jay at the bottom.

He pushed the earth back over it, patting the hillock down with the back of the trowel, and went back inside.

This time, it took longer for Gabriel to calm down and disengage from the here and now. But he persisted, repeating the mantra and waiting …

13

... he felt the slip as an almost physical shift as he entered a zone of awareness somewhere between waking and sleeping.

He pictured himself in a limitless expanse of blackness, lit by a single, tall candle whose tulip-shaped flame burned steadily, not flickering by so much as a millimetre. He extended his mind, searching for the clearest and most recent memory of the man who raised him from the age of ten.

From out of the darkness, the stooped form of an old man appeared, wearing a cinnamon-coloured kung fu suit with bright-blue flashes on the arms.

He sank into a cross-legged pose in front of Gabriel and smiled. Gabriel heard his old mentor's words, though the elderly man's lips didn't move.

– *Now Peter Nesbitt is dead, how are you going to find Ponting?*

– *I don't know.*

– *Think, Wolfe Cub. Think hard.*

– *He was in his thirties when he quit the RHKP. But he would still have had a pension pot, even a small one. Maybe he opened an account in Spain and arranged for it to be paid in there when he reached the official pension age.*

– *Good. So you can trace him via the financial system. How will you do it?*

– *There'll be a few cops who retired down there, but not many from Hong Kong. He was corrupt, so he might have changed his name when he fetched up there, but the original records would all be in his true name.*

– *Ask your friend Wūshī to research the banks on the Costa del Crime. Especially local ones. Fewer security protocols than the big global brands. Easier to corrupt with payouts to poorly paid officials, too.*

Gabriel looked into Master Zhao's eyes. They were clear and alert. No milkiness that one often saw in the very old.

– *Master, I'm sorry I brought Sasha Beck to your door. You died because of me. Can you forgive me?*

Zhao Xi placed a hand over his heart.

– *Wolfe Cub, I am not really here. There is only you in this place. You are asking yourself, not me. The question you must ask is, do you forgive* yourself?

– *I am trying, Master. Eli says I must. The past has happened, she says. Let it go. Build our life together.*

– *She speaks wisely. But then, you already knew that. Listen to her, Wolfe Cub. Listen to Eli. Every human story reaches the same point: we all die in the end. It is not dying that should concern you, but living. Let me go. I lived my time. Focus on your own life. Your life with Eli. Consider what sort of a future you might create together.*

– *Do you mean children, Master?*

But Master Zhao offered an unreadable smile.

– *It is not I who means anything in this conversation, Wolfe Cub.*

The darkness lightened, replaced by sunlight streaming in through the bedroom window. Gabriel opened his eyes.

It was morning. He'd slept in his clothes, without dreaming. As Gabriel was eating breakfast, his phone rang. It was Mei.

'I've been thinking. If you're going after Ponting, you need backup. I want to come, too.'

'You're sure? Not quite the business trip people would expect Alice Lang to be making.'

'Look, if he's some fat old retired cop swilling pornstar martinis in a beachfront bar, it'll be easy to take him. You won't need me, but I want to be there,' she said. 'But if he's protected, you'll need support. You know what I did for a living. We'd make a pretty good team, I'd say.'

'OK. Let's find him first, then we can think about what to do next.'

Later that day, Gabriel called a Metropolitan Police number. Its owner answered in a spiky South London drawl that could have stripped battle grime off an assault rifle.

'Good God, it's my favourite HR consultant. How are you, Gabriel?'

Gabriel smiled. It was good to hear Penny Farrell's voice. The last time they'd met had been right here in Hong Kong. She'd been calling herself Valerie Duggan then, working undercover in the Golden Dragon. They'd swapped legends, he an executive search consultant, she something in telecoms. Both had tumbled to the other's lie within seconds of meeting.

'I'm good, thanks, Penny. How's the world of digital network sales?'

'Oh, you know, mustn't grumble. More than my fair share of utterly despicable low-lifes but *c'est la guerre* and all that.' As she'd done once before she deliberately mangled the French pronunciation so it came out as *sailor gayer*. 'Is this a social call? You about to ask me out for another lunch?'

'Afraid not. Or not right now, anyway. I'm in Hong Kong again and I wondered whether you might be able to help me.'

'With what? I don't have access to the armoury if that's what you're thinking. Us financial crime bods are strictly laptops and spreadsheets.'

'Funnily enough, it's more of a laptops and spreadsheets type of enquiry.'

'You've piqued my curiosity now. Go on.'

'I need to track down a corrupt former Special Branch officer. He was seconded to the RHKP to protect my parents and instead helped a triad kidnap my baby sister.'

'Bloody hell! You do squeeze a lot of info into a little story, don't you? What did you think I could do for you? Not—' she continued quickly, before he could answer, 'that I'm making any promises, by the way.'

'Understood. I thought, maybe if he'd had a pension, I could trace him through that.' The line went silent for a few seconds. All Gabriel could hear was his own breathing. Had she hung up? 'Penny? You still here?'

'Yeah, yeah, sorry. I was thinking.' He heard the sound of her sucking her teeth. 'You saved my life before. I owe you. There's someone I can talk to. I'll have to think up a decent reason but give me a couple of days and I'll call you.'

'Thanks, Penny. This means a lot.'

'Yeah, well, you can stand me another plate of frogs' legs next time you're in the Smoke, then, can't you?'

He laughed. 'It would be my pleasure. One last thing. Would there be a photo of Ponting on the Met's database anywhere?'

Her answer didn't surprise him. 'No digital records of officers before the late nineties.'

The call ended, he returned to the issue that had risen to the top of the list. He needed a recent photo of Steve Ponting. After wasting a couple of hours searching online, he gave it up as a bad job. The photo could wait. First they had to track Ponting down.

14

ALDEBURGH

By the time Penny called back, Gabriel was at home in Aldeburgh. He and Mei had flown back on separate flights, she using her new alias of Alice Lang, he one of the several identities he maintained as a Department operative.

Penny explained she'd passed Gabriel's details to a colleague in the Met's vast administration who handled pensions for all cops who'd performed duties overseas. Apparently the tax situation was more complicated.

She didn't bother with the details, for which he was grateful. What mattered was that this colleague, 'Naz', was looking into Ponting's files and would contact Gabriel with details of the receiving bank he'd given for when his pension eventually became payable.

Pensions research? It felt a million miles from the up close and personal style of mission Gabriel was used to. Although he realised with a jolt that his last few ops had involved more desk research then he'd been used to.

While he waited for Naz to come back with the next link in the chain he hoped would lead him to Ponting, he took Mei to visit their parents' graves.

* * *

The churchyard sat on the edge of a village deep in the Surrey countryside called Morseby Parva. Gabriel parked in a fenced-in gravel patch behind the church. Outside, the air smelled as clean as it did in Aldeburgh, but without the tang of the sea. Something greener; a reflection, perhaps, of the multitude of trees just coming into leaf all around them. The foliage of the ash, sycamore and alders was bright green, almost fluorescent, as though the life flooding up from the warming ground was too much for them to contain.

For the visit, Mei had dressed in black: a long skirt that swept the ground beneath a jacket with a nipped-in waist. She'd pinned her hair up, too, and overall Gabriel thought the effect was theatrical, as if she hadn't been sure how to play her role.

He'd initially put on a newish pair of indigo jeans and a leather jacket, but when she'd come downstairs that morning, he'd hurriedly excused himself and gone upstairs to change. Now, like her, he wore a suit, charcoal grey rather than black, over a white shirt and navy tie.

'They're over there,' he said, pointing to a section of the graveyard towards the western edge, shaded by a yew tree almost as tall as the church tower.

As they walked across the soft, springy grass, he realised he hadn't been back here since his parents had died. He searched his feelings to see whether guilt lay among them, but it was absent. He pointed at a polished black granite gravestone. The grass around it, as all the others, had been recently cut. Gabriel thanked whichever groundsperson saw to it that even unvisited graves were not left to fall into disrepair. Bare of ornament, no angels or lambs for the Wolfes, its text was picked out in gold.

IN LOVING MEMORY

GERALD ARTHUR WILLIAM WOLFE
12th May 1954–18th May 2002

LIN WOLFE
29th October 1956–18th May 2002

IF YOU STAND STRAIGHT,
DO NOT FEAR A CROOKED SHADOW.

Brother and sister stood shoulder to shoulder for a minute or two. Gabriel listened to a blackbird singing from the lower branches of the yew. For no reason he could fathom, its sweet, trilling song brought tears to his eyes.

He hadn't cried at the funeral. His girlfriend at the time, Robyn, had clutched his arm and whispered that it was OK to show emotion. She didn't know that rather than holding anything in, he was simply empty of feelings. There was no emotion to show.

Mei slid her left hand into his right and interlaced her fingers with his. He squeezed and received an answering pressure. He glanced at her. She was dry-eyed, much as he had been nineteen years earlier.

She stretched out her free hand and pointed at the inscription.

'I like that. Is it from the Bible?'

He shook his head and swiped the tears away with the back of his other hand. 'No, it's an old Chinese proverb. Master Zhao's favourite. He made me memorise it.'

'Huh. I've never heard it before. Are you sure he didn't just make it up?'

Gabriel shrugged. 'Maybe he did. I wouldn't put it past him. He had a massive store of them. One for every occasion, every challenge.'

'I wish I could have known him like you did.'

'He would have liked you.'

'Why do you think he never mentioned me?'

Gabriel turned and looked into his sister's eyes. 'I don't know. I've been asking myself the same question ever since I realised who you were. I think they'd all decided it was best to keep me and Michael innocent of your existence,' he said. 'There was nothing to gain by telling us, especially as I was so young when you were kidnapped.'

'Yeah, but I still think it's weird.'

Gabriel sniffed. '*Everything* about our family is weird.'

She smiled at him. 'True.'

He looked back at the proverb. Had Master Zhao invented it? A useful way of imparting a moral lesson to his young charge? It would be easy enough to check. A quick internet search would yield proof one way or the other. As he stared at the ten gold words cut into the stone, he realised how true they were as they applied to his and his sister's lives.

'We've lived under a crooked shadow our whole lives, Mei,' he said. 'Our whole lives! Ponting's shadow. What's more crooked than a bent cop? He was crooked as hell. Everything that happened, happened because of what he did.'

As he spoke, he clenched his fists. Mei winced and disengaged her left hand.

'We're going to find him,' she said.

'And we're going to kill him,' they said in unison.

* * *

Two days elapsed before Naz called Gabriel on his mobile. He'd tracked Ponting's pension. The file had never been flagged with a 'deceased' tag: Ponting was still alive. The receiving bank he'd allocated when he left the service was a tiny local outfit on the Costa del Sol: Banco Sombra Málaga. It only had three branches in the city that gave it its name and was privately held.

Gabriel made a note. A tiny outfit like that would have far less in the way of oversight than one of the big national or global banks with their compliance departments, rafts of lawyers and brand values of 'transparency' and 'integrity'. Perfect for a bent cop.

Ponting had chosen a bank that would pay lip service to written contracts and the rules laid down by external regulators, but would use handshakes and words of honour to actually shape its relationships with its clients.

But banks like that were easier to penetrate than their global cousins, so Gabriel was happier Ponting had gone down that route.

'I don't suppose you have a photo of Steve Ponting?' he asked Naz.

'Sorry, no. The system's been updated and rebuilt a handful of times since the eighties but, in any case, we don't attach photos of the scheme members.'

He called the bank, introducing himself, in deliberately poor Spanish, as the senior assistant pensions coordinator for the Metropolitan Police.

The person who answered switched effortlessly to English. From the sound of his voice, Gabriel pictured a man in his seventies, dressed, despite the heat, in a suit and tie and leaning back in an antique leather wing chair.

'How can I help Scotland Yard?' he asked. 'I hope we are not being investigated.'

He laughed at his own joke and Gabriel detected the roughened timbre of a life-long smoker. The chink and rasp of a lighter, and the crackle of igniting tobacco in his earpiece confirmed his intuition.

'Hah ha! No, nothing like that,' Gabriel said, getting into character. 'I've been asked to trace members of one of our departments who emigrated to Spain in the 1980s. Apparently there was a problem with the original entitlement calculation. One of them, a Mr Steven Ponting, listed your bank on his pension forms. We don't appear to have a forwarding address and I was hoping you could help me.'

'Give me your number. I'll have my secretary look into it and call you back.'

'I don't suppose you could have someone look into it now for me?' Gabriel asked. 'I'm happy to hold.'

He heard the man take a long, luxurious drag on his cigarette. 'I'm afraid not. As I said, give me your number and I promise she will return your call.'

Gabriel rattled off a fake number and ended the call with profuse but entirely insincere thanks.

'Shit!' he said with feeling.

'What?'

Mei had just come in from a run and placed a mug of coffee by his right hand. Gabriel explained where he'd got to with the Spanish banker.

'It doesn't matter,' Mei said. 'We can just track him down in person. Between us, it shouldn't be too hard.'

* * *

Enrique González replaced the handset and stared at it for a few seconds. He took another drag on his cigarette, then called a lawyer friend of his.

'I had a call just now from Scotland Yard. They were asking about Señor Ponting. They were looking into his pension, apparently.'

'Apparently?'

'There's a cat locked up, Teo. I can't explain why.'

'OK, thanks, Kiké. I'll call him.'

González replaced the handset thoughtfully and finished his cigarette. He hadn't risen to, and held for years, his esteemed position in the family firm by spilling his guts to every foreign cop who came sniffing around the bank's clients.

15

MÁLAGA, COSTA DEL SOL, SPAIN

Even though the temperature in Málaga was a balmy 21 Celsius, and a light breeze was keeping him cool, Gabriel still didn't enjoy queuing for a hire car. In truth, he hated queuing anywhere, for anything.

He'd left Mei sitting on a sunlit bench checking her messages. She was running her company from her phone and whatever the deal in Singapore was about, it was days away from being signed.

In front of and behind him, tourists and business-types chattered about holidays, family reunions, conferences and sales targets. The thought of their reactions if they could have overheard his and Mei's conversation earlier that day made him smile.

  — Do we kill him at his house or take him somewhere?

  — It depends if he's got muscle protecting him.

  — Why would he have?

  — I don't know. But if he stayed bent all this time, then he's either part of a crew or he's done well enough for himself to hire one.

Gabriel wondered whether killing Ponting would finally close the book on the bleak history of the Wolfe family. Would he and Mei feel some tangible sense of freedom from the long, crooked shadow Ponting had cast over their respective lives since Christmas 1983? Or was it too late? Maybe the scars were too old and too integrated into their personalities to ever be transcended.

He felt nothing but hatred and contempt for Ponting. Killing him would be a pleasure. How could someone be so greedy, so venal, as to discard all sense of duty, of honour, for a few thousand pounds?

Wanting to know what a sergeant in the British police earned in 1983, he'd checked online and found a record of a question asked in Parliament of the Home Secretary. The annual basic pay for sergeants at that time ranged from £9,369 to £10,749. So Ponting had betrayed the Wolfes for a year's salary.

It didn't seem enough to Gabriel. Though he struggled to imagine what sort of sum would tempt him to betray Eli. There wasn't one large enough.

He reached the desk and began the process of exchanging a wealth of personal information for the keys to a Seat León. He'd been hoping they might have a sporty option, but when the smiling sales clerk finally proffered a black plastic fob attached by thin string to a dogeared cardboard label, she explained it was for a 1.4 litre petrol model.

Smiling, and offering her a 'Muchas gracias,' he turned and left the chilly, air-conditioned office. Collecting Mei, he followed the clerk's instructions to the parking bay housing their new ride and was leaving the airport's precincts a few minutes later.

Following the A-7 towards Algeciras and Cadiz, it took them an hour to make the forty-six-mile trip to San Luis de Sabinillas, the little coastal town where Jack Webb had said Roy McAllister owned his bar.

Gabriel parked on the street and got out to stretch his legs. Now things started to get real. The telephone research, the pretending to be a pensions administrator, the keeping a careful distance: they'd got them this far. Now it was time to fall back on more practical skills. And he knew that at some point, once he and Mei started asking questions, word would get back to Ponting.

If he was here in Spain, Gabriel thought he could live with that. He'd bet on his and Mei's ability to find Ponting before he skipped the country against his ability to evade them any day of the week. But what if Ponting wasn't here at all? If he'd only lived here for a while after Hong Kong, then the odds changed drastically in Ponting's favour. *Better hope he's here, then*, he thought.

They found a cheap hotel a few streets back from the beach. Clean tiled floors everywhere and a welcoming elderly lady owner who, once she'd shown Gabriel and Mei their rooms, disappeared into the cubby hole in the lobby where they'd found her.

Gabriel opened the window and looked down into a courtyard filled with glazed pots holding scarlet and deep-maroon geraniums. He caught a waft of their sharp lemon scent and thought immediately of Eli. He hoped she was OK. Pointless trying to figure out what she'd be doing.

They'd agreed not to try once their relationship became serious. It was counterproductive, imagining your partner lying dead in a dusty backstreet, or dumped in the ocean from a black-painted helicopter.

Mostly, Gabriel could manage it. But Eli had been talking enthusiastically about setting a date for their wedding before she left on her latest op, and the conversation had cemented the reality in his head.

He wanted it so much, and the thought that she might be taken from him, like so many of those he'd loved already had been, was becoming harder and harder to bear. He retreated into the cool of his room, shutting the window behind him.

He and Mei had agreed on a cover story that would stand a halfway decent chance of allowing them to probe Ponting's defences.

They were film-makers. She the producer, he the screen-writer. The legend explained Mei's appearance and serviceable but not fluent English. Everybody knew Chinese money was behind all sorts of projects around the world these days, from nuclear power stations to Hollywood blockbusters.

Their subject, which was bordering on outright truth, how organised crime figures had made the Costa del Sol their own. The angle, the growing impact of new waves of crime figures and their displacement of the 'old guard': British hard men from the sixties, seventies and eighties.

Target number one: McAllister's bar. Jack Webb hadn't been able to come up with a name. But he'd been helpful with approaches that might work.

'If I were you,' he'd said, 'I'd look for places with a really obvious British look. Pubs called the Royal Oak, or the King's Head, that sort of thing. Either that, or, if he went upmarket, it'll be kind of obviously stuck in the past. Like an eighties pop video. Those guys never had much imagination.'

Gabriel and Mei met up outside the hotel half an hour later. Gabriel wore tan chinos and a white linen shirt. Mei had opted for something more formal: a sage-green silk trouser suit over a lemon-yellow silk T-shirt. Three-inch heels completed the outfit.

'Does this say Chinese finance to you?' she asked with a grin.

He nodded, smiling back. 'It's perfect. You look like you could buy the whole town twice over. Maybe you should act like it, as well.'

'Treat you like the hired hand, you mean?'

He shrugged. 'I'm used to it.'

They walked down the sloping street towards the sea. Mopeds buzzed alarmingly close. Gabriel noticed Mei had her right arm clamped over her handbag, a neat little black quilted number with the distinctive linked 'C's of Chanel for the clasp. He pitied any lowlife street criminal who fancied their chances nicking her bag. He'd be lucky to escape with all his bones intact, if not his eyes.

'How do you want to do this?' Mei asked, as they strolled down the pavement between the beach and the bars, restaurants and ice-cream parlours lining the other side of the road.

'Let's just observe today. I don't want to trip anyone's early warning system by asking questions,' he said. 'We should split up. Take a picture of anywhere that fits Jack's theory for a bar a guy like McAllister might own. We can compare notes later.'

She nodded, looked up and down the street then turned back to Gabriel. 'I'll start at the far end and work my way back to here. You do the same, then we can go one street back and do it again.'

Gabriel grinned at his sister.

'What?' she asked, eyes wide.

'Told you I was used to being treated like the help.'

'If the cap fits,' she said, then turned on her stiletto heel and stalked off towards the end of town.

Calle Duquesa de Arcos was typical of the seafront streets on that part of the Spanish coast. Low-rise buildings painted white, yellow, cream or *café con leche*. Palm trees, their scaly trunks neatly trimmed of dead fronds. A pavement crammed with outdoor cafe furniture and tables with paper cloths held on by spring clips.

The smells of grilled chicken, fried fish and garlic mingled with the universal tourist aroma: coconut sun cream, expensive perfumes and aftershaves and summer sweat.

Gabriel sauntered along, hands in pockets, looking around him, imagining he was location-scouting for the movie he was writing. As he strolled, returning the smiles and occasional greetings of restaurant staff stationed beside their menu-stands, he tried to come up with titles.

Past Glories sounded good. *The Coastal Elite*. Very satirical. Or maybe something simple would work: *Costa*. He smiled. Ridiculous. It sounded like an ad for the coffee chain.

He caught the glance of a young waitress laying a table by the front door of one of the restaurants. Perhaps imagining his smile was for her, she returned one of her own, white teeth in a honey-coloured complexion.

'Table for one, sir?' she asked.

He shook his head. 'Maybe later. What's good here?'

She straightened and pushed a strand of dark hair back behind her ear. 'We have wild sea bass. Caught early this morning. The chef bakes it in a salt crust. Beautiful. Very moist. Very tender. We call it Lubina a la sal.'

Gabriel repeated it, trying to nail the regional accent.

Her eyes widened.

'Very good! Hablas Español como un local.'

He thought she was being kind saying he spoke like a local. Though fluent in Spanish, he didn't think he'd nailed the southern twang.

'No tan bien como tú hablas Ingles,' he replied. *Not as well as you speak English.*

She cocked a hip and gave him an appraising look. Her gaze fell to his left hand. Back to meet his eyes again.

'You are not a tourist, are you?' she asked, switching back to English.

He smiled. 'I'm a screenwriter. We're doing research for a new movie.'

A middle-aged woman appeared in the doorway of the restaurant. Hands on her ample, aproned hips, she looked left and right. On spotting the waitress, she raised her voice to be heard above the chatter from the surrounding tables.

'Alba! Deja de coquetear y vuelve al trabajo!'

Gabriel held his hands out in mock surrender. If the boss lady wanted Alba to stop flirting and get back to work, he'd better make a suitable apology.

'Lo siento, señora. Fue mi culpa. Ella estaba tomando mi reserva para esta noche.' *I'm sorry, señora. It was my fault. She was just taking my booking for tonight.*

This did the trick. She offered him a beneficent smile. 'Hasta luego, señor!' she called before disappearing back inside. *See you later!*

Gabriel asked for a table for two, outside, at seven that evening, gave his name as Gibson, and left Alba to her tables. On an impulse, he turned back.

'Busco un pub Inglés. Muy tradicional. Imagen de la reina y la cerveza Británica.' *I'm looking for an English bar. Very traditional. Picture of the Queen and British beer.*

Her eyes lit up. 'Sure! There are two. One is even called The Queen's Head.'

'And the other?'

She hesitated, looked up for a second. 'It's a bar, really. A funny name. La Luz Azul. That means…'

But Gabriel knew what it meant. The Blue Light. He thought he'd just found McAllister.

16

NOVI SAD

Popović leaned back in his chair and stared at the small, irregular pieces of cardboard scattered across the table in front of him. He'd been working on this particular puzzle for a couple of days and was close to giving up. He picked up the box lid again and scrutinised the picture.

His wife came in from the garden and stroked a cool hand over the skin at the back of his neck. He looked round and smiled.

'Are you still stuck?' she said.

'It's this bloody sky,' he exclaimed with a hint of petulance. 'Who puts a sky like that in a painting? Not a single cloud. How am I supposed to do it?'

She leaned over him, exposing her deep cleavage, which he stared at greedily as though she were a new girlfriend and not his soulmate of twenty-eight years. She stretched out her hand and selected a piece. She placed it in a corner of royal blue fading to turquoise and tapped it in with a long, pink nail.

'Like that,' she said with a grin. 'Lunch in half an hour, OK?'

He nodded, grinning. As she turned she lingered just long enough for him to pat her behind. Milena knew him well.

He went back to his jigsaw, scanning the array of blues before him and trying to repeat Milena's trick. His phone rang, drawing a brief curse from his lips. Then he saw the name on the display and frowned. He hadn't spoken to Teodoro Marín for, what? It must have been ten years, easy.

'Teo. Long time no speak,' he said, using English for the first time in weeks.

'Yes, my friend. How are you? And your fine family?'

'I'm good. They are, too.'

'Your boys. They must be young men now.'

'Vlado's twenty-two. He's studying Business Administration at the University of Belgrade. I'm preparing him to take over when I'm too old. Andrej just turned eighteen. He's working with me already. More on the enforcement side, but that was always his talent.'

The lawyer laughed, a whispery sound in which he could hear many years of good brandy and better cigars.

'Every man has one, Steven. Mine is watchfulness,' he said, his voice becoming serious. 'A friend phoned me from Banco Sombra. Scotland Yard called him. They were asking about you. Trying to trace your whereabouts.'

'Did this friend of yours tell them anything?'

'No. Kiké is discreet. He called me, that was all. But he said something that worried me.'

'What?'

'He said something did not feel right. We say in Spanish *hay gato encerrado*. It means there's a cat locked up. In English, maybe the expression is, there is something fishy?'

After ending the call, Popović stared down at the half-completed jigsaw.

'Fuck!' he shouted. Then he swept the pieces onto the floor with a violent backhand swing of his arm.

17

'We need a gun,' Mei said over breakfast the next morning.

'Don't you think we have what it takes to deal with a retired cop?' Gabriel replied.

'Yes, but we might end up killing him if he decides to fight. People obey you when you point a gun in their face.'

Gabriel had to concede. They'd both pointed enough guns into enough people's faces to know her assessment of human behaviour was accurate. Even a chess-playing pacifist might hurl the board at you if you threatened him with a knife. Show him the business end of a nine and he'd do whatever you told him to.

The same went for most people with a services background. Most, Gabriel thought, But not all. There were some, like him and his former colleagues in the Regiment, like Eli, who'd been trained how to disarm all but the most determined gun-waver.

'Who has guns?' he asked Mei.

'You can buy rifles and shotguns legally. Other than that, it's the police, military and criminals.'

'Cops are easier to track down than bad guys.'

'We're not going to kill any cops.'

Mei shrugged. 'You're in charge, BB. I'm just saying, if you want to get hold of a pistol quickly, finding a cop is going to be a hell of a lot easier than hanging around some scuzzy area waiting to get robbed,' she said. 'Plus it'd probably be some smackhead with a dodgy purse-gun that'd blow your hand off if you pulled the trigger.'

Gabriel nodded. He thought he knew of a way they could relieve a cop of their gun without any bloodshed.

Later that day, around noon, when the roads above San Luis de Sabinillas were deserted, Gabriel pulled over at a gravelled viewpoint next to the gates to a vineyard.

He and Mei got out. They wandered over to the guardrail and looked down, across the scrub-covered hillside towards the sea. The smell of wild rosemary, thyme and lavender drifted up from the sun-warmed ground before them. Everywhere bright-yellow and hot-pink flowers bloomed on thorny bushes clinging like limpets to the slope.

Mei had gone into town after they'd formulated their plan. She'd returned with a glossy carrier bag in black with hot-pink ribbon handles. It contained the outfit she wore now: a leopard-skin mini-skirt and a wide-shouldered, buttercup-yellow leather jacket.

Mei pulled a blonde wig from her bag and adjusted it until it completely covered her own hair, which she'd pinned up before leaving the hotel. With over-sized sunglasses and a vivid slash of shocking pink lipstick, she'd transformed her appearance from Hong Kong Chinese bodyguard-turned-CEO to Eurotrash princess.

'How do I look?' she asked Gabriel.

'Like your name ought to be Diamante, or maybe Chardonnay.'

She grinned. 'That's good, right?'

'You look like you stepped straight off a Russian oligarch's yacht.'

'Or a Chinese billionaire's.'

'Or that,' he agreed.

For his own persona, that of a D-list celebrity, Gabriel had clad himself in a white suit with garish mauve lining over a burnt-orange T-shirt. He'd also donned mirrored aviator sunglasses, and had spent half an hour in the bathroom bleaching his hair. The effect, while shocking, was perfect: all trace of the old Gabriel Wolfe had gone, to be replaced with 'Tony Van Der Weyen' from Chelsea.

Their object was simple; overload the unfortunate cop with so many blaring visual signals that he'd give a hugely confident and radically incorrect description of the two people he'd encountered high in the hills above the town.

'Make the call,' Gabriel said, pushing up the sleeves of his suit jacket.

Mei breathed in and out rapidly a few times, then called the emergency number.

'Hello, er, buenos días. We've been robbed. Mugged!' she panted.

Gabriel heard the operator's question as a buzz from the phone. *Where are you?*

'Camiño del Pocillo,' Mei said. 'Just after the roundabout. What? You don't understand? Hold on.' She turned to Gabriel. 'What's the Spanish for roundabout?'

Gabriel checked the sign at the gates to the vineyard. It told visitors, in English and Spanish, Welcome to the House of Goats Vineyard.

'Tell her, rotonda por la casa de las cabras viñedo.'

Word by word, and maintaining her breathless diction, Mei repeated their location to the call centre.

'Thank you so much,' she said and ended the call.

'Well?' Gabriel asked. 'And by the way, your Oscar nomination is in the bag.'

'I'm enjoying myself,' Mei said with a grin. 'They're sending someone. She said no longer than ten minutes.'

They waited in the car, leaving the doors open to admit the soft sea breeze blowing up the hill.

Gabriel checked his watch. Seven minutes had elapsed since Mei made the fake emergency call. Then he heard the sound of a big motorbike engine. Not under strain, but being ridden fast. He turned to Mei.

'Showtime!'

They got out. A white bike with green stripes was slowing as it approached the viewpoint. It was a BMW, Gabriel saw, noting the cylinders of its flat twin engine sticking out sideways through the fairing.

The cop heeled out the kickstand and dismounted, lifting the whole front of his helmet as he swaggered towards them. Sun glinted off his mirror-polished knee-boots. Gabriel glanced at his left hip and was relieved to see a black leather holster, its strap fastened over a black grip of a handgun.

As soon as he arrived, Mei went into overdrive. Sobbing, she related in deliberately garbled English and Spanish a story of a long-haired mugger who'd held them up at gunpoint and taken her bag and her friend's wallet, plus two Rolexes. She grabbed his hi-vis vest and then swung an arm round and pointed up into the hills. *Thataway!*

Politely, but firmly, the cop disengaged her clawed hands from his jacket. Gabriel intervened. In Spanish he told the cop he'd seen the mugger tearing off on foot towards a small housing development. He added a few details to Mei's description and urged the cop to give chase.

But as the cop listened, Gabriel was introducing commands in a different pitch, interspersing them among the words of the surface story. He matched them with a precisely coordinated sequence of movements of his head and hands, flicking his gaze from the cop's right eye to his left, then back again.

This was a technique of *Yinshen fangshi*: the Way of Stealth. Master Zhao had drilled him for years in its intricacies; always patient, never shouting, but relentless in his tutelage, until the teenaged Gabriel Wolfe could put his own master into a temporary hypnotic trance and relieve him of a jade figurine he clasped in his hand, replacing it with a walnut.

Zhao had been adept in the art, and when Gabriel had finally beaten him, admitted he'd been powerless to resist. Compared to Master Zhao, the cop was as biddable as a sheep. His eyes wandered after only a few seconds and his lower jaw dropped a little so that Gabriel could see his tongue. Slowly, a thin trickle of saliva crawled down his chin and dripped to the hot earth beneath his boots.

Gabriel had also been shopping earlier in the day. Now he pulled his purchase from the waistband of his suit trousers. Without taking his eyes off the cop, he unsnapped the press stud closing the retaining strap over his 9 mm and lifted it clear, before replacing it with a very realistic matt-black air pistol.

He snapped his fingers, twice, right between the cop's eyes.

'No deberías estar persiguiendo al atracador? Se fue por ahí,' he said indignantly. *Shouldn't you be chasing the mugger? He went that way.*

The cop blinked. 'Por supuesto! Espera aquí.' *Of course! Wait here.*

He ran back to his bike, thumbed the starter and then flipped his visor down and roared away, heading further up the hill.

As soon as he was out of sight, Gabriel stashed the purloined pistol, a scuffed but serviceable Beretta 92 9mm, in the spare wheel well.

He pulled out and drove carefully back into town, slipping on a black wig at the same time as Mei was removing her blonde one. They were back in the hotel fifteen minutes later, clinking beer bottles in the bar.

'That was an impressive little trick,' Mei said.

'Master Zhao taught me.'

'When do you think he'll notice you swapped his pistol?'

Gabriel shrugged. 'Next time he draws it, I suppose. For a traffic cop in a small town like this, it could be months from now.'

She nodded. 'And if he remembers us at all, his description won't be worth shit.'

Gabriel pointed to his hair, which was itching beneath the wig. 'What do you think? Should I keep the spikes?'

Mei shook her head, grinning. 'I'll go into town in a minute and get you some brown dye.'

Gabriel pouted. 'I think they make me look cool.'

She rolled her eyes. 'Moving on. Once we talk to McAllister, we'll have to hold onto him until we locate Ponting in case they're in contact.' She took a swig of her beer. 'Or we could just kill him.'

'No. He's done nothing to us.'

'But holding him means splitting up. And what if Ponting's not here? What if he's not even in Spain?' Mei hissed. 'I'm not going to play gaoler for a week, let alone a month.'

Mei was right. Even though she'd assumed it would be her left behind with McAllister, the whole scenario didn't work. He ran through a possible chain of events. They interrogated McAllister. He gave up Ponting. As soon as they left him, he called Ponting.

– *I've just been beaten up by two people looking for you, Steve.*

– *What did they want?*

– *They wouldn't say.*

Ponting would wonder about the enemies he'd made since moving to Spain. Maybe if he was still involved in criminality, he'd pissed off the wrong people. He'd think they were coming for money, or to exact punishment for a double-cross.

But if he'd gone straight, then what? He might have bought a bar like McAllister. Opened a boat hire business. Or retrained as a homeopath. Stranger things had happened.

He'd think his past was catching up with him. The question was, how far back would he go in searching for an answer? All the way to a baby and her three-year-old brother?

Gabriel didn't see it. That wasn't the way memory worked. Adults framed their sins in terms of other adults. A bent cop on the straight and narrow would imagine other cops coming for him. That or villains he'd framed, extorted or been in business with.

Either way, how would Ponting react to McAllister's warning? He'd get skittish. He could run, or he could double-down on whatever security he had. Wait for the battle to come to him.

Gabriel had an idea.

'Once he's given us Ponting, let's tell McAllister to warn him we're coming.'

Mei's eyes popped wide. 'What? Are you crazy? Why would we do that?'

Gabriel smiled. 'We go and see McAllister. He tells us where Ponting is. If he's in this part of Spain, I'll go and stake his place out. Once I'm in position, I'll call you and you let McAllister make the call. You wouldn't have to hold McAllister for more than a few hours.'

Mei nodded eagerly. 'He tells him we're on our way and asks him what he's going to do.' She paused, frowned for a second. 'I'll get him to put Ponting on speaker, then we know what Ponting's going to do. If he runs, you can follow him and I'll catch you up.'

'Exactly. And if he says he's going to stay put, you can come and join me straightaway.'

'Yeah, but what if he calls him again as soon as I leave? Tells him we know his plans.'

'I don't think it matters. He still only has the two options. If he says he'll stay and then runs anyway, I'll be on his tail immediately.'

'What if he's somewhere else? Up north, or in another country?'

Gabriel looked up, into the cloudless sky. What would *he* do if someone from his own past was on his trail, out for blood? And God knew, there were plenty of those.

Most of the major players were dead. Lizzie Maitland. Max Novgorodsky. Sasha Beck. Comrade Liu. But there were loyal lieutenants he hadn't killed. People who might have acquired vast wealth or undreamed-of power, but for Gabriel's interventions.

Run? He didn't think so. He'd realise that the kind of people capable of tracking him down once could do it again. He wouldn't want to spend the rest of his life running. He'd find a way to neutralise the threat. Either a pre-emptive strike or by digging in and waiting for his pursuer to arrive.

To neutralise a threat you'd have to know where that threat was coming from. Difficult for Ponting. Mei and he had arrived in Spain with fake identities. Even if McAllister managed to recall their appearance with one hundred percent accuracy, what use would it be to Ponting? There'd be no chance he could translate their adult features into those of two tiny children.

But Mei had inherited her half-Chinese mother's looks, whereas some quirk of genetics had given Gabriel entirely Caucasian features. He lacked even a trace of the epicanthic fold at the inner corners of his eyes to give the game away. His father had always said it showed the strength of the Wolfe genes.

Would Ponting seize on McAllister's description of 'a Chinese bird' and make the connection to the kidnapping thirty-seven years earlier? More to the point, would it matter? These possibilities were too many branches down the decision-tree to be useful for planning purposes. Gabriel drew back towards the trunk.

McAllister would warn Ponting to expect a man and a woman who were out looking for him and prepared to use force to acquire his location. That would spell danger. The one thing Gabriel was certain of was that Ponting wouldn't go to the police. They'd ask too many questions.

Suddenly, Gabriel knew what Ponting would do. He'd stand his ground, in Spain or elsewhere. He had to. If he wasn't armed already, he'd acquire a firearm. And he'd get cautious. Start changing his routine. Maybe hire some muscle if he could afford it.

But paranoia was the friend of the pursuer, not the pursued. It screwed up people's risk perception and interfered with their ability to think rationally. A disorganised enemy could be defeated by their own panic.

Gabriel thought that, after all these years, he was starting to think – and sound – like Master Zhao.

'What?' Mei asked. 'Why are you smiling?'

'We're going to get him, Mei,' he said. 'I can feel it.'

18

It took Gabriel less than two minutes to discount The Queen's Head. The owners were a retired couple from Durham. He spoke to the wife. Her husband had worked for the council for thirty-five years.

La Luz Azul occupied a corner site facing a pretty square dominated by a white church at its far end. A scruffy white-and-tan terrier was lying in a patch of shade beside the front door. It raised its whiskery snout from its front paws long enough to look up at Gabriel, wagged its tail a couple of times, then settled back down and closed its eyes again.

Gabriel pushed through the door and entered the brightly lit interior of the bar. As he'd predicted in his idolised description to Alba the day before, a photo of the Queen hung dead centre behind the bar. It was flanked by racks of backlit glass shelves in acid yellow and lime green displaying several dozen bottles of spirits and liqueurs.

Surely this was McAllister's place. Then Gabriel noticed something that clinched it for him. A blue bubble-light of the type American cops slapped onto the roofs of their unmarked cars was screwed to the wall above a blue-and-white plastic sign.

The sign read 'West End Central', the name of a police station a few blocks from Trafalgar Square. Gabriel looked around. A few afternoon drinkers looked up, but mostly he was clearly a figure of no interest.

He pulled out his phone and took a picture of the sign. This small action did elicit a reaction. A silver-haired man who'd been sitting in a corner working on a set of account books with an oversized calculator came over.

'Can I help you?' he asked.

Years of living the good life in Spain had smoothed off the corners of a Cockney accent. The tone was amiable. The look wasn't overtly hostile. Not yet.

Gabriel turned, pasting a wide smile on his face. The man facing him was a couple of inches over six foot, and in good shape. Fifteen, maybe sixteen, stone and with a build that spoke, if not of sessions in the gym, then at least a certain restraint when it came to sampling his own wares.

'Are you the owner?' Gabriel asked as if he was in the presence of the Spanish king.

'I am. Like I said, can I help you?'

The friendliness was still there in his voice, just. But there was an edge of, what, threat? Not quite. But wariness. Understandable, if he was who Gabriel thought he was.

Gabriel introduced himself and delivered a short version of his legend.

'We're looking for people who know their way around that world,' he said. 'To act as consultants while we develop the main character's backstory. Paid, of course,' he added with a smile. 'Can I ask your name?'

'It's Roy,' the guy said. 'McAllister.'

Still suspicious. But Gabriel thought the double promise of involvement with a Hollywood film and the lure of some easy money would be working on him from within now.

'Maybe I could get a beer, then, Roy. If you've got five minutes, I can tell you a little more about the film.'

McAllister nodded and signalled to a barman. 'Dos Cruzcampo.'

He turned back to Gabriel. 'Take a seat.'

The barman brought the beers over and they clicked bottle necks. Gabriel took a pull on his beer.

He outlined the entirely fictional story of a British crime figure relocating to Spain in the eighties then being drawn against his will into gang warfare with incoming Russians.

Throughout, McAllister watched him with hooded eyes, nodding occasionally, but otherwise keeping completely still. Gabriel could imagine it a powerful incentive to talk for the people he'd formerly pursued before going rogue and joining them.

'It sounds like a good idea, but I'm afraid I can't help you. The people you're talking about, well, the ones who are still alive, they're mostly up the coast in Marbella,' he said. 'Maybe a few scattered about, but all that was a long time ago. They're old men. Most of 'em have either popped their clogs or they've got Alzheimer's.'

Gabriel nodded. He desperately wanted to ask about bent cops but if he did that, he might as well cut out the middleman and throw himself out of the bar.

'I understand,' he said. 'It's a shame, really. I mean I'm a writer, obviously, so I can,' he mimed tapping frenetically on a keyboard, 'make it all up. But without that edge of realism the punters can just tell, you know?'

McAllister shrugged, then drained his beer. 'I wish I could help you, Joe. Sorry.'

Gabriel felt the window closing fast. He had to squeeze through before it shut completely. 'Look,' he said, leaning across the table towards McAllister and lowering his voice to a conspiratorial whisper. 'I shouldn't be telling you this. My director would fire me if he even *thought* I was saying anything. But if you knew who we've got lined up to play the gangster, well, let's just say he *cruises* along in the A-list, if you know what I mean.'

McAllister rolled his eyes. 'As a retired East End gangster? Are you serious? Never mind the height, what about the accent?'

'I'm deadly serious, Roy. T—, I mean this actor, he's been having dialect coaching for six months to get it right.'

'Yeah, well, good luck with that.'

'Sorry, I didn't explain myself properly. It's just, one of our production crew, her uncle was in the police,' he said, deliberately allowing himself to get flustered. 'He said to Rosie, that's her name by the way, lovely girl. There was a guy who if we could talk to, he'd unlock the narrative arc. Really give us the insights we need into the whole Costa del Crime culture. You see,' Gabriel looked both ways, wondering as he did so whether he was overcooking the 'need for secrecy' act, 'he's an ex-cop. Apparently he retired down here. And when I saw your bar, well, naturally, I thought he might be one of your patrons.'

McAllister looked unconcerned. He pursed his lips. 'Got a name, has he? This ex-copper?'

'Hold on,' Gabriel said, pulling out his phone and consulting a note-taking app. 'Yes, here it is. His name's Steven Ponting. I think that's right. Bloody autocorrect, you can never tell nowadays, can you? It could be Postman for all I know.'

McAllister shook his head. 'Sorry. If there is a bloke by that name, he doesn't drink in here. Or not to my knowledge.'

Gabriel frowned, letting his lower lip protrude a fraction: just the suggestion of a creative person pouting out of frustration.

'Crap! Oh, well,' he said, brightly. 'If you don't ask, eh? Look, I need to meet the producer in twenty minutes, but thanks for your help. How much do I owe you for the *cerveza*?'

McAllister flapped a hand languidly. 'On the house. What did you say the film was called again? I'll have to look out for it.'

'It's just a working title,' Gabriel said as he got to his feet. 'Looper's Chase.'

Outside again, he strolled away from the bar without a backward glance. He imagined McAllister standing in the doorway following his progress down the street before pulling out a phone and calling Ponting to warn him, then dismissed it. The story was beautifully simple. And he'd played it with just the right combination of movie industry arrogance and bumbling Englishness.

He called Mei and explained he'd already found McAllister. They met up in ten minutes at a bar fronting the sea, sitting at a table shaded by a palm tree.

'I think he's lying,' Gabriel said as Mei signalled a waiter.

'Why?'

'Look, we know from Jack that McAllister's bent. Or was. So was Ponting,' Gabriel said. 'What are the odds two bent cops who moved down here at the same time wouldn't know each other?'

Mei ordered two coffees. 'Low. Probably. But you said Ponting's bank was in Málaga. That's up the coast from here. Maybe he's there.'

Gabriel stared out at the sea, squinting as the sun bounced slivers of bright-white light into his eyes. Mei was right. He'd leaped to conclusions because it was the shortest way between two points. Him being one and Ponting being the other. What if Ponting wasn't in Spain at all? It was entirely possible. But that was why it was so important to pick up his trail.

Their coffees arrived. Gabriel thanked the waiter and took a sip. It was the best he'd tasted in quite a while. Strong and nutty with that indefinable quality that came from drinking in a sun-warmed outdoor cafe on the Mediterranean coast.

'If *I* was a bent cop,' Mei said, 'and a stranger came sniffing around my bar asking questions about *another* bent cop, I'd blank him. Even if McAllister did buy your screenwriter story, he had no reason to give up Ponting.'

Gabriel frowned. 'Maybe you're right.'

Mei rolled her eyes. 'Listen, BB. I know corrupt cops, OK? I had dozens on my payroll. It's like a club. They don't squeal unless they're under pressure.'

Gabriel nodded. If McAllister wasn't willing to help voluntarily, maybe they'd have to try a more direct approach. He looked at his sister. The way she'd said 'pressure', made him think she wanted to apply some.

'You think we should pay him another visit?' he asked.

'Not now. Later. Early tomorrow morning.'

'Three?'

'Perfect.'

* * *

La Luz Azul closed its doors at 1.00 a.m. In navy and dark-grey clothes, Gabriel and Mei sat in the hire car parked across the road and a few doors down from the bar. Both wore dark baseball caps pulled down low over their foreheads.

Gabriel watched as the stream of punters leaving the bar dwindled to a few couples and solo drinkers. After nobody else emerged from its blue-lit interior during a ten-minute wait, he turned to Mei. She nodded back at him.

'He should be out soon,' he said.

He imagined McAllister having a final drink at the bar while the staff cleaned up and stacked chairs on tables ready for the morning cleaners. Loud laughter made him look up. Three young bartenders in black trousers and white shirts came out from the front door, laughing and kidding around, giving each other piggy-backs.

They made their way down the street, presumably in search of a bar they didn't work in where they could let off steam and relax before going home.

Mei nudged him. She jerked her chin in the direction of La Luz Azul. McAllister was standing with his back to them, locking the door. Gabriel hoped he walked to work. If he had a car, they'd stick out following him: the town was virtually deserted and there'd been hardly any traffic while they'd been sitting outside the bar.

19

McAllister walked up the road towards them. Gabriel slumped lower in his seat. If he spotted them and came over they'd have to adopt new tactics at speed. He was ready for it, but would prefer it if they could stick to the original plan.

In the event, McAllister turned left up a narrow side street. Gabriel got out, Mei following, and wandered down until he could look up the side street. As he reached the spot opposite the turning, he heard a powerful car engine turn over and then saw bright car headlights. He dashed back to his own car, Mei at his heels.

McAllister appeared at the junction behind the wheel of a bulky Mercedes coupe. An eighties SL in silver, Gabriel saw; noting the car's long, low stance. McAllister indicated left then swept out and accelerated away from his bar. Gabriel had to execute a hurried three-point turn and was a few hundred yards back from the Merc by the time he'd got the Seat facing the right way.

Either McAllister was in a relaxed mood after a night schmoozing his clientele or he was always a cautious driver. Given the late hour and total absence of traffic, let alone cops, Gabriel was surprised he didn't put his foot down. Especially given the performance the SL could deliver.

He tailed the silver coupe for five miles, staying as far back as he dared without losing visuals on the target. Mei was looking at the route on her phone, giving him a running commentary on upcoming junctions, allowing him to drop back where there was an unbroken stretch, only closing with McAllister if there was a risk he'd turn off and lose them.

Eventually, McAllister made a right turn into a driveway of a two-storey house and stopped. Gabriel pulled off the road and watched as the car's rear lights dimmed and winked out. They gave McAllister five minutes to get inside and pour himself a drink or grab something from the fridge, then, on foot, made their way along the scrubby verge to the driveway.

It was 1.30 a.m.

Reaching the gate to the house, Gabriel squatted down in the lee of a sprawling bougainvillea that scrambled through a chain-link fence. Mei joined him, facing the road.

'How do you want to get in?' she asked, looking over her shoulder at the house.

He took a look at the house himself. 'We could go in through the roof. Those barrel tiles look like they'd lift off easily. Or we can go in through the door.'

Gabriel had bought a set of lock picks in the same, mildly dodgy shop where he'd found the air pistol currently snug in the Guardia Civil officer's black leather holster. He would have loved to see the expression on the cop's face the next time he pulled it. He hoped it would be on the range or for an inspection. He also carried a lock-knife and the cop's pistol tucked into the waistband of his trousers.

'Maybe easier than that if he's left a window open,' she said. 'We should check whether he's got a burglar alarm.'

Gabriel nodded. 'Let's wait until three and then come back for a quick look round. Whatever looks easiest, we'll do.'

Back at the car, they climbed in and closed the doors softly. Gabriel buzzed his window down, admitting the scent of some sweetly perfumed shrub and the incessant chitter and whine of nocturnal insects.

'You remember those christening gifts you gave me?' Mei asked.

'The horse and the rabbit, yes, of course.'

She reached into her T-shirt and pulled free a little silver horse on a fine chain. 'I wear it every day,' she said. 'The rabbit sits on my desk at the office.'

'I hope he brings you good luck.'

'Seems to have, so far.' She turned to look at him. 'What about you, BB? You're getting married.'

'Yep.'

'Is that all you can say? "Yep"? Eli's lovely!' Mei said indignantly. 'I didn't get much time to talk to her last time she was there but I can see why you love her. What's wrong?'

'Nothing's wrong.'

She rolled her eyes. 'Come on, it's me you're talking to. Maybe we were separated for all those years, but I have a sister's sense. I can tell you're not happy.'

'I *am* happy. It's just—'

'What?'

Gabriel struggled to put his feelings into words. It was something he hadn't shared with Eli. But maybe, sitting here in the dark with his sister, the words would come. He stared out of the windscreen and tried to get out of the way, to let his feelings speak for themselves.

'I'll be a married man! That's supposed to be about stability, isn't it? Regular hours. Living the suburban dream. How can I accept that and still do the job I love?'

'You don't know many married people, do you?' Mei said. Gabriel detected more than a hint of sarcasm.

'Not many, no. Don and Christine. A few people in Aldeburgh. That's it.'

'Let me tell you something about triad life, BB,' she said. 'If a husband runs drugs for the Coral Snakes, his wife works for them, too. Maybe in the accounting department. If a wife is a croupier in one of their casinos, the husband works the door.'

'What's your point?'

'Marriage is *here*,' she said, emphasising the last word by rapping her knuckle against her side window, which she hadn't lowered.

'Work is there.' She pointed at Gabriel's door. 'Separate, yes? Do you think soldiers, spies and firearms cops don't get married? Only bank managers and librarians?'

'No. Of course not.'

'Then what? Why can't you and Eli tie the knot and still carry on working for Don if that's what you want?'

There it was. The killer question. Why *couldn't* they? What was nagging at him like a dull toothache? Not quiet enough to ignore, but not so painful you wanted to do something about it. The kind of ache you'd keep prodding at with your tongue, taking the odd painkiller, hoping it would settle down of its own accord.

But it wouldn't. It would just grumble away until one day, or, more likely, night, it would wake you up with a lightning bolt of pain that would send you scrambling for codeine, alcohol, whatever you had in the house while you counted down the hours until you could call the dentist and try to book an emergency appointment.

'I don't know. Not exactly. I just have this feeling of unease,' he said. 'As if we're making ourselves bigger targets by getting married.'

'There can't be anyone left who wants you dead,' Mei said. 'You killed them all.'

'It's not that.'

'What is it, then?'

'It's leverage, isn't it?'

'Explain?'

Gabriel thought back to an unpleasant few days he'd spent in the basement of the Iranian Ministry of Intelligence and Security in Tehran. To get the ball rolling, his captor had nailed Gabriel's hand to a table.

'I was tortured once,' he said. 'I survived. I went inside myself. Used techniques Master Zhao taught me. I could do it because it was just me they were hurting. But Eli's like a whole other level of vulnerability. In Chile, under Pinochet, do you know what the secret police used to do to get information out of dissidents?'

'Something horrible, I expect.'

'They had this device called the grill. A shallow box like a metal bed frame. What they used to do was lock the prisoner in it, face-up. Then they brought in their wife, or husband, shackled them to the top of the frame and then tortured them.' Gabriel paused, trying to slow his pulse, which had started racing. 'The prisoner was close enough to hear every breath, let alone scream, to feel their loved one writhing with pain, to smell their fear, get their blood on them. Nobody held out. Everybody broke.'

'And you're frightened that could happen to you and Eli?'

'Yes! I am! How could I deal with it, Mei? I couldn't,' he said. 'I'd break. I'd betray the op, Don, The Department, my country, you, everything I love and hold dear. Just to save her a second's pain.'

Mei stayed silent once he'd finished his impassioned speech. He could hear her breathing alongside the high-pitched song of the crickets and cicadas. Finally, she spoke.

'One day, I hope I find a man who loves me as much as you love Eli.'

Gabriel contented himself with a nod. Godammit, why didn't love come with a manual? Why couldn't you strip it down, take it to pieces and figure out how it worked? And how to fix it if anything went wrong?

He checked the time. An hour to go. He closed his eyes. Time to snatch a little sleep.

It was surprisingly cold outside the car. Probably the snow. He saw a red-haired figure in a long black fur coat walking towards him, kicking up powdery sprays of white with her boots.

She met him halfway between the car and McAllister's place. A fresh, flower-strewn grave separated them. Oxeye daisies, cornflowers and field poppies as bright as arterial blood carpeted the recently turned earth. He looked down and read the name off the headstone. Britta Falskog. Odd. They must have made a mistake. Here she was, as large as life.

– *Mei's right,* she said. *You're wrong.*

– *About what?*

– *About love.*

– *Because?*

She grinned, revealing a gap between her front teeth.

— Silly, boy! Because love isn't a rifle or a radio set, that's why. You can't field-strip your emotions. You just have to enjoy them. If you can't enjoy them, you have to bear them. There is no other choice.

— You sound like Fariyah.

Britta pulled up a turquoise hijab and tucked her streaming coppery hair beneath its silky folds.

— You should listen to her. You should listen to us all. Marrying Eli won't weaken you. Or her. I have to go. I don't think you'll be seeing much more of me.

She turned and walked away, rounding McAllister's house. He saw her moving steadily up the hillside away from him through the snow. Felt wetness on his cheeks. And someone nudging him. He coughed and opened his eyes. Found the dampness was real and dashed away the tears.

'Time to go,' Mei was saying.

He nodded and climbed out of the car.

20

Up here, away from the town, there were no streetlights to cast a yellow pall over the hillside. A crescent moon hung over the sea, sending a wobbling line of silver sickles across its surface towards the shore. Stars were out, but their light, combined with that of their waning sister, did little but glaze the ground with grey.

Gabriel and Mei waited until their eyes had adjusted and then, on silent feet, ran down the sloping driveway to the house. He looked at the roofline, saw no winking red light, breathed a little easier. Caught the scent of rosemary and thyme. He signalled for Mei to go left; he went right.

As he crept along the side of the house, his eyes searching the walls for the light of a burglar alarm, Gabriel wondered whether this was how Fang Jian and his accomplice had felt as they prepared to take Tara Wolfe from her crib.

Snake and Donkey: that's how they'd been known when they were nothing but blue lanterns – junior members – of the Four Point Star triad. Now the Snake was dead and the Donkey had disappeared far into the reeds of the British witness protection programme. But their legacy remained. Decades when Gabriel and

Tara had been unaware of each other's existence. And the deaths of the three other members of Gabriel's family.

He stepped on a twig which snapped, sending a shiver of anticipation through him. Every muscle locked and he slowed his breathing as he waited for McAllister to appear at the door bellowing, 'Who's there?' Nothing happened. Cursing his inattention, he made his way to the rear of the house. On the way, he noted three windows, all closed and apparently fastened securely from the inside.

McAllister didn't have a back garden as such: no fence, no lawn, no flower beds. Instead, a cleared patch of rocky hillside dotted with spike-leaved plants.

Mei had just appeared at the opposite corner of the house and they met in the centre of the rear wall.

'He's left a window open a crack on my side,' she murmured.

Gabriel nodded. He followed her back the way she'd come, touching the pistol tucked into his waistband on the way. Would he have to use it? He didn't know. He hoped not. Or not for its intended purpose at any rate. McAllister would die if it became necessary, but he'd not wronged Gabriel and, for that reason, Gabriel wanted to spare his life.

Propped open by a long-handled wooden spoon in place of a stay, the window led into a kitchen. Gabriel peered in through the pane next to it, careful not to press any part of his face against the glass. The only obstacle was the stainless-steel sink directly in front of the window. He looked down: no dishes. A small but significant blessing: it meant they could climb in without risking a crash from disturbed crockery.

He put his gloves on, held the window open with one hand and slid the other through the gap, lifting the wooden spoon free. He was about to lever himself over the sill when Mei put a restraining hand on his shoulder.

She pointed a finger at her own chest. *Me.*

Mei was right. She was smaller and lighter than him. Possibly more agile. He held the window wide and kept a watch to left and right as she slithered through the gap. The only sound a whisper of fabric as she slid her hips over the edge of the sink.

She pointed to her left: he understood at once. He closed the window silently and waited for Mei to open the back door. In the distance a dog barked three times, a deep-bellied, mournful sound. Gabriel imagined a Rottweiler, or a big German Shepherd, chained outside and miserable at being denied the comforts of an indoor bed, or even a rug on the floor.

The scratch of a key in a lock brought him back to the task at hand. The door opened slowly. McAllister maintained his house well: no squeak or protest from un-oiled hinges.

Inside with Mei, he pulled out the pistol. He pointed towards the door at the other end of the kitchen and then flicked his finger left and right. Mei nodded. Shoulder to shoulder, they advanced across the terracotta tiles and left the kitchen through an open archway.

They checked the rooms leading off a wide hallway that led to the front door. Gabriel entered a large, open-plan sitting room. Paintings crowded together on a wall above expensive hi-fi components including, when he peered closer, an amplifier studded with glass valves: a mini-cityscape of transparent skyscrapers glinting in the faint light filtering into the room.

Back in the hallway, he pointed at the stairs, a curving flight of tiled steps with a white bannister. He led the way, pistol in hand. Three doors led off the landing: all were open. Gabriel turned to Mei and put a finger to his lips. He closed his eyes and listened.

Yes. Above the beat of his own heart, he heard breathing. Not the light, easy inhalations and exhalations of a clean-living citizen: these were stertorous rasps, halfway between a grunt and a groan. He chose to believe McAllister suffered from bad sleep as a direct result of his own corruption, though the truth was probably a combination of his age and his lifestyle.

They entered McAllister's bedroom in single file. Gabriel rounded the king-sized bed, keeping an eye on the sheet-clad form sprawled across the centre. Mei went right and took up a position in the shadows of the far corner, between a large, heavy wardrobe and a cheval glass, its oval mirror reflecting two desperadoes back at Gabriel.

Pulse elevated slightly, he pulled a simple wooden chair out from the wall, tilted it so the jeans and shirt slung across the seat slipped to the floor, and placed it a few feet back from McAllister's head.

He settled himself, crossed his legs and let the pistol rest on his right knee.

And then he spoke.

'Mr McAllister? Wake up.'

He waited, tasting the sharpness of adrenaline at the back of his throat. Enjoying it.

McAllister clearly did not have a problem with sleeping. The juddering breaths faltered, then resumed.

Gabriel leaned forwards and knocked the pistol's muzzle against an ankle that had escaped from the sheet.

The leg jerked away; the movement appeared involuntary, as if he'd touched some kind of sensitive plant.

'McAllister! Wake up!'

This time, McAllister heard him. With a strangled moan he heaved himself upright, then reared back, banging his head against the white wall behind him with an audible clonk. He lurched sideways, reaching for the top drawer of a wooden nightstand and pulling it open.

Mei stepped forwards and kicked the drawer shut, drawing a yelp of pain and surprise from McAllister. She withdrew into the shadows again. McAllister turned back to Gabriel.

'Who the fuck are you? What do you want?'

'Where is Ponting?'

'Who?'

'Where is Ponting?'

'I don't know anyone called Ponting.' A beat. 'Wait. You're that smarmy little cunt who came to my bar earlier.'

By way of answer, Gabriel racked the slide. The metallic scrape was loud in the room and McAllister's eyes widened so that Gabriel could see the whites clearly.

'Where is Steve Ponting?'

McAllister held his hands out. 'I don't know, OK? I don't know!'

'This pistol doesn't have a silencer,' Gabriel said. 'The cop I killed to get it didn't have one. Of course he didn't. What kind of cop would carry a silenced weapon?'

'A corrupt cop,' Mei said.

McAllister's head jerked round a second time.

'Look, I don't know what you people want, OK? But all that was a long time ago,' he said. 'I'm a legit bar-owner now. That's all. I serve drinks and tapas and put on the odd bit of live music.'

Gabriel continued as if neither Mei or McAllister had spoken.

'If I shoot you, it's going to make a hell of a noise. It might wake up the neighbours. And all the dogs of the neighbourhood will go crazy. But I know how to improvise. It's my training. A pillow works wonders.'

'Please!' McAllister gasped. 'I don't know where Steve is.'

There it was: the slip. People always slipped. Some took longer than others.

'Steve?'

In the silence that followed this simple question, Gabriel could hear the thought processes occupying McAllister's brain. Sell out a mate to an armed stranger? Or stay quiet and sacrifice himself for a bent cop's notion of honour among thieves? But if Ponting survived, he'd come for McAllister himself.

It was a dilemma, for sure. And there was no completely safe way out of it. Both choices had consequences. The only question was, what sort of man was McAllister? Gabriel had a shrewd idea he knew.

'I knew him back in the late eighties,' McAllister said on a long out-breath. 'When we'd both just arrived. Expats always find each other. Cops do, too. Make that bent expat cops and we might as well have moved in together.'

Now he'd started talking, the words flowed. Gabriel sensed that McAllister was fed-up with keeping secrets. He let his man talk.

'I wanted to open a bar. Steve knew a few people. He hooked me up with a couple of investors. But you've got to understand, I wasn't in his league. Yes, I was corrupt. I admit that,' he said. 'But it was low-level stuff. I was in financial crimes. I was taking money from bankers to look the other way when their dodgy deals got caught up in an investigation. I tell you, compared to me, those boys were the real criminals. I mean, we're talking millions. Tens of millions!'

'I'm not interested in your CV,' Gabriel said. 'Now, I've asked you, very politely, three times to tell me where he is.'

'And I told you—'

'Please let me finish. Maybe you don't think I'm serious. So, let me share a little of *my* career history. I killed a general in the Iranian Revolutionary Guard Corps with a six-inch nail. I beheaded a Russian Mafiya boss with an ornamental Cossack sabre. I killed a CIA paramilitary specialist with a knife you'd use to peel oranges. And I have lost count of the men I've killed with one of these,' he said, lifting the pistol up so McAllister could get a good look down the barrel. 'My colleague is no slouch either. What I'm saying to you, Roy, is this. I don't *care* about your previous crimes. I don't *care* whether you've gone straight or you're running the biggest protection racket on the Costa del Sol. All I care about is finding Steve Ponting. If you tell me now, we'll go the way we came and you'll never see us again. If you don't, first, we'll cause you a great deal of pain. Then, you'll tell us where he is. And last, because by then we'll have over-committed already, we'll kill you, cut you into pieces and feed you to that hellhound down the hill.'

'Please. You have to believe me. I don't know where he is.'

Mei stepped forwards smartly and delivered a ringing slap to McAllister's left cheek. Of all the blows she could have inflicted, of all the ways she knew to hurt a man, this was probably near the bottom of the list. But she'd put enough force behind it to swing his head through ninety degrees to smack against the wall again. Only this time at considerably greater speed. It also had the effect of utterly humiliating him. A slap? From a girl half his size?

'OK!' he shrieked. 'He left! He fucked off in ninety-one. To Serbia. Belgrade, I think. He had family there.' Mei took a step closer. 'No wait,' he looked pleadingly at Mei, 'don't hit me again. Yes, it was definitely Belgrade. Said he was going to establish a business out there. I didn't get the impression he meant a dry cleaner's either. Unless it was for money-laundering, if you catch my drift. That was the last time we spoke. I tried to call him once, but he must've changed numbers.'

Gabriel nodded. McAllister was telling the truth. He could see it behind the eyes. And he'd said three things that interested Gabriel. Ponting had left for Serbia one year before the outbreak of the Bosnian War. He'd moved into organised crime. And he had family out there.

'Tell me about his family.'

'I don't know much. Just cousins, I think. His parents were both dead. Killed by Croats or the other ones, the Muslims,' he said, in full flow again. 'You know what the Balkans are like. They bear grudges for hundreds of years.'

'Name?'

'What?'

'What was his family's name? Was Ponting even his real name?'

'Yeah, yeah, it was. His dad was English. But his mum was Serbian. Oh, shit, what was her maiden name? Pop-something? Popper—?'

'Popović?'

McAllister nodded vigorously. 'That's it! Popović. How did you know?'

'Educated guess.'

McAllister clutched the sheet tighter about his chest. 'Look, I've told you everything I know. Honestly. If I knew anything else, I'd tell you. No point holding back now, is there?'

'No, there really isn't.'

Gabriel got to his feet.

'We're leaving now,' he said. 'I strongly advise you not to do anything silly like call the local cops or the Guardia Civil. They won't find us and we'll pay you another visit. Clear?'

'As mud. Don't worry. I know how these things work. Just leave me alone, OK? And leave my bar alone.'

'You won't see us again.'

Gabriel waited for Mei to precede him out of the bedroom, then he followed her. As he reached the door, McAllister spoke.

'What did Steve do to you?'

Gabriel put his right hand on the door jamb and thought for a moment. Then he left without answering. They wouldn't have to worry about McAllister warning Ponting. That made things marginally less complicated.

21

NOVI SAD

Popović drove out into the forest behind the wheel of his battered blue Toyota pickup. It had served him well for a great many years. He'd had other cars, but the Alfa Romeos and the BMWs didn't stir his blood the way the Hilux did.

Maybe because they'd never had a Soviet-era heavy machinegun mounted in the back, its cradle a custom-job welded up in his workshop. With the fir trees closing in on both sides of the road, he let his thoughts drift back to those few years in the early nineties when, for the first time ever, it now seemed to him, he had felt truly, gloriously alive.

Partly it had been the fighting, of course. He'd thrown up the first time he'd killed a man, a member of a ragtag group of Bosnians attacking their position with AK-47s and grenades.

But after that, and the elation that kicked in as he and his men celebrated their victory with looted scotch, he'd plunged headlong into the war with an enthusiasm more suited to one of the teenage volunteers in the Black Eagles militia than a forty-year-old ex-cop.

Their commander, a heavyset ex-commando with a milky left

eye from a knife-fight, went by the name Redbeard. The moniker would have suited him even without the bushy ginger facial hair. Redbeard was notorious for smearing the blood of his dead enemies over his face before going house to house to rape their womenfolk.

Three years in, Redbeard was shot by a sniper. Popović was standing close enough to receive a portion of the dead man's brains full in the face. The whistle of the round caught up with it just as he was opening his mouth to scream.

By unanimous vote, the men elected him their new commander. He'd led them for the remainder of the war. In skirmishes with Bosnians, Croats, even British troops on one memorable occasion. In house-to-house fighting in Sarajevo. And in a Godforsaken place called Srebrenica. That, he would remember until his dying day.

They'd lost all trace of reason, of humanity, that day. The men and boys they took away to the forest were all Muslims, and at the time that had seemed justification enough for what followed. But as the news leaked out, and the International Criminal Tribunal for the former Yugoslavia ground into operation, Popović detected the change in the wind long before the rest of his men did.

He left them at a heavily fortified position deep inside Bosnia and told them he was flying back to Belgrade for orders. In fact, he went home, buried his weapons in the woods, raised his boys, established a little black market business and sat out the rest of the war. While others died in battle or were arraigned on charges of crimes against humanity, he prospered, setting up the Golden Bough with other former commanders and moving from warfighting into organised criminal activities, a subject with which he was already familiar.

The memories and the present collapsed into one. The forest into which they'd taken the Muslims became the forest through which he was driving now. They even shared the same thick mist that swirled in from those straight-trunked trees with their foliage so deep green it was almost black.

He sighed. He'd built a good life in Serbia. His roots were here, and, as soon as he'd stepped onto Serbian soil, well, concrete, at

Belgrade Nikola Tesla Airport, he'd felt a surge of connectedness flowing up through the ground and into his boot soles.

And now the old firm were looking for him.

What the fuck did Scotland Yard want with him? He hadn't been a cop for the last Christ knew how many years. Even then, he'd been in the RHKP attached to Special Branch. Or was that it? Was it some ambitious anti-corruption officer with a degree in Criminology or Finance and a hard-on for closing cold cases?

Popović had arrived in Hong Kong an innocent, more or less. But he'd left with a soul rotted out by greed, lust and the ability to sate whatever depraved appetites he could conjure. Money had always been the prize, but he hadn't stinted himself in other departments, resulting in several visits to a discreet private medical clinic. He'd chased the dragon a few times, but pulled back from the abyss while he still could.

And then, the plan that would have opened up a whole new line of business. The Wolfe job was supposed to be a proof-of-concept. Take it to the triads, show how easy it was and then line up every millionaire in the colony on the target list. Instead, it had all gone to shit. Not his part. That had gone fine. But those morons had entrusted the baby to a couple who clearly couldn't be trusted to run a Chinese laundry.

After that, and the heat it generated, Popović fled, fearing both retribution from the triads and from the honest elements of the RHKP.

And now someone had trodden on a little pressure-plate he'd buried in his past. A bank account he no longer used but which remained the only link between the old and new versions of himself. The plate had given a little and activated an alarm that sounded all the way from the good old Costa del Crime to Novi Sad.

He pulled up in a clearing and turned off the engine. From the glovebox, he withdrew his pistol, the one he'd carried all through the war. He climbed out into the cool mountain air and nodded.

Let them come. The rookie anti-corruption cop with his designer suit and his stupid degree. The big boss with his official Jag and plenty of tinsel on his shoulder boards. He'd faced down worse than them: men so frightening you'd piss yourself with fear.

The target, a metal plate with a hole drilled through the rim, was where he'd left it: suspended by a length of nylon para cord from the lowest branch of a towering fir.

Popović stood twenty-five feet back from the plate. He raised the pistol, took aim and fired. The report was deafening in the silent clearing. The bullet spun the plate round. The round had bitten a chunk out of the rim. *Winged*.

He fired again. With a clang, the plate swung up and back down again, spinning at the end of the cord; as it came to rest briefly before unwinding, he saw a fresh hole four inches from the centre. *Wounded*.

He stuck the pistol in his waistband and walked towards the tree. Ten yards out he smiled, held his arms wide and stopped before reaching round, whipping his gun arm up and loosing off three closely spaced shots.

The plate leaped and danced on its tether. Three more holes. *Dead*.

He turned a full circle in the clearing breathing deeply with satisfaction and enjoying the sharp smell of the fir trees. This was his land. His family came from here. And nobody – not Scotland Yard, not the ICTY, not his rivals in the shadows of Serbia's criminal underworld – was going to take it from him, or him from it.

He ran a hand over his beard. He'd left Hong Kong in eighty-four. He was thirty then; sixty-seven now. Nobody from the UK had seen him in those intervening years, or not to get a proper look. Certainly no photos existed. The man he'd once been had all but disappeared.

22

BELGRADE, SERBIA

Gabriel and Mei stepped down onto the airport's golden Tarmac: it bounced the sun into their eyes, adding a portion of its own stored heat like a radiator stuck permanently on FULL.

As they walked amid a crowd of mainly Serbian nationals towards the terminal building, Gabriel felt the sweat trickling down his ribcage. The heat and humidity reminded him of Hong Kong.

There it had felt like just another part of being home. Here, surrounded by perspiring matrons in over-bright colours and florid makeup, and businessmen in badly cut suits and comb-overs, it felt like an imposition. As if the country itself was trying to keep him out. Tough. He was here. And when he left, Serbia's citizenry would be short by one.

After picking up their hire car, Gabriel drove away from the airport. The perimeter road took them past the cargo terminal and here, all the glamour of the international airport fell away like powder flaking from an ageing actress's face. The Tarmac was cracked and weedy, acid-yellow flowers blazed out from the silver-grey road surface.

To their left, he spotted a clutch of rusting planes: two prop engines apiece, snub noses and fat, cigar-shaped bodies. He pegged them as Douglas C-47s, antiquated troop transports missing their rudders, one with its Yugoslavian YU-AD tail number still visible on the sun-bleached olive-drab paint.

The car's aircon needed a re-gas: the feeble stream of tepid air pushed out by the fans was worse than useless so he buzzed down the window. The throat-clogging smell of oilseed rape filled the cabin. Mei pulled a face.

'My initial impression of Serbia is that it's a shithole,' she said. 'Ugly, fat people, zero customer service and now bad smells.'

'I booked us into the Hyatt Regency. Best I could find.'

'Good. I like their style.'

* * *

After unpacking and showering the sweat off, Gabriel donned one of the Hyatt's soft white dressing gowns and lay back on the king-sized bed. He folded his arms behind his head and stared at the ceiling.

They were on Ponting's home ground now. Advantages: he'd be relaxed, which could make him over-confident and under-prepared. And above all else, they were closing in on him. Disadvantages: Ponting, or whatever he was calling himself nowadays, would have access to all the resources he'd have built up in the intervening years since leaving Spain.

Then there was the vexed question of the man himself. Gabriel didn't have a photo to consult. Without one he and Mei would be hampered in making a positive ID.

Gabriel could almost see the funny side: pick a random stranger and look them up online and you'd find holiday snaps, professionally shot pictures on LinkedIn, corporate photos on websites, plus the never-ending stream of selfies on Instagram, Twitter, Facebook and the rest.

But for people who either made a conscious choice to avoid leaving a digital footprint, or who were simply members of a pre-internet generation, the evidence of their existence might simply not be available online.

What about non-digital sources? Where would Gabriel find a printed photo of Ponting – at any age? If he were an American, a school yearbook. But he wasn't. Strike one. If he were a musician, an album cover. But he wasn't. Strike two.

Aware that the baseball metaphor he found himself using wasn't binding, nevertheless Gabriel paused before reaching for a third, equally ludicrous idea.

He closed his eyes, letting the hum from the air-conditioning unit above his head act as white noise, silencing the rushing thoughts in his head and allowing him to just *be* for a few minutes.

Gabriel conjured the figure of a man and had him stand before him. The man wore generic black clothes, a sweater, jeans and boots. Tall, well-built. About thirty years of age.

But where his features should have been, there was only a smooth cream plastic face like a shop window dummy fresh off the production line. A bald pate with a satin sheen. No bone structure to speak of. Certainly no skin tone, wrinkles or disfigurements. Vague outlines of eyes, nose, mouth.

Where are you? I want to see your face, Ponting. Your adult face.

Yeah, I just bet you do, the unreachable, unreadable man said. *Trouble for you is, landing the job of nursemaiding your parents and their ever-expanding brood was the last vaguely high-profile job I ever did.*

Gabriel pondered that remark. Then dismissed the faceless mannequin and opened his eyes.

He still had the contact details in his phone for a freelance Hong Kong journalist called Sarah Chow. He checked the time. Just after 5.03 p.m. in Belgrade would be 00.03 a.m. in Hong Kong. Briefly he considered emailing Sarah, but then called her. If she was sleeping, she'd have silenced her phone and would pick up his message in the morning.

'Hello? Gabriel?'

She sounded wide awake. Maybe she was working on a story.

'Hi, Sarah, yes it's me. I want to hire you again. A small research project. Have you got time?'

'I guess it depends. What's the project?'

'I need to track down a photo of a British Special Branch cop who was working with the RHKP in the early eighties.' He gave her what little physical description he could manage. 'His name's Steve Ponting. Better make that Steven. He was in charge of my parents' security. My father was a trade commissioner, so I was wondering whether the *South China Morning Post* might have a story in its archives.'

'Early eighties? Can you narrow it down?'

'He would have left Hong Kong on or shortly after 16 December 1983. That's your upper bound.'

'And the lower?'

'That's easier: 10 July 1982.'

'OK, so just seventeen months. I don't know how much of their print archive's been digitised. If it's paper or microfiche, it's going to take a while.'

'Can you make a start? Same terms as before for the fee?'

'Yeah, great. I followed your advice, by the way. I never negotiate with myself now and I even put my prices up. Guess what?'

'What?' Gabriel asked with a smile, knowing the answer.

'I'm busier than ever.'

'There you are,' Gabriel said. 'Success is fifty percent talent and fifty percent knowing your own worth. Call me if you get anything, any time of the day or night.'

He dressed and walked down the corridor to Mei's room, his feet sinking into thick, soft carpet. She answered his knock. Like him, she'd changed into cooler clothes, in her case, a linen blouse and a navy skirt. She smiled and held the door wide.

'Enter,' she said, executing a small bow. 'I approve of my room.'

'Well, we can't have the CEO of Lang Investments slumming it, now can we?'

'Drink?'

'Yeah, a beer, please.'

Mei opened the minibar and grabbed two bottles of a beer with the unpromising name of Lollipop. She popped the tops off and handed one to Gabriel. The bottle itself came wrapped in pink paper, twisted at the neck and decorated with a graphic of a green and pink lollipop.

Gabriel regarded it with suspicion. 'If this tastes of apple and strawberry, it's going down the sink.'

She grinned.

'Don't be so stuffy. Try it. You might like it.'

'What, and you have, I suppose.'

'I might have. Go on, drink it. Drink it, drink it, drink it!' she chanted.

Shaking his head, Gabriel raised the neck to his lips and took a swig. To his surprise, the beer tasted nothing like the garish confectionery on its wrapper. Just a pleasant, hoppy IPA, as, he could now see when he read the text on the back, the brewery claimed it was.

Mei took a long pull on her bottle, screwed up her face and emitted a huge belch, then stilted her head on one side.

'Well?'

He shrugged. 'It's all right, I suppose. I prefer bitter.'

'Of course you do,' she said. 'Nice warm beer. Only the British could get away with calling their national drink "bitter", don't you think?'

'For a start, I think the national drink is tea. For second, no, I don't think that. We're not a bitter nation. If anything, I'd say we're unusually relaxed about life.'

She put her bottle down on a glass-topped table between their chairs. She was frowning.

'What is it?' Gabriel asked.

'Am *I* British?'

Gabriel drank some more beer before answering. It was a good question. And not an easy one to answer. Not after everything that had happened.

'We have the same parents, so the same genes,' he began, feeling his way towards an answer he thought would need them both to agree on. 'I think of myself as British. But that's more because I think I always focused more on Dad than Mum. Plus I went into the army at eighteen and moved to England when I resigned my commission.'

'That's the thing, though, isn't it? *I* grew up in China. On the mainland. I never even knew Mum and Dad. And I look much more Chinese than you.'

'What do you feel like you are?'

'Until last year I would have said I was Chinese. Not even a Hong Konger.'

'And now?'

'Now, I don't know.'

'You could say you have Chinese-English heritage.'

'I could, but it doesn't get me any closer, does it?'

Gabriel could sense without Mei needing to say it that she was struggling with an age-old problem. Who she really was. It affected him, too, but in a different way.

Mei was thinking about her past. Where she came from. And what that might make her. Gabriel was looking at his future, though with the same basic question framing his enquiries. Who, and what, would he become when he married Eli?

'I don't think "British" suits you,' he said finally. 'If anything, I'd say you were half-English, half-Chinese, whatever that means.'

She finished her beer and looked away, staring at the view of downtown Belgrade through the floor-to-ceiling picture window. 'It doesn't matter. So, what's the plan? How are we going to find Ponting?'

'I think he went into organised crime. That's more your department than mine.'

'Hey! Legitimate businesswoman now, thanks very much.'

'Seriously. How would you find him?'

'I'd reach out through the White Koi's international network. Ask if anyone knew of a British cop who came to Belgrade in the early nineties and muscled in on the action.'

'Is there anyone left, or did you completely dismantle it?'

Mei smiled. 'There's a few people I can talk to.'

23

Over the next three days, Mei spent hours with her phone glued to her ear. She put the word out that she was looking for Ponting. She gave each of her contacts the same information: his English surname, his Serbian family name and his probable location. Everyone promised to let her know if they found anything. Nobody did.

Gabriel spent the time mooching around Belgrade's seedier quarters, hanging out in bars, the dodgier the better, drinking and chatting to anyone who looked up for a conversation in return for a beer.

His enquiries were as fruitless as Mei's, whether because the men and women he drank with were frightened, cagey or genuinely ignorant; it was impossible to judge. He met one old geezer in a park and plied him with vodka, but the stories he received in return were gibberish.

Walking back to the Hyatt from another dead-end conversation, his phone rang. Sarah Chow.

'Please tell me you found him,' he said.

'I did!' she said, the excitement evident in her voice. 'On Tuesday August 3rd, 1982, the *South China Morning Post* carried a story about a big new garment manufacturing contract being signed. Your father was there to officiate. There's a guy in the background who I think might be Ponting.'

Gabriel felt it then: the first flicker of adrenaline that told him the hunt was on.

'Why do you say that?'

'He just looks the part. Everybody else is smiling into the camera. He's facing the right way, but his eyes are off to one side. And he isn't smiling. He looks like a cop.'

'Anything else? I mean, why are you sure? You are sure, aren't you?'

'Yeah, I am. You said he used to box, right?'

'Yes.'

'This guy has a busted nose and thick, not eyebrows, but sort of ridges. Like he got punched in the face a lot. I just sent you the photo.'

Gabriel's phone pinged. He put Sarah on speaker and opened the attachment. She'd included two photos with her email. The first was the whole image from the *SCMP*. There was Gabriel's father, beaming with a polished diplomat's smile.

Gabriel felt a pricking behind his eyes. He was a handsome man. Not movie-star handsome, but possessed of a certain English style. A well-cut suit, short dark hair. And intelligence radiating out from his eyes, which Gabriel realised he'd inherited.

And behind Gerald Wolfe and the managing director of the textile factory was a tall, thickset man in a grey suit, white shirt and dark tie. Gabriel tapped the second photo. Sarah had enlarged a section and cropped in tight on the bodyguard. Blonde hair cut even shorter than Gerald Wolfe's, eyes, as Sarah had said, off to one side, a firm set to his unsmiling mouth and, the clincher; a lumpy, offset nose, surely the result of a defeat in the ring.

He sighed.

'Everything all right?' Sarah's tinny voice asked from the phone's speaker.

'Yes, yes. Sorry, Sarah. This is him, I'm sure. Thank you so much. Send me your bill, yes?'

Sarah didn't reply at once, and Gabriel could hear background noise of boat klaxons. He wondered where she was. Down at the harbour, maybe.

'Actually, Gabriel, this one's on the house. It wasn't hard to find after all,' she said. 'They'd digitised the whole of the eighties and someone had done a brilliant job of tagging every photo with keywords. I just searched on Gerald Wolfe and it came up.'

'Come on, Sarah. You know that's not the deal. You did the work. I want to pay you.'

'I found some other stories while I was looking,' she said in a low voice. 'About when Tara was kidnapped. This is in connection with that, isn't it?'

'It is, yes.'

'I want to help. I owe you. Your advice helped me make more money last year than I did in the previous three. Please, accept this as a gift. My way of saying thank you.'

Gabriel didn't want to throw her generosity back in her face. She was in charge of her own business, so he accepted.

'Thank you. Maybe one day I can return the favour.'

'I hope you get him, Gabriel.'

'I think we will.'

* * *

At the hotel, Gabriel knocked on Mei's door.

'We've got him,' he said as soon as she answered.

She let him in and he showed her the image on his phone.

'Couldn't it be a private bodyguard?'

He shook his head. 'No way HMG would allow diplomats to hire protection. They'd have insisted on a Special Branch protection officer. That's Ponting.'

'OK, but he's how old in that picture, twenty-eight, twenty-nine?'

'Yes, give or take a few months either way.'

'He's sixty-seven or eight now, then.'

'I've got a plan for that. I'm going to ask Wūshī to artificially age it. He's bound to have some specialist software,' he said. 'Did any of your contacts come back with anything?'

'Nope. I think I'm,' she switched to English, '*persona non grata*' back to Cantonese, 'since I took the White Koi legit.'

'Maybe I'll have more luck. I'll call mine again this afternoon.'

Gabriel went back to his own room and sat at the desk to make some notes for his conversation with Wūshī. He'd found a promotional site online for face-ageing software and tried it himself. The options were limited to smoking, drinking and tanning. In order, the program hollowed out his cheeks and turned his skin grey, added jowls and pouchy eyes and made his skin look like well-worn suede. He guessed the full-fat version would be configurable in much more detail.

He made a short list of lifestyle factors to give to the Wizard. It wasn't exact, and much was guesswork, but he thought it wouldn't be too far off the truth, based on Ponting's being an ex-cop who'd no doubt picked up bad habits only partially offset by his boxing.

24

Andrew Glover peered down the microscope at one of the grains the Serbian police had couriered over to his lab outside Edinburgh. He'd need more detailed analysis to be sure, but even from an optical examination it was clear to him he was looking at khorasan.

The ancient grain was making a comeback in the west as healthy eating enthusiasts searched for more 'authentic' foodstuffs. He himself was more of a burger 'n' fries kind of a guy, but each to his own.

Over the next few hours he subjected the sample to a range of tests while he waited for the DNA profile.

The printout from the sequencer confirmed his initial assessment. Yes, this was indeed khorasan. Increasingly common in Western markets where there were enough foodies to make it a viable commercial product, but less so elsewhere. And Serbia? If anything, he felt it was more likely that a tiny family farm somewhere had simply never stopped growing it.

He typed up his report, keeping it as short and concise as possible, and emailed it off to the Serbian cop who'd contacted him through Interpol and the Met.

* * *

Pacariz downed the last of his tiny paper cup of espresso and opened the email from Andrew Glover that had just popped up on his computer screen. After an infuriatingly long wait, for which he roundly cursed those corrupt bastards in IT procurement, the document opened.

He read it slowly, frowning as he struggled over some of the unfamiliar English words. But Glover had kept it nice and short, and, in any case, the one sentence he cared about was right there in nice bold type.

Species: Triticum turgidum subsp. turanicum. "KHORASAN".

Glover added that this was grown commercially in the US under the brand name 'Kamut' and was, in his experience, rare outside of developed Western agricultural systems.

Rare was good. Rare meant Pacariz wouldn't be visiting hundreds of wheat farmers all over the fucking country. Rare, he could work with. He looked up the number for the Institute of Agricultural Economics in Belgrade.

A day later, he had a list of twenty-five farms who were registered as farming khorasan wheat commercially. Most were in the south, clustered, for reasons he neither fathomed nor cared about, around the city of Niš. But two were located within fifty kilometres of Novi Sad.

He sent Stan up to one while he took the other. He chose his for no other reason than it was closer by five kilometres as the crow flew to the branch of Erste Bank where the unfortunate Herr Kanstner had been dumped.

Stan struck out. The farmer did indeed grow khorasan, milling it on his own farm. As for the straw, he had a chopper on the back of his combine harvester to return the stalks to the land.

Pacariz did better. The guy he interviewed sold his straw to a neighbour who farmed livestock to use as bedding. But he had sold a load to another man a week or so earlier. Who was this man? Pacariz asked. Oh, just a distant neighbour. The farmer professed not to know him at all. But he'd paid cash and taken a whole truckload.

Pacariz asked if he remembered what he looked like. Of course, the farmer replied. He wasn't senile yet. The guy was in his late sixties. Piercing blue eyes that looked right into your soul. And cropped silver hair. Beard and 'tache to match. Pacariz thanked him for his help and returned to Novi Sad. Because unlike the farmer, he *did* know the neighbour. By reputation, at least. A check of the local property records confirmed it.

The farmer's neighbour was one Ratko Popović. A man with his filthy fingers in every dodgy pie in Novi Sad. Yet who, whenever the police invited him in for a chat, would appear with hands as clean as a priest's. And a man who, local barfly gossip hinted, had blood on those lily-white hands from the war. A lot of blood.

Maybe Pacariz's luck was changing for the better. And Popović's for the worse.

He took thirty minutes to compose, laboriously, and with much recourse to a Serbian-English dictionary, a thank-you email to Glover. Thinking that here was an opportunity to curry favour with Interpol, he copied in his contact. It would be good to show the shiny shoes in Lyon that not every cop in the Balkans was a beer-swilling oaf who solved every problem with a fist, a boot or a bullet.

* * *

And in that glass-and-stone edifice on Quai Charles de Gaulle overlooking the Rhône, home to so many 'shiny shoes' Interpol officers, an Israeli detective, seconded from Jerusalem, received an alert on her computer screen. It related to a case in Serbia, the murder of a German banker, in which a contact of hers in Zurich had expressed an interest. She called him and relayed the details.

He, in turn, rang Gabriel Wolfe, delighted to be able to offer hard intelligence.

'A banker named Erich Kanstner was burnt to death the week before last,' he said. 'His charred corpse was dumped on the steps of Erste Bank in Novi Sad. Something about the crime sent my antennae twitching, so I followed it up. Here's where it gets interesting. Ready?'

'Yes.'

'The police found a stalk of ancient grain wheat in the body's mouth. Khorasan,' he said. 'Interestingly it originated in the region of the same name comprising modern-day north-eastern Iran, Afghanistan and Central Asia. Anyway, I digress. It would appear that khorasan straw was used to incinerate poor Herr Kanstner. And the buyer of the load used was a Ratko Popović. Now, this Popović is—'

'A Serbian gangster based in Novi Sad. And the man I'm looking for. Thank you, Amos. Once again, I'm in your debt.'

Amos brushed off the young man's thanks.

'Just make sure I get a kiss from your bride at the wedding.'

25

His spirits rising from the slump into which they'd descended, Gabriel thanked Amos and reiterated his standing invite to the wedding, though right now that seemed like a whole other life.

'Let's go and buy some guns,' he said to Mei.

'OK. Sounds like fun. Where?'

'There's a town about thirty minutes' drive north-west of the city. Stara Pazova. Small enough not to have much in the way of a police force, big enough to have a black market in second-hand weapons.'

'How come there's so many?'

'Blame the war in Bosnia in '92. Most of those guys weren't in regular armies. They were just militias at best and armed gangs at worst. When it was over they just went home and took their guns with them.'

'What's the going rate for an AK?'

Gabriel shrugged. 'I couldn't find exact figures. Probably in the high hundreds of dollars. But you can get a pistol – a Tokarev, say, or a Makarov – for maybe a hundred.'

'Ponting will have plenty of men. I say we get an AK and a pistol each.'

Gabriel enjoyed planning with his sister. They'd had radically different childhoods, and their careers could scarcely have been more different, yet beneath it all they were of the same blood. And their training, on each side of a dividing line separating the lawmakers from the lawbreakers, encompassed a lot of overlap. Certainly when it came to weapons and tactics.

Maybe on the strategic front they would have been better with a long-time triad boss like Fang Jian. Or a major rather than a captain, Gabriel's rank when he resigned his commission. Maybe. But he felt this mission would be almost entirely about tactics.

* * *

They arrived in Stara Pazova at 1.30 p.m. Driving through a crossroads of two wide avenues, Gabriel saw three distinct styles of architecture scrapping for dominance.

First, what he assumed was the town's original nineteenth-century formal buildings: a church, what might have once been a town hall and some ancient shops. These were built from a golden sandstone, replete with ornate carvings above the doors and windows and topped with turrets and towers. Gabriel could imagine prosperous burghers going about their business, stopping for conversations on street corners or in coffee shops.

But in the fifties, the Soviets had imposed their brutalist vision of a workers' paradise onto this town as with so many right across Eastern Europe. Stone was out of favour – too bourgeois, probably – replaced with featureless grey concrete, now stained by water leaks and the ravages of the climate. Their watchword had been function – from flat roofs to endless ranks of unadorned windows – never mind that less than eighty years later this much-vaunted efficiency looked drab, and on the point of collapse.

Finally, in a post-Perestroika world, when the Soviet Union had collapsed, a bright, brash, glitzy commercialism had taken root, spreading upwards from street level like weeds colonising a bomb-site after a civil war.

Advertising hoardings – *Funky Burger!* – *His Style!* – *Discount wood stoves!* – clung, limpet-like to the facades of the older, elegant buildings and their dreary modern counterparts.

A branch of McDonalds occupied the site of a classical building complete with triangular pediment balanced on two fluted columns. And, in common with every other European town of comparable size, global brands – Western Union, Nike, Sony – had established beachheads. Their desire for profits dovetailed with the desires of a populace starved for so many years of decent quality in anything and everything, from banking to shoes.

Gabriel drove through the crossroads, swearing – and swerving – as a delivery truck made an unadvertised turn across the centre of the junction, almost T-boning him in the process.

He was looking for somewhere where they could begin their search. And although a regular market didn't seem like the place where firearms would be on open sale, he had a shrewd idea the stallholders would be a helpful source of intelligence.

After cruising round the network of streets for ten minutes, Gabriel pulled in by a bus stop and buzzed the window down. Most of the people queueing were middle-aged or elderly, clad in grey, black and brown. They'd speak Serbian and maybe one or more of the minority languages and dialects. That was no good to Gabriel, whose only language from this part of the world was Russian.

Towards the back of the drably dressed queue, a couple of teenagers, a boy and a girl, were standing together, their heads bobbing in unison as they shared a set of wired earphones plugged into a phone. Their Western-style clothes popped with turquoise, pink and royal-blue: peacocks amid a flock of crows.

He hoped his guess about their language skills was on the money.

'Hey! Excuse me,' he called out to them in English, drawing curious stares from the adults in front of them. 'I need a little help.'

They removed their earphones in sync as if they'd choreographed the move for just such a moment, and ambled over.

'What do you want?' the boy asked in American-accented English.

'We're looking for a market. You know, fruit, vegetables, clothes, maybe? Pet stuff?'

The boy smiled, revealing wire braces around upper and lower teeth.

'Sure! Go down this street about five hundred metres, yes?'

Gabriel nodded, feeling sure the boy imagined anyone over thirty must be deaf, stupid, or suffering with dementia — possibly all three.

'Got it.'

'Make a left, drive along till you come to a building with a big tree outside with red leaves, yes?'

'Uh-huh.'

'Make another left and you come to the market. But you better hurry. All the good stuff is gone by this time usually.'

'Thanks.'

The boy grinned. 'Hey! That's solid info, yeah? Gotta be worth a ten spot?'

The accent verged on parody, making Gabriel smile.

'Dinars?'

The boy laughed and his friend joined in.

'Benjamins, man. The mighty dollar!'

'Fair enough.'

Gabriel reached for his wallet and took out five one-dollar bills from the cache he always carried wherever he was travelling. No currency, apart from gold, would be guaranteed to get you out of a tight spot more than greenbacks. From Mozambique to Lebanon, Colombia to the Russian interior, he'd always found a sheaf of dollars would unlock doors, loosen lips and, occasionally, persuade guards to look the other way.

He held them out of the open window to the boy, who accepted them with an appraising nod.

'Hey, there's only five here.'

'It was five dollars' worth of info.'

'Gotta be worth seven, at least,' he said, winking at his girlfriend.

Gabriel warmed to the boy and his upfront confidence.

'Tell you what. Answer one more question and I'll give you the ten you asked for.'

'Cool.'

'You look like you might've watched some gangster movies, am I right?'

'Sure. *Scarface, Goodfellas, The Godfather.* Was that the question?'

'No. If I was looking for the Serbian equivalent of those guys, where would I go outside of Belgrade?'

The boy frowned. He turned to the girl and spoke rapidly in Serbian. She held her hands wide. Then her eyebrows shot up. She muttered something back to him. He nodded and turned back to Gabriel.

'We don't know exactly. But Nadja's dad's a history teacher. He goes on about the war. She says the guys who run everything used to be militia commanders. That's all we know.'

It wasn't much, but it was better than nothing. Gabriel smiled and held out another five dollars, which the boy took, counted, folded and stuck in his hip pocket with the rest of his earnings.

'Thanks,' he said with another braces-baring grin. 'Maybe we'll get a taxi home today.'

Gabriel nodded, then put the window up and pulled away.

Five minutes later, he and Mei were strolling between gaily decorated market stalls, their canopies a riot of rainbow-hued plastic flapping in the breeze. Old women held out sheaves of fresh herbs, grinning from toothless mouths. Others proffered small spring cabbages like pale green grenades.

A heavily tattooed, swarthy guy presided over a stand groaning with shallow brass bowls of spices: pyramids of red, gold and beige powders, plus knobbly dried seeds, berries and flowers. Gabriel recognised the distinctive five-petalled shapes of star anise and inhaled deeply: his brain sparkled with the aromas of the Middle East.

'Finest spices in Stara Pazova,' the guy called out to Gabriel, in English. 'Try, try!'

Gabriel stepped closer. If the spice merchant spoke English then he was worth a try. Gabriel leaned closer, right across the bowls of paprika, ground coriander, ginger and cumin.

'You want to buy some paprika? Peppercorns? Allspice?'

Gabriel shook his head. 'I need some information.'

'Information?'

The man packed a lot into that one-word question. Interest. Suspicion. Appraisal. Commerce.

Gabriel nodded. 'May I?' he asked, nodding towards the side of the stall, where empty plastic crates teetered in a metre-high pile.

'Yes, yes, my friend,' the guy said with a grin.

Leaving Mei to keep watch in the aisle between the stalls, Gabriel squeezed into the tight space between the flapping canvas sidewall and the table.

'Do you know where I could buy guns?' Gabriel asked, seeing no point in dressing up the request in euphemisms the man might not understand.

The man looked over Gabriel's shoulder, first at Mei, then up and down the thronging alleyway.

'Guns? Not here. Tomatoes, herbs, baby clothes, spices,' he said, waving a large hand out across his wares.

Gabriel took out his wallet. 'Actually, I think I might need some spices after all,' he said, pulling out some dollars. He handed over a ten. 'How much would that buy me?'

The note disappeared into the man's pocket.

'Maybe I do know where you could get a gun after all. You want an AK? Pistols? What?'

'Both of those. Maybe something else, too. Do you know where I could find such things?'

The man eyed Gabriel's wallet. Another ten passed between them.

'Tolstojeva. There is an empty warehouse halfway down the street. Go round the back and knock on the black steel door.'

'Do I need a letter of introduction?'

'What?'

'How do I get past the security?'

The man smiled, tipped his head towards Gabriel's wallet. A third ten made its way to the man's pocket.

'You say you are there to buy Mikhail's chickens.'

Gabriel smiled. Mikhail would be Kalashnikov, the designer of the rifle that bore his name, so indestructible that whacking recalcitrant parts with a hammer was universally agreed to be a perfectly valid method of fault correction.

He handed over a fourth ten-spot. 'Here. Thank you.'

In return, the man plucked a handful of glassine packets of spices from a shelf behind him.

'For you, my friend. Though maybe your life is about to get hotter already.'

He winked, then laughed uproariously at his own joke and turned away to serve a shawled housewife with a basket over one plump arm.

Gabriel and Mei walked back to the car and checked the street map on his phone for the location of the arms dealer.

'How did you know to ask him?' Mei asked as she settled herself in her seat and did up her seat belt.

'You saw all the ink?'

'Yes.'

'He had a Russian army one. *Ubey ikh vsekh*. It means, "Kill 'em all". A lot of their veterans have it. It was a good bet he'd know who was shifting black market weapons.'

Tolstojeva was a ten-minute drive. As they neared their destination, the urban landscape shifted perceptibly. The cosmetics of Western sophistication began wearing off, revealing a drabber, down-at-heel face to the world.

Here, the only cars visible were rusted-out Ladas, Tatras and Wartburgs. The owners of these decrepit Soviet-era relics held their rides together with silver duct tape, bungee cords and, in the case of one spectacularly moth-eaten old banger, a purple nylon clothesline, looped around the bonnet and secured to the chassis through the front wheel arches.

He drove a circuit of the block and slowed as he spotted the warehouse. Five underfed teenagers in faded denim slouched around the entrance, hips cocked, arms folded. They looked like they were auditioning for a particularly low-rent production of *West Side Story*.

Feeling that to park the shiny new rental car there would be inviting either a half-assed extortion attempt or a comprehensive parts-strip, he opted to leave the car out the front. At least there, the presence of passing traffic and pedestrians might inhibit the most obvious attempts at theft.

He and Mei walked back to the access door. One of the teens slid off the dumpster he'd been lounging on and approached them. A couple of others fell into step by his side.

He reached towards his pocket but then Mei glared at him and uttered a lurid and prolonged threat in Cantonese. Catching its import, if not its precise meaning, the boy backed away, signalling for his lieutenants to follow suit. It was a smart move. A life would still be possible for him with his balls removed and stuffed down his throat, but it would be far from comfortable.

Gabriel hammered on the steel door, which clanged like a mission bell. He looked for a slider: a small grille behind which some heavy's ugly mug would scowl, demanding to know the password. Instead, with a metallic shriek from a sliding bolt on the other side, the door shuddered and then swung inwards.

Now they did meet the muscle. Near seven foot tall and half as broad. He looked down at Gabriel and Mei from coal-black eyes shaded by a thick brow ridge.

In Cantonese, Mei said, 'I didn't know they had gorillas in Serbia.'

'We've come to buy Mikail's chickens,' Gabriel said, using phonetic Serbian.

The gorilla shuffled aside, and admitted them. Up close, he smelled strongly of garlic. The door banged closed behind them.

The space was vast, empty save a grimy, once-white caravan in the centre. High windows on the side facing the Main Street allowed a thin, pale light to enter. Much of its power was lost by the time it reached the litter-strewn concrete floor, puddled here and there with dark, rainbow-filmed water.

The gorilla stretched out an arm as thick as Gabriel's leg and pointed at the caravan.

On the thirty-yard walk to the caravan, Gabriel scanned left and right, knowing that beside him, Mei would be doing the same. But he saw no additional bodies. No hidey-holes where reinforcements might lurk. No gangways or balconies from which snipers might perch and observe visitors. Obviously, the dealer was sufficiently confident not to need much in the way of protection. Or much beyond the Incredible Hulk.

Side by side, they reached the slab side of the caravan. Feeling slightly ridiculous as he did so, Gabriel reached out and knocked on the thin door.

It opened outwards. He stepped back and got his first look at the arms dealer.

26

The dealer smiled down at him. Thick, dark eyelashes half-obscured widely-spaced eyes of a vivid shade of green. Wet-look lip gloss in a deep, plum-red enhanced a full, sensuous mouth. She was mid-thirties, dressed in tight-fitting stone-washed jeans and a white sweat-shirt emblazoned with a Coca-Cola logo.

Not for the first time, Gabriel admonished himself for making assumptions.

'Well, you found me, so please, come in,' she said in English. The mid-Atlantic twang told him she, like so many others behind the former Iron Curtain, had learned her English watching American TV shows.

Gabriel and Mei stepped up and into the caravan. In contrast to the exterior, everything was spotless. They followed the woman down a shoulder-width corridor and into a cramped living area. The space was kitted out as an office, with black ash furniture including a desk and filing cabinet, plus a glass-fronted display cabinet. Beneath a concealed downlighter, a recent-model Kalashnikov assault rifle gleamed.

'I am Duga,' she said, after seating herself behind the desk.

'Toby,' Gabriel said. 'This is Lizzie,' he added, gesturing to Mei.

'Would you like some tea?'

'Why not?'

'Good. Tea first, then we talk.'

She yelled out in Serbian, then returned her gaze to Gabriel.

'English?'

'Yes.'

'And you?' she asked Mei.

Mei glanced at Gabriel before she answered. 'Chinese.'

'Long way from home,' she said with a smile and a lowering of these impressively long eyelashes.

Mei shrugged.

Duga turned to Gabriel.

'Why are you here?'

'We need guns.'

The caravan door opened and a pocket-sized version of the gorilla who'd admitted them appeared on the threshold of the office. Gabriel wondered if they were brothers, with one having bagged all the genes for over-developed physical size, leaving the other with the dregs of the parental gene-pool. He carried a cardboard tray with three lidded takeaway cups wedged into its punched-out pockets.

'*Hvala vam*,' Duga said.

He nodded at her thanks and retreated down the little corridor.

Duga handed out the teas before removing the lid from her own cup and taking a quick, catlike sip.

'If I *could* help, and I'm not saying I can, by the way, how do I know you're not police?' she asked Gabriel.

'Do the police know about your operation here?'

She shrugged. 'I pay them to look the other way.'

'Why would they be interested, then?'

'Maybe not the locals. Maybe you're INTERPOL. They have a special division who take pleasure in shutting down businesses like mine,' she said. 'They call themselves Illicit Arms Records Management System.'

Gabriel looked up as he worked through the initials and figured out what the INTERPOL management were on about. He laughed.

'Wait, I-ARMS? Seriously? God, those bureaucrats love coming up with cool-sounding names, don't they?'

It was the right move. She grinned back at him. He felt the route to the weapons solidifying beneath his feet.

'Maybe you're not cops,' she said. 'But I still have to be sure.'

Mei leaned across the desk.

'Listen, we don't have time for all this bullshit. You want proof we're not cops? OK, bring some lowlife in off the street and I'll shoot them for you.'

Duga's eyes narrowed, so that those emerald rises disappeared beneath the canopies of her lashes.

'You're serious?'

'As a bullet.'

'Fine.'

She picked up her phone and made a call. Frowned at the initial answer. Spoke again, with more authority in her voice. Glanced at Gabriel.

'*Da, da,*' she said, then ended the call. 'Goran will bring one of those kids from out the back. Come outside.'

She led the way, and, as Gabriel stood, he caught Mei's eye and raised his eyebrows. He couldn't read the look she gave him in return.

He fell into step beside Mei as she marched across the concrete to a spot where Duga waited for them. The metal door leading to the outside screeched in protest and swung inwards.

The gorilla – Goran – strode in, slamming the door behind him with his free hand. The other was clenched around the scrawny bicep of the teenaged hoodlum who'd tried his luck when Gabriel and Mei arrived. He was struggling and swearing mightily in his own language, but he might just as well have tried to free himself from a full set of prison chains and leg irons.

Arriving in front of Duga, Goran let the kid go and retreated a few paces. The kid's wild, white eyes scanned the three adults before settling on Duga.

She pulled a small black pistol from her jacket and handed it to Mei.

'Go on, then. Shoot him.'

Mei accepted the pistol and racked the slide. A round pinged out of the extractor port and flew into one of the greasy puddles. So Duga carried a loaded pistol ready to go.

She turned to the boy. First she pointed the gun at his forehead, then at the ground.

'Down!' she barked.

Trembling, he complied. All power of speech had deserted him, though his pleading eyes never left Duga's face. She was watching Mei, an appraising look that Gabriel had seen on the faces of unarmed combat instructors and other trainers from his time in the SAS. Did she have the bottle? That's what the look said.

Pulse heightened, he wondered what Mei would do next. She was ruthless, he knew that. But if she shot the little wannabe gangster, they'd be creating additional complications, not to mention murdering an innocent kid.

She took a step back and then extended her right arm out and down until the muzzle of the little pistol was six inches from the boy's left eye.

'*Zbogom mali prijatelju,*' she said.

The boy flinched and cried out.

'*Ne! Mama!*'

Mei's index finger tightened on the trigger. Gabriel watched as the blood left the knuckle.

'That's enough!' Duga shouted.

Mei lowered the pistol, though not before closing the gap between its vicious little mouth and the boy's eyeball to half an inch. She turned to Duga and handed the pistol back.

'Satisfied?'

'Let's go inside.' She turned to Goran and muttered a command in Serbian.

He nodded, dragged the boy to his feet and frogmarched him to the door. Gabriel and Mei followed Duga back inside the caravan.

'What do you need?' Duga asked.

164

'Two AKs, two pistols.'

'Did you bring money?'

'Of course. Dollars OK?'

Duga smiled. 'The best. The mother hens are two thousand apiece. The chicks are two hundred each.'

Gabriel knew an opening position when he saw one. She'd just quoted way above the market price, even allowing for his sketchy information.

'Two thousand? If we were in the US, I could buy a new one for half that.'

Duga merely inclined her head.

'I'm sure you could. If you were in the good old US of A. But you're not, are you Toby? You're in the bad old Republika Srpska, aren't you? And here, the price is two big ones. Each.'

'We'll pay you two-four for the AKs and you throw in the Tokarevs for free.'

'Three-eight, and I'll let you have the Tokarevs for a hundred each.'

'Two-seven for everything. Final offer. We could just tour around the farms hereabouts,' he said. 'I'm sure we'd find some old soldier with a bunch of guns in his hayloft who'd love to make some hard currency the easy way.'

Duga pursed her lips. She looked down at her phone and then back at Gabriel. He returned her gaze, not smiling this time. What he'd said was true; they *could* find an alternative supplier. But it would take time. And it only needed one suspicious or particularly law-abiding farmer to call the cops and everything would get immeasurably more complicated than it already was.

'Three-five. *My* final offer. I can just call Goran and have him show you out. I have no debts and plenty of other customers. I can wait to make the sale at the right price.'

Gabriel leaned back in his chair, throwing Duga an appraising glance. Time for a little playacting. He turned to Mei, who had been sitting impassively through the haggling, and spoke behind his hand. He kept his eyes on Duga the whole time.

'Do you fancy steak tonight?' he asked her in Cantonese. She nodded. 'Good. Me, too. You think she looks happy?' Another nod.

He straightened. 'OK. Deal.'

'Let's see the colour of your money.'

Gabriel took out an envelope from his inside pocket and counted out thirty five-hundred-dollar bills.

'Let's see the livestock,' he said.

Duga rose from her chair and left them alone together.

'What did you say to the kid?' Gabriel asked Mei.

'I said, "Goodbye, little friend".'

'I didn't know you spoke Serbian.'

'I learned it specially.'

'That was your plan all along?'

'You're not the only one with a tough background,' she said.

'Noted.'

'What if she tries to stiff us?' Mei asked, jerking her head towards the door.

'I don't think she will.'

'But if she does?'

'What do *you* think we should do?'

'We come back later and trash the place, kill the muscle, threaten her with torture and leave with the money *and* the guns.'

Though this brief, brutal plan was well within their capabilities, they had no need of it. Duga reappeared a minute or two later cradling a long black nylon holdall. It sagged where her arms weren't supporting it. She dumped it on the desk with a clank and unzipped it.

'Take a look,' she said, reaching between Gabriel and Mei to scoop up the cash.

While Duga re-counted the money, Gabriel took the firearms from the bag. Two clean and freshly oiled AK-47s, bearing the scuffs and scratches of much use, and a pair of black Tokarev TT-30s. He worked the charging levers on the AKs while Mei racked the slides on the pistols.

'All good?' he asked.

'Mm, hmm. You?'

'So far.'

Working methodically, and in silence, they field-stripped the weapons, laying out the parts on the desk. Gabriel was pleased to see that the internal components were in good condition. Not box-fresh, but these were Kalashnikovs. They could withstand being submerged in a bog for decades, or run over by a tank. They'd do.

He turned in his chair to look up at Duga.

'We're going to need eggs to go with our chickens,' Gabriel said.

Duga shook her head, smiling. 'AKs and Tokarevs I can do. But ammunition? No. Not my line, I'm afraid.'

'No? Then forgive me, but why are we here? If we wanted clubs, we'd have gone to a sports store and bought baseball bats.' He turned to Mei. 'Come on, Lizzie, we're wasting our time here.'

Mei nodded and rose from her chair.

He held his hand out. 'I'll take our money back, please.'

'Hold on! Don't be so hasty,' Duga said. 'I don't sell ammunition, but I know where you can find plenty.'

'Where?' Gabriel said.

'It's more of a who,' she said.

'Explain.'

'His name is Osman. He owns a bunch of clubs and bars downtown. He's usually drinking in one of them.'

'Osman? Is that a common name in Serbia?'

'Sure! But if you ask for Osman and say Duga sent you, people will know who you mean.'

'Where would you suggest we start?'

'Try Hipshot on Jana Sikore.'

Gabriel nodded. 'Thank you. I think we're done here.'

After handshakes, Gabriel and Mei left the caravan with their new flock. Goran was waiting by the warehouse door to let them out.

Gabriel blinked in the sunlight, shifting the holdall from right to left hands as the heavy door slammed shut behind them. The mini-goodfellas had all disappeared. He couldn't blame them after the move Mei had put on their leader.

'I'll get the car,' Mei said.

Five minutes later she drove down the access road, stopping a few hundred feet away from the warehouse. Gabriel stashed the weapons in the boot and climbed in next to Mei. They nodded at each other in synchrony. Next stop, Hipshot.

27

They waited until 9.00 p.m. before tackling Hipshot. Gabriel pushed through the double doors after being given the once-over by the leather-jacketed heavy on the door.

The interior of the bar, which was hot and humid from much human sweat and a heating system clearly left over from Soviet times, was themed around a pinball machine.

Oversized graphics had been expertly applied to the sweating walls. Aliens battled space-suited cosmonauts. Triple-breasted maidens with glowing orange eyes and antennae sprouting from their bald heads aimed 1950s-style ray-guns out at the viewer. Flippers, bumpers and knock-down targets glowed with airbrushed neon. And chrome wire ball-runs swooped and swirled up and over the ceiling.

Techno music blasted from the PA system and the mid-evening patrons were getting into it on the dance floor. Gabriel inhaled a heady mixture of cigarette smoke, cheap perfumes and clumsy aftershaves. He caught a whiff of cannabis, too.

He turned to Mei.

'We're never going to find him in the middle of all this!' he shouted.

She nodded. Then crooked her finger.

Gabriel followed her through the crowded dance floor. She slid between dancing couples, without needing to deploy shoulders or elbows, just seeming to meld with the music on her way to the bar. He tried to emulate her rhythm and mostly succeeded.

Then he mistimed a lunge into a gap and ended up colliding with a tall, buff young guy in a red leather jacket and white jeans. He had the thick neck of a US Marine Corps 'jar head'. He scowled and shoved Gabriel hard in the chest, sending him cannoning back into other dancers who yelled their disapproval and shoved him back.

Feeling that the situation was about to get out of control before he'd even made it to the bar, Gabriel regained his balance then held his hands up in surrender. He offered a sheepish smile and wormed his way under the guy's left arm and on to join Mei. There'd be time to dispense physical correction on this trip, but the middle of a crowded nightclub wasn't it.

'Everything all right?' Mei asked, as soon as he arrived at her right elbow, one eyebrow raised.

'Fine. Just befriending the locals.'

'Really. Because from where I was standing it looked like some provincial thug in a truly horrible outfit was besting a former Special Forces soldier.'

He shrugged. 'You think I should have broken his arm? Maybe popped an eyeball out of its socket?'

She shook her head. 'No. But maybe you should stay close to your little sister while we're in here. This is my sort of place, after all.'

He offered a jaunty salute. 'Yes, Ma'am.'

She passed a bottle to him. He glanced down at the label: lemons and limes with childlike smiling faces. He clinked necks with her and took a sip of the sweet, fizzy drink.

Mei turned her back to the bar and leaned against it, elbows on the scratched and dented zinc top. Gabriel followed suit and together they scanned the dance floor and the booths around the edge. He was looking for a figure who'd resemble in style, if not precisely in looks, the late and unlamented boss of the White Koi triad.

When Fang Jian had run his business from the Golden Dragon, he'd spend part of each evening entertaining guests or business partners at a private table in the club's main room. Resplendent in a gold dinner jacket, his booming laugh and expansive hand gestures let anybody in his eyeline or within earshot know who was in charge.

Gabriel saw nobody giving off Alpha-male vibes. But he did register a table towards the rear of the room at which a group of four dark-suited men were engaged in an intense discussion, bordering on an argument.

Though expansive, their gestures looked rehearsed. Fists thumped on the tabletop. Index fingers jabbed in faces. Hands spread wide in theatrical gestures of innocence. So it wasn't just the teenagers who learned their moves from American films.

Each man had a tumbler of amber spirit in front of him; a dozen or more long-necked green beer bottles littered the space between them like off-duty soldiers waiting for orders.

He nudged Mei and jerked his chin towards the men.

'I don't think they came here for the music,' he said. 'You think we should introduce ourselves?'

She nodded.

Tuning into the music this time, and employing moves from the wealth of *Yinshen fangshi* techniques he'd acquired under Master Zhao's tutelage, Gabriel navigated the crush without incident. He and Mei arrived side by side at the table. All four men looked up. Their expressions were different, but drawn from a range stretching all the way from suspicion to outright hostility.

Gabriel smiled and tried out some of his hastily acquired Serbian.

'Dobro veče. Tražimo Osman,' he said, trying to emulate the local accent. *Good evening. We're looking for Osman.*

Suspicion deepened. Hostility intensified. Gabriel waited. Breathing evenly. Despite what Duga said, he knew neither Mei nor he looked like a cop. But that left only a handful of other possibilities. 'Business' rivals. Assassins. Suppliers. Or customers.

He noticed a couple of hands drop beneath the table. He didn't think they'd start waving ordnance around in here, but there was always the possibility of an impossible-to-refuse invitation 'out back'. It wasn't a problem in terms of engaging them. But he was concerned not to lose the slender advantage they'd gained towards their ultimate goal of finding and dealing with Ponting.

One of the men spoke in English, forming the words around a freshly lit cigarette, blinking away the smoke.

'The fuck are you?'

'Friends of Duga.'

Shoulders dropped. Narrowed eyes relaxed. Hands reappeared on the table top.

'Duga who?'

'Duga who helps struggling chicken farmers acquire livestock. Now we need some eggs to go with our chickens. She said we should talk to Osman.'

'Yeah? Well he's not here.'

'Any idea where we can find him?'

The man shrugged, before turning to his drinking buddies and exchanging a few sentences. Gabriel couldn't hear a word over the music and his lip-reading skills weren't up to decoding mumbled Serbian. He could imagine the conversation easily enough.

This guy wants to speak to the boss.

Do we trust him?

No, but what if he's legit? Osman could lose it if we don't hook them up.

Better tell him something.

Nodding to his neighbour, the guy turned back to Gabriel.

'Osman's got other clubs in town. Try these.'

He fished out a scrap of paper and a stub of pencil from his jacket pocket and scribbled down half a dozen names before sliding the list across to Gabriel.

'Thank you. We'll let you get back to your drinks.'

Gabriel and Mei turned their backs on the table of gangsters and threaded their way through the dancers and out onto the street.

The list of nightspots they looked at beneath a streetlight revealed Osman's taste for cheesy, out-of-date, Americanised pop culture:

Silver Starz
    Klub Tropikana
    Red Sox Sports Bar
    Harvey Wallbanger's
    Top Gun
    Cheers!

Mei scrutinised the list. 'It's going to be quicker if we split up.'

'You're sure about that?'

'Of course! Why, you think I can't take care of myself?'

'No, it's not that.'

But of course it *was* that, wasn't it? He had to admit she'd caught him out. And not for the first time. He realised he'd been thinking of her, still, as that kidnapped baby, stolen in the dead of night from the one place where she should have been safe. Her family home.

She linked arms with him as she led them away from the club.

'Listen, BB. You don't need to worry about me, OK? I haven't been a soldier like you. But I worked for Fang Jian for a long time. Believe me, I dealt with some very dangerous people. And I'm still here to tell you about it. They're not.'

He smiled. 'Fair point. So, which clubs do you want?'

She shrugged. 'Tear off the top half. They're probably all as bad as each other, anyway.'

He divided the scrap of beer-stained paper between them.

'If you find him, text me or call. Any trouble—'

'Text you or call, yeah, I get it.'

'Well, do it, then. Let's meet back at the car at three if neither of us has found anything by then.'

Mei summoned directions to her first call then set off at a trot.

Gabriel watched her until she disappeared round a corner, then looked at his own portion of the list. Harvey Wallbanger's. Top Gun. Cheers.

They reminded him of a couple of places he'd hung around in on an op in Estonia. He'd secured some door-work at a place called Jonny Rocketz in Talinn's red light district while working undercover. The joint opposite was called Nitro.

That mission had ended well. Hostages rescued unharmed, if shaken. Hostiles all dead. Please God let this one end with the same scoreline.

Of the three places on his list, Top Gun was closest: just a couple of blocks away. He zipped up his jacket against the cool of the evening and strode on.

28

It was after midnight when Mei walked into the Red Sox Sports Bar. Her two previous stops had proved fruitless. The barman in Silver Starz had grudgingly admitted to knowing Osman, but claimed not to have seen him for a few days and told her to try Hipshot. The music in Klub Tropikana had been so overwhelmingly loud that conversation was impossible.

She'd considered going behind the scenes and searching out the management offices, but rejected it as an unnecessary escalation while she still had one more place to check.

The decor was based on the legendary baseball team. Pairs of white-heeled socks in varying shades of red were pinned up over the bar, and the red-white-and-blue logo, or at least a competent knock-off, adorned the walls. Half a dozen huge flat-screen TVs were suspended from the ceiling, each showing a different sports event: some local soccer plus what looked to be American baseball and basketball games.

The clientele was mostly male. Their raucous, beer-fuelled cheers made it hard for her to make herself heard when she asked the pretty young girl behind the bar if she knew Osman's whereabouts.

The girl shook her head, smiling, then pointed to the beer taps. Mei shook her head. She'd had enough pop to leave her in need of frequent visits to the ladies' rooms in the two previous nightspots and she didn't want any more. Especially as she could imagine all too easily the level of care the management here would have expended on the minority interest's facilities.

The girl shrugged, mouthed something that Mei felt sure was Serbian for 'suit yourself', and sashayed off to serve a gaggle of young guys leaning over the bar and waving banknotes at her.

She didn't want to return empty-handed. Gabriel thought he was top dog, just because he was older and had his black ops government job and military training. But he had a lot to learn about Mei and she intended to teach him. She loved him, sure, but he just didn't understand her, or her life.

Maybe returning with a bag full of ammunition would convince him she was more than capable of taking care of herself *and* dealing with any flavour of bad guy the world could conjure up.

But where to start? She scanned the room. If it was one of Fang Jian's old places, she'd start on the more exclusive spots. The booths. The tables on raised platforms discreetly screened by bamboo or money trees in vast glazed pots. The private rooms guarded by deadly young women dressed head-to-toe in white leather.

In a dark corner she saw what she was looking for. A plain wooden door beside which stood an over-muscled dude in the standard-issue black leather bomber jacket and black jeans. He affected a watchful grimace – eyes narrowed, mouth set in a lipless line – that he probably imagined made him look like a Secret Service agent out of some 'Protect the President' movie.

She made her way over, but halfway there an argument broke out at a table of five or six young men. One stood up suddenly, toppling beer bottles and thrusting his chair back right into her path. She threw her hands out to steady herself as she stumbled and swore in Cantonese.

'Fucking arsehole!'

He whirled round and, on catching sight of her, spat out something in the local language.

'Odjebi, koso oko!'

The other men at the table roared with laughter, and she caught one of them pulling the outer corners of his eyes out wide: a schoolkid's cruel parody.

The meaning of the insult was as clear to her as if he'd used classical Mandarin. *Fuck off, slant eye!*

He put his hands on his hips and jerked his chin towards the door.

'There is Chinese restaurant on Partizanska,' he said, in English this time. 'Fuck off and bring me some chow mein.'

And then Mei's right fist jabbed him hard in the solar plexus. He jack-knifed over his corpulent waist, emitting a startled groan as his wind left him. His stubbled chin met her up-rushing knee with a crack audible above the noise of the bar as his teeth smashed together.

He toppled sideways, hands clutched to his midriff. Mei skipped back into a space that had magically appeared around her. The other men had all jumped to their feet and were rounding the table, teeth bared, fists bunched.

She felt bad for what was about to happen. What if the carnage put her in Osman's black books? They'd never get the ammunition and BB would have another reason to give her a lecture on military discipline or some such crap. It couldn't be helped. If you bruised the beautiful plum you had to pay for your bad manners.

The first to try his luck swung a punch so amateurish she almost laughed. She moved out of range with a backwards tilt from her waist. Time slowed down, allowing her to watch the fat sausages sail in front of her face.

As the momentum of his arm twisted his torso, she moved in again and chopped him on the side of his throat and followed up with a hammer-strike to his left temple. Not too hard: she didn't want to kill him. But enough to switch the lights out for a few minutes.

She stepped back as he collapsed almost vertically in front of her and seized the wrist behind an incoming bottle. Two hands this time. One to stabilise the two thin bones of the forearm, the other to snap the wrist with a vicious clockwise wrench that drew a howl of agony from her attacker's lips.

He retreated, but not before she drove a kick into the top of his right knee that accelerated his progress towards the floor, where he kicked himself away using his remaining good leg, right hand flopping from its smashed joint.

She spun round just as the remaining boys closed on her. One held a narrow-bladed knife in his right hand, the other a broken chair leg. She dodged the chair leg, feeling air moving past the tip of her nose as it scythed left to right, millimetres from her face. The knifeman was advancing too, making feints with the switchblade and grinning evilly.

He half-looked as though he knew what he was doing. She grabbed the chair leg as it came back in on its return journey and broke its wielder's thumb with a sharp snap of her fist. She struck him between the eyes with a foot-long cylinder of wood and hooked his right foot out from under him for good measure.

The knife-point caught her left bicep, drawing blood through her jacket. Her *good* leather jacket.

She stepped inside his reach, stretched an arm out and grasped his knife-hand then pulled it down and across her left knee. Grabbing two of his fingers in each of her own hands, she splayed them until they broke and he dropped the knife with a squeal.

It was in her fist half a second later, not having reached the floor. And then his right quadriceps muscles, three inches deep and almost striking the bone. She took care to avoid the femoral artery, but he'd still be experiencing a very particular kind of pain.

She shoved him away from her, letting his momentum pull the blade free of his insulted tissues. With his hands clamped around his thigh he could only stare up at her, eyes wide, nostrils flaring like a calf about to be slaughtered in the meat market.

She stepped back and turned, readying herself for any further attacks, however unwise. She became aware for the first time in the two minutes since the violence had erupted that the other punters, far from scattering, had formed a circle around them, eyes glittering with some kind of bloodlust.

'Stop!' a man shouted.

Mei turned. The muzzle of the pistol looked huge in the light from the flat-screen overhead. At least a .45. Its owner was far wiser than the variously disabled and wounded thugs she'd just sent to the floor. He was standing out of range of either her fists or her feet. He looked amused rather than angry, red lips quirked upwards in a handsome face marred by a harelip scar that he'd half-covered with a black moustache.

He raised a hand and snapped his fingers. The music died.

'Enough,' he said quietly in the sudden silence. 'Before you kill all my customers. Who are you, my lady? And what do you want so badly?'

'Are you Osman?' Mei asked, trying to get her breathing back under control.

'I *know* Osman,' he countered. 'I ask you again, still politely, for now. Who are you?'

'I am a guest in your bar. In your country. That idiot,' she aimed a toe at the first man to attack her, 'insulted me.'

'And so you nearly killed him and his friends? Not the behaviour of a respectful guest – to a bar *or* a country.'

'Do you want to debate ethics or do you want to do business?'

'So *that* is why you are here looking for Osman.'

'Yes. But I don't want to discuss it with the help,' she said. 'I want the boss.'

He laughed, shaking his head. 'OK, OK, I get it. You've got bigger balls than every man in this place. Come with me. Let's find somewhere quiet to talk and maybe I introduce you to Osman.'

29

Somewhere quiet turned out to be a small office behind the bar, exactly where Mei would have expected to find it. Her host tucked the pistol into his waistband and walked across the richly patterned Turkey carpet to a glossy wooden cabinet.

'May I offer you a drink? You must be thirsty after your,' he hesitated, 'exertions. Is that the right word? My English is a little rusty.'

'I'm not tired,' Mei said. 'And your English is fine, don't pretend it isn't.'

'As is yours.' He unlocked the door of the cabinet to reveal a few decanters and the white door of a concealed mini-fridge. 'What's your poison?'

'Water, please. Sparkling if possible.'

He raised his eyebrows. 'Nothing stronger? I assure you the gun was merely a precaution. You are in no danger.'

She gave him a tight smile in return. 'Water.' A beat. 'Please.'

He sighed. 'Very well. But I am going to indulge myself.'

He poured himself a couple of fingers of a deep-brown spirit and cracked the cap of a bottle of Perrier, which he poured into a plain glass and handed to Mei.

'This is your office, isn't it?' Mei asked. 'You're Osman.'

He nodded as he rounded the desk and sat in the heavily padded chair behind it.

'Guilty as charged. And now, after I drink your health,' he raised his glass to her before swallowing half its contents, 'I think it is time for you to do me the courtesy, *as my guest*, of introducing yourself. Truthfully,' he added.

Mei took a sip of the sparkling water. She placed it on the desk in front of her.

'Lizzie. Wong.'

'Lizzie,' he said with a half-smile. 'A traditional Chinese name?'

'Hong Kong Chinese. My dad was a big fan of the Queen.'

'Well, Lizzie Wong. I am Osman Zeravica. And as you have made such obvious efforts to find me, I feel I should hear you out.'

There didn't seem any more point being coy. This was the big boss, Mei could tell. The body language was enough even before he'd admitted his identity.

'My brother and I bought some guns from Duga earlier today. Now we need some ammunition.'

Osman steepled his fingers together in front of his face. Mei felt sure that, having passed Duga's scrutiny, she wouldn't have to repeat the whole rigmarole with Osman. But was she right? Or would he make the weapons' dealer's caution look like devil-may-care unreason?

'Calibre and quantity?'

Good. That was settled, then. He trusted her.

'We've got AKs and Tokarev pistols, so that's 7.62 for the rifles and I don't know about the pistols. Russian junk. I myself only ever use NATO small arms.'

He smiled. 'The TT-30s also take 7.62. But in a 25 mm cartridge instead of the AK's 39.'

'I'll take three hundred for the AKs and one-sixty for the pistols. Plus spare magazines if you have them. Otherwise boxed is fine.'

Osman's black eyebrows ascended high. 'Are you planning on starting a new war in Bosnia?'

'I was in the Girl Guides. You know the motto? Be prepared.'

'A good motto. But I don't suppose many Girl Guides ever went off camping with enough ammunition to start a small war.'

Mei sipped from her glass of water. 'If you can't handle such a big order, please just say so. I will find another supplier.'

Osman shook his head. 'Oh, I can meet your needs, Lizzie. Quite easily. The question is, can you meet my price?'

'That depends. What is it?'

'What do you think that much ammunition is worth? I mean, given that you're not choosing to look at the licensed route?'

It was a transparent negotiating ploy. Get the buyer to reveal their budget. And when selling a second-hand car or domestic appliance to an inexperienced negotiator, a good way of opening discussions. But Mei was far from inexperienced, and before shifting to the side of the angels, had concluded plenty of arms deals of her own.

She looked up at the ceiling while making a few quick calculations. The going rate on the Hong Kong black market or the dark web was ten to twenty HK dollars a round, depending on calibre and quantity. That equated to roughly 120–240 Serbian dinars. Multiply that by a round 500 and she was looking at somewhere in the region of 90,000 dinars. Or if, as she suspected, he preferred a harder currency, just under a thousand US dollars.

Expensive compared to shop-bought ammunition. But then, as Osman had pointed out, she wasn't waiting for the nearest sporting goods shop to open. Discretion cost.

Mei spread her hands. 'I don't know. I imagine it's pretty plentiful given how easy it was to pick up the AKs. Why don't you tell me your price and we'll go from there?'

Osman took another pull on his drink then rubbed vigorously at the bony part of his nose.

'Two thousand dollars.'

Mei pushed out her lower lip. 'Osman, Osman,' she said. 'I am a guest. I'm not an idiot. I'll give you a thousand, but for that I want three spare magazines each for the AKs and two each for the Tokarevs.'

Some minutes of good-natured negotiating followed, at the end of which a hammer price of 1,350 dollars was agreed, and shaken upon.

While Mei counted out the cash, Osman swung a large and very ugly abstract painting out from the wall behind his desk, revealing a dull-green safe door. He blocked her view with his body while he spun the combination wheel. She caught a glimpse of plain grey cardboard boxes stacked inside the safe and returned to counting out the dollars.

A solid clunk made her look up. Osman had placed his pistol on the desk near his right hand.

'You know,' he said, smiling wolfishly, 'I could just shoot you and keep the ammunition *and* the money.'

She nodded. 'You could try, of course you could. And maybe you'd succeed. But then when he didn't receive my pre-agreed phone call, my brother would come here and kill you, and every one of your men and, depending on his grief, your customers and any police stupid enough to intervene. Then he would torch the place and go to your house to take care of your family.' She paused, smiled. 'He and I are very close.'

He finished stacking the cardboard cartons and laid the empty steel magazines beside them in an unsteady tower.

'I'm sure you are. And forgive my poor attempt at humour,' he said. 'So, will you tell me who or what brought you to Serbia to buy illegal firearms?'

'It's a hunting trip.'

He laughed then took a moment to finish his drink and pour a second.

'What sort of beast are you hunting with automatic rifles? Must be dangerous.'

Mei stared at Osman. Could he be helpful to her and Gabriel? Might he know of Ponting, in either his old, or new identity? Could he direct them straight to their target? Or was he in business with him, ready to call and warn him the moment she left the sports bar?

'A beast who attacked our family many years ago and did us great harm.'

'And who now lives in Serbia, you think?'

'We do. Maybe in Novi Sad.'

He frowned. 'Oh, well that explains it. They're animals up there.'

She felt her pulse quicken. 'Why do you say that?'

He paced a large hand over his heart. 'I am a Muslim, yes? Osman, my name? It means "Most powerful". But my people were the weakest in the Bosnian war. Eight thousand Bosniak men and boys were massacred at Srebrenica by the Serbs. When the war ended, those who weren't caught and tried went to Novi. Now all the crime gangs there are run by former militia commanders. Sadistic bastards, every motherfucking one of them.'

The boy Gabriel had spoken to in the bus queue had mentioned militia, too. This sounded promising.

'But you live in Serbia. You work among them.'

He shrugged. 'Business is business. Plus my wife is Serbian. Love works in strange ways, no?'

'So do you sell to them?'

He shrugged. 'Business is business. Do I love them as my brothers? Do I wish them long and happy lives? Do I pray for them to have many children and grandchildren? No!' He slammed his fist down on the table, toppling Mei's empty Perrier bottle. 'I wish them all dead.' He took a breath. 'But until then, I take their money.'

Mei made a decision. 'My brother and I only wish one of them dead. His name used to be Ponting. We think he might be calling himself Popović now and living in Novi Sad. He's some kind of gangster.'

Osman frowned. 'Popović?'

'Yes.'

'It is a very common surname.'

Something about the way Osman paused before speaking made Mei believe he knew more than he was admitting.

'Maybe it is among the general population,' she said. 'But what about organised crime? Organised crime in Novi Sad? Do you know him?'

'Novi Sad is a big place. Not as big as Belgrade, but still...' he tailed off.

Now Mei was convinced he knew and was simply holding out for more money.

Her phone rang. Irritated at the interruption, she pulled it out and glanced at the screen.

BB

She answered.

'Hey. What's up?'

'I struck out. You?'

'Pay dirt. I'm with Osman now. Can you get over here?'

'Which club?'

'Red Sox Sports Bar.'

'OK. I'll be there as soon as I can.'

Mei looked upon at Osman. 'You can meet my brother. He's coming to join us. Maybe you could make sure he gets back here without having to fight his way in?'

Osman smiled and picked up a phone on his desk. He spoke rapidly and nodded a couple of times before replacing the receiver.

'Your brother…' He paused and raised an enquiring eyebrow.

'Toby.'

' – will be received warmly. No need for any more violence.' He frowned. 'Tell me, Lizzie, where did you learn to fight like that?'

'I was a bodyguard for a triad boss.'

He nodded. 'Was?'

'He died. Of a heart attack.'

'My condolences.'

'It was me that attacked it.'

Osman stroked his moustache, fingertips lingering over the crooked scar on his lip.

'So you have no employer anymore?'

'No.'

'I could use someone with your talents in my organisation. Head of security, for example. I could pay well. How does that sound?'

Mei inclined her head. It wasn't the first job offer she'd received since killing Fang Jian. She imagined she could buy out Osman's little operation ten times over out of petty cash, but saw no need to insult the man.

'I'm flattered. But I have my own business interests in Hong Kong.'

'A dangerous place to live these days. Especially for entrepreneurs.'

'I manage.'

He smiled. 'Well, I won't insult you by pressing you any further. Tell me, have you eaten this evening?'

She shook her head. As she did so, her stomach, perhaps awakened by his question, emitted a low rumble she hoped wasn't audible on his side of the desk.

'Then let me offer you some hospitality. Now that our business is concluded, we can eat as friends, yes?'

'OK. I'd like that.'

She meant it. She sensed she'd found an ally who would help her and Gabriel get to Ponting. Maybe she'd end up hiring Osman rather than the other way round.

30

Ten minutes later, there was a knock at the door. Osman shouted something in Serbian. It opened to reveal a young woman in a Red Sox-branded baseball jersey, cream shorts and a dinky red, white and blue apron tied round her waist. She carried in a large, circular, stainless-steel tray, smiled at Osman, then at Mei, and placed it on the desk between them. She bobbed a little curtsey and left.

Plates were crammed onto the tray. Grilled chicken thickly dusted with brick-red paprika. Golden pastry dumplings emitting a fragrant steam of herbs and pork. Thin lamb cutlets crusted with herbs and sesame seeds and blackened under a hot grill. Flatbreads, blistered here and there with cratered bubbles where the wafer-thin crust had burst. A chopped salad of cucumber, tomatoes, yellow and red peppers, spring onions. And a bowl of creamy-yellow noodles beneath a melting blob of herby garlic butter.

This time the squawk of protest from Mei's stomach was loud enough for Osman to hear. She blushed, but he roared with laughter.

'You poor girl! The fight really took it out of you, eh? Help yourself, please. I would be failing in my duty as a host if I let you go hungry for a second longer.'

She folded a flatbread around some of the chopped salad and a couple of pieces of the chicken and took a bite. Instantly her mouth flooded with saliva. Beneath the hot, smoky, paprika, the succulent chicken carried its own strong flavour.

This wasn't an industrial product, shorn by selective breeding and meagre conditions of its texture and flavour. It was a farm bird: she'd tasted exactly the same in her childhood on the Chinese mainland. Healthy creatures: not scrawny, but not the overfed, hormone-plumped, bland specimens that the *gwáiló* seemed to enjoy so much.

'How is it?' Osman asked her through a mouthful of lamb.

'Good,' she managed, as the lemony tang of the salad dressing pricked at her mouth just behind the angles of her jaw. 'Really good.'

He smiled. 'My mother is the cook here. A proper family business. I will tell her you enjoyed her cooking. It will make her happy.'

'She is very talented.'

'Your own parents,' he said, gesturing with the cutlet bone. 'They are still alive?'

Mei shook her head. The lump of meat she was chewing had suddenly lost its savour. With an effort, she swallowed it.

'They should be. They *would* be. But Ponting, or Popović, or whatever his name is, placed a curse on our family.'

Alone with this virtual stranger, thousands of miles from home, boxes of ammunition and a deal-cementing feast laid out between them, Mei felt a rush of grief overtake her. Hot tears tracked down her cheeks and dropped into her lap.

Why? Why was this happening now? The quest for vengeance had been Gabriel's motivation, not hers. Yes, she wanted to spend time with him and help him close the chapter of this life that had started all those years ago. But the complex tangle of emotions binding him to Hong Kong long after he'd left for England? Of those she shared nothing. Or so she'd always thought.

Her parents, if she had any at all, were the elderly Chinese woman who'd raised her on the mainland in Shenzhen — Mummy

Rita — and Fang Jian. They were both gone, one mourned, one not.

And then she realised. No. Those people were not her parents. Her real parents lay dead, cold, under the ground in a drab English churchyard under skies the colour of old knife blades.

When she'd visited their graves with Gabriel, the emotions passing briefly through her had been curiosity and a desire to comfort Gabriel. He'd been visibly moved as they stood shoulder to shoulder staring at the slabs of black stone. Now, as the tears continued to roll down her cheeks, with a Serbian arms dealer regarding her with an unreadable expression in his eyes, she thought she understood.

You needed to know where you had come from. You needed to feel a connection to all those who had come before you. To those who'd contributed their own small gifts to you that would manifest in your character. Shaping your personality and the way you met each new challenge life threw at you.

She looked down at her hands, turning them palm upwards and flexing her fingers. Her fingerprints, unique to her; the old scars overlaying the intersecting lines denoting life, love, fortune, and all the variables the old fortune teller ladies on Temple Street would explain to you for a couple of dollars.

Then she raised them to her face. Still staring at Osman, yet not really seeing him, she traced the pads of her fingers over her features. Her high, smooth, domed forehead. Her eyebrows, so soft to the touch, like cat's fur. Her eyes, round for a Chinese, the legacy of her father, yet still hooded at their inner corners by the epicanthic folds she'd inherited from her mother. The pronounced groove beneath her nose that led down to her lips and her pointed chin.

All this ... all this and every other square inch of her, every gene, every cell, every muscle fibre, bone, nerve and blood vessel ... all that made her *her* she owed to her parents.

She felt it then. Nothing more than a twitch in her right eye at first. Then a faint ringing in her ears. The hands that a moment earlier had been tracing the bones beneath the skin of her face were now clutching the arms of the chair, the knuckles whitening, the tendons standing out like the taut ropes tethering the cargo ships to the docks in Victoria Harbour.

She tilted her head left, then right, aiming to ease the tension in the muscles of her neck, which had knotted up. Her neck cracked twice, high-pitched pops in the quiet of Osman's office like distant pistol shots.

She thought back to a Chinese New Year dinner she'd once hosted where the centrepiece of each table was an elaborate display of indoor fireworks. The head of each table lit a single fuse that wormed among the brightly coloured cones, cylinders and stubby cuboid fireworks.

In turn they glowed, streamed, fountained and crackled, emitting showers of gold, silver and red sparks, writhing snakes of powdery green ash, even translucent turquoise paper parachutists that ascended a few feet on columns of hot air before spiralling down to land among the champagne glasses and discarded lobster shells.

The displays culminated in chrysanthemum blossoms of sinuous blue-white flames that emitted light, but not heat. She encouraged her guests to pass their hands through the 'cold fire'. They gasped, then laughed delightedly at the tickling sensations.

Burning brightly in her chest was a relative of that same incendiary chemical: a fiercer, brighter, more dangerous version that didn't burn her but which would, she knew, she *swore*, annihilate Steve Ponting.

'Lizzie, are you all right?' Osman asked, finally.

His voice seemed to lag the movement of his lips as she focused on his face again. She blinked, and the sound and vision snapped into alignment.

The door opened. She turned to see Gabriel nodding his thanks to a coarse-featured man who then withdrew, closing the door after him.

31

Gabriel took in the scene in a couple of seconds. Mei had obviously done the deal. Boxes of ammunition and empty magazines lay in a tidy stack at one end of the wide wooden desk. She and Osman had been eating. The food smelled incredible. He detected Middle Eastern spices: paprika, toasted sesame seeds, ground cumin, cinnamon.

Mei jumped to her feet and embraced him, squeezing so hard he gasped before she let him go.

He glanced at Osman then back at her.

'Are you OK?'

'I'm fine. I'll explain in a minute.'

She turned to Osman and introduced him. Gabriel shook the older man's hand and pulled up a chair to sit beside his sister.

'Mei, what happened?'

'First of all, big change. I want you to call me Tara from now on.'

'What? But you told me—'

'I know what I told you,' she said, smiling. 'But I've changed my mind. When I get back to Hong Kong, I'm going to see my lawyer.

I'm going to change everything from Wei Mei to Tara Wolfe. The letters of incorporation for the business, everything.'

'Wow,' he said, smiling and realising how happy her decision had made him. 'But why? What changed?'

He looked at Osman but he merely shrugged his shoulders while gnawing at a fresh lamb cutlet.

'I don't know exactly,' she said. 'We were just talking and it hit me. Hard. Like a train. I felt them, Gabriel, here.' She placed her open hand over her heart. 'Mum and Dad.'

Struggling to process the news, Gabriel nonetheless felt himself able to relax for the first time since they'd touched down in Serbia. He had news of his own to impart. Although his own trawl through Osman's holdings in the town had proved fruitless, while he was walking between Top Gun and Cheers! his phone had buzzed with an incoming email. Wūshī had come up with a digitally aged photo of Ponting.

The face staring out of the screen at him bore a resemblance to the grainy newspaper image, but overlaid with a patina of time-wrought changes. Lines, liver spots, sunken cheeks and an eerie cast to the eyes had appeared courtesy of whichever software Wūshī had used to add forty years to the former Special Branch officer.

He pulled out his phone, swiped up the image and turned the phone round, showing it first to Mei – Tara, he corrected himself – then Osman.

'Do you recognise that man?' he asked him.

Osman took the phone and studied the photo.

'He looks like a robot but, yes, underneath it, I see him. His full name is Ratko Popović, and if you are going to kill him then I will gladly help you any way I can.'

'We think he's based in Novi Sad.'

'Yes, your sister told me. I do not know his exact location, but he has a house in a very expensive district. International bankers, sports stars, celebrities, you know?'

'What's it called, this district?'

'Paragovo.'

Gabriel noted it down. He could feel the end-game coming into view. With weapons and ammunition and whatever intel Osman was willing to provide, he could almost taste victory over the man who had wreaked such damage on the Wolfe family.

'What can you tell us about him? Do you know how many men work for him? What sort of arsenal he has?'

'That's a lot of questions. Please, eat and I will tell you what I know.'

Gabriel took one of the cutlets and bit into the smoky, spicy meat. 'Fire away,' he said through his mouthful.

'Popović commanded maybe fifty men in the war. About ten stayed with him afterwards. They regrouped in Novi Sad. They call themselves the Golden Bough now, but in the war they were known as the Black Eagles,' he said, wrinkling his nose. 'He has plenty of low-level operators on his payroll, but they're just chaff, blowing in the wind and sticking to whoever will pay them a living wage. They won't risk their lives for him, or anybody else. You can forget about them. When the bullets start flying, so will they.'

'What's the command structure?'

'He has two sons. Vlado's the older one. He'll take over when Popović retires. Got a business brain. Andrej is younger, just a kid, really. He likes the rough stuff. Like his father. But the man to watch is Saša Lukić. He's the number two in the organisation and a total psychopath.'

'What about guns?' Tara asked.

Osman shrugged. 'What you would expect. They all carry pistols. Then there are AKs like yours. Maybe heavier stuff. I don't know, I'm sorry.'

'Don't be,' Gabriel said. 'This is all useful stuff. Does he have anything that makes him vulnerable, do you know?'

'Well, his sons, obviously. And, I don't know if this counts, he is mad about football. Like half his countrymen, he follows Red Star Belgrade. But for him, it's an obsession. He is fanatical.'

'What about his wife?' Mei asked. 'Is he still married to the mother of his children?'

Osman nodded. 'He is. And it's a good question. Do not, under any circumstances, discount his wife. Milena is tough,' he said.

'When Ratko is away on business, she runs things. Serbian women are fearless, but Milena, she takes that to a whole other level.'

Gabriel checked his watch. It was late, or maybe early. After 2.00 a.m. anyway. He wanted to make an early start the next day and all their gear was back in Belgrade.

He looked at his sister. Tara returned his gaze and he sensed the connection between them, stronger than before. She nodded. Stood.

'Thank you, Osman,' she said, holding out her hand which he shook warmly, grasping her forearm with his free hand.

'May God's peace and His blessings be upon you,' he said in a formal register that made him sound almost priestly.

Gabriel followed Tara's lead, shaking hands and receiving the same blessing from Osman.

Osman opened a desk drawer and pulled out a bundle of supermarket carrier bags, which he filled with the cartons of ammunition. Gabriel and Tara divided the bags between them. He hadn't carried a combat load for a while and enjoyed the reassuring weight of the brass, lead, copper and gunpowder as they tightened the handles into thin plastic strings that cut into his fingers.

How many would they expend before Ponting was dead? The answer was brutally simple.

Enough.

32

Gabriel and Tara were on the road out of Belgrade by 7.45 a.m. the next morning. The A-1 meandered northwest for seventy-five miles through a fertile agricultural plain. Vast fields of sunflowers and maize bordered the motorway, stretching to the horizon.

'How are we going to do this?' she asked, pushing her seat all the way back and then sticking her booted feet up on the dashboard.

'Get to Ponting?'

'Yes.'

'We need to make a positive ID first. The picture isn't bad, but it's not enough. I don't want to target the wrong guy.'

'So how do we do that?'

'After we find somewhere discreet to stay, we check out the residential area Osman told us about: Paragovo.'

'And how do we do that without arousing suspicion? We can't just loiter around the place pretending to be tourists, can we?'

'Osman said it's very upmarket, right? Lots of footballers, celebrities, that type. So, you'll be a Chinese movie star and I'll be your agent. Call it a variation on a theme. We're looking for somewhere you can rent while you're making a film.'

'In Serbia?'

'Why not? It's a spy film set in the Cold War. We'll say Serbia is standing in for Soviet Russia.'

She turned to him and grinned. 'That's actually not bad.'

'Thank you! I thought of it all on my own.'

'And then what? Full-frontal assault or stealth attack?'

'Two of us versus ten or more loyal soldiers plus more on tap? I'd say option two.'

'How?'

'Not sure yet. Ideally, I'd like to draw him out, get him away from his men.'

'That won't be easy. Men like him like to surround themselves with protection at all times. Fang did.'

'True. But we still got to him, didn't we?'

'We did. But if I hadn't realised you were my brother, I would have killed you instead of Fang.'

Gabriel rolled his head on his shoulders. He pulled out to overtake a flatbed truck overloaded with bales of straw. Loose pieces were swirling in its slipstream as Gabriel floored the throttle to pass it.

'Let's find him first, then we'll come up with a plan to extract him.'

'And you still want to kill him, not take him back to the UK and hand him over to the police?'

'Listen, Tara,' Gabriel said, finding it surprisingly easy to use his sister's given name. 'If I thought we'd get justice – for you, for Michael, for Mum and Dad – then, sure, I'd say let's make a citizen's arrest or whatever they call it out here and find a way to get him out of Serbia and into the UK. But then what? We'd have to make a complaint first. The police would have to investigate it and they'd only arrest him if they found enough evidence to suspect him on the kidnapping. How's that going to happen after so many years? And even if they *did* arrest him, the chances of the Crown Prosecution Service agreeing to try him are tiny. And— '

Tara interrupted before he could go any further.

'I get it, BB, I get it! Then he'd have to be tried. And found guilty. And then he'd probably get a ridiculous sentence and serve only half of it,' she said, emphasising with a thump of her boot heel on the dash each precarious link in the judicial chain that might, just, lead to Ponting's incarceration. 'Then he'd be out again and looking for payback.'

'Why did you ask, then?'

'Because if it was just me, I'd take him out to the woods and cut his head off after telling him why he was going to die. But before I did that I'd tell him I was going to go back and torture his wife and sons to death.'

'You wouldn't, would you?'

'No. But I'd make sure he believed me, so his last moments on Earth were filled with despair,' she said, her voice grim. 'But it's not just me. So I wanted to make sure we agreed on what we were going to do with him.'

'We do.'

* * *

They arrived in Novi Sad at 8.58 a.m. and found a cheap, but clean, family-owned hotel on the outskirts of the commercial district. The owner, a keen-eyed lady in her late middle-years, seemed perfectly happy to accept a large advance payment in cash without the need to see passports or anything else in the way of ID.

'We need a different car,' Gabriel said, sitting on the bed in Tara's room while she stood at the window and looked down at the street. 'Something flashy to go with the story. Any preferences?'

'Lambo,' she said at once. 'If Novi Sad can supply one, that's what I want. Nothing succeeds like excess, right?'

Smiling, Gabriel tapped in a search term on his phone.

'OK. Looks like we're off to visit Dragan Luxe Hire on Bulevar Cara Lazar. I'm going to change into my sharpest suit. Have you got anything that says Chinese film star?'

Tara grinned. 'Leave it with me. I brought just the thing.'

Ten minutes later, Gabriel was fastening sapphire and white-gold cufflinks in the French cuffs of his shirt. He adjusted his jacket sleeves to leave half an inch of the snowy white cotton visible, the bling glinting oh-so-discreetly beneath the soft pale-grey wool. He laced his mirror-polished black Oxfords then straightened and checked the knot of his sea-green silk tie in the mirror.

He nodded to himself. From the newly washed and gelled hair to the polished toecaps of his shoes, he was every inch the A-lister's agent. Then he picked up the Tokarev he'd brought up in his suitcase, racked the slide and stuck it into the back of his waistband. OK, almost every inch.

He knocked on Tara's door.

'Wait one second. OK, come in!'

Her voice sounded different. Imperious. Not angry exactly. But on a short fuse. So she'd got into character already. That was good.

He went in and took in his sister's transformation. She'd packed her Lotus Blossom outfit. A white leather biker jacket with quilted lapels, plus matching jeans and low-heeled boots. He registered the slash in the left upper arm.

He frowned. 'I'd hoped we'd be reasonably inconspicuous.'

'You don't like it?'

'It's not that. And it screams movie star. But we're really going to stand out.'

'Listen, BB. He doesn't know we're coming for him. He doesn't even know we exist,' she said. 'Last time he saw either of us, you were three and I was a baby. So what if we get noticed? The story's good. If he asks the agent, they'll just confirm it.'

It wasn't what Gabriel wanted, but he knew there'd be no point in arguing with his sister. He was learning a lot about her on this trip, including that she didn't like backing down.

'Have you got room for a pistol in there anywhere?'

She nodded and held the left-hand side of the jacket out wide to reveal the black grip of the Tokarev. 'Built in shoulder-holster. Fang's tailor did a special run for us.'

'We'll stick with our aliases, OK? Lizzie Wong and Toby Sutherland. This way our legends are in place well before we get within shooting range of Ponting. If he asks around, the story holds.'

She nodded. 'You do all the talking. I'll just play the diva,' she said, tossing her head. 'In fact, I think I'm going to enjoy this. I get to boss you around and there's nothing you can do about it.'

Gabriel shook his head. It turned out highly skilled assassins and bosses of recently-turned-legit investment houses could also be incredibly juvenile little sisters when it suited them.

33

The car hire showroom occupied the ground floor of a mirror-glass-fronted office block. The top of the block was emblazoned with a green and gold bank logo.

Standing across the road, having just locked the rental, Gabriel imagined thousands of cubicle-drones inside, shackled to desks. What did they do all day? He pictured rows of smartly dressed, immaculately groomed men and women slaving away over keyboards, staring at banks of trading monitors and scrolling information feeds. Yammering into phones clamped under their chins as they moved ones and zeroes around the global financial markets making money for their employer.

It was a world he knew virtually nothing about. He'd flirted with the advertising industry after leaving the army and it hadn't turned out well. Since then, his life had been a mixture of operations for The Department and freelance missions. The latter either on his own account or that of wealthy clients who needed the sort of unorthodox services only an ex-SAS member with an exotic portfolio of additional skills could provide.

They'd all be married, he imagined. Married or expecting to be one day. Looking for the next rung on the housing ladder. Angling for a bigger mortgage, higher ceiling on their credit card, better personal lease contract on the BMW or the Merc. Saving for private school fees, that second property on a lakefront or somewhere in the countryside. Planning their foreign holidays, maybe on the Black Sea coast or heading west to the Med.

And it struck him. Was this what he should be thinking about? Aiming for? Was this what married life meant? Eli had been adamant it didn't. Fariyah had told him as much. But were they right?

Were there married agents? Happily hitched firearms officers or Special Forces personnel? He'd never met another Department operative so it was hard to tell. But Don had seemed pretty sanguine about the prospect of two of his people tying the knot.

Tara nudged him with her elbow.

'Hey! Stop daydreaming. We've got a Lamborghini to rent and I bags the first drive.'

He spotted a pedestrian crossing fifty yards to their left and turned toward it. Tara had other ideas.

Head held high, oversized sunglasses reflecting the clouds, she stepped off the kerb and strode directly across all four lanes, making a bee-line for the showroom. The traffic was light, Novi Sad's limited rush hour already having subsided, but she still brought a silver VW screeching to a halt, its driver leaning on the horn and waving a fist at her from behind the windscreen.

Gabriel ran to catch up with her, swearing under his breath, holding up his hands in a gesture he intended to convey part-apology, part-don't-blame-me-she's-the-client helplessness. More cars and the odd truck either stopped dead like the VW or swerved around her, but Tara carried on as if she were walking down a red carpet.

Under a barrage of yelled Serbian expletives, Gabriel escorted Tara to the far kerb.

Reaching the safety of the pavement, she burst out laughing.

'What the fuck was that?' Gabriel demanded, his heart pounding.

'Lizzie Wong, she not wait for nobody! She big, big movie star!'

Tara said in a terrible Chinglish accent lifted straight from kung fu films.

'Really? You're in character already? You could have been killed, you idiot!'

She spun round, hands on hips, eyes blazing. 'Number one, yes, I'm in character. In case you hadn't noticed, we're waist-deep in enemy territory. Number two, no I couldn't have been killed. I've been watching them all morning. They drive like they've all got Ming vases on the bonnet. And three, don't call me an idiot. Ever! OK? I took over the White Koi triad, in case you don't remember. I moved the whole thing legit in a couple of years and nobody died in the process. Nobody important, anyway. Now I'm CEO of Lang Investments. What have *you* done that's so clever you get to call me an idiot?'

Gabriel held his palms out in surrender for the second time in a couple of minutes, only this time he meant it. Her outburst had taken him completely by surprise.

'Look, I'm sorry. I didn't mean it. I shouldn't have said it. I was just … concerned, that's all. We won't be able to get Ponting if you're nursing a busted leg in the hospital.'

Tara adjusted her sunglasses. She inhaled sharply through her nose.

'Yeah, OK. I'm sorry, too. I don't know where that came from. I spent a lot of years being at Fang's beck and call. I guess I don't like a man – *any* man – giving me orders or telling me off.'

'Noted,' Gabriel said dryly. 'You ready? Maybe you could channel some of that attitude into your new persona.'

Side by side they marched up to the double plate-glass doors. Gabriel made sure he arrived fractionally ahead of Tara and held the door wide for her to precede him to the showroom.

'Showtime!' he muttered as a black-suited saleswoman clicked across the polished white floor towards them.

Over the woman's shoulder Gabriel clocked the half dozen low-slung sports cars arrayed in a chevron pattern. A gun-metal Aston Martin sat shoulder to shoulder with a Ferrari in the Italian marque's signature Rosso Corsa. They reminded him of a sober-suited hedge fund manager showing off a trophy girlfriend. He couldn't see any Lamborghinis, however. Maybe 'Lizzie Wong' could be persuaded to settle. Right. Because *that* was going to happen.

The saleswoman – makeup flawless, scarlet lips as bright as the Ferrari behind her, blonde hair swept up into an elegant chignon – cast swift, appraising glances at her two new customers. Evidently satisfied she was dealing with potential clients and not time-wasters, she beamed a high-wattage smile at them, revealing teeth as white as the floor tiles.

'Good morning, sir, madam,' she said in unaccented English. 'I am Emina. Welcome to Dragan Luxe Hire. Do you have a specific car in mind or would you like to look around?'

Ignoring her, Tara stalked off towards the cars, running a fingertip down the paintwork of a glittering black Porsche as if checking for dirt.

'Good morning,' Gabriel said, watching his sister playing her role up to and beyond the hilt. 'These are all very classy cars, but what I'd really like is a Lamborghini. I don't suppose you have any available? My client is rather insistent I find one for her. She's a movie actress,' he added in an undertone. 'Very picky.'

She smiled and nodded. 'I understand. We have two Huracans. One is out, but other is in our Belgrade branch. I can have it brought over within the hour if you are sure you want to take it?'

'Can I ask what colour it is?'

'It is Verde Mantis. Very bright green.'

'Let me check with Miss Wong. One moment, please.'

Gabriel left Emina and went over to Tara, who'd settled herself behind the wheel of a silver Mercedes SLS, its gull-wing doors opened high above the roof.

'Enjoying ourselves, are we?' he asked quietly. 'Emina wants to know if *Miss Wong* is happy with a pearlescent lime-green Lamborghini Huracan.'

In reply, Tara swore at him loudly and inventively in a filthy Hong Kong street dialect for twenty seconds, waving her hands around and buffeting him about the shoulders.

'Tell her I wanted white,' she added in a calmer voice at the end of the tirade, with an impish smile only he could see, 'but slime green will do.'

He sighed and rolled his eyes, then retraced his steps between the couple of million quid's worth of automotive bling-for-hire to rejoin Emina at the front desk.

'Miss Wong was hoping for white,' he said, 'to match her outfit. But the Verde Mantis will be fine.'

'Very good, sir. The rental is one hundred fifty-five thousand dinars per day or six-fifty for seven days. For convenience we can invoice in dollars or euros if you prefer. We also require certain financial sureties: deposit, fifty percent advance payment and so on. Then there is insurance—'

'That's all fine. We'll take it for a week, please,' he said. 'If you could sort out the paperwork while the car is being brought up from Belgrade, I'll sign everything then.'

'How will you be paying? We take all major credit cards.'

'Miss Wong prefers to deal in cash. It's a cultural thing,' he added in a whisper. 'I assume American dollars are OK? We can pay the full amount in advance if that would help. And if there's any additional charge for the inconvenience, then of course just let me know and I can pay that on top.'

It was a fairly unambiguous invitation to add a little something on for herself, but, as it turned out, unnecessary.

'Cash is perfectly acceptable,' Emina said. 'Many of our clients are like Miss Wong. Cash is king, that is what they say.'

Gabriel sensed an opening. People who liked to hire over-the-top Italian wheels and pay in cash often inhabited the shady side of the street.

'Can I ask you something, Emina?' he began, casting a glance over at Tara, who'd now exited the SLS and was sitting in a leather and stainless-steel armchair making a great show of checking her phone.

'Of course,' she said with a smile. 'I am here to help. Is Dragan brand value.'

'The film we're here to shoot. It's a big budget Cold War spy movie. We'll need many extras. I don't suppose any of these clients of yours who prefer dealing in cash are…' he deliberately left a gap and rubbed his chin nervously, 'that is to say, the director is looking for some authentic inhabitants of what you might call the *demi monde.*'

She frowned, grooving three lines in her otherwise smooth forehead. Gabriel wondered whether she used Botox.

'I'm sorry. Demi who?'

'Oh, no, *I'm* sorry. I lived in Paris for six months. Always dropping into French. I mean we need, and not to beat around the bush, some actual, real-life,' he dropped his voice into a hiss, '*gangsters.*'

Her eyes widened. 'I'm afraid I cannot help, sir,' she primly. 'All our clients are legitimate businesspeople. Celebrities. Entertainers. No criminals.'

'Oh, of course, of course. I understand. Forgive my clumsy language. But, Emina, come on, you know what I mean,' he said. 'Let's say all your clients *are* legitimate businessmen and women. But if I was looking for someone who could walk around Novi Sad and the police wouldn't be able to lift a finger against them, even though they wanted to, who would that be?'

She stiffened. 'I am sorry, sir. I'm afraid I don't know of such people.'

Gabriel had come this far, he felt it was worth one final try. He pulled out his wallet and separated two hundred-dollar bills from their stablemates.

'I understand. Truly, I do. Look, you said you didn't need an inconvenience payment because we were dealing in cash, but how about making it a little side deal? Just between you and me,' he said. 'I'll overpay your invoice by this two hundred dollars. And you can tell me where I might go if I wanted to find the kind of man I'm talking about. How about that?'

Her eyes flicked down to the notes in his hand then back to his. He watched her sorting through the pros and cons of his offer. He had no idea what a sales lady made at a car rental place, however upmarket, in Serbia's second city. But he didn't think it could be much. Maybe two hundred bucks would pay for a nice holiday somewhere, or an online Business Studies course.

She came to a decision and deftly relieved him of the bills.

'There is bar on Bulevar Cara Lazara. It is called Crvena Zvezda. That means Red Star. Very popular sports bar. One of the most legitimate,' she made air quotes round the word, 'businessmen in Novi Sad likes to drink there when Red Star Belgrade are playing. I cannot say any more. You understand?'

Gabriel nodded. 'Of course. And thanks,' he whispered. Then, at a conversational volume, 'How long will it take for you to get our Huracan here from Belgrade?'

She checked her watch. 'Can you come back at midday? I will have the car valeted and ready for you to drive away, plus all paperwork ready.'

He nodded, shook her hand and retrieved Tara from her perch on the designer armchair.

'Good to go. Back here at noon,' he said as he escorted her towards the doors, turning his head to smile at Emina.

34

Two hours later they returned and swapped a bundle of large-denomination dollar bills and half a dozen fake signatures for a garish green Lamborghini that came up to Gabriel's midriff.

As she'd promised, Tara took the keys. After adjusting the driving position, she snicked the transmission into first gear and peeled away from the side of the road, lighting up the tyres and sending a deafening roar from the exhaust bouncing off the plate-glass frontage of the showroom.

She turned a corner into full sun. The razor-sharp lines of the bonnet blurred as the pearlescent paint flared in the bright light. Gabriel flipped down the visor. Tara drove just inside the speed limit but she'd locked the transmission in second and the howl from the engine had heads turning all the way along their route towards Paragovo.

He leant back in the quilted seat, which, like the rest of the interior, was constructed from black and lime-green leather, and tried to enjoy being driven by his kid sister in the least discreet set of wheels he'd ever ridden in. Compared to the Lamborghini, his old midnight-blue Maserati was a stealth fighter.

As they approached a crossroads, the traffic lights turned red. Tara brought the car to a smooth stop and turned to Gabriel.

'How's my driving?'

'It's good. Although I think there's a couple of people in the northern suburbs who didn't hear you leave the showroom.'

'Ha! Very funny. Seriously, though, what do you think?'

Gabriel twisted in his seat to look at Tara. He realised she was completely serious. She wanted his opinion. And his approval? He hadn't detected much in the way of insecurity so far. In fact, her outburst when he'd called her an idiot suggested she had a brittle edge when it came to criticism. He told the truth.

'You're an excellent driver. There are plenty of people who've wrapped these things round lamp-posts minutes after taking delivery. You're handling it like a pro. It's not your first time, is it?'

She grinned.

'Nope. I have one of these in Hong Kong. Well, a Gallardo, but it's still the baby Lambo. Mine's Arancio Borealis. That's—'

'A very loud orange. I speak Italian.'

'So you do.'

'It's funny we both like fast cars, though, isn't it? We've led totally separate lives yet we've followed similar paths.'

'You think? The British Army and the White Koi triad are similar?'

'Not exactly, but think about it. At the personal level, we've led what you'd have to call violent lives, at least part of the time.'

'I've *used* violence. I wouldn't say it was a violent life.'

'Fair enough. Dangerous lives, then. Martial arts, skill with weapons, and we've both ended up with more than our fair share of money: do you think there's something in that? It can't all be luck and coincidence, can it?'

A sleek black Mercedes S-class drew up next to them, a whale beside a shark. The side windows were blacked out. Gabriel looked across, wondering whether the man they sought was on the other side of the privacy glass, staring out at him. The Merc's engine revved, emitting a throbbing rumble from some large-capacity V-engine under the bonnet: an eight, Gabriel thought, or just possibly a twelve.

Mei responded in kind, blipping the throttle and producing a rasping bark from the Huracan's exhaust.

'Tara, no. Please,' Gabriel said. 'Let them go. We're drawing enough attention to ourselves already. If the police get involved, our cover story won't hold. They could be in Ponting's pocket, too. Think of that.'

'Relax, BB,' she drawled. 'I'm just winding him up.'

She blipped the throttle again, harder this time, sending a shimmy of torque through the car and into Gabriel's stomach. She took her foot off the brake for an instant, too, so that the car snapped forwards by half a foot.

The Merc began rolling forwards and, as the lights changed, surged ahead of them, engine bellowing.

As if taking her driving test, Tara drove with exaggerated caution across the junction, barely reaching thirty by the time they reached the far side.

Gabriel laughed. 'OK, you've made your point. Now, can we just get to Paragovo like normal film stars and their agents?'

She accelerated, letting the transmission decide when to change gear.

'What you said back then,' Tara said. 'About our lives. Were you asking if I believed in fate?'

'Yeah, I guess I was. Do you think we would *ever* have ended up in white-collar jobs, doing the nine-to-five, paying the mortgage and raising kids?'

'Well, for a start, I'd have had to *not* be kidnapped when I was a baby.'

'And I suppose I'd have had to *not* be raised by Master Zhao.'

'That would only have happened if Michael hadn't died.'

Gabriel sighed. 'Yeah. Poor little Michael. You know, even though I remember him now, it's like watching an old video.'

'What do you mean?'

'I can't feel him. In here.' He thumped his chest. 'I can see him now. Pictures of him in my head. But the connection's long gone. I don't think I'll ever get it back.'

'At least you remember him. By the time he was born, I was in China,' she said. 'Anyway, where's this all coming from? Because we're closing in on Ponting?'

'I suppose so.'

'But?'

'What do you mean?'

'Oh, come on, BB. I can hear the "but" every time you speak about your personal life,' she said, making a right turn and heading up a long, straight hill towards Paragovo. 'What is it? Wait. You just asked about mortgages and raising kids. This is about Eli, isn't it? You asked about this before and I told you about how it works in the triads. Are you going to back out of the wedding? Because if you are I'll kill you myself.'

There it was. The question he'd been avoiding for weeks. He loved Eli. No question about that. He loved her in a way he'd never loved anyone before. If it weren't such a soppy phrase, he'd call it 'the real thing'. But there was love and then there was marriage.

Eli would want kids, he just knew it. How could they carry on as before? *'Kiss Daddy goodbye, children. He's off to Yemen to kill terrorists. I don't know when – or if – he'll be back and they might torture him, so be prepared for him to come back with bits missing.'*

'Oh, shit! You are, aren't you?' Tara asked, when he stayed silent.

'No! I want to marry her. More than I've wanted anything else in my life,' he said, realising at that point how much he truly meant it. Emboldened by the realisation, he plunged ahead. 'I know what you said about different ways of living to the normal, but what if we have kids? How the hell do I protect them given what I do for a living? What would happen if I got killed? Or Eli did?'

'I guess the other one would have to give up work to raise them. Like in any family. Listen, BB, shit happens. You should know that better than anyone. People die all the time. Not just soldiers and gangsters and Department operatives. Truck drivers, too. Teachers.

Civil servants. Artists. Chefs. Politicians. Bankers. Everybody dies in the end.'

'Jesus! That's bleak.'

'Is it? Or is it just the truth? The story ends the same for everybody, BB. The only question is when and how. There's no "if" about it.'

'So what are you saying? Just be resigned to it?'

'No, dummy! I'm saying get on with your life. I'm saying marry Eli. Have kids if you both want them. Carry on working for Don Webster or resign and devote the rest of your life to charity work. People will thank you for it whatever you decide. But stop worrying, OK?'

Gabriel scragged his fingers through his hair. It felt odd getting life advice from his sister. But he had to admit her philosophy had plenty in its favour. Maybe he could try living in the present and forgetting all those terrifying 3.00 a.m. 'What if?' questions.

'I'll try,' he said. 'Take the next left. There's a sign for Paragovo.'

Five minutes later, they were cruising along a wide, tree-lined avenue. The houses were all set well back, boasting lush front lawns, when they could see them behind tall fences and security gates. Such cars visible from the street confirmed the impression of a well-heeled neighbourhood. Plenty of high-end 4x4s, sleek German and Japanese saloons and a smattering of close cousins to the Huaracan, though none approaching its screeching 'look-at-me' paint job.

'You think Ponting's behind one of those doors?' Tara asked.

'Could be.'

A Mercedes S-Class with blacked-out windows pulled out from a side street and came towards them. Gabriel checked the licence plate. It was the car they'd almost raced at the traffic lights. He glanced at the driver, caught a generic male face behind mirror shades and a set to the jaw that spoke volumes for his profession. Driver, yes, but also muscle. A man willing to swing a punch, or a cosh, if his boss needed it swung. The man looked back at him. The grim set to his jaw didn't waver. Then the two cars passed.

Gabriel suddenly wanted very badly to know who sat in the Merc's rear seat. But with so little traffic on the roads in this quiet residential neighbourhood, tailing it was out of the question. He corrected himself, tailing it *covertly*. So forget the covert aspect.

'Turn round and follow the Merc,' he said.

'You think he's in there?'

'I don't know. Just do it.'

Tara pulled in to a side road and then backed the Huaracan out facing back the way they'd come. The Merc was disappearing over the brow of a hill, so she accelerated until she had its fat rear end in sight once more.

'They'll know we're following them,' she said.

'If they're ordinary rich folk they won't be suspicious. If they're Emina's friends it doesn't matter. When they stop I'll go and give them our story,' he said. 'Say we're looking for the right real estate agent and ask for a recommendation. If you want you can lay on your act again, as thick as you like. That type respect money and power above all else so you can go for the Oscar.'

'And if they don't buy it?'

'We can make this ridiculous car work in our favour. Does it *look* like the sort of wheels an out-of-town mob would use to keep a low profile?'

'Good point.'

Keeping a respectful fifty yards back from the Mercedes, Tara trailed it as it wound higher into the hills above Novi Sad. It neither accelerated nor slowed and Gabriel began to relax. Either the occupants were really just a legit business exec plus chauffeur or they weren't worried about picking up a tail. Either worked for what he had in mind.

Finally the brake lights came on and the Merc slowed to a stop outside a pair of grey-painted solid steel gates. As they swung inwards and Tara brought the Huaracan to a stop, Gabriel jumped out, taking care to adjust his jacket to cover the Tokarev's butt and ran over to the Mercedes.

He ran a hand through his hair, then rapped on the rear window.

The black glass descended with a faint hum. A woman stared

out at him. Mid-thirties, heavily made-up and with immaculately styled ash-blonde hair. He took her for a TV show host.

He stood back a couple of feet, not wanting to alarm her.

'Da? Mogu li da vam pomognem?'

She spoke Serbian, but the question was close enough to Russian for him to be able to translate. Though anyone with half a brain could have managed. *Yes? Can I help you with something?*

'Govorite Engleski, molim?' *Do you speak English, please?*

'Yes,' she replied cautiously.

Gabriel could see the driver turned round in his seat. His hands were out of sight, but he could imagine a small pistol gripped in his right fist. He suspected it was the presence of a fluorescent-green Lamborghini that was staying his hand. Stalkers tended not to have the money for such trappings.

'Thank goodness!' Gabriel introduced himself, or rather his fictional persona and explained about his pressing need for an upscale estate agent.

'Try Kovak & Vuković,' she said, then issued an instruction in Serbian to her driver and buzzed up the window.

Back in the car with Tara, he looked up the estate agent and gave her the address.

On the way back into Novi Sad, they had to slow as they came upon a procession of cars, all hooting their horns. Joining the tail end of the convoy, Tara could only crawl along, waiting for a chance to pass. The cars began pulling off the road and she moved slowly along the outside of the column.

At its head, in a layby outside a church, was a white open-topped carriage pulled by two dappled horses, their manes tied in plaits by blue and red ribbons.

Gabriel looked sideways to see a young girl, who couldn't have been more than eighteen or nineteen, being helped down by a middle-aged man in a dark suit. She was enveloped in a fluffy white wedding dress, her face half-hidden by a net veil clamped to her luxuriant blonde hair by a circlet of ox-eye daisies. And then the road ahead opened up and Tara put her foot down.

35

Gabriel waited until the real estate agent had shown them two houses before moving the conversation round to the real reason for his and Tara's interest in Paragovo.

'I've heard there are some quite interesting people living in Paragovo,' he began. 'I'm trying to find someone who could act as a consultant on the film we're making. Maybe someone who knows the criminal underworld. Would you know anybody like that?'

He'd resigned himself to a denial like Emina's. After all, it made sense. Blabbing about the gangster living among your celebrity clients might earn you a swift and direct trip to the bottom of a lake, or the foundations of a motorway flyover. So the young man's answer surprised him.

'You mean Ratko Popović, I suppose. Many people know of him. He has many business interests in Novi Sad. Some are, what do you say, on the level?' Gabriel nodded, trying not to punch the air in his delight at finally landing a solid lead on Ponting. 'But everyone knows where he makes his real money.'

'And he lives here in Paragovo,' Gabriel said.

'For sure.'

'Do you know his address?'

The man shrugged. 'You need a consultant, you said?'

'That's right.'

'Must pay well, being a movie consultant.'

'It does. And do you know what?' Gabriel got his wallet out. 'Acting as a middleman does as well.' He handed over another two hundred dollars, which disappeared into a pocket.

'He lives on Sonje Marinković. The last house before the forest.'

Gabriel smiled warmly. 'Thank you.'

'So, you want to take one of the houses I've shown you?'

'Let me talk it over with Miss Wong. I've got your card so I'll get back to you.'

After saying goodbye to the estate agent, Gabriel drove the Huracan back to their hotel, parking it in a small courtyard shielded by high walls from curious passers-by.

'We'll go up there tonight in a taxi and scope it out,' he said.

Later that same evening, Ratko Popović received a call during dinner. He checked the screen, then looked across the table at his wife.

'Sorry, Milena, I have to take this.'

He leaned back and accepted the call.

'Uncle Ratko? It's Emina. Something odd happened at work today. Two strangers rented a Lamborghini. They were acting weird. She was Chinese and he was English. He said she was a film star, but then he was asking questions about gangsters. Said the director wanted to talk to someone who knew the underside of Novi Sad. Anyway, it's probably nothing but I thought you'd want to know.'

'Thanks, Emina. You did the right thing. How's your mum?'

'She's fine. Says to send you her love.'

'Tell her I'll drop by soon for a coffee, OK? I'll bring some almond cakes.'

'OK. Thanks, Uncle Ratko. I love you.'

'I love you too, darling. By the way, these strangers. Anything else stand out about them?'

'Not really. He had a scar on his cheek and she was wearing this all-white leather outfit, fitted, you know? Which I guess fits with her being a movie star. Other than that, nothing.'

'What sort of age were they?'

'Late thirties? Oh and, Uncle Ratko?'

'Yes, darling?'

'They asked where gangsters like to hang out. I told them you watch the football in Crvena Zvezda.'

'Good girl.'

He put the phone back in his pocket and went on with his meal. Emina was a smart girl and no mistake. Presumably they'd offered her some cash for information: she'd pocketed their money and sent them to the wrong bar. Good for her!

'What did she want?' Milena asked.

'We might have trouble. Remember I said someone had been sniffing around down in Spain?'

'The account?'

'That's right. Well, Emina said two people hired a car today, a Lamborghini. They were asking about where they could find gangsters, if you can believe it. Said they were movie people.'

'You think they're connected?'

'I don't know. Maybe, maybe not. But Emina's got a good head on her shoulders. If she thought it was worth calling me then I'm going to check it out.'

'Surely if they were after you they wouldn't be so blatant? A car like that is hardly under the radar, is it?'

'Double-bluff? I don't know.'

'What are you going to do?'

'I'm going to speak to Saša,' he said, wiping some gravy from his chin with a starched white napkin. 'Set him on their trail. If they're really just nosy celebrities he'll find out. But if there's something else going on he'll sniff them out in a heartbeat.'

'And then?'

'And then we figure out a way to deal with them.'

'You can't just kill them. We need to know who they are and where they're from,' Milena said, standing up and stacking his plate on top of hers. 'They don't sound like cops, do they?'

Popović shook his head. 'If there's a police force anywhere in the world that would authorise a couple of cops to hire a Lamborghini, I've yet to hear of it.'

'Who then? Scouts for some Belgrade outfit looking to move in on Novi?'

He wrinkled his nose. 'I can't see it. For a start, Emina said the woman was Chinese. Does that sound like a Belgrade mob to you? And why would they show their hand like that to a bloody car hire saleswoman?' he asked, throwing his hands wide. 'It doesn't make any sense. They'd head for the bars and clubs like we would if we were moving in on their territory.'

Milena shrugged, then took the plates and cutlery out to the kitchen and returned with a fresh-baked pie, the pastry top golden and jewelled with brown sugar.

'Mm, that smells good. Is it—?'

'Plum. Your favourite. Here,' she said, serving him a slice.

He cut into the crust with the edge of his spoon and scooped some of the soft fruit and pastry into his mouth, scattering flakes onto the tablecloth. Milena had balanced the tartness of the plums from the garden, frozen since last year, with dark-brown sugar, cinnamon and cloves.

'Not cops. Not a Belgrade firm. One English, one Chinese,' he said, summarising what he knew as much for his own benefit as Milena's. 'What does that say to you?'

Milena frowned, not answering immediately. He'd always valued that in his wife. Others would leap to conclusions, offering half-assed theories because they thought the boss would prefer instant answers to considered ones. Milena always preferred to take her time when a problem presented itself.

After the war, when they got married, it was Milena who'd advised him on the best way to stay clear of the ICTY investigators. While other militia commanders had been rounded up and put on trial at The Hague, he'd melted into obscurity, beyond their reach.

It was she who'd put him in touch with the people he needed to set up his operation in Novi Sad. And when the existing gangs, mostly rubbish little outfits content to run a few dealers or half a dozen girls had protested, it was Milena who'd devised the strategy to contain, neutralise and eventually wipe them out.

He remembered one night in particular. Golden Bough had spent three months skirmishing with one of the old-established family firms in Novi Sad. They'd reached a bloody stalemate. Milena had prevailed on him to invite the patriarch of the opposing outfit to a dinner under a flag of truce.

The old man had arrived with three of his sons, strapping lads of twenty-two to twenty-eight, all tempered in the fires of war as well the ongoing conflict on the streets of the city for control of drug territory and swathes of the vice trade. Or, what did the city council and the cops call it nowadays? The night-time economy?

Ha! That was a joke. Back when he'd been a wet-behind-the-ears cop in uniform on the Met, he'd worked the Soho beat for a few months. Vice was vice, pure and simple. Pimps, prossies, nonces, rent boys. Porn barons, punters, junkies, pushers. Call them what you liked, it changed nothing.

People had needs they couldn't admit to in polite society so they went down to where they could find *impolite* society, and get their needs taken care of. And if a few people got clipped as a result, either for their cash or, in extreme cases, their lives, well, nobody said the trade was safe, did they? It's why it was called vice.

So, old man Stanković had arrived with a couple of bottles of Vranac red and his sons in tow. What had Milena muttered to him just before opening the front door?

'Here he comes and look, he's brought Huey, Dewey and Louie with him.'

The thought made him smile even now. At the time, he'd laughed aloud as she winked, then turned to admit their enemies.

The dinner had gone well. Milena had served veal soup with lots of garlic and freshly chopped parsley. Then *sarma*, cabbage leaves rolled and stuffed with rice and minced pork and braised in a rich beef stock. And finally, as the guests' faces were shining from the food and the strong red wine they'd brought, pudding. Milena had baked a huge *vasina torta*, a rich, creamy walnut and chocolate cake. She served it with tiny cups of coffee, sludgy with fine grounds, and home-brewed *rakija* made from plums off the same tree that had supplied the fruit for tonight's dessert.

Stanković and his sons had partaken liberally of the wine and the fiery spirit that Milena poured for them all evening. The flag of truce was a time-honoured tradition and they believed in its protective powers utterly. The absence of any muscle from the Popović side must also have reassured them. Had they been a little less trusting, they might have observed how very little their hosts drank themselves.

After everyone had been offered, and had refused, second helpings of the *vasina torta*, Milena rose to clear away the final round of plates and spoons.

'I have one last surprise for you,' she said with a smile as she went into the kitchen.

'Milena, we're full,' Stanković slurred. 'If I eat another mouthful, I'll—'

'Explode?' she asked from the doorway.

She was holding a shotgun, and before any of the four visitors could react, she blew the old man's head off.

Faces spattered with their father's blood, the sons screamed, rearing back from the table. With no guns of their own – because that was one of the rules of truce, wasn't it? – they were defenceless.

Milena could have let them go. But what good would that have done? She'd killed the patriarch and sent a message to his followers, but created a triumvirate of vengeful young Turks in his place. And we all know what to expect from a Turk with a grievance.

She racked another shell into the breech and turned her weapon on Novak, the youngest, blowing a fist-sized hole in the centre of his chest and obliterating heart, lungs and part of his liver. A second shot tore his abdomen apart.

Rodavan fell next, half his face missing as Milena's third blast took away the right-hand side of his head.

The stink of blood, and shit from Novak's split-open belly, permeated the room.

Roaring with grief, shock and animal rage, Spiridon had rounded the dining table and was halfway across the room to Milena. Teeth bared, fingers clawed, he had the wild-eyed look of a wolf backed into a corner by a hunter.

Milena pumped the gun a third time, but the action jammed. Spiridon was on her a second later, his hands around her throat, choking the life out of her in a frenzy.

Which is when Ratko, finally given something to do, left his chair and stabbed the younger man over his left kidney. He pulled his blade free and repeated the move again and again and again, on both sides, slicing into Spiridon's vital organs and pulling forth from his stretched mouth an inhuman howl of agony and shock. His hands fell from Milena's neck: she collapsed backwards and sank onto a wooden bench against the back wall.

Spiridon went down in a disorganised pile of limbs at incongruous angles, blood sluicing from the rents in his back. The light was going from his eyes but Ratko still bent towards him and opened his throat from ear to ear, cutting almost down to his spine. As the eyes filmed over, the piercing blue turning to a milky slate, Ratko whispered into the dying man's face.

'The city is ours now.'

That had been twenty-three years ago. Since then they'd had no serious competition in Novi Sad. Any time anyone tried their hand at setting up in business, a Golden Bough enforcer would arrive at their house in the middle of the night. They'd ring the doorbell, hammer on the door, shout through the letter box until someone let them in.

And then a short, quiet, simple conversation would take place, in which the householder's attention would be secured through the presence of a large-calibre handgun aimed at their face. The Golden Bough enforcer would explain the consequences should the householder decide to persist in their business strategy; if he judged it necessary, he would produce visual aids, taken on the night when the Stanković outfit had lost its patriarch.

The concluding part of the presentation would be an invitation to choose one of two courses of action. Join the Stankoviċes. Or Golden Bough, as a licensed franchisee.

Of course, in the moment, everybody chose wisely. But inevitably there would be backsliders. People whose greed, or faith in their own abilities, outstripped their instinct for self-preservation. And then the evening news would carry a report of a body found in a suitcase under one of the city's underpasses. Or left, in pieces, in a public park. Or dragged, bloated to twice its original size, from the Danube.

Milena's voice dragged him from his reminiscing.

'They're not cops. And they're not rivals either. I know the firms in Belgrade. They're all Serbian,' she said decisively. 'Well, that or Croats. Montenegrins, maybe. Even a few Albanians. But an Englishman? And a Chink? No.'

'Who, then?'

'Either they really are from the movie business—'

'Or?'

'Or they're here for you specifically.'

'To kill me.'

'To kill you. So who have you pissed off who'd go outside our world and hire foreign contractors?'

He poured them both a slug of the *rakija* and drank his glass off before refilling it. The spirit heated his belly and as the fumes rose into his eyes making them water, he thought, hard.

36

In truth, everyone in his and Milena's world who he'd pissed off was dead. Everybody else knew what to expect if they tried forging their own path. And the idea that one of them might try anything as *mad* as staging a hit on Ratko Popović – no. He couldn't see it.

He'd pissed off, if that was the right phrase, the city's government and what remained of its uncorrupted police force. But they were powerless against him and his team of lawyers. Even if they thought they did have a chance at a prosecution, they'd send detectives to arrest him, not a pair of cartoon characters in a twenty-million-dinar Italian sports car.

So if it wasn't locals, it must be outsiders. He considered, briefly, relatives of some of those who'd been at Srebrenica. No. The notion was ridiculous. Those Bosniaks were no good in a fight and hardly likely to come up with the wherewithal to hire contract killers.

He forced himself to reach deeper into his imagination. Who, Steve? Who?

He frowned. Steve? That was odd. He'd stopped thinking of himself as Steve a long time ago. He was Ratko now. He'd embraced and been embraced in return by his Serbian heritage. He felt the soul of the country running in his veins as it had in those of his ancestors.

So was that it? Was the clue to his mystery pursuers' identity somewhere in the past? Before he settled here? Spain, then? Plenty of bad lads down there who might want revenge on a bent cop. But he'd never crossed any of those guys. Not in Spain. Not in London. He'd spent most of his service in Special Branch, protecting diplomats, politicians and royalty.

He closed his eyes and pinched the bony bridge of his nose, feeling the misshapen lump where a sixteen-stone bruiser from the West Midlands Serious Crimes Squad had broken it for him in '77.

CID had rejected him, but surely he had enough nous to think his way through this puzzle. An Englishman and a Chinese woman. Late thirties. Male with a scar. Female in some tight, white leather getup.

Something about the woman was setting off an itch deep in his memory. The leather outfit. He'd seen it before. On a Chinese chick. Where the hell was it? And then, like a shaft of sunlight spearing through a grey cloud to illuminate a familiar landscape, he saw her.

A club in Hong Kong. Jesus, that was going back a bit. What was it called? He pictured a gaudy entrance: two eight-foot-high golden dragons, mouths agape. Two massive, slab-sided doormen in front, managing the velvet rope. That was it, wasn't it? The Golden Dragon. And now the memories surged back from the early eighties as if fresh-minted.

The Golden Dragon was where the boss of the White Koi triad conducted his business. He'd always had a couple of dolly-birds around dressed in skin-tight white leather. More than decorative, they were his own close-protection officers, ready to deter or, if necessary, disable or kill anyone their master wanted shot of.

He'd done the odd bit of business with the WK, but for his final attempt at a score, he'd turned to one of their rivals, the Four-Point Star. Picked a couple of likely lads to kidnap that diplomat's daughter. But it had all gone sideways and he'd had to get his skates on and leave the island in a hurry.

So why was the White Koi triad sending people to Novi Sad asking about him? People who didn't sound like they were in Serbia to offer him a film deal.

The answer was obvious. As obvious as if a ranking White Koi member found themselves under the scrutiny of a couple of Serbians who'd pitched up in Hong Kong. It was a hit.

But why? He'd been out of circulation for decades. He'd never crossed anyone on the island, either inside the law or outside of it.

He needed to think harder.

Milena had disappeared. He hadn't even noticed her go. It was after midnight. He refilled his glass. He took a sip, then rose from his chair, pleased to see he was rock-steady on his feet, and crossed to an old-fashioned bureau in the corner of the dining room. He unlocked the top drawer and pulled it open on well-waxed wooden runners.

A Glock 17 pistol lay atop a file of papers. One of several he kept around the house, upstairs and down. One could never be too careful. He took it out and returned with it to the table.

Absent-mindedly, he began to field-strip it. With practised moves that had become automatic over the years, he dropped out the magazine, cleared the action and separated the slide from the frame. The recoil spring came next, then he poked out the barrel. As he worked the five pieces of metal and plastic, he let his mind wander where it wanted to, sure it would lead him to the answer he needed. The timeline, then.

He'd left Hong Kong aged thirty in mid-1984. So it stood to reason that was the last date he could have caused enough offence to a triad boss for them to want him dead. And even if that were true, why wait thirty-seven years? It didn't make any sense.

On the one hand, she was dressed like a White Koi bodyguard. On the other, the current boss would have no reason to even *know* about Ratko Popović, much less want him dead.

What if it wasn't official triad business? What if this was a personal grudge? And then, slowly, like one of the big lake pike he liked to fish for up at the castle, rising through the green water to take a lure, it came to him. Not all at once, but in pieces that connected as soon as each made itself visible.

A woman dressed as a White Koi enforcer. In her late thirties, so born in the early eighties...

On a personal mission to rub out Ratko Popović aka Steve Ponting...

Who'd fled Hong Kong in the mid-eighties after a botched kidnapping...

Of the daughter of an English diplomat and his half-Chinese wife...

Who was a babe-in-arms at the time...

With a three-year-old brother...

Their names came to him like invisible ink turning brown above a candle flame. Tara and Gabriel.

Good God! The baby girl had grown up and joined the White Koi. It was she who'd rented the car from Emina. And the Englishman must have been her brother. He looked at his hands. The Glock was sitting in his right fist, reassembled, the trigger covered by his curled index finger. He laid it on its side with a muted clunk.

He called Saša.

'Boss?'

'I've got a job for you, Saša. Intelligence-gathering.'

'OK.'

'There's a guy in Novi Sad at the moment and if I'm right about him, he's here to kill me. He's got a woman with him. Their names are Gabriel and Tara Wolfe. I don't think you'll find out much about her, but he might be traceable. He grew up in Hong Kong. He would have turned eighteen in, wait, 1998. Maybe a year either way. Father was a British diplomat. That's all I have at the moment.'

'Should be enough.'

'Good man.'

'You want me to kill them?'

'No. Not yet. Just find out everything you can about them.'

He ended the call. Before going up to join Milena, he went outside and did a circuit of the house, Glock in hand. Then he went inside again and locked all the downstairs windows and put the security bar across the front door. He thought about getting a handful of men out of bed and up to the house, but dismissed the idea. Forewarned was forewarned, and he reckoned that meant he, Milena and Andrej could handle a couple of rich kids with a grudge.

37

Gabriel looked over his shoulder at the assembled guests. Everyone had made a real effort. The guys from the Regiment all looked fantastic in their dress uniform. Creases in their trousers sharp enough to shave with. Medals competing with brass buttons as to which could shine brighter. Sand-coloured berets shaped by hand above steaming kettles and swept, dashingly low, over the right eye.

The old girlfriends had snagged a bench to themselves: Robyn, Petra and Annie, giggling behind their hands and whispering something about him. Something that brought a flare of heat to his cheeks.

Amos Peled and Saul Ben Zacchai were there, deep in conversation, wearing ragged, grey-and-black-striped morning suits with yellow roses in their buttonholes.

He looked around. No sign of Eli yet. Fashionably late. Why she'd chosen a pass high in the Afghan mountains was a puzzle he hadn't solved yet. They were unprotected. Exposed. He felt a breeze on his back. He shivered and looked down at himself. Coming naked to his own wedding was a bold choice. Bev had encouraged him, handing him a Greek shield; 'if you feel like covering your modesty,' she'd said with a wink.

Now he knew what his exes were laughing about. Jesus! Was it too late to go and change? He turned to his right. Smudge was there, staring straight ahead, stroking his jaw. Great guy to have as his best man. Rock steady.

'You got the rings, mate?' he asked under his breath.

Smudge turned to him and nodded. He pushed back on his chin. It emitted a click as the latches under his ears popped and he pulled it down and away from his face. He tilted the jaw towards Gabriel. The two gold rings lay just behind the lower row of teeth.

'Safe as houses, boss,' he said with a grin, before reattaching it.

Gabriel felt an unpleasant squirm of anxiety in his stomach. This wasn't right.

Too late. Eli was stepping down from a horse-drawn SAS Land Rover. Her dress matched the ancient Pinkie's salmon paint. Beside Eli, her chief bridesmaid carried a vast bouquet of blood-red roses that obscured her face. Long coppery-red tresses flickered up above her head in the wind. She lowered the flowers and offered a gap-toothed grin.

The blood issuing from the massive head wound ran down her freckled nose, over her top lip and in between her two top teeth. She licked it away. He wanted to scream.

'Stay calm, Gabriel,' Fariyah said from the front row of chairs. 'There's nothing to be scared of – except your own fears. You're among friends, here.'

'Then why do I feel we're all in danger?'

'Why don't you tell me?'

'Because of him!' he shouted, extending his arm and pointing at the dark figure standing to one side of the congregation. He wore the deep-navy uniform and pointed Sentinel helmet of an old-fashioned British bobby. But where his face should have been there was a compass, its four cardinal points picked out in gold. He was cradling a baby in his arms.

In the last seat of the nearest row, Gabriel's mother was straining to reach the policeman, her husband only just managing to restrain her. Beside them, Michael, now a successful banker in his thirties, though still dressed like a schoolboy and with a schoolboy's physique, was engrossed in his phone.

'Ignore him,' Eli whispered from his left. She took his left hand in her right and squeezed. 'Master Zhao's waiting.'

Gabriel tore his eyes away from the police officer and looked straight ahead.

Eli was right. His old master was here to officiate. His features crinkled with pleasure as their eyes met.

'Wolfe cub. You are ready.'

'Master, I—'

Zhao Xi shook his head. 'It was not a question.'

Then someone behind him screamed. Gabriel spun round, relieved at least that he'd regained his uniform. The faceless copper dropped the baby, which fell to the ground with a muffled cry. In its place he gripped a pistol. He began shooting.

Gabriel's parents were the first to die, blood spurting from wounds in their chests, right over the heart. Michael fell next, toppling off his chair and falling to the ground, clothes soaking wet, hair tangled with seaweed.

One by one, the faceless cop murdered every single guest until the air was thick with smoke that smelled of burnt meat.

Gabriel turned, hoping Eli at least had escaped the carnage. But she was dead, too, sprawled in the dirt with Britta beside her. He looked around frantically for Mei. But she was nowhere to be seen.

'It's just you and me, kid,' the faceless cop said, aiming the pistol at Gabriel.

'You came here to kill me. But maybe I'm not ready to die, yet. Maybe it's not my *time* to die. Maybe it's yours.'

The cop pulled the trigger. Again. And again. Fast. A triple-tap.

Gabriel flinched. But nothing happened. The cop had missed with all three rounds. The fallen infant threw back its wrappings and tossed a concealed pistol up to Gabriel, who caught it, racked the slide and fired in one, continuous motion.

As the bullets struck the policeman in the centre of this chest, the compass points shimmered and faded. Features appeared, gaining solidity and definition like shapes forming out of gun smoke. And Gabriel recognised them. They were his own.

He screamed and dropped the pistol.

Unhurt, the policeman laughed and fired again. And this time Gabriel felt the impact as the hollow-point round tore into him, smashing its way through his ribcage and slamming into his heart.

The cop approached, free hand outstretched, and reached into the wound, closing his fingers around the ruined pump before extracting it and holding the pulpy mess up to Gabriel's eyes.

'You lose,' he whispered.

The breeze intensified until it was a howling wind. The sun brightened to a blinding white light. Its heat was so intense, Gabriel could feel his skin burning, crisping, peeling away from his muscles.

'No,' he moaned. 'No, no, no!'

'NO!' he shouted, sitting up in bed, drenched in sweat, heart racing, mind possessed by the nightmare and unwilling to let him escape its gore-soaked clutches.

He fought to free himself from the soaked tangle of bedding and staggered across the room to the sink. There, he ran the tap and splashed icy water over his face and neck, shivering, whether from the cold or from residual fear he couldn't tell. He staggered to the window and dragged the thin floral curtains wide. The sun was up. He could feel its heat through the glass.

People were walking along the narrow street below his window. An elderly woman towed a wheeled wicker shopping trolley, brimming with paper-wrapped parcels of groceries. A young mother pushed her baby in a stroller, one hand busy with her phone. Two young men in business suits carrying briefcases stepped off the pavement to make way for the babushka with the trolley.

Slowly, Gabriel's breathing settled. He muttered a calming mantra to himself, forcing his overstressed system to adopt a normal rhythm. As his senses returned to normal, he felt the tatters of the nightmare unwind themselves from his mind.

'That was a bad one,' he said to the empty room as he buckled on his watch. 'I thought I was cured of the PTSD. It can't come back. Not now.'

He cleared his throat, turned back to the sink and scooped some of the still-cold water into the palm of his hand and drank. Then he dressed in running gear, laced on his shoes and left the room. It was 7.45 a.m.

Out on the street, he ran along the edge of the pavement, taking to the road to avoid the other pedestrians and weaving among the slow-moving traffic.

What the hell did the dream mean? It seemed clear. He was still frightened that the wedding would weaken him and the bad guys would win. But then he thought more carefully, raising a placatory hand as a dustcart negotiating the narrow street tooted its horn at this crazy guy jogging down the middle of the road.

It was *his* face beneath Ponting's helmet. So *he* was the enemy. Gabriel had been shot by another version of himself. He really wished he had the real Fariyah here in Novi Sad to talk to. But he'd have to conjure up a virtual shrink. What would she say? Wait! She'd spoken to him in the dream. What had she said?

He turned off the little street and found a small park. He dodged a couple of elderly gentlemen, one of whom carried a chessboard, the other a wooden box, and entered the green space. Tall, mature trees leaned over the central grassed area. Apart from Gabriel and the two chess-players, the park was empty, surrounded by black, wrought-iron railings.

He headed for the corner furthest from the old guys, who were setting up their game. He knelt on the grass, springy with moss, and closed his eyes. Initially he simply focused on his breathing, allowing the breath to come any way it wanted: deep inhalations and sighing exhalations as his heart and lungs regained the oxygen they needed.

Gradually it slowed, and he began to manage the flow of air, a familiar pattern that soon took him into a tranquil, meditative state he'd learned to enter long ago in the dojo of Master Zhao's hillside house.

Fariyah's features coalesced in front of him. Her chartreuse-yellow hijab of rough silk framed her plump face, on which her customary enquiring expression played. He imagined a conversation, using her to speak for one side of his personality.

– What did you tell me in the dream, Fariyah?

– That your own fears were the most frightening thing.

– And if I let them go, everything will be OK?

– No. But if you let them go, you can live in the present, with Eli.

– Because nobody knows whether the future will be OK, even one second from now.

– That's what Master Zhao would say, isn't it?

– He would.

– And he was right.

– You're saying live now.

– I'm saying now is the only place any of us can ever live. Everything else isn't living, it's wondering. Leave wondering for philosophers. You have a fiancée. A sister. A life. Take it. Live it.

Slowly, he let his eyelids flutter open. A robin hopped on the grass just a few feet from him. It cocked its head to one side and fastened the little black bead of its eye on him. He looked back at it.

'She's right,' he said to the bird. 'It's time to let go of all the "What if?s" and live in the here and now.'

He got to his feet. The robin flew off to the safety of a shrub in the flower bed. He jogged across the grass, towards the gate, offering a 'Dobro jutro,' to the chess players, who smiled and said good morning back to him. Then he jogged back the way he'd come, towards the hotel, where he and Mei needed to plan the final stage of their operation to avenge their parents and Michael on Ponting.

38

It had been Gabriel's idea to cover their camouflage gear with black shell suits. Two bus-rides and a fifteen-minute walk later, he and Mei had reached the outer fringes of the select housing development in Paragovo where they'd posed as house buyers. This time, there was no cover story. Just cover.

Finding a dense copse of hazel trees, they pushed their way in and unzipped the shell suits. These they stuffed into day sacks. The camo gear beneath they'd purchased from an army surplus store in a scuzzy area downtown, straight after leaving the hotel. Keeping to the wooded hillside, Gabriel led them along a ridge looking down at the big houses with security gates and tall fences at the front, and swimming pools and vast landscaped gardens at the rear.

They found Popović's place without much difficulty. As the young real estate agent had said, it was the last house before the woods. From their vantage point, Gabriel took his time with a pair of binoculars, noting the different elements of the perimeter. Brick walls nearer the house, six-foot fence panels slotted into pre-cast concrete posts along the sides, and a much-taller hedge of glossy green laurel at the rear of the property.

The hedge looked thick, but it was still organic. All they'd need to get through it was a pair of everyday garden secateurs, loppers at worst, if the branches were too thick.

In a notebook, he drew a simple schematic of the property and marked the position of the security cameras as Mei pointed them out to him. There were four in all: one at the front aimed at the drive, another on the back corner aimed down the property line, and two more screwed on the wall above a back door, pointing down the garden.

He could see black wires leading away from the cameras, stapled to the walls. That was good. If Popović had opted for wireless cameras, their job would have been far harder. As it was, they could simply cut the wires. It would raise suspicion, but would give them precious minutes to gain access to the house.

'I can't see a kennel,' Mei muttered from beside him.

'No dog toys either,' Gabriel replied, scanning the ground for chews, tug-ropes or those oddly shaped rubber objects dogs loved to chase as they bounced and bumbled randomly across the lawn.

'He feels secure up here,' she said, 'among his A-list neighbours. Probably loves playing the bigshot businessman like Fang used to.'

'We can use that to our advantage.'

They stayed in position for the next eight hours. Gabriel filled page after page of his notebook with detailed records of the people who came to the house. Their age, sex, build; how physically fit they appeared to be, rated on a scale from one to five; whether they appeared to be armed; and whether they seemed familiar with the house or appeared to be irregular or first-time visitors.

They repeated the process for the following five days and nights, digging down into the hide they'd pulled together from fallen branches and soft foliage clipped from the underbrush in the woods. They returned to the hotel to eat and shower at a different time each day.

At the end of the period, they'd established that the only three permanent residents at the house were Popović, his wife, Milena, and the younger son, Andrej, who rated a five on Gabriel's fitness scale.

A further five men, all aged between twenty and forty were

regular visitors: members of the Golden Bough's inner team, Gabriel assumed.

One day, as they lay on the ripstop groundsheet, with nothing going on down at the house to distract them, he started wondering about the origins of the organisation's name. It sounded poetic, like a triad.

He knew from talking to British cops that traditional big city gangs often just went by the name of their founding family. The Krays and the Richardsons in the sixties up to modern outfits like the Wilkses and the McTiernans.

'Golden' symbolised wealth in dozens if not hundreds of cultures worldwide. But 'Bough'? He Googled the two-word phrase and the only hit that made even vague sense was a book about mythology and religion. Somehow he didn't see Steve Ponting aka Ratko Popović as a religious man.

He tried again, seeing the two-word phrase as a whole, but nothing would come. He knew a man who'd lick his lips at the prospect of solving it. Johnny 'Sparrow' Hawke had served with Gabriel in the SAS. He'd spent the time waiting for things to happen solving cryptic crosswords.

What would Sparrow have made of the little word puzzle facing Gabriel? The book angle was a bust. The 'golden' part was obvious. So he'd look at 'bough'. Gabriel rolled onto his back and stared up into the tree canopy. Boughs were all about him. Tree boughs. When the bough breaks, the baby will fall. Down will come baby…

Boughs were branches. A golden bough was a valuable branch. A special branch. He almost laughed, it was so simple in the end. Ponting hadn't forgotten his roots. He'd just turned them into a joke. Well, the joke was on him. Or would be in a couple of days.

If there was any doubt in his mind they'd misidentified their target, it vanished now. The silver-haired man they'd caught snatches of disappearing into the back of the black Range Rover was the same man who'd organised Mei's kidnapping. And soon he would pay for all the damage that had flowed from that one act of greed.

* * *

Inside the house, Saša was sitting at the kitchen table, thumbing 7.62mm rounds into the curved magazine of an AK-47. It smelled of gun oil, which pleased him.

'You should get out for a bit, boss,' he said. 'Until we've killed them.'

'You worry too much, Saša.'

'No. I don't. Did you even hear what I just told you?'

'Yes, I heard,' Popović said with a smile. 'Parachute Regiment, then in 2005 he disappears but isn't discharged from the British Army until 2012.'

'That means Special Forces, Ratko. I know about these things. They don't publicise it, but most likely that's where he went,' he said, slotting the magazine home. 'The Parachute Regiment's a prime recruiting stream for the British. That means SAS, most likely, maybe Special Boat Squadron.'

'You worry too much, old friend. Maybe he *was* in the SAS. But that was almost ten years ago. Soldiers are like cops. Out of harness, they lose their edge. Or are you frightened you and your guys can't handle him and that sister of his?'

Saša offered his boss a sardonic smile.

'Don't bother trying to wind me up, Ratko,' he said. 'It didn't work in the war and it won't work now. You know what I'm talking about. And for the record, no, I'm not worried about him. I'm just thinking of what's best. Milena agrees with me, don't you, Milena?'

She put down the Glock she was cleaning.

'Don't assume you know what I think, Saša,' she said sharply. 'We didn't let those ICTY jackals lay a finger on Ratko, did we? Or the gangs who were here before we arrived? And he went through the war without a scratch.'

But Saša wasn't ready to give up. He argued his point over and over again, employing new lines of reasoning as each was batted away by the husband and wife team at the head of the Golden Bough.

Back and forth the three old friends went, never straying beyond the bounds of civility, but not holding back with each other, either. At one point Milena broke out a bottle of *rakija*. As they argued about the various ways they could take out the Wolfe siblings, none was aware that their targets were in turn surveilling them from the woods at the side of the house, completing their map of the CCTV cameras and plotting how to get inside.

* * *

At 7.00 p.m. that evening, Gabriel and Tara packed up their gear and walked out of the woods, away from the houses of Paragovo. They left the district via a wooded valley that led down to a road into the city. There, clad once more in their anonymous black shell suits, they caught a city bus and took it all the way to the centre where they disembarked and jogged the last few blocks to their hotel.

Later, they sat in Gabriel's room, finalising the plan to take out Popović. Like all good plans, it was simple. From midnight to seven thirty, nobody outside the immediate family was inside the house. They'd wait until 3.00 a.m. the following morning before infiltrating.

39

Not being a religious man, Gabriel didn't pray for cloud cover that night. But when he and Tara left the hotel and he looked up to see moon and stars obscured by a thick, dark blanket, he nodded with satisfaction.

Leaving the Lamborghini tucked away in the courtyard behind the hotel, where the owner had set her extended family to watching over it like a baby, Gabriel drove to within five hundred yards of the Popović house in their other, altogether more anonymous, rental. Unlike the Huracan, it had a boot that would hold more than a weekend bag. They intended to make good use of it later.

Currently it held two black market Kalashnikovs plus spare magazines, an entrenching tool and heavy-duty black refuse sacks. A black daysack held equipment they'd need to get inside the house, plus bottled water and energy bars. The Tokarevs, he and Tara carried under their shell suits. In the pockets of their camo gear, green, black and brown greasepaint sticks, black zip ties and a roll of black duct tape.

Gabriel turned to Tara as he started the engine.

'Ready?'

She nodded.

'Payback time.'

They reached the woods in under fifteen minutes, so quiet were the streets. If Novi Sad had night-time police patrols, they were busy downtown: Gabriel and Tara's progress in what, in a bigger, more populous city might have attracted unwanted attention, went totally unremarked.

Gabriel turned off the smooth residential road in Paragovo onto a small track snaking away from the upscale housing across scrubland. He clenched his jaw to stop his teeth clacking together as the road surface deteriorated. Patchy Tarmac turned to potholed rubble. Rubble to rutted earth studded with melon-sized flints whose chalky shells resembled human skulls. Beside him, Tara was bracing herself with a hand clamped onto the grab-handle above her head.

The track ended in a clearing. From the tracks they'd studied earlier in the week, it appeared to be a start-point for off-road bikers to streak around on the miles of forest tracks and open hills to the north of the city. Wide, rough-treaded pickup tyres were interspersed with narrower, knobbly rubber. They'd even been able to pick out two sets of boot prints.

Gabriel turned the car around, backed up to a narrow path leading into the woods, then killed the engine. As before, he and Tara stripped off the shell suits, only this time they dumped them in the boot.

Gabriel turned to Tara. 'Come here. Make-up time.'

She stood in front of him, face upturned and allowed him to paint her face with streaks of the camo greasepaint. He worked quickly, applying random streaks until every square inch of her pale facial skin was darkened with the sticky pigment.

'My turn,' she said.

While she applied the makeup, he stared past her left shoulder into the woods. A few hundred yards further down the track sat the house in which Steve Ponting/Ratko Popović lay sleeping with his wife and teenaged son. Now it was his turn to be snatched from his bed in the darkness, ripped away from his family.

Like Tara, he'd be spirited away from those who loved him. Like Gerald and Lin Wolfe, those left behind would forever wonder what had happened. Unlike Gabriel himself, they would never discover the answer. Would they assume it was a hit by a rival from Novi Sad's criminal underworld? It was the most likely scenario.

But Gabriel had been digging into Popović's history during the five-day lurk in the woods overlooking his house. And what he'd discovered had suggested a second, entirely plausible, reason why someone might want him dead.

Osman the arms dealer had told him Popović had commanded a militia called the Black Eagles during the Bosnian war. But that had only been to give context to his available men in the Golden Bough organisation. In the long hours doing nothing but waiting, Gabriel had dug into UN and Bosnian campaign group websites, human rights blogs, and Wikipedia entries, including all the hyperlinked references in the footnotes. What he discovered horrified him.

Though by no means alone in their use of such tactics, the Black Eagles had become specialists in using punitive rape as a weapon of war. Women, children, the elderly, the infirm: anyone not away fighting was fair game for the barbaric men who invaded villages in 4x4s and set about reducing them to ashes. Several survivors had identified a particularly vicious individual. A dogged Belgian ICTY investigator had added a name to the description they'd given him: Zoran Kordić. Gabriel recoiled from the witness testimony, but forced himself to keep reading.

One article included photographic evidence of the atrocities the Black Eagles had committed. He'd had to steel himself not to scroll past the full-colour images of desecrated corpses, where trophies had clearly been taken by the marauders.

Other militia leaders, Serbian generals and indeed national politicians up to and including the president had been indicted and brought before the Tribunal. Once again, Ratko Popović had evaded justice and entered into the third phase of his criminal career. From bent cop to perpetrator of war crimes to gang boss.

But his luck was about to run out.

Tara dabbed a final fingertip onto the bridge of Gabriel's nose, nodded, pleased with her handiwork, then capped the stick of camo paint and stuck it in a pocket.

They each took an AK and slung it over their back. Gabriel added the daysack with the kidnap gear to his own load. Then they simply walked down the narrow track until they reached the edge of the wood. Owing to the favourable topography, they could sit in tree cover about fifteen feet above the roofline of the house.

Tara handed her rifle to Gabriel. Then, in an unbroken series of flowing moves, she climbed a youngish birch tree. Stretching for impossible-seeming holds on slender branches that gave a little as she hauled herself higher, she was twenty feet above Gabriel's head within a minute.

She'd spotted the tree on their third day observing the house.

'There's my route in,' she'd said to Gabriel.

At the time he'd been doubtful. Though it loomed high over the roof owing to its position on the wooded slope, it seemed far too thin to bear her weight. But he'd quickly seen that was Tara's intention. The tree was immature and full of sap. It would bend but not break.

Now, as he craned his neck to watch her ascend, her astute analysis bore fruit. The trunk began bowing as she climbed. By bracing her feet against it and swinging her weight to and fro, she encouraged it into a swaying motion that grew more pronounced with each cycle, like a kid sloshing the water from one end to the other of its bath.

On the next swing, the top third of the birch arched over in a graceful curve that brought the soft soles of Tara's shoes within a few inches of the roof. She dropped silently onto the slates, releasing the tree, which sprang back to the vertical with a hiss and rustle of new leaves.

Catlike in the silence, she worked her way over to the rear pitch of the roof. From a pocket she took out a pot of Vaseline and smeared the lens of the camera nearest the woods. They'd decided, in a last-minute change of plan, not to cut the wires. It would send too obvious a signal that the house was under attack should anyone be up late monitoring the screens.

From there she crept along to the next camera, and angled it outwards by a tiny amount. Even were somebody inside to be watching, they'd have to be hyper-alert to catch the change in angle. She repeated the process with the next camera along.

Now, although both cameras were still sending feeds inside, their overlap had vanished. In its place, a blind spot – an alley, really – that stretched from the hedge at the far end of the garden all the way up to the house.

Completing her preparations at the rear of the house, she snipped the wire to the motion-activated floodlight angling down towards the garden. Five minutes later and she'd disabled the front-facing camera too, using the Vaseline and a sprig of foliage she'd clipped off the birch tree.

Was it perfect? No. Could it still ring metaphorical alarm bells? Yes. Might it give them precious extra minutes or seconds? Absolutely.

Tara knelt up on the roof and gave a thumbs-up to Gabriel. His signal to move. Shouldering Tara's AK, he made his way round and down through the woods, emerging at a spot behind the laurel hedge.

He began cutting through the thicker stems of the hedge, leaving intact the whippy new growth that faced the house. When he'd finished, he'd created an opening through which a man could pass with a captive, yet which, from the rear windows of the house, appeared not to exist at all.

* * *

Ratko Popović slept on, oblivious of the assault taking place on his property. He dreamed he was playing on the right wing for his beloved Red Star Belgrade. Milosević crossed the ball to him and he dribbled it from the halfway line towards the Sarajevo goal.

One after another, the opposition's defenders tried to relieve him of the ball – Babić, Kunarac, Miletić – and he defeated each of them in turn, a bullet to the head each, leaving them sprawled in their own blood.

Finally, only the goalkeeper stood between him and glory. The man was terrified. The yellowish whites of his eyes blared from a faced streaked with gore. Strugar's gloves, once white, were stained wine-red. Behind him, dozens of balls distended the back of the net, each marked with a distinctive triangle of black holes.

Lining up his shot, he tapped the ball forward, following its bobbling progress for a couple more strides before drawing back his right boot and smashing it home.

The ball shattered midway on its journey, spraying blood and brains everywhere. Screaming with triumph, he punched the air as it sailed high over Strugar's head into the top-left corner of the net.

Spattered with human tissue, he turned with a wide grin on his face to accept the embraces of his team-mates. And the crowd roared on.

'Pop-o-vić! Pop-o-vić! Pop-o-VIĆ!'

40

From her vantage point on the rear pitch of the slate-tiled roof, Tara caught the slight movement in the laurel hedge at their end of the garden. Good. BB was making the opening they'd need to spirit Popović away.

Moving crabwise across the slope, she made her way to a small window at the side of the house. She swung herself out and over the guttering, letting her feet dangle in mid-air, searching with her toes for the wide stone window ledge. Finding it, she manoeuvred her body until she could crouch, sideways on, using one hand to steady herself on the guttering.

She attached a quick-release suction cup to the centre of the window, then scored around the frame with a glass cutter. Like cracking an egg without breaking the yolk, the secret to removing a window cleanly was to deliver precisely the right amount of force at precisely the right speed. Too much or too little of either quantity and the glass would either stay put or shatter.

It took a minute to get into a position where she could bring her knee into play. After that, it was a straightforward matter of applying a sharp blow and letting the glass fall in a little way before stopping it with the handle of the suction cup.

Congratulating herself for having maintained her strict physical training regimen, Tara slithered, snakelike, through the small, square aperture and into the box room on the other side. The room smelled of laundry starch. It was empty apart from an ironing board and a row of dress shirts hanging on a free-standing rail. She rolled her head on her neck then drew her pistol.

Four steps took her to the door, which she opened a couple of inches, placing her ear to the crack. Stilling her breathing, she strained to detect any sounds that might indicate the presence of a wakened sleeper. From somewhere distant, she heard the mechanical ticking of what sounded like a large, wood-cased clock. But that was all.

As she made her way along the hallway, she realised that the man they'd come to kidnap was sleeping behind one of the closed doors she was passing. She could burst in to each bedroom and shoot whoever rose from their bed on the other side, unless it was him. The wife, the kid, then Popović.

Killing the family wouldn't bother her. She'd sent every kind of human being to their grave in her years working for Fang: men, women, the young, the old. Hong Kongers, mainlanders, *gwáiló*; even on a trip to South America, thirty or so Colombian drug cartel members.

Now *that* had been carnage on a grand scale. After the Colombians had convened for some high-level meeting inside a luxurious house beside a reservoir, Tara – or Mei as she was then – and her two assistants had detonated M112 demolition blocks of C4.

But Gabriel was more squeamish about creating collateral damage than she was. He'd had those military ethics drummed into him. When she'd suggested wiping out the whole family and any hangers-on in a coordinated attack, everything on full auto, he'd got on his high horse with her. She'd had to remind him that she wasn't his little sister any more and nor was she under his command. After all, *she* was the one who'd been kidnapped, not him.

She'd still agreed to follow the plan. And it made sense. She wanted Popović to know exactly who was killing him and why.

Maybe she'd increase his pain by telling him that after he was dead, they'd go back and kill the wife and sons anyway. Just because they could.

So, with the lightest of treads, and keeping to the edge of the staircase, she descended to the ground floor. The door leading to the kitchen was open, admitting into the downstairs hallway just enough illumination from a couple of glowing appliance lights for Tara to see by.

The key to the back door wasn't in the lock. Nor on a hook to either side. Those were merely the two most obvious places and Tara was a long way from panicking. She looked around, saw what she wanted: drawers beneath the worktop. Cutlery, pots and pans, crockery. She shook her head and moved along to the next set.

The top drawer contained a mess of screws, clips for closing plastic bags, a torch, bottle openers, a pack of playing cards, a ball composed of rubber bands, and a Glock 17. Nodding her appreciation, she stuck it into the waistband of her trousers. Beneath the Glock, her questing fingers closed on a bunch of keys.

The rules of the Universe dictated that whichever key she started with, the one that would unlock the door would be the last on the ring. In fact, after two misses, she got a hit. She opened the door wide and then waited.

* * *

As soon as he saw the door open, Gabriel pushed through the thin scrim of leaves hiding him from the house. He sprinted up the centre of the lawn, the two AKs on his back, hoping he'd hit his mark for the blind spot. Nothing for it now, though. If it all got kinetic, he and Tara were ready.

He slipped inside and closed the door behind him. Tara took one of the AKs and nodded.

They'd just reached the hallway when Gabriel heard footsteps coming from the upper storey. His heart pounding, he yanked back the AK's charging lever and crouched, rifle at his shoulder.

A dark shape appeared at the top of the stairs. Then it passed and continued on, out of sight, along the hall. *Must be Popović needing an early-hours piss*, he thought.

He signalled to Tara they should head for the stairs.

Then all the lights went on. Shit! Change of plan. No knocking out the wife and son and snatching the father. Shouting in Serbian shattered the calm. Then a figure sprinted from left to right at the top of the stairs along the gallery, firing down into the hallway with a pistol.

Gabriel and Tara returned fire, two overlapping bursts that filled the downstairs with gun smoke and added their own deafening noise to the cracks from the pistol. Splinters of wood and plaster chips rained down on them.

A second figure appeared behind the balusters upstairs. Automatic fire rained down and Gabriel retreated around a corner, seeing Tara mirror his actions at the far end of the hall.

He poked the barrel of his AK around the corner and loosed off a quick burst, just as Tara, as if reading his thoughts, did the same. He heard a scream. The automatic fire from upstairs stopped.

'Cover me!' he yelled, then broke cover and rushed up the stairs, firing bursts to left and right as he went. Tara laid down suppressive fire, allowing him to get to the upper landing.

A body lay on its front, curled into a foetal position, blood pooling under the torso. No time to check the sex, but it looked to be a young man. So possibly the son, Andrej.

He ran down the hallway, and kicked out at the first of the bedroom doors. The room was empty, the bed undisturbed. He heard more gunfire. Tara's AK and more single shots from a pistol. He raced out again, and caught sight of a silver-haired man ducking into one of the bedrooms. Popović!

Tara was still downstairs, covering the stairway.

'He's up here!' Gabriel yelled down.

'Go and get him. I'll cover you from here,' she shouted back.

She was right. If Popović had had time to summon reinforcements, Gabriel would need her downstairs to keep them at bay while he snatched their boss.

He crept along the hallway and stood to one side of the door. Raising his own pistol he fired two shots high into the wood.

An answering burst put five holes through the thin panelling, which splintered outward, allowing beams of dusty light to spear across the smoke-filled hallway.

Gabriel stood back, readied his AK and fired a long burst through the door. Without hesitating, he kicked it in and ran into the room, pistol at the ready. The silver-haired man had pulled over a tall antique wooden wardrobe and was crouching behind it. Gabriel could just see the top of his head. No returning fire, so either his gun had jammed or he was out of ammunition.

'Time's up, Ponting,' Gabriel growled. 'Throw the gun over here then come out with your hands up.'

He readied himself to take charge of his prisoner, working out how to transfer his grip on the pistol to access the zip ties and secure Ponting before he could do any damage.

Then a black cylinder arced over the top of the fallen wardrobe and bounced across the wooden floorboards towards Gabriel. Grenade! He dived sideways, aiming for the double bed and what limited cover it would provide, when the device detonated with a blinding white light and an ear-burstingly loud bang.

He flinched, imagining the incoming shrapnel ripping through his unprotected limbs and soft tissue, but felt nothing beyond the percussive impact on his eyes and ears. He thought he heard more flash bangs but it could have been mental echoes of the one that had just exploded.

Then Ponting was up and firing. The bullets were ripping into the bedclothes, puffing out the quilt where it dropped over the side of the mattress. Gabriel shuffled underneath and fired a double-tap at Ponting's ankles. Blood spurted and he went down with a scream. Yelling with defiance, he aimed at Gabriel's head along the floor.

Gabriel fired first. The round took Ponting full in the face, obliterating the lower half altogether. As blood flowed copiously from the horrific wound, Gabriel slithered away from the corpse and stood up.

'Tara!' he called. 'It's over. He's dead.'

He ran from the room and over to the gallery. He looked over the bannister but saw no sign of Tara.

He called out her name. Nothing.

He ran for the stairs and descended carefully, AK reloaded and sweeping left and right. Then he heard tyres screeching.

He ran to the front door and threw it wide just in time to see a black 4x4 with blacked-out windows peeling away down the street, sending a pall of blue smoke drifting into the still air.

Shit! Shitshitshitshit! No. This wasn't supposed to happen!

He ran out to the roadside only to see the 4x4's red brake lights flick on briefly as it took the bend at the end of the street.

And then the reality of the situation asserted itself. Sirens screamed from down the hill and he could see blue lights flaring. Whatever had happened to Tara, he wouldn't help her by remaining here a second longer.

He ran back inside, pausing momentarily at the trail of blood drops leading from the last place he'd seen Tara towards the front door. Of her Kalshnikov there was no sign, so her assailants had been calm enough to collect that, too. He retraced his steps through the kitchen and back door, ran down the back garden, heedless of the CCTV cameras now, and was through the laurel hedge and climbing around the perimeter of the garden to the birch tree a minute after that.

The sirens were close now and the police lights were turning the treetops turquoise in regular pulses. He reached the rental car and opened the boot. He scrambled into the shell suit, snagging both boots in the legs and swearing constantly as he jammed his feet down hard enough to rip the cheaply made trousers. In the space where Ponting should have been dumped, he laid the AK and his daysack then climbed behind the wheel, started the engine and pulled away.

He checked the mirror out of habit and saw his own nightmarish face staring back at him, eyes wide in that mask of earth-coloured camo paint. Take the time to clean himself up or drive off now and hope whatever police were descending on the Popović residence had already arrived?

Every fibre of his being was screaming 'go, now!' But from somewhere deep inside him, a place from which he'd always heard the whisperings of his training under Master Zhao, came a quiet, still voice. *Arrested, you can't help her.*

He stopped the car, fished out the cleanser and spent five precious minutes wiping every trace of the camouflage makeup off his face.

After taking the trouble to recreate at least the semblance of a law-abiding citizen, albeit one driving around at dawn in a car loaded with small arms, he didn't see a single police car all the way back to the hotel.

Back inside his room, with the gear from the op pushed under the bed, he sat and stared at himself in the mirror above the little wooden desk. He shook his head. This wasn't happening. He'd killed Ponting but lost Tara again. The henchmen had arrived too late to save their boss but they'd taken a prize.

Except…

That made no sense.

Why would they take Tara and leave without at least trying to save the man who paid their wages? The man who'd called them in? They couldn't have known he was already dead. And if they'd taken Tara, why hadn't they forged on and gone after Gabriel as well?

And then a horrible doubt surfaced in Gabriel's mind. A shark, lazily surfacing and looking for prey after cruising down in the cold, black depths of his consciousness.

Was it even Ponting that he'd shot?

During their five-day lurk, they'd definitely identified him against the CGI image Wūshī had sent Gabriel. The bone structure looked right, as did the features.

So it ought to have been him in the bedroom asleep when Gabriel and Tara infiltrated. The man who'd fired on Gabriel certainly resembled Ponting. But he reminded himself, that had been in the heat of a firefight and one silver-haired thug in his late sixties might easily pass for another.

And what did 'resembled' even mean in this context? Looked like a digitally aged image of a grainy black-and-white newspaper photo from the eighties? It was hardly what a lawyer would call of evidentiary value. By the time Gabriel had been close enough to make a positive ID, everything below the bridge of Ponting's nose was red mush and white bone fragments.

He sat for half an hour with his fists clenched between his knees, rerunning the minutes they'd spent inside the house, struggling to believe that at the very least he'd killed the man he and Tara had come to Serbia to find. But the shark wouldn't dive deep again, back to where it had come from. It was enjoying the light and scenting blood in the water.

He had to find Tara. But he had no leads. No friends in Serbia. Nowhere to turn. Nobody to talk to.

Finally, realising that unless he slept, he'd been of even less use to Tara, he collapsed sideways, still fully dressed and closed his eyes.

He'd imagined sleep would elude him and he'd have the rest of what remained of the night to worry. But as soon as his head hit the pillow and his eyes fluttered closed, all the lights went out.

Gabriel awoke five hours later to a huge bang that set his pulse racing. Sun was streaming into his room through the thin curtains. Odd though how the light was flickering like that. Then there came a furious knocking on his door. He stumbled to the door and opened it to find the hotel lady standing there, eyes wide.

'Mr Lang, so sorry,' she said. 'There is crash. A drunk man. Your car.'

He followed her downstairs envisaging the Huracan blazing like a fluorescent green bonfire. Then he remembered the Lamborghini was parked at the back of the hotel, whereas his room was at the front overlooking the street.

His landlady opened the Main Street door and he followed her outside. His rental Toyota was ablaze: a battered old Skoda joining it at a right angle making a perfect T. The driver's door was open and he could see a figure slumped against the wall of the shop next door to the hotel. Passers-by had obviously dragged the drunk from behind the wheel before he burnt alive.

As the flames gradually ate their way back to the boot, he was glad he'd unloaded the gear the night before. The police would have had more than a few questions for him had hundreds of rounds of ammunition begun exploding out of the boot to mow down the good people of Novi Sad. As it was, he had nothing more awkward than some insurance documents to deplete. They could wait.

A fire engine arrived, sirens blaring. As the firefighters unrolled hoses and set about extinguishing the fire, he went back inside. Somewhere, the remains of Ponting's gang were holding Tara. And Gabriel thought he knew where.

41

Gabriel packed his gear and descended the narrow staircase. As usual, the owner was sitting in her little cubbyhole to one side of the reception area. She rose when she saw him.

'Mr Lang, is OK about car?'

'Yes. All good,' he said, making a circle of thumb and forefinger for added emphasis. 'I have to go. Can I pay, please?'

She frowned. 'No sister?'

He shook his head. 'She had to leave early.'

After settling his bill, he stooped to pick up his bag only to collide with the old lady as she stepped around the desk to embrace him. He straightened, awkwardly, his arms pinioned by his sides. She kissed him three times on the cheeks, left, right, left, before releasing him.

'Hvala vam,' he said. *Thank you.* He'd studied the language during the stakeout of Popović's house, adding to his meagre stock of phrases, but this most basic of courtesies was definitely appropriate here.

She beamed up at him. 'Nema na čemu.' *You're welcome.*

He walked to the courtyard where the Huracan sat waiting for him. It had seemed like a ridiculous extravagance when they'd hired it, but now he was grateful for a fast car. Grateful that the secluded courtyard offered him protection from prying eyes, or goggling locals who might want to take photos for their Instagrams, he loaded his gear.

Gabriel stood back, wondering how he was going to store the AK-47, currently wrapped in a black bin liner he'd cadged from the hotel cook. The Lamborghini hadn't been designed with luggage in mind. No boot to speak of and although the AK would sit happily enough in the passenger footwell, he didn't fancy having to explain its presence to a nosy traffic cop. Somehow he doubted a cheery 'Hunting trip, officer,' would cut it.

No rear bench either. But as he peered over the tall headrests of the seats, he saw it had a narrow shelf just wide enough to accommodate the rifle. In it went. He draped his jacket over it. Perfect. With the seat ratcheted back, it was barely visible, let alone the weapon underneath it.

With his bag occupying the passenger seat, and the daysack in the tiny compartment beneath the hood, he was ready to go.

The Huracan's engine woke with an eager bark and he was rolling across the cobbles and out onto the street with renewed purpose. Popović's castle was 120 miles southeast of Novi Sad. He estimated it would take him no more than three and a half hours to reach it, no matter what sort of traffic he encountered on Serbia's less-than-stellar roads.

With a wave out of the window to the hotel owner's grandkids, he goosed the throttle and accelerated smoothly into the traffic with a howl from the car's highly tuned engine.

It took half an hour to free himself from the clutches of Novi Sad's urban roads, and the congestion that rendered them passable at little more than walking pace. Then he reached open country and took the Huracan up to eighty as the traffic thinned to the occasional vegetable truck and ancient Skoda or VW.

The men who'd taken Tara would be expecting him. Not just the men, either. Osman had told him not to underestimate Milena, the wife. If Gabriel had killed her husband, would she be in charge? Did she even know he'd been killed? It didn't matter. Gabriel was one against many. Osman had said that Popović could count on perhaps fifty men. Those were appalling odds.

A full frontal attack was obviously out. Stealth was the only viable option. Or no, maybe not the only option. Combining stealth with subterfuge might help to inch the odds a little in Gabriel's favour. Could he draw out some of the defending force? Send them off on a wild goose chase while he extracted Tara?

As the miles unspooled in front of him, and the flat agricultural countryside began to undulate, first in gentle, grassy waves and then in more pronounced hills, he turned the problem over and over in his mind.

What would they be expecting? That was the critical question. That he would want his sister back, of course. But what of his tactics? His approach? Much as he had, they'd have discounted a direct attack on the castle. But as he had no way of contacting them, nor they him, what else *could* he do?

His burner rang. His pulse jumped. Only Tara had the number. No, wait. Because he'd given it to two others. The sales woman who'd rented them the Huracan and the real estate agent.

He pulled off the road, ABS brakes juddering as the tyres slid on the gritty shoulder. He took the call.

'Hello, Toby?' A female voice. Local. He thought he recognised it.

'Yes.'

'It's Emina from Dragan Luxe Hire. Emina,' a beat, 'Popović.'

It was a common enough name in Serbia. But why had she leaned on it so heavily? He began to suspect he knew the answer.

'What can I do for you, Emina?'

'How are you liking Huracan?'

'It's fine.'

'And Miss Wong? She likes it also?'

'Yep.'

'She is with you now? In car?'

'Not right now, no.'

'Pity. To lose employer in foreign country.'

'Who said I lost her?'

'My mistake. Anyway, I have message for you,' she paused, 'Gabriel Wolfe.' There. That confirmed it. 'Message is from my aunt Milena. If you want to see Tara again, bring one million US dollars to city of Niš at five in the a.m. tomorrow. There is bridge over river Ništava six kilometres out on east side of town. Take E771.'

'How do I know she's still alive?'

'You must trust, yes?'

'No. I want to speak to her. Tell your aunt it's that or no deal.'

'No deal means they will kill your sister.'

'Then your aunt won't see a cent and I'll come for her anyway. And you. Tell her.'

The line went dead.

Gabriel leaned back against the car, waiting. Trying to imagine the young woman's hurried call to her Aunt Milena. He didn't think his request would go unmet. Milena would know how these things went down. You made the ransom demand. The family asked for proof their loved one was still alive. You put them on the phone or maybe treated a photo with that day's paper held up.

Fourteen minutes and twenty-one seconds passed before the phone rang again.

'Hello?'

'BB it's me. I'm—'

'Tara!' he said. 'How—'

A new voice came on the line.

'Your sister is fine, Gabriel. For now. Bring the money or she won't be.'

The speaker was male. Older. Gabriel could hear a trace of a British accent under the local vowel sounds.

'Who is this?'

'Who do you think it is?'

He detected mockery as well as a stronger British accent. And he knew who he was speaking to. Knew that whoever it was in the swanky house in Paragovo lying dead with half his face missing, it wasn't Ponting. Knew that his sister had fallen into the hands of the man who'd arranged the original kidnap in '83.

'Ponting.'

'You know, Gabriel, it's been a long while since anyone called me by that name.'

'If you hurt her, I'll find you. Then I'll kill you.'

'Looks like we better work out a deal then, doesn't it?'

'Yes, it does.'

'There's only one problem.'

'What?'

'Let me ask you a question. Why are you in Serbia looking for me? Because I'm pretty sure it wasn't to share memories of Hong Kong in the good old days before the Chinese got their hands on it again.'

Ponting had put his finger on it, hadn't he? Gabriel frantically tried to construct a lie that would be credible to someone steeped in deceit and criminality. Ponting no doubt suspected Gabriel and Tara were in Serbia to kill him. Gabriel had to persuade him otherwise. or the whole thing would blow up in his face.

He had one chance. He went for the only thing he thought might work with the leader of an organised crime group.

'Money.'

'What?'

'You heard me. I saw my father's papers. You demanded a million Hong Kong dollars ransom when you kidnapped Tara. We decided to find you and demand the same sum back. In sterling.'

'Or you'd kill me.'

'Exactly.'

'Why not take the money, always assuming I'd pay it, then kill me anyway?'

'You're not worth it, Ponting. Besides, Tara's alive. I only take an eye for an eye.'

'Very Biblical. So what are you suggesting?'

'I'm *telling* you that I want my sister back and a million pounds.'

Ponting laughed. 'Here's the thing, Gabriel. You don't have the right to make demands anymore. Maybe when you arrived in Serbia you did. Or you thought you did. But when you attacked my house and killed one of my men and we captured your sister, you lost it. Now it's all got a bit more tricky, hasn't it?'

'Do you want to die, Ponting?'

'Not particularly. But if it's my time, I'm ready for it. My wife'll cope. How about you?' Gabriel thought of Eli. It caused him to pause for a fraction before answering. Ponting caught the hesitation. 'I see. Got a girl waiting back home, have we? Ties that bind and all that?'

'No. It's just me, and I'm as ready to die as you are.'

'I don't think so. I can hear it in your voice. Not cowardice, just reluctance. I think you're bluffing. Me? I'm not like you. Any scruples I had got burnt out of me years back. I'll kill your sister if you force me to. You, too, if I can,' he said.

Gabriel was running out of options. He sensed Ponting knew it, too.

'How about you give me back my sister and we forget about the money?'

'Now why would I do that?'

'To stop me coming for you.'

Ponting sighed. 'I've made a massive mistake, haven't I?'

'What do you mean?'

Gabriel tried to keep his voice level, because in his resigned tone Ponting seemed to be moving away from a kidnap and towards a murder.

'I'm sure you can work it out. If I give her back to you then you both come for me and mine. If I kill her now, you come on your own,' he said. 'Either way there'll be a fuck-off firefight and a lot of claret all over the walls. But at least if I shoot her now, the odds are better and we can prepare a welcome committee for you.'

Gabriel thought of Eli a second time since the start of the conversation. He realised how much he wanted to live. To marry her. And, yes, if she wanted, to have children with her. Then he saw it. The way to get to Ponting.

'You're right. I have got a girl at home. But no kids. I'm not a family man like you. You said you're ready to die, and maybe that's true. And Milena will, what, grieve and move on? But what about your sons? What about Andrej? What about Vlado? Are you happy for them to die?' Now it was Ponting's turn to hesitate. Gabriel sensed his advantage. Pressed it. 'Only one of us is going to get out of this alive, Ponting. We both know that. But if you play fair, I promise you, I won't touch your family.'

'Play fair?' Ponting laughed dismissively. 'This isn't a game of fucking cricket.'

'But we can have rules, just the same. I'm going to come for you,' Gabriel said, 'you know that. If I come out on top then find out you've killed my sister, I will hunt down your sons and I will torture them to death. In front of their mother. If you've left Tara alone, we'll leave and never come back.'

'And if I come out on top?'

'Then you're free to do whatever your burnt-out morals tell you to.'

Gabriel kept his breathing steady, though it cost him hugely. He wanted to yell and scream at Ponting. To threaten him with all the agonies of the world, every disgusting, horrific, pain-inflicting act that had ever been dreamt up by humans in their insane pursuit of victory over others for their looks, their beliefs, their race or just because they found them in the wrong place at the wrong time.

Finally, Ponting broke the thick silence that hung between them.

'I hope you've brought lots of bullets.'

Then he hung up.

42

Zoran's thick fingers stabbed the buttons on the controller and swore at the advancing zombies on the plasma TV as their heads exploded in a welter of digital gore.

'Fuck you! And you! And,' he grunted with the effort, 'you!'

A female undead got within biting distance and his avatar screamed as she bit through his arm.

'Shit! Fucking bitch!'

Though it was still only 11.00 a.m., Zoran was high. The hash they trafficked from Afghanistan into Western Europe was, by his estimate, *el primo*. Say what you like about those rag-heads, and Zoran never missed an opportunity, they cooked up magnificent drugs. It always struck him as funny that they were doing business with a bunch of Muslims after sending so many of them to meet their Maker at Srebrenica.

Smiling to himself and shaking his head, his thoughts turned to their campaign in Bosnia. The violence. How Zoran had enjoyed it. No, strike that. Because he hadn't just enjoyed it, had he? He'd *loved* it. Got high on it, just like he was now on the Islamics' hash.

Best of all was when they went into a village to deal with the women. He always picked the young ones. Pretty if possible. Nice

ANDY MASLEN

juicy tits and an arse you could get hold of. And why not? He was only seventeen himself. He couldn't be expected to do the old ones, could he?

The memory made him horny. And that made him think of the Chink the boss had locked up. She was just his type. And get that! The boss had her stashed in a real, actual dungeon. Most hard men used nightclubs as their bases. Not the boss. He had a genuine castle. How did the Yanks say it?

'Gen-you-wine!' he said aloud in what he reckoned was a damn good American accent.

When Zoran had been a kid, he'd loved those Hollywood movies with sword fights in old-timey castles. The good guy was always locked away in a dungeon with a fuck-off wooden door with beefy iron studs. He'd escape somehow and fight his way out, usually ending up in a one-to-one with the evil duke or whatever.

Zoran and his brothers used to wait till that word 'Fin' scrolled up across the final image, then rush outside into the countryside with their wooden swords and act it all out again. Zoran always played the hero. Anyone who tried to challenge him for the role ended up in the dirt with a bloody nose or a black eye. Zoran was the youngest, but it didn't matter. He was the biggest, the boldest and always the readiest for a scrap.

He got up from the couch and dropped the gaming controller to the floor. Fucking up zombies could wait. He had a better idea.

Leaving the ground floor of the castle was like travelling back in a time machine. The boss made sure they had all the home comforts: proper heating, carpets, decent furniture, TVs, decent kitchen, WiFi, all that. But once you left the living accommodation and descended the stone staircase off the entrance hall, well, let's just say you knew you weren't in Kansas anymore.

The stone walls were freezing, damp to the touch. Even in the heat of summer you'd be chilled through if you stayed down there for more than ten minutes. The boss could easily have sprung for electric lights down here. But he'd left the iron wall sconces in place.

If they had a *guest* – he chuckled at the boss's sense of humour – they made wooden torches with oil-soaked rags wrapped around them and lit them with matches. Proper old school. The boss said it was more effective for putting the frighteners on the people they wanted to talk to.

Zoran fished out his battered brass Zippo and thumbed the wheel. As trusty as his old AK, it immediately produced a smooth yellow flame. He lit a torch waiting by the door and descended the stairs.

Those old guys knew how to build, he gave them that. They'd built the castle on a hill and its dungeons were carved out of the rock. As his boot soles scuffed the gritty treads, he imagined he was one of those first gaolers. He'd be marching some sad-sack prisoner down here, ignoring his pleas and delivering an old-fashioned smack to the back of his head to keep him walking.

He rounded the final corner and emerged into a narrow corridor. A couple of the torches were burning. Their oily stink merged with the pungent tang of those cheap Russian cigarettes Draž liked so much.

Draž was leaning back against the wall on a tipped-back chair, blowing smoke rings towards the ceiling. Zoran personally couldn't see why the boss insisted on armed guards for the girl. It wasn't as if she was going anywhere, was it? And it made his life just that little bit more difficult today.

Draž looked round and jerked his weight forward so the chair's front legs clacked down onto the stone flags.

'Hey. What're you doing down here? I'm not due to be relieved for another hour.'

'I'm bored with the new game. Thought I'd relieve you early.'

'What, because it's more interesting down here?'

Zoran aimed for a nonchalant shrug. Really, he just wanted Draž to fuck off so he could give the Chink a good seeing-to, but Draž was a pain-in-the-arse stickler for the rules.

'Look, I'm offering you a favour, OK? I'm gonna smoke some dope and chill out. Mio was getting on my nerves while I was playing. I wanted to get away, if you must know.'

Draž got to his feet and dropped his cigarette to the floor before grinding it out with the toe of his boot.

'Relax. I'm going. I owe you.'

He clapped Zoran on his broad back as he went past him.

'Hey! Aren't you forgetting something?' Zoran said.

'What?'

'The key, dummy!'

Draž grinned and handed him the heavy key on its steel ring. Zoran waited until he couldn't hear Draž's footsteps on the stairs then, feeling his hunger for the woman growing inside him, wandered over to the barred door and looked in.

She was sitting cross-legged on the floor. Jesus! She must be freezing her fanny off. He grinned. He'd soon warm it up for her. She was so still. He'd have marked her down as dead if it weren't for the fact she was upright.

He stared harder. Her ribs were moving in and out. Not much, but he could see the tiny movements.

The pressure in his groin was building. He'd had enough of peeping. He drew his knife and scraped its spine down one of the iron bars. At the metallic screech, she turned her head, saw him and stood. It was like she was a marionette being pulled upright by a puppeteer hiding above her, out of sight. She didn't seem to use any muscles. One minute she was sitting on the floor, the next, she was standing facing him.

He frowned. He'd been expecting the same expression as they always wore. Eyes wide, lips trembling. Face so pale you could see the blue veins beneath the skin.

Her eyes were round for a Chink, and so dark he couldn't make out the pupils. She was looking at him the way a cat would. Well, he'd make her purr all right. That or yowl like a molly getting fucked six ways from Sunday by the neighbourhood tom.

He stuck the thick black key in the lock and turned it. Disappointingly, the mechanism gave with a quiet series of snicks. Old-fashioned, maybe, but the boss insisted every piece of kit worked like it should. He'd been hoping for more of a squawk, just like in the movies.

Grinning at her, he let himself inside and locked the door behind him, pocketing the key.

* * *

Tara had heard the new guy coming down the stone steps. A heavy tread, with an irregular beat, da-*dum*, da-*dum*. A limp. Bad for him. Good for her.

As he approached the current guard, she lifted her chin and sniffed the air. He smelled the way they all did. Sour sweat and bad food. Something else, too. Hashish smoke. He was bantering with the guard, but it sounded forced. She didn't have Gabriel's knack for languages, but she caught the impatience in his tone, even if his words were all spiky-edged rubbish.

Guard number one walked off. Number two shot out an indignant demand. She heard a metallic *plink*. He'd asked for the key on its steel split-ring.

She kept her face to the wall, preferring, for now, to use her other senses to define and measure her latest target. The young guy hadn't given her a single opening. Nor the one before him. Something told her this one would be different.

When he drew a knife, the steel whispering as it slid out of the leather sheath, she readied herself. Impatience, plus hash, plus a knife, plus a demand for the key all added up to one thing. Then he scraped the knife down one of the bars to the cell. She turned her head to get her first look at him then stood in a fluid motion, using the strength in her legs to push up from the floor without using her hands.

What she saw confirmed her initial impression. The guy had one thing on his mind. The front of his jeans was distended. His pinkish eyes were battened onto her chest. And he was breathing heavily, the roughness of a heavy smoker evident in each sawing inhalation. If he'd had a sign round his neck, he couldn't have made his intentions any clearer.

He locked the cell door behind him, keeping those lazy predator's eyes fixed on hers. Then he pulled a pistol from the back of his waistband. A crappy Type 54. Not even a genuine crappy Russian Tokarev like she and Gabriel had bought, either. A Chinese knock-off they used to call 'Black Stars' back in the day, on account of the five-pointed star moulded into the black plastic grips.

He closed the distance between them to a foot or so and pointed the pistol at her face. Leering, he said something to her she couldn't translate but fully understood. She waited. Deciding maybe she should at least try to look worried, she tightened the muscles around her eyes and turned her mouth down.

'Please don't hurt me, Mr big tough gangster-man,' she said pleadingly, in Cantonese, pleased to see him relax still further.

He ran the tip of his tongue across his top lip and pushed her chin to one side with the pistol's muzzle. Then she felt the tip of the knife prodding in the region of her groin.

He grunted out something else, and looked down at what he was doing with the knife. Just for a second. She could tell he wasn't worried. After all, how could an unarmed woman do anything to an armed man in just a second?

43

Back behind the wheel, Gabriel slammed his foot down on the throttle, sending the Huracan's offside tyres scrabbling for grip on the loose grit at the side of the road. Trying not to think of what a bunch of thugs working for a former militia commander might do to Tara, he took the car up to 110 mph. He had to back off when the undulations in the road threatened to send him and the Huracan careering across the moorland and into a ditch. Or a tree.

As it climbed higher into the mountains, the road folded up on itself into a series of tight S-bends. Gabriel rarely got much beyond 40 mph, and, as the bends narrowed into hairpins, had to crawl round or risk smashing the car into the rock wall.

He found himself driving along a straight stretch of road between towering sheer rockfaces on both sides. He tried to ease the tension that had built from between his shoulder blades up into the muscles of his neck, rolling his neck from side to side and listening to the pops that emanated from between the cervical vertebrae.

The sun was directly behind him and suddenly it flashed off something high on the ridge ahead of him and to the right. Nothing natural made reflections like that. No herder or hunter would be up there on barren rock. It was either optical lenses or something metallic. Mirrored sunglasses. Binoculars.

Or a telescopic sight.

Shit! He was trapped between hundred-foot-high cliffs of solid rock and a sniper high above the road. Nowhere to turn even had the Huracan not had the turning circle of a London bus. And nowhere to run, either. There was only one option.

He jammed his foot down, grinding the throttle pedal into the mat beneath his right foot. With an angry yowl, the engine let rip, propelling the Huracan forward with such force that Gabriel felt the compression in his eyeballs.

Less than four hundred yards ahead lay the exit from the canyon. He glanced up at the mountain top. Another wink of sunlight against the crystalline blue of the sky. Then a puff of white smoke. He flicked his eyes back to the road then risked another look upwards.

Drifting upwards now, the puff had been joined by a streak of white smoke like an upside-down exclamation mark. It appeared to be descending almost vertically. Then he realised it was just the foreshortening effect of the distance between them. The rocket was coming straight for him.

The needle of the tachometer bounced off the red line as the Huracan's transmission upshifted with brutal speed, slamming Gabriel's internal organs against his ribs each time. His right foot was cramping with the effort of crushing the throttle pedal as he searched for even a millimetre more travel.

If he could coax a fraction more petrol into the cylinders, he might outrun the incoming munition. Because if he didn't, the warhead would turn the Lambo, and its passenger, into so much flying debris of metal, plastic and bone. The canyon exit was widening ahead of him, the narrow V broadening out as perspective shifted and gave a truer picture of the geometry of his route to safety.

With mounting desperation, and the noise inside the cabin deafening him, Gabriel realised he wasn't going to make it. No chance to exit the canyon, swerve off the road and take his chance in a 180 mph supercar on rough moorland. But there were a couple of final options. It came down to the experience and skill of the RPG's operator.

Had he been leading the car? Making mental adjustments to plant the rocket where the Huracan would be seconds into the future? It would make sense for someone who knew what they were doing.

RPGs were dumb missiles, purely ballistic. No onboard guidance, no heat-seeking capability. They went where they were pointed. Aim at a moving car and the grenade would arrive where it had been when the trigger was pulled. At this range, a huge miss.

Gabriel straightened his arms, locking his elbows and switched his right foot from throttle to brake. He ground his boot down, pivoting his hips and sliding partway under the seatbelt to exert maximum force.

Even though he was wearing heavy-soled boots, he could feel every contour of the brake pedal, a small piece of ridged aluminium all that stood between him and his imminent destruction.

Gabriel gasped in a breath and got a lungful of the acrid smoke filling the cabin as the treads of the car's fat tyres began melting from friction. The steering wheel juddered in Gabriel's hands as the ABS struggled to prevent the car skidding.

The rocket was almost upon him. The smoke trail bloomed in front of the car. At the last moment, Gabriel screamed out in defiance and squeezed his eyes tight shut. Then the car jerked to a halt, throwing him forwards then back as the over-stressed suspension decompressed.

With a terrifying loud *crack-boom*, and a flash of white so bright Gabriel saw its shape through his eyelids, the RPG detonated ten feet in front of the Huracan. The high explosive threw the car into the air, spinning end over end, before smashing down onto the Tarmac on its roof.

Gabriel opened his eyes. He had no idea if he'd blacked out. It didn't matter. He had to get out.

He could smell petrol now, a heady top-note to the burnt-rubber smell of the sticky tyres. Even at their best, Lambos had a nasty habit of bursting into flames when a fuel pipe got too close to the engine or exhaust. This one's risk-rating was far, far worse.

Through the windscreen, crazed and bellied towards him like a wet sheet, the flames were roaring up from the bonnet, *quite pretty, really scarlet bluish-green like a peacock's tail a sort of lemony-orange now what colour would you call that Bev would know what with her being an artist and what about those women in the cafe in Aldeburgh chatting him up because one of them had bought the painting Bev'd done of him in his birthday suit bloody silly idea really the lads'd have a field day if they ever found out*

'Fuck!' he shouted, snapping his consciousness back into sharp focus.

Where the hell had he been? The bloody car was about to explode. This was no time to be going for a little shock-dream.

He reached down, up, and jabbed his thumb against the seat belt latch. Miraculously, it released instantly and he dropped onto the roof, twisting his neck as he crumpled upside down against the headlining. He squirmed round, cursing the Italians for making their cabins so snug you couldn't even leave one without turning yourself into a fucking origami animal.

An angular green bird, a swan, appeared before him. If you gently tugged on its tail and head, the wings flapped. Master Zhao smiled at him. 'Now you try, Wolfe cub.' Then the swan caught fire and the flames were so intense they started burning Gabriel's face.

'No!' he yelled out. Then again, louder this time. 'No!'

He stretched out his hand and yanked the door release lever. But the impact must have damaged the door frame. It wouldn't give. Flames were creeping up from beneath the car. Bits of the bodywork had ignited and were burning fiercely.

The smoke was thickening. Not just rubber, either. Gabriel's throat caught as the sickly odour of burning plastic swirled into the cabin. A bout of violent coughing seized him, and with eyes streaming he wriggled closer to the door, which was hot to the touch, trying once more to operate the lever.

He kicked out at the door, heavy blows delivered with as much force as he could muster. The heat was intensifying. Flames were licking all around the cabin and he could feel his unprotected skin burning.

'Come on, you bastard!' he yelled. 'I am not dying in here like a fucking ready meal.'

The coughing redoubled, leaving him nauseous and gagging as he inhaled another lungful of the toxic smoke.

He tucked his knees up as tight to his chest as the limited space would allow then convulsively straightened both legs, driving out through his boot heels and screaming out a lungful of over-heated, smoky air as he did so.

The impact jarred his ankles, knees and hips, but the door remained immobile, wedged into the frame. He kicked out at the drop glass and after three attempts it shattered, falling out onto the roadway with a crunch of broken glass.

But the impact when the car landed on its roof had squashed the opening and he realised there was no way he'd be able to exit via that route. Oh, he might get his head out, but then his shoulders would jam and he'd be incinerated, leaving the cops to find a half-burnt corpse.

The heat was dizzying and the smoke had thickened to a whitish mist. He closed his eyes and gathered himself for a final effort. Then the light through his closed lids dimmed before brightening and he was back in Hong Kong again, drinking cocktails with Britta Falskog, Smudge Smith and the assassin Sasha Beck at the bar in the Golden Dragon.

It didn't matter to him that all three of his companions were dead. They themselves seemed remarkably well adjusted to their non-alive status. In fact, they were getting along famously, laughing and swapping stories about just how they came to be residents of the Underworld.

Gabriel felt out of place among such unfettered good spirits and took a sip of his cocktail, a Flaming Lamborghini. The alcohol burnt his throat on the way down and he winced. But it was numbing the pain of his loss and that had to be good, so he took another sip. And another. And *another and another and another until he felt himself dissolving and merging with the others in their blithe acceptance of death as just one more waypoint on this great journey we were pleased to call exist—*

44

With the Type 54's muzzle jammed against her jaw and a wicked-looking hunting knife at her crotch, Tara needed to do twice as much work as normal. And quickly.

She visualised the map of pressure points on the inside of the human arm. In her mind's eye, the model was a naked male, though without genitalia. Every part of his anatomy was divided and subdivided with coloured lines like the Beijing Metro. But instead of stations, the coloured dots marked acupuncture points.

Shiatsu therapists focused on the points for spleen, kidney, gut, heart and so on. But people in Tara's line of work had developed overlays focused on the 'dark' points, where pressure, correctly applied, would produce sensations ranging from mild discomfort through the most exquisite agony to death itself.

She let herself sag in the man's arms, and as he rebalanced himself to take the added weight she loaded onto his muscles, she struck.

Her left hand closed around his right wrist, the fingers wrapped over the top aligning her fingertips with the blood vessels, nerves and tendons beneath the skin. She dug in hard, knowing the pain would be so extreme he'd find screaming impossible. As it turned out.

His eyes popped wide with shock, his mouth gaped like a tuna on a fishmonger's slab. But all that issued forth was a peculiar wheezing hiss. She straightened her arm convulsively, taking his out wide with it. The Type 54 was locked into his paralysed fist, its muzzle now pointing ineffectually at the wall.

Her right hand had been acting independently of its sister, reaching down towards her groin and digging deep into the muscle between his thumb and index finger. She felt the thick tendon give under the pressure as she twisted his hand outwards. As the wrist rotated, the fingers opened and the knife was in her hand instead of his.

The first thrust took him just above the pelvic girdle, through the muscles that, in all but the fittest, grew soft with age. The needle-point slid in as if she were cutting the fatty belly-meat of the fishmonger's tuna.

With the knife plunged hilt-deep in his side, she relieved him of the pistol and jammed it deep into his throat so that he gagged on the cold steel barrel. She pushed him down onto the flagstones, maintaining pressure on the gun until he was sprawled before her while she knelt at his side.

'You speak English?' she asked him.

He tried to nod, eyes rolling in his skull, but the barrel made the movement impossible, the only result being his upper incisors grating against the front sight. Then he choked out a single syllable round the Type 54's muzzle that might have been, 'yes'.

'You're a disgusting man. A rapist. Worse than a beast. I'm not your first, am I?'

He said nothing.

'Am I?' she shouted.

A sound emerged from his stretched lips – 'oh'.

She leaned towards him.

'No. But I'm your last.'

Now she withdrew the blade. Now the blood flowed, a dark river that pooled beneath him, staining his pale jeans maroon. He whimpered, writhing before her, though the pistol in his mouth prevented him from moving far. Without breaking eye contact – that mistake was only for amateurs – she slit open the front of his jeans.

'Pull it out.'

He tried to shake his head so she stabbed him a second time, just a testing blow, nothing major. She didn't want him bleeding out. Not yet.

'Do it!' she barked.

She followed the movement out of the corner of her eye, catching the pale, blurry shape. And then, with a fast slicing motion, she passed the knife beneath his fist, separating him from his penis. She pulled the pistol out of his mouth allowing him to draw in a huge, panicked breath. Before he could scream it out again, she stopped his mouth with his own member and clamped his jaws shut around it.

The blood was flowing freely, but not fast. And it was time to leave. She used the knife a fourth time, this time opening his throat, bisecting the carotid artery on both sides. Some of the scarlet arterial blood spattered her outfit.

She didn't watch him die. That was for amateurs, too. He was already dead. He just didn't know it yet.

His eyes drooped and his head lolled to the left. Not long now. A few seconds. She patted him down and came up with his phone. Picking up his limp hand she pushed the thumb against the On button and was rewarded with the home screen. He was dead by the time she'd finished disabling its security.

Leaving, she closed and locked the cell door, tossing the key over towards the corpse. She dropped out the Type 54's magazine and pushed down on the topmost round. It didn't give at all. Excellent. Now, how many did these old Norincos hold? Seven, was it? Eight? Not great. But add in the element of surprise, plus the knife and her fighting skills, and she was reasonably confident she'd be out of the castle within the hour in one piece.

The men who'd taken her at Ponting's house were hard, reasonably fit, well trained, and experienced in armed combat. But that was just it. *Armed* combat.

They needed AKs, grenades, a 4x4 to escape in and the support of a crew to feel confident. Whereas Tara was happy operating alone. Preferred it in some ways.

And though a gun was always nice, it had never been a must-have for her. Her hands and feet, and improvised weapons from whatever local environment she found herself in, would always suffice.

As she crept along the corridor, a breeze from somewhere up above swirled down the stone staircase and set the torches flickering. Torches! How ridiculous! Even Fang Jian's lurid imagination had only stretched as far as gilded dragons and ceremonial swords. His club was lit with electricity, above *and* below ground.

A door opening upstairs might have caused the breeze. But they only changed guards twice a day and it was too soon after the last changeover for another to be on his way.

Six steps into the climb up the staircase she heard a good-natured shout and laughing from above her. She reversed direction, reached the bottom on silent feet and hid beneath the curved underside of the staircase where it curled round a pillar as thick as a tree trunk. Someone was descending the stairs. Maybe it was guard number one, back to check on how his mate was getting on with the prisoner. The gait sounded about right.

His feet were right above her head, the sound of his footsteps muffled by the stone but then reproduced as a hard echo off the walls further down the corridor.

She picked up on the double-scuff as his boots hit the gritty floor. He called out.

'Hej, Zoran! Završili ste je vec?'

Then he laughed coarsely.

She could work it out. He wanted to know if his friend had finished fucking the prisoner yet.

She emerged from her hiding place, stepped quietly up behind him, clamped a hand over his mouth and, just as she had with the repulsive Zoran, slit his throat right down to the bone. This time she was clear of the blood, which jetted out with such force it painted the ceiling. She lowered his lifeless body to the floor. After taking his pistol – a Beretta M9, much better – she restarted her ascent.

At the top of the stairs, she paused and put her ear to the rough wooden door. She could hear the roar of high-performance car engines and competing with it, male voices. Two. No, three.

She listened for a few minutes. These were subordinates. None was using the tone of command. None was giving orders while the others listened and replied in monosyllables as befitted underlings. They were bantering. Troops off duty, gassing while the leadership were elsewhere making the strategic decisions.

She stuck the Type 54 into the front of her waistband. That left her with the M9 in her left hand and the hunting knife in her right.

Stepping back a little, she pushed the door open, inching it wider until she could step through it into the cavernous hall on the other side. And back into the twenty-first century.

No more bare stone and wrought iron. This place was outfitted like some sort of luxury bachelor pad with cheesy framed prints of semi-naked girls on motorbikes and a massive plasma TV dominating a wall above a fireplace. On its screen, realistic-looking sports cars, including a bright-orange version of the Huracan she and Gabriel had hired, were racing round a track fringed by thick forest.

In a corner, its red mouth a grotesquely distorted 'O', a partially deflated sex doll sat in a chair, a blonde wig sliding off its head.

Directly in front of her was a wide leather sofa facing the TV. Ranged along its squashy back rest were the backs of three heads: the owners of the voices she'd heard from the other side of the door to the dungeon. The heads' owners were still laughing and elbowing each other as they fought for the best lines round bends.

Sliding her feet over the thick carpet, she arrived behind the men in utter silence. Even had she made a sound, the revving engines and howling exhausts blaring from the surround-sound system offered perfect cover.

She stabbed the right-hand player hard and fast into the side of his neck, pulling him over sideways as she withdrew the blade. He groaned in shock and pain.

As his neighbour turned, distracted from his progress around the racetrack, she plunged the knife into his left eye socket, cracking the thin bone at the back with a sound like bursting bubblewrap, and driving the point deep into his brain.

The last guy was halfway to his feet when she struck for the third time, an upcurving blow that took him under the ribcage. His eyes bulged as the knife pierced his heart. He would have screamed had Tara not pulled the knife free and stabbed him in the larynx.

'Game over,' she said.

Breathing heavily, she heaved the bodies back into position and replaced the game controllers in their laps. The effect wasn't wholly convincing. Too much blood had sprayed out and doused the furniture, sheepskin rugs and the plasma screen. She shrugged. Couldn't be helped.

Then she ran for the door.

She'd arrived hooded, hands cinched behind her back with cable ties. Sighted, and free to move as she wished, she saw the castle courtyard for the first time.

45

From his vantage point above the ravine, Jako Orić watched as the bright-green Lambo leaped into the air like a hooked pike breaking the surface on Lake Zavoj. He hadn't fired an RPG in years and he'd been sufficiently worried about his aim to retro-fit a telescopic sight. In the event it had gone fantastically well.

He'd followed the car's progress on his phone thanks to the tracker those guys at Dragan installed on all their motors. Smart, really, when you thought about it. It wouldn't be too hard to swagger in there, hire a Ferrari or whatever, take it over the border and move it on to some Russians without getting caught. That Emina, she was a smart girl, too. Calling her uncle at the first whiff of fish.

When it became obvious which way the Englishman was coming, he'd ridden up to the ridge on his bike with the RPG slung over his back. Not the best weight distribution, but the BMW was nice and heavy and as sure-footed as a goat on the mountains. He'd never really had any concerns.

He followed the trail of white smoke all the way down in a graceful, feathering curve, before the grenade detonated and fucked up that beautiful piece of Italian ass.

Shame, really. If Jako ever got that kind of money, he'd always promised himself the first thing he'd buy would be a properly decent set of wheels. The sort that would have the chicks flocking round him. He knew he wasn't that good-looking, but pussy couldn't resist a flashy motor, everyone knew that.

The explosion looked like one of the splashy flowers in his mum's garden. Petals unfolding and stretching up and out on an orange stalk then collapsing inwards as the fire sucked oxygen in to feed its hunger.

The boom came next, a second or two behind the visuals, which at this remove looked somehow less impressive than the ones you got on *GTA* or *Call of Duty*.

On the other hand, the car rotating in the air: that *did* work. Four or five complete revolutions, bits of bodywork flying off in all directions, before it landed on its roof and burst into flames. He sat, eating a chunk of cold beef with his knife, enjoying the sight of the lime-green paintwork blackening.

At this distance, it looked a bit like a dying insect, one of those shiny beetles with long spiky black legs you got on the bushes near the castle. He tried for a bit to make some sort of similarity between legs and wheels, but gave up: he'd never been one for reading, much less writing. He shrugged. The boss hadn't picked him for his literary talents, had he?

He watched for bit, half-hoping the Englishman would crawl out from under the car so he could ride down there and finish him off with a couple of bullets to the face. But as the minutes passed and nobody – Ha! No body! – appeared, he got bored and turned away, walking back to the bike leaning on its kickstand.

In the over-excitable voice of his favourite football commentator on Arena Sport 1 he announced the results of his own most recent match:

'English Arsehole nil, Golden Bough one. The winner, a blinding shot from three hundred metres – get that, sports fans, three hundred fucking metres – from star striker Jako Orić.'

Shaking his head at his own wit, he re-slung the telescoped RPG over his shoulder. Down in the canyon he heard a second rolling boom: the gas tank igniting. Well, if the RPG hadn't done for him, that would, for sure.

He mounted the bike and rode away. He spent the journey rehearsing different ways of confirming the kill to the boss, wondering if he'd get first go with the Chink as his reward.

46

Reality swam into focus again, though Gabriel could tell it would be for the last time.

Mustering as much force as he could manage and suppressing the coughing just long enough for the effort, Gabriel kicked out again. This time, the door gave a little, unlatching and springing out by a couple of inches. He booted it once more and with a squawk of protest from the damaged hinges, it popped out.

Gabriel scrabbled through the opening onto the burning roadway. Even with the risk of being immolated if the car blew, he looked back for a second and snatched the pistol from its resting place in the centre of the roof. The AK was wedged behind the damaged seats. That was lost.

Then he ran, splashing through the shallow lake of petrol spreading out beneath the car. He glanced up at the ridge. The shooter must have gone, convinced he'd achieved his goal. No rifle fire, no incendiary rounds to detonate the petrol. That was...

WHOOMPH!

The explosion as the petrol ignited and the flames tracked back to the fuel tank knocked Gabriel off his feet, sending him sprawling onto the Tarmac, hands outspread.

He tucked into a foetal position and rolled away from the vibrant-orange fireball rising from the wreckage of the Huracan. On hands and knees he watched as the heat sucked white-and-black smoke up to follow the flames, creating a mini-mushroom cloud that boiled up between the rock walls. He got to his feet, staggering as his balance deserted him for a moment. His ears were ringing, adding a high-pitched whine to the roar of the flames. He shook his head and started walking away from the pyre.

'Probably not worth worrying about the collision damage waiver,' he said aloud.

Then he laughed, a lunatic bark in the empty canyon that bounced off the walls and reflected his own crazed merriment back to him.

At the end of the stretch of road enclosed by the towering rock walls, the moorland landscape reasserted itself. Gabriel took a path down to the left because he could see a twinkling thread a few hundred feet below him that he thought – hoped – might be water.

Though the gradient was steep, the going was easy thanks to the springy turf underfoot. Patches of bushy purple and yellow heather dotted the ground and as he navigated a path between them he saw rabbit droppings on the ground. He realised he was hungry. With more time and equipment he'd have considered fashioning a trap: nothing like fire-roasted bunny to chase the old pangs away.

But time was the one commodity he didn't have. Strike that. He also lacked food, *as previously noted*, he thought, medical supplies and drinking water. He looked down at his jeans, which had scorch marks all over them, not to mention rips and tears through which bloodied skin was visible, added a change of clothes to his list of 'haven't gots'.

The twinkling line was resolving as he drew closer and he could make out the meandering line of a stream. At least that was something to be grateful for, and he mentally crossed off drinking water.

His balance was improving. Maybe he'd just needed to get rid of the poison the smoke had deposited into his bloodstream. He picked up the pace, and broke into a trot when the stream, now audible as well as visible – splashing over flat stones and larger, sharper rocks – made its way across the hillside.

Arriving at the water's edge, he knelt, ignoring the protests from his road-scored knees and scooped up the ice-cold water in cupped hands to slake his thirst. After drinking for a minute or so, he dashed a double-handful of water against his face, rubbing at it and then tipped more over his head.

The water running off his chin and dripping back into the stream was a deep rose pink. He felt around on his scalp, before yelping as his fingertips grazed an open wound that was sticky with congealed blood. Head wounds were 'proper bleeders' as they used to say on active duty. But this one was weeping rather than gushing, so he left it alone, hoping it would heal itself.

Heaving a sigh, he sat back and began a systematic inspection of his body, looking for wounds. That wing mirror embedded in his shoulder felt like a lifetime ago, but the fact he'd not noticed it until someone else had pointed it out showed the anaesthetic power of shock. He didn't want to make the same mistake again. Although if he *did* have a Lamborghini windscreen wiper sticking out of his back, he thought, on the whole, he'd rather not know about it.

Both feet were fine: the boots had stood up admirably. He ran his hands up his left shin and calf, finding minor cuts here and there but nothing you could call serious. He worked his way up his thigh and then the other leg, again finding nothing worse than you might get on a vigorous circuit of an assault course.

He took his jacket off and removed his T-shirt, wincing at the pain as he lifted his arms above his head. Nothing on his torso, or nothing he could see at any rate. He stretched up and over, feeling down over his shoulder blades.

The stitches from his earlier injury felt ragged. He tested them by teasing at the thread with thumb and forefinger and a loop came free. He touched the wound and inspected his fingertip. No blood. So it had healed over. He left the remaining stitches in place. No sense in tempting fate by asking for an infection to set in.

After a few more minutes, he determined that, by good luck, divine intervention or a miracle of Italian safety engineering – the thought made him huff out an ironic laugh – he'd survived an RPG attack. And minor wounds even a rookie Boy Scout without a single badge to his name could patch up with the contents of a home first-aid kit. Result.

The burns were sore to the touch and weeping with plasma. But not dangerous. What the medics called 'superficial' when talking to soldiers or 'first degree' amongst themselves.

So, the body was in reasonable shape, all things considered. The mind was holding together, more or less. But his materiel was looking seriously depleted. The AK-47, with its sniping and automatic fire potential, gone. The spare mags for the Tokarev also gone. That left the seven rounds already loaded in the grip and bugger all else.

If Ponting's men had given up on him, figuring he'd not survive the inferno engulfing the Huracan, he'd be OK for now. But if they were still hunting him and armed with anything longer than a pistol, he'd be within range well before they'd be in any danger from the Tokarev. Hell, they could just stand up and aim while his bullets dropped to the ground ten feet in front of them.

He looked around. Was there anything out here he could use as an improvised weapon?

The stones in the stream would make decent clubs and if he could knap one with another like some old caveman, he might be able to fashion a crude hand axe.

Trees were scarce, and the ones he could see were gnarled, twisted things that the wind had trained into identical sideswept forms, like full-size versions of Bonsai trees. Not a straight branch anywhere, which meant fire-hardened spears were out, always assuming he could get a blaze going.

Ironically, the single source of all the things he needed was the same as his destination: Ponting's castle. The paradox that he needed to attack and defeat his enemy in order to get the kit he needed to attack and defeat his enemy wasn't lost on him. He felt sure Master Zhao would have had a useful saying for just such a puzzle. In fact, maybe he did. *Surely* he did.

Gabriel crossed his legs and closed his eyes. He worked to still his mind, easing his focus away from the myriad aches and pains that suddenly fizzed and sparked into brighter life now he'd shut down his dominant sense.

What should I do, Master?

He didn't strain to hear an answer. That only led to frustration. Instead he waited, focusing on his breathing. Slowing it down until he gained that familiar controlled rhythm: in for four, hold for one, out for four, hold for one.

He thought he heard the sound of a vehicle engine high above him. A big diesel. Maybe a truck, then. It would come upon the blackened wreckage of the Huracan and, what? Call the cops? Skirt it and carry on?

He resisted the urge to listen closer and went back to his breathing. And asked again.

What should I do, Master?

Nothing. He tried to avoid thinking about Tara. She was alive. Of that he was sure. Nothing else mattered. Whatever else they did to her, as long as they didn't kill her, she'd be fine. Not the same, not necessarily, but she'd survive it.

Once more he asked, though the pull of reality was growing stronger.

What should I do, Master?

This time he did hear the answer. From somewhere deep down in his memory, Master Zhao's voice, half-amused, half-serious, grew in volume until he could hear his mentor as if he were sitting beside him.

A paradox is merely a trap for the unschooled thinker. Remain inside its boundaries and it offers only two choices. Each contradicting the other. Step outside it, however, and you can look for a third option. Use it to solve the problem.

Gabriel let his eyes flutter open, as he'd been taught, holding onto the sound of Master Zhao's voice for as long as possible. God, how he missed the old man. They'd not spoken much, even after Gabriel had rediscovered his existence. But he'd been there, always ready to offer advice or simply to listen. And that had been worth more to Gabriel than he thought he could ever put into words.

Somehow, the simple exercise of stepping away from the problem for a while had allowed him to reframe it. It was only a trap if you stayed inside its walls. To find what he needed to attack the castle, attack the castle.

OK, so step outside and triangulate the problem. Find the third option. He was *here*, by the stream. The castle was *there*, wherever 'there' was: and if his mapping app still worked, he'd find it. What he needed was a third location. Another *there*. Somewhere he could rest, re-equip and refocus on the mission.

He got to his feet, relieved that his vision stayed sharp and there was no swaying or staggering as he walked away from the stream. Turning in a circle, he scanned the horizon in all directions. Maybe someone lived up here. A hermit? Did they even have those anymore? If they did, he thought this might be the sort of place some grizzled old geezer with a long grey beard and a mahogany suntan might choose. He saw nothing.

The sun was bright. Feeling he might have missed something in its glare, he shaded his eyes and tried again. This time, maybe half a mile distant, he caught a distant cousin of the RPG's smoke-trail: a fine column of bluish smoke drifting at a forty-five-degree angle. He'd missed it the first time because its colour blended in with the shadows on the hillside beyond.

Feeling suddenly optimistic and imagining a settlement, maybe a village with a bar or a cafe, he strode towards the smoke. As he walked, he practised some of the Serbian phrases he'd learned.

'Molimo vas.' *Please.*

'Hvala vam.' *Thank you.*

'Želim pivo i sendvič sa šunkom.' *I'd like a beer and a ham sandwich.*

'Mogu li kupiti Kalašnjikov?' *Can I buy a Kalashnikov?*

He laughed at the absurdity of the thought. Some dinged-up stranger walks into your village looking like he just took a bath in burning petrol and broken glass, and the first thing he asks is where he can lay his hands on an automatic weapon?

Why, of course, sir. Let me direct you to Vlastimir's place. He's the best dealer for miles around. Not the cheapest, but he sells only the best ex-Soviet gear.

And while you're at it, do you need wheels? We have a fine ex-Yugoslavian army 4x4 up for grabs.

Smiling, despite the gravity of his situation, he covered the distance in twenty minutes. As he got closer, the ground rose in front of him, masking the source of the smoke. Doubts crept in. Maybe it was peat burning underground. Those things could go for months, years, even. Or the remains of a hunter's cooking fire.

He strode up the hill, all thoughts of a village, with or without a friendly neighbourhood arms dealer, fading fast. Nearing the top he slowed, almost unable to take the last few steps that would reveal to him whether his third option was fact or fantasy.

Then, from behind him, in the distance, he heard the one sound he'd hoped to avoid.

Shouts. Men's shouts. *Ponting's* men's shouts.

He hunkered down and turned to scan the horizon. Though they were still a good five hundred yards distant, the men stood out on the barren moor so clearly they might have been signposted with red arrows drawn by an invisible hand.

No attempt at camouflage, either. Brightly coloured jackets predominated. He counted five, moving in a widely spaced line. Not good. Not good at all.

47

A gritty concrete courtyard separated the castle from its surrounding wall. Four big 4x4s occupied one corner: two blocky Merc G Wagons, a Toyota Land Cruiser and a Range Rover. All black. Predictable.

Tara considered taking one, but a glance over towards the double wooden gate convinced her to leave on foot. Unbolting it and disabling the security would almost certainly have men running out, guns drawn. She didn't think the Norinco would be enough to keep them at bay.

She shot a look back towards the castle. Nothing stirred. Maybe the others were sleeping off hangovers or checking weapons.

She didn't have the tools or the time to start cutting brake lines. But she could slow them down almost as effectively with a simpler and much lower-tech method beloved by Hong Kong street kids looking to hold up the island's wealthier occupants.

Crouching between the high wall and the first of the G Wagons, she sliced through the tyres, moving on to the next as soon as the blade cut deep enough to release a hiss of pressurised air. The heavy vehicle sagged sideways as the tyres deflated and she scurried along to the next in line.

She'd slashed the rear tyre when she heard the scuff and scrape of approaching feet. Shit! She balled herself up and waited.

The door locks on the first Merc clunked open and the door opened then shut. The engine started with a cough and a roar. It idled for a few seconds, and the pitch deepened as the driver put the transmission into Drive, then it cut off.

She knew exactly what had happened. The driver, maybe going into Novi Sad for supplies, had been about to pull away when he'd realised the 4x4 was canted over. The door opened again. He was getting out. In a moment or two he'd be bending to check the tyres before moving round to find the damaged pair. And Tara.

She got onto her belly and pulled herself under the second G Wagon, then slithered beneath it and crossed the foot or so of open ground to its neighbour. From her vantage point beneath the stricken 4x4, she could see the driver's feet as he moved round the back. His boots disappeared, hidden by the huge car wheel, before reappearing again halfway between rear and front tyres.

He swore under his breath. His right knee touched down onto the concrete. Followed by the left. So he was going to check underneath.

He poked his head under the sill and came face to face with Tara. His eyes widened and he opened his mouth. Presumably he intended to say something like 'What the fuck?'

She couldn't allow that. Grabbing a hank of his thick blond hair, she jerked his head up, smacking it into the chassis, and down again, hard, mashing his face against the oily grit.

The blows had disorientated him, but that was all. There hadn't been enough space to get much speed behind the movement. His right fist came round in a low, sweeping curve. Even fully functioning, he wouldn't have done much damage. As it was, Tara met the punch with the point of the hunting knife. He moaned as it slid between his knuckles. Tara choked off the sound with a pincer grip around his throat, pushing thumb and finger towards each other around the back of his windpipe.

He flailed his left arm, trying to free himself from her stranglehold. Then she hauled him under the car, grabbed the back of his head and flipped herself over in a half-roll that severed his spinal cord with an audible snap.

It took another couple of minutes to drag the rest of the body beneath the Merc. When it was done, she shuffled herself out backwards and finished slashing the tyres of the remaining vehicles.

She needed to leave now. She'd done all she could, short of taking the fight to the remaining men inside the castle, and without knowing the numbers decided now was the time for a strategic retreat. Gabriel would be on his way. All she had to do was hole up somewhere, wait for him to arrive, then join him in the final assault that would see Ponting pay, finally, for his crime.

Checking that she was unobserved, and that nobody else was coming out to check the vehicles, play football, start a barbecue, or whatever Serbian gangsters did in their spare time, she darted along the wall. The sun was almost directly overhead, casting sharp-edged but truncated shadows.

She kept tight to the wall, where the shadow was almost black. Halfway round the side of the castle, she heard shouts and stamping boots. What? Were they drilling? She stopped, then crept forwards, hugging the cool stone of the wall until she caught a glimpse of the men making all the noise.

Twenty or more men, a ragtag army in mismatched camouflage, stonewashed denim and sports gear, were standing to attention. A guy stood in front of them, silver hair cropped short, looking like he'd always wanted to star as the drill sergeant in a movie about US Marines.

They weren't carrying rifles, but she saw one or two pistols tucked into waistbands or sitting in belt-mounted black nylon holsters. This wasn't the time or the place for an attack. Eight pistol rounds and a knife against that lot? She'd take maybe half of them down before she fell, but those were no sort of odds.

She retraced her steps, finding a shallow niche in the wall where she could flatten herself and remain invisible except from a spot directly between her and the castle itself.

The massive front gates were locked. The squad drilling

prevented her moving any further in that direction. That left only one option for escape. One option and one direction. Upwards.

Emerging from the little alcove, she looked up. The wall was only thirty feet or so high at this point. There'd be a walkway at the top. She could see turrets spaced every fifty feet or so around the top. Maybe she'd find a rope in one of them.

Castles were designed to be impregnable against a full-frontal assault and their thick walls resistant to cannon balls. But over the centuries, the stones this one was built of had weathered badly. She visualised a route out encompassing dozens of hand and footholds where the crude mortar had fallen out or frost had split the stones themselves.

She took a final look around, but, apart from the drill squad, there was nobody about.

She placed her fingers into the lowest cavity and pulled herself up. Flattening herself against the wall, she zig-zagged up the wall like a gecko. The effort must have worked the Type 54 loose because as she neared the top, it fell out her waistband. Swearing, she rolled over the inner retaining wall, little more than a kerb, really, got to her feet and, keeping low, ran for the nearest turret.

At a loud shout from the courtyard, she threw herself face down. They'd discovered the vandalised 4x4s. Crap! Change of plan. Forget about ropes. If the outer surface of the wall was in as bad condition as the inner, she'd be fine. As more men came running, she slid through a wide gap in the outer retaining wall where a couple of blocks had fallen, or been blasted away.

Pulse racing, she descended as fast as she could, having to search with her toes for the next foothold. One of her favourite methods of keeping in shape in Hong Kong was to visit the climbing wall at ATTIC V on Yip Fat Street. Grateful for the practice now, she switched grips, shifted her weight and, when necessary, let both feet and one hand dangle while she twisted to look down for the next hold.

Nevertheless, she sighed with relief when her questing right toes brushed the grass at the foot of the wall. She dropped into a crouch, reseated the Type 54 and sprinted for the thickets and scrub breaking up the rocky mountainside thirty or so yards from the castle wall.

She pushed her way through the thick foliage, ignoring the whipping thorny branches that scratched her face, then took a few seconds to scan the landscape in front of her for the best route to safety.

Behind her she heard metallic clanks and then a massive double bang as the castle gates were thrown back against the outer wall. Without vehicles, they'd be only as fast as she was. But what they lacked in speed they made up for in numbers. And that was still a problem for Tara.

The route dead ahead was across open country, with only sporadic cover provided by thinly spaced thickets like the one in which she was sheltering. No good. They'd have rifles by now, and no doubt at least one of them was a marksman good enough to pick off a lone running figure at the sort of range she'd offer.

Over to her right, two hundred yards distant, a spine of grey rock interrupted the thin soil, knobbly boulders bursting up like broken bones through skin. They rose into a tall formation that fell away on its far side in a gentle slope. A patch of deep shadow suggested a possible exit from her predicament. She ran for it, leaping the rocky bed of a stream at one point, and keeping low to the ground. Behind, the shouts and cries were growing stronger.

48

Tara's heart lifted. Unlike the others thrown by the rocks around it, the patch of shadow didn't lighten as she drew near. It remained an impenetrable black. She could see why as she arrived before it. It was a cave entrance. She cast a hurried glance over her shoulder and saw blonde heads bobbing into view above a ridge of grass and moss.

She cut a thickly leaved branch from the nearest tree, wincing as an inch-long thorn stabbed into the soft flesh at the base of her thumb. Dragging it into place behind her to obscure the entrance, she ducked inside. She activated the torch on the phone she'd lifted from the first Serb she'd killed and held it at head height. The cave widened a little, but she still had to stoop as she made her way deeper into its welcoming maw.

It was cold in here, despite the warmth out in the open air. The cave smelt old. Earthy. Not unpleasant, no trace of decay, either animal or vegetable. No faint trace of cigarette smoke that would indicate herders or hunters used it as a bad weather shelter.

She ducked under a low rock that brought the ceiling to within four feet of the floor then her eyes widened and, despite herself, she let out a small cry of wonder.

The roof seemed to vanish. She tilted the phone up and saw that it had curved away from the floor to maybe ten feet above her head. Smooth creamy stalactites dripping moisture from their tips hung from the roof like blunted spear points ready to drop and impale the unwary visitor.

To her left a narrow passage led away from this vaulted cavern. That was the only exit, unless she wanted to retrace her steps. She executed a full circle, taking in the miraculous subterranean architecture formed by nothing but the forces of earth and water.

Heavy footsteps echoed towards her from the passage leading back to the open air. Her pulse bumped in her throat. It wasn't over yet. She clambered over the boulder-strewn floor towards the exit tunnel and made her way along it. Behind her, a man was muttering. Just one voice. He'd seen the cave and come to investigate. The crisp click as he racked a pistol slide bounced off the walls.

He'd reach the cavern in a few seconds. If he pushed on down the tunnel, he'd eventually find her. Maybe she could kill him silently, but if he even got one shot off, the noise would bring his friends running. In numbers.

Then they could do whatever they liked. Starve her out. Send dogs in. Bring jerry cans of fuel over from the castle and torch the place. Roll a couple of boulders across the entrance and seal her up like a mediaeval wise woman accused of being a witch and punished for healing the sick.

She couldn't let them gain the upper hand. Not here. Not now. Not while Ponting still breathed. Some words of Fang Jian's came back to her.

When in a tight spot, remember you exist in three dimensions, not two.

She'd asked him to explain. He'd smiled indulgently.

Trapped by enemies, most people look ahead. They look left. They look right. They look back, he'd said, miming these four actions with theatrical swivels of his head. *That is simply a horizontal plane. Two dimensions, yes? The x and the y.*

She'd nodded, comprehension dawning.

So I must look down and I must look up. Three dimensions. The x, the y and *the z.*

Fang had beamed, his gold teeth glinting.

Exactly. A ladder, a branch, a fire escape, a tunnel, a manhole. All could offer a route to safety. In my younger days, I was known as Snake. I climbed everything I could find. Trees, scaffolding, bridges, radio masts. I learned to think in 3-D. You must, too, if you are to survive in my world.

Tara looked up. A formation that climbers at ATTIC V called a chimney stretched away from her. The narrow crevice, ending in blackness, was just wide enough for her frame.

She hauled herself up, wedging her fingers into a narrow crack in the wall. By jamming her back against one side and bracing with her feet against the other, she was able to inch her way up into the gloom. She turned off the torch and focused on steadying her breathing.

Her pursuer's footsteps grew louder. He swore repeatedly, keeping up a steady stream of expletives and she smiled to herself as she heard a particular loud yelp of pain followed by an intensified burst of Serbian oaths.

He must have twisted his ankle. Good. He'd be losing heart and growing impatient to be out of there. Only his fear of his master's displeasure and the slender chance he could get the glory of killing the escapee was driving him on.

And then he entered the tunnel.

His voice gained a special kind of clarity as if he were talking to her face to face. Some quirk of the acoustics this far underground. He was repeating a single, short phrase as if chanting a mantra, except he was spitting the words out like cherry stones.

'Jebena pička, jebena pička, jebena pička.'

She didn't know the precise meaning, but she could translate the tone. He'd be using the word a man always did when a woman had got the better of him. Calling her the worst name he, with his limited imagination, could think of.

A muscle in her right thigh started twitching, and she knew cramp was arriving. The twitch turned to a pulse and then it hardened into a grinding contraction that had her biting her lip to stifle a cry of pain.

Then he was below her. The smell of sweat and stale cigarette smoke rose off him, entered the chimney and was drawn into her nostrils. She wrinkled her nose and stared down through the narrow gap between her thighs.

If he looked up, she'd drop onto him and end his life with a knife thrust. Then we'd see who was the *yebenna peeska*, and who wasn't.

He craned his head forwards, peering into the gloom, using his phone just as Tara had used the dead man's. In the feeble illumination he'd see how the tunnel narrowed.

She tightened her leg muscles, willing herself to ignore the cramp.

He glanced over his shoulder. As if she might be creeping up on him. Two dimensions. The x and the y. She readied the knife.

She visualised herself dropping like a hunting spider ambushing a small bird. Legs either side of his head, yank his head back by the hair and slice across his unprotected throat left to right then ride his lifeless corpse to the ground.

Then he shook his head, muttered, 'jebena pička' a final time and turned. Tara waited until his footsteps had faded to silence before letting herself down from the chimney's embrace. Swearing quietly to herself, she massaged feeling into her screaming quads. She waited fifteen minutes before making her way back to the vaulted cavern.

She stayed there for another hour, alert to any sound, however slight, from the clatter of pebbles to the sniffing of hounds, but heard nothing beyond the steady drip from the stalactites.

She checked the phone periodically, but there was no signal. As if! The tech companies had made amazing strides, but even China Telecom wouldn't be able to feed enough electromagnetic radiation this far down to permit her to call Gabriel.

At 3.00 p.m., she ventured back along the passageway through the cave that led to the outside. Gun in hand, she neared the entrance. The branch was gone.

308

In retrospect it had been a mistake to cover the opening. It signalled that someone had gone inside. The guy who'd followed her in must have assumed it was her, then, on finding the place empty, blamed a local for covering it up.

She shrugged. What did it matter? She was free. The Serbs had retreated inside their fortress. Gabriel was on his way. All she had to do was make contact and then wait.

The landscape was empty apart from her and a couple of wild goats, cropping the scabby lichen from some of the nearby rocks. They regarded her incuriously with those weird horizontal pupils of theirs before returning to their grazing.

She tried the phone again. Success! In the top-left corner of the screen the precious legend, Telenor 4G, and four bars. From memory, she tapped in the number of Gabriel's burner.

Nothing. She waited, pulse bumping. He had to be there. It was just the Serbian network being slow. Seconds passed and still nothing.

Swearing, she ended the call and immediately retried. She counted to seven before giving up.

'Come on,' she muttered. 'You're giving me four fucking bars!'

She hit redial and, as if unable to understand what all the fuss was about, the call connected instantly. Holding her breath, she listened to the soft purring of the ringtone and willed her brother to answer.

49

Not caring whether he was heading for an abandoned campfire or a chemicals plant, Gabriel scrambled to reach the brow of the hill.

The smoke was issuing from the chimney of a broken-down stone cottage fifty yards from his position. He sprinted towards it, dodging rabbit holes in the turf and grey boulders that broke the surface like teeth from a rotten brown gum.

The wind changed, bringing the sweet smell of woodsmoke. He allowed himself to hope he'd find a friendly face within.

The windows in the wall facing him were shuttered. He raced around to the front of the cottage where he found encouraging signs. A muddy quad bike. Boot prints leading away from it to the front of the cottage.

He stepped up to the door, whose sky-blue paint was blistered and peeling, and knocked. If there was no answer, he'd break in. Maybe he'd strike it lucky and find something he could use as a weapon. He could always leave some cash or come back another day and make things right with the owner.

But he'd no need. He heard footsteps approaching from the other side. Straightening up and pasting a smile on his face, he assembled the necessary words into a phrase aimed at disarming the occupant. Possibly literally.

The door swung inwards to reveal a solidly built man with fluffy white hair standing up round his tanned scalp like a halo. From the wrinkled skin of his face, Gabriel put his age anywhere from seventy to eighty, but he had the stance and musculature of a much younger man.

'Da?' he said, white eyebrows raised.

He didn't seem particularly surprised to see a burnt and dishevelled visitor on the threshold of his cottage.

'Ubiće me! Molim vas pomozite.' *They will kill me. Please help.*

The old guy could have asked, 'who?', or 'why?' Or 'what do you mean?' Instead, with a glance over Gabriel's shoulder, he drew him inside by the elbow and closed the door behind him.

The door opened into a living room. It was furnished simply, with two armchairs flanking a log fire. A rifle leaned against the wall in a corner. The old man pointed to one of the chairs. Gabriel took it, grateful not to have to scrape around for further Serbian to explain his predicament. Or not yet, anyway.

'English?' the old man asked.

'Yes,' Gabriel replied, not quite able to believe what he was hearing.

The man held out his hand. Gabriel took it. The skin was worn and callused and the grip was iron-hard, like grasping something mechanical rather than flesh and blood.

'Danilo,' he said, placing his palm over his heart.

'Gabriel. Da li govorite Engleski?'

'Yes, I speak English. I was a teacher for many years. Who wants to kill you?'

'They're gangsters. They work for a man called—'

'Ratko Popović,' Danilo said, curling his lip. 'That bastard is a stain on this country's honour for what he did in the war.'

'You know about that?'

'Of course I know! I was fifty-six the year the war broke out. Too old to fight, but I had my hunting rifle. I defended our village. Popović claimed to be defending Serbia but what he did, what they all did…' Danilo hawked and spat onto the stone floor. 'My daughter married a Muslim boy. Ali. He was kind. Learned. He wanted to be an engineer. Instead, he ended up in a mass grave at Srebrenica. Svetlana killed herself on the first anniversary of his death. Grief took my wife three months later.'

Gabriel nodded, aware of another family destroyed by Ponting's actions. 'His real name is Steven Ponting. He is English but his mother was Serbian.'

'And what have you done that he sends men to kill you?'

'It's what he did that matters. He kidnapped my sister when she was a baby. My whole family died as a result. She and I are the only ones left. We tracked him to his castle. Now he has her again.'

Danilo nodded. 'You came here to kill him. Well, I don't blame you. They'll be here soon. There is a root cellar left over from when people lived here,' he said. 'It's only my hunting place now. You must hide. When they get here, I'll say you came knocking but I sent you away with a bee in your ear.'

Danilo's little slip reminded Gabriel fleetingly of Britta and her knack for tweaking English idiomatic phrases into something comical. He got to his feet and followed Danilo through a door that led into a small, beaten-up kitchen. Danilo drew a threadbare rug aside and lifted an iron ring in a wooden trapdoor. He heaved it open, letting it rest against a chair.

Gabriel looked down as a dank smell wafted up and filled his nose. Wooden steps led down into the gloom. Lighting his way with his phone's torch, he descended into the darkness, ducking so Danilo could lower the door. As he reached the earth floor he heard a muffled swish as Danilo replaced the rug.

He shone the meagre beam of light around the low-ceilinged space. Wooden shelves lined the walls. All bare now, bar a couple of large glass jars containing dark globular shapes in some evil-looking purple liquid. Beetroots? Onions? Hell, they could have been human kidneys. Maybe he'd just allowed himself to be locked into a cannibal's killing room. Still, better one cannibal than five heavily armed mass murderers. And he still had his pistol.

With nothing else to do, he sat cross-legged on the cold floor and field-stripped the Tokarev. First in the light from his phone, then again in pitch darkness.

Did he trust the man into whose gnarled and powerful hands he'd just entrusted his life? He found that he did. Unreservedly. The venom with which Danilo had denounced Ponting came from a place of raw, undiluted pain. He'd seen the expression many times before. That level of honesty was impossible to fake.

Psychopaths and serial killers, terrorists and corrupt politicians: he'd met monsters of every description, and though some weren't bad at feigning normal human emotions, something always betrayed them. A twitch of a smile on lips pushed downwards into a grimace of anguish. A gaze unable to meet his own for more than a second. A blankness behind the eyes into which a person could fall and never emerge whole.

From upstairs came a thunderous hammering on the front door. Gabriel pictured the group's designated leader using the butt of a pistol or the heel of his hand. Fearing retribution from his boss if he returned without a confirmed kill. Anxious not to appear weak in front of the others. Ready to bully some peasant into revealing all.

Would Danilo make good on his promise? Gabriel knew he'd want to. But if the men decided to use violence, he'd break. It was unreasonable to expect anything else. He was an ex-teacher. That was all.

He backed into the corner of the cellar furthest from the steps, laid the pistol across his lap, and waited.

The door scraped open. A muffled male voice. The tone friendly, enquiring. Danilo's reply. Long. Angry. He caught a single word. 'Da.' *Yes.* They would have asked him whether he'd seen a guy on foot, looking like he'd been through the wars. And Danilo had just told them 'yes'? But then what? *Yes, and I sent him away?* Or *Yes, and I tricked him into hiding in my cellar?*

Gabriel tensed, holding the pistol out in front of him, aiming at the midpoint of the steps. If they came down, he'd have ample warning as Danilo drew the rug back and opened the trapdoor. Anyone descending from the kitchen would be backlit, framed, a perfect target. One bullet, one man. But the rest would retreat to consider their options.

Why not just push the stove over the trapdoor and leave him there to die? Or chuck a grenade down? Gabriel had seen what happened to tank crews when that happened, or they took a direct hit from an armour-piercing shell. In the first case, men became meat. In the second, pink mist that the blast blew back out through the entry hole.

Yet, despite Danilo's agreement that, yes, he had seen a fugitive, silence reigned. No thumping boots from the room above his head. No sudden splash of blinding light. No automatic fire from a spraying AK-47.

He heard the front door open and close again. Then footsteps. Then the swish of the rug, the clink of the iron ring and the scrape and thud as the trapdoor fell back against the chair again.

'Gabriel, come out. They have gone.'

Blinking in the light, he climbed the steps, sticking the pistol into his waistband.

Danilo pushed a glass of clear spirit into Gabriel's hand. He took a cautious sip and coughed. Some home-brewed firewater that tasted of cherries and almonds.

'Thank you,' he said, raising his glass.

Danilo raised his own and they clinked rims.

'I told them I'd seen you. Said you'd come to the door and I told you to leave. Pointed them towards town. It's miles away. You can be far gone before they come back.'

He led Gabriel to the sitting room and they sat in the chairs flanking the fire again. They might have been two hunting buddies, enjoying a relaxing tot before cooking up the game they'd shot that day. Gabriel winced as the Tokarev dug into his back. He leaned forwards so he could free it and lay it on the floor beside him.

'I still have to find my sister,' he said. 'And then we're going after Ponting.'

'Then you will need more than that pop-gun,' Danilo said, pointing to the Tokarev. 'I have something you can have. Something nice and quiet. Better for the work ahead, I think.'

He rose from his chair and left the room. Jesus! Did the old guy have a suppressed rifle? Strange weapon for a hunter. Danilo returned, clutching a crossbow.

But this was no wooden-stocked replica of a medieval weapon. The old man held an ultra-modern hunting bow with a woodland camouflage pattern to the stock, fore-grip and limbs. A quiver slung beneath the cocking stirrup held six bolts fletched in red and white plastic. Best of all, it was mounted with a telescopic sight.

Danilo passed it to Gabriel. He accepted it and inspected the various components. Had it not been for the complex arrangement of limbs, pulleys, criss-crossing cords and the bolts, he'd have said it looked more like a modern AR-15-style rifle than a bow of any kind.

Turning away from Danilo, he held it up and aimed at the window. The pistol-grip fitted his hand snugly and as he sighted through the scope the weapon seemed to merge into his arms as surely as his old M-16.

'It's a fine weapon,' he said, turning back to Danilo.

'EK Archery Guillotine. I use it for roe deer. The arrow velocity is four hundred feet per second. Probably not much worse than that Russian pistol.'

'Effective range?'

'Eighty, a hundred metres? A little more if you're a good shot.' He paused and scrutinised Gabriel. '*Are* you a good shot? Something tells me, yes.'

Gabriel smiled. 'Not bad.'

'Army?'

'That's right.'

'Me, too.'

'I thought you were a teacher.'

'I was. But we had National Service here back when I was young. I left school at eighteen and went straight in. You had to do six months, but you got paid more if you signed on as a regular. So I did.'

'Did you enjoy it?'

'I did,' Danilo said with a smile. 'Good money, good food. Well, bad food but plenty of it, which was fine for young men. I was a designated marksman. I used to hunt with my father, you see.'

Gabriel pointed to the thin aluminium stirrup protruding from the front of the bow. 'Is that how you cock it?'

Danilo nodded. 'Just like in books, yes? You put your toe through, stand on it and pull the string back with both fists till it latches. Slot the bolt into the groove, there, and you're ready to fire.'

'How about the scope? What's it zeroed for?'

'Eighty metres.'

Gabriel pulled one of the bolts out of the quiver. It ended in a sharp-pointed broadhead: three razor-sharp blades with an acute angle at their leading edges and a shallow one behind. He held it up to the sunlight entering the room through a cloudy window. The edges glinted, revealing the minute striations of a grinding wheel.

'I can't guarantee I'll be able to return it to you, Danilo,' he said, placing the bow on the floor beside the Tokarev, 'but I can pay you for it.'

Danilo shook his head.

'I have a better idea. When you find Popović or, what did you call him?'

'Ponting.'

'Before you kill him, tell him this is also for Ali Ibrahimović.'

Gabriel nodded. 'I can do that.'

'I will let you have a dozen spare bolts, too. And do you need food, water?'

'Thank you. Both would be good, if you can spare them. And if you have a spare knife, I could use that as well.'

Danilo nodded grimly.

Ten minutes later, Gabriel turned to wave to Danilo, who stood at the side of the cottage, watching him go. The old man raised a hand and held it there for a few seconds before letting it fall by his side. Gabriel turned around, shouldered the rucksack containing the supplies Danilo had provided and walked away.

When he glanced over his shoulder, the old man had gone.

His phone rang and he snatched it out of his pocket, almost dropping it in his haste. Only one person had the number.

'Tara?'

'Hey, BB, how are you?'

'What? Yes. I'm fine. Where are you?'

'I'm in a cave. Actually, I'm just outside. It's quite nice, really. I've just had a rabbit and some blueberries. Very tasty.'

'Jesus! How did you escape?'

'No time for that, I'll tell you later. But Ponting's down five men, so the odds are better than they were yesterday.'

'Text me your GPS. I'll come and get you.'

Ten seconds later, his phone beeped. He tapped the coordinates and the mapping app opened. Smiling at the thought of being reunited with Tara, he strode on, up the hill, clapping his hands at a crew of wary-looking goats who scattered before him, bleating their disgust.

Climbing steadily, Gabriel entered a trance-like state, leaving part of his mind aware of his surroundings while the other looked ahead, weighing options, considering tactics.

With no accurate intelligence on the enemy's forces, he had to rely on an estimate. Osman had said Ponting could rely on up to fifty men. But would they all be available? Within reach of the castle? Surely a gangster couldn't afford to bring his entire operation to a halt while he defended himself against one or at most two attackers?

Gabriel wouldn't. He'd hand-pick a small squad of his best fighters depending on the situation. This was no infiltration, more of a siege. That meant marksmen. Guys who were skilled in hand-to-hand combat if the enemy breached the perimeter and got inside. Above all, loyal men who wouldn't desert if things got hairy.

How many then? That was the question. Gabriel decided to be pessimistic. Ponting keeps half his forces on routine duties, extorting money from businesses, trafficking drugs, weapons and people. And he pulls the other half in to help him repel the attack. Twenty-five men, then. Tara said Ponting was five men down, so Gabriel knocked the total down to twenty.

But two against twenty were atrocious odds. In the Regiment, they'd always gone in with overwhelming numbers. Nine to one.

The popular image was of a small group way behind enemy lines. And it was true, for covert ops involving harrying the enemy or blowing up materiel, small, agile squads were the order of the day. But in anything approaching a firefight, standard operating procedure was to blitz the foe with superior numbers, tactics and firepower.

He shrugged. Couldn't be helped. Two was all they had.

50

Ascending a scrubby rise with the wind in his face, he heard men's voices. Had to be his pursuers. They must have given up on the idea of chasing a ghost into town and decided to admit defeat and return to the castle.

He caught a whiff of woodsmoke and another smell that had him salivating: brewing coffee. Obviously they weren't in too much of a hurry to get back and face their master's displeasure.

He crawled up to the lip of the ridge and peered over the other side. In a shallow, grassy depression two men sat opposite each other across a small fire. Above it, suspended on a simple cradle, a coffee pot was boiling. Their AK-47s lay on the ground beside them. He saw pistols at their hips. One was busy texting, the other leaned back on his elbows, face tilted to the sun.

He slid back down the slope a few yards and considered his options. The pistol's rapid fire capability would make it more effective at shorter range, but it would also be noisy and might bring the other three gangsters running. Plus, a Russian pistol, or possibly a Yugoslavian knockoff of same, was hardly a weapon designed for pinpoint accuracy.

Even straight from the factory, it was a close-combat weapon.

This one might be decades' old. And the two men Ponting had sent to kill him were forty metres away.

He shucked the crossbow off his shoulder. Lying on his back, he stuck his right boot through the cocking stirrup and drew the bowstring back towards the pistol grip. It latched with a muted click.

Breathing slowly, he slid a bolt out of the quiver and slotted it along the flight groove. He belly-crawled up to the lip once more, this time with deadly intent.

A centre-mass shot was the sensible choice at this range with an unfamiliar weapon. But he had no idea of the damage a broadhead crossbow bolt would do to a man. It would be messy, but instantly fatal? Only if he hit a major artery or pierced the heart.

Gabriel sighted on the man facing him, positioning the cross hairs over his right eye. Danilo had said the scope was zeroed for eighty metres. Gabriel made the necessary mental corrections for the reduced range and downhill trajectory.

He inhaled, let the breath out, waited for a heartbeat, and squeezed the trigger. The bolt flew with a sharp slap from the bow as the pulleys snapped the limbs forward. A scream of agony pierced the silence, followed by a shout.

Without waiting to see where the bolt hit, Gabriel rolled onto his back and re-cocked the crossbow, slotting a second bolt home and returning to his firing position. He popped up over the ridge, sighted on the second man who had jumped to his feet and was kneeling over his fallen comrade.

The bolt hit him just to the left of his thoracic spine. With a screech, he jerked upright then arched over backwards, his hand scrabbling over his shoulder to find the arrow that had just pieced his lung.

Gabriel charged down the hill, the hunting knife in his hand. The first man he'd shot lay on his back. Motionless. The second man was staggering towards his rifle. Gabriel couldn't let him reach it. If he fired, the noise would bring reinforcements.

He covered the last few yards at a sprint, barrelling into his enemy and knocking him onto his back. Gabriel fell on top of him but was thrown off again as the guy rolled. He jumped to his feet and moved in, knife grabbed for a killing blow, edge uppermost. But there was no need.

The man lay as still as his former comrade, eyes staring. The three razor-sharp blades of the broadhead pointed at Gabriel from the centre of a blood-soaked patch of T-shirt.

Twenty had just become eighteen.

A mobile phone pinged. The guy texting must have received a new message. Gabriel grabbed the phone from beside the fire and read the text.

Ima li znakova o njemu?

A moment's work with Google Translate and he had it in English. *Any sign of him?*

Gabriel busied himself with the two apps again before replying. He kept it short to avoid trapping himself with bad Serbian.

Imam ga. Uz kafu. Pridružinam se

Got him. Having coffee. Join us

He added the GPS coordinates. Then he took one of the AKs and retreated a hundred yards to a lone tree, bent almost horizontal by the prevailing winds, and climbed into the cover of its branches.

Gabriel had worked with Kalashnikovs many times. He checked the position of the long, pressed-steel fire selector lever. Its previous owner had it in its central position for automatic fire, revealing the Cyrillic characters

АВ

Gabriel pushed it down with its characteristic loud click to semi-automatic.

ОД

He remembered a story told to him by Vinnie Calder. Vinnie had been in the US Marines then, and training with a Russian defector who'd enlisted as an army cadet. The man joked that they always said the CIA had designed the Kalashnikov's safety because, 'bloody loud noise gives away shooter's position'.

Ten minutes later, he heard male voices, laughing, joking, sounding like a great and worrying weight had been removed from their shoulders. *Sorry, boys. Guess it's not your day.*

The first man to arrive stood on the brow of the hill. He stared down at the bodies of his two friends who, from that distance might have been sleeping. Then, crying out, he ran down the hill, stumbling, tripping and ending up rolling half the remaining distance before coming to a stop in an untidy heap, elbow-to-elbow with the man Gabriel had shot through the chest.

He checked his pulse, head cocked to one side, then stood and rushed to the first man. No pulse-checking this time. A crossbow bolt to the skull sent an unmistakable message.

He turned a full circle, then yelled out, 'Pomozite! Brzo!'

It was close enough to Russian that Gabriel could understand him easily. *Help! Come quick!* Well, what else was he going to shout?

Two more men appeared at the top of the rise then ran down to join him. Each man had a Kalashnikov slung over his shoulder. They took them off now and whipped round, this way and that, searching for their comrades' killer…

…who brought the Kalashnikov up to his shoulder, aimed, and fired. The first round took the leftmost man high in the chest. He fell backwards, blood fountaining from the entry wound.

The other two were better trained than their casual dress indicated and split apart, dropping to their knees and aiming back towards Gabriel's position.

Bursts of automatic fire raked the branches, shredding leaves and sending a rain of macerated foliage and wood down onto his head. He fired again, dropping one of the men with a headshot that covered the man next to him with blood and tissue.

He fired wildly towards the tree. Gabriel dropped out of the branches into a crouch, then got down onto his belly and lined up his next shot.

Without any cover of his own, the final Serb was a sitting duck. Perhaps realising this, he jumped to his feet, yelled out a battle-cry and charged towards Gabriel.

Gabriel fired again and again, missing with the first shot then hitting the man in the right shoulder, sending a gout of blood up into the air above his head where the sun caught it, turning it garnet.

The impact spun him round and he dropped his rifle. Gabriel got to his feet and walked towards the fallen gangster. He was scrabbling at his waist to release a pistol, but it was too late. Gabriel shot him dead from ten yards out: a double-tap to the chest. Arriving beside him, he delivered a coup de grâce shot to the head.

Fifteen.

He collected a second AK for Tara, then removed the bolts and magazines from the other three and stuck them in his rucksack. The magazines for the pistols followed. He left the scene with the smell of gun smoke pricking his nose. His ears rang from the gunfire but that would pass; there'd be more before the day was done, anyway.

Did he feel anything for the men he'd killed? No. This was far from honest combat between opposing armies. Between enemies who could still respect each other when the fighting was over. Or when prisoners were taken.

If what Danilo, Osman and others had told him was correct, they were the worst kind of sadistic killers. Gabriel had no way of knowing whether they'd been among the triggermen at Srebrenica. Or were they just willing participants in everything that went on around it at that blood-soaked time?

But they'd developed a taste for murder, seasoned it with punitive rape, and carried their evil into a new occupation under Ponting's protection. They'd escaped justice at the hands of the ICTY. He hoped they were being judged for their crimes somewhere now.

He checked his phone. Tara was barely fifteen minutes away. He picked up his pace, pausing only to drop the spare rifle bolts into a patch of boggy ground, where he trod them out of sight into the waterlogged sphagnum moss.

Gabriel felt optimistic for the first time in days. He and Tara would be armed, rested and fed, and they'd have surprise on their side. Ponting's men had met their fate. Soon, so would he.

51

Gabriel arrived at the cave mouth at just before 6.00 p.m. The sun was low, turning the undersides of a few high clouds a brilliant mix of pink and orange. A straggling V of birds, black against the pale-blue sky, moved westwards, pushed by some imperative imperceptible to human senses.

He entered the dim space, from which virtually all of the remaining daylight quickly disappeared. Using the torch on his phone, he weaved between the rocks strewing the floor until he reached a vaulted cavern, its ceiling prickling with stalactites. The smell of roasted meat assailed his nostrils.

'Tara?' he called. 'It's me.'

She emerged from the shadows, sticking a pistol into her waistband. Grinning, she ran to him, leaping a boulder, and threw her arms around him.

Gabriel returned the embrace, squeezing back.

'Hey! I didn't come all this way only for you to bloody suffocate me,' he said, laughing and heaving in a breath to loosen her grip around his ribs.

She released him and stepped back.

'You OK?'

ANDY MASLEN

'Yeah. I met this old hunter. He hid me and gave me this,' he said, turning his back to show her the crossbow.

He slid the bow, the two rifles and the rucksack off his back, sighing with relief. The gear wasn't so much heavy as awkward, and he was glad to be able to get it off his shoulders.

'He give you the AKs, too?' Tara asked, picking one up and sighting along the barrel.

'Courtesy of five of Ponting's men. They won't be needing them anymore.'

Tara nodded. 'He's down by ten men.'

'I think he may have as few as ten left.'

'How do you figure that?'

Gabriel explained the reasoning behind his estimate of Ponting's forces. But Tara pursed her lips.

'He'll have found the men I killed by now. In his shoes I'd have sent for everyone else.'

'Even if he has, they'll have to make their way here. We should hit him tonight.'

'Agreed. But soon, OK? I know cops and soldiers always think you should go in at 3.00 a.m., but we tried that at his place in Novi Sad and it was a complete fuckup.'

She'd echoed Gabriel's own thoughts. And Ponting was both ex-police and ex-military – of a sort, anyway – so would be expecting them to hold off until just before dawn. The wrong time was now the right time to attack.

'When the five who were chasing us don't come back to the castle, he's going to get properly spooked.'

'Good. Let's use it. Frightened men aren't thinking straight.'

Gabriel and Tara left the cave, one Kalashnikov and one Tokarev apiece, plus spare ammunition. Gabriel also carried Danilo's crossbow and the spare bolts. He gave the hunting knife to Tara. Everything else they left hidden in a cleft between two boulders. It wouldn't do to leave themselves bottled up if Popović's men came out looking a second time.

* * *

By 9.00 p.m. that night the sun had disappeared over the horizon. Clouds had moved in, too, dampening still further the dying light. On their way again, their faces and hands smeared with mud, the Wolfe siblings blended into the background. Were they invisible? No. But unless someone pointed their night-sight in the right direction, the chance of a stray movement catching a guard's eye had shrunk almost to zero. That was good enough.

The castle loomed into view. In the darkness, its sheer sides were black, rising out of the ground in an unbroken wall of stone. The huge gate was closed.

By now Gabriel's eyes had adjusted to the lack of light and he could see clearly the crenelated ramparts. The situation felt unreal, as if the men they were attacking might appear at the battlements dressed in chainmail and surcoats, wielding swords and maces instead of automatic weapons.

He patted the air, signalling Tara to crouch down beside him. Scanning from left to right and back again, he strove to see an outline above the stonework that would indicate Ponting had set sentries up there. It's what he would have done. Had done many times, in fact. But then he would also have erected a perimeter protected by Claymores. Ready to blow any intruders into their constituent atoms if they were foolish enough to try and break through.

He tapped Tara on the shoulder and indicated that they should split up and circle the castle. She nodded, and crept away to his right. He watched her go. He moved away on a clockwise circuit.

What was he hoping to find? A back door? Hardly likely. It wasn't as if the people who'd built the castle would have been so accommodating. But it had to be done. A recce might yield a single piece of intel that could help them gain entry. And once they were inside, they would track down Ponting.

He met up with Tara at the rear of the castle. He raised his eyebrows in mute enquiry. *Anything?* Tara shook her head.

Gabriel looked up at the forbidding wall in front of them. The stonework was rough, the blocks weathered over time. Could they climb it? He went closer and stretched out a hand to feel the outline of one of the massive blocks at the base of the wall.

His fingers slipped into a crack at least three inches deep between the block and its neighbour. It was wide enough to get a toe in. He looked up. Darker lines between the stones indicated the presence of more imperfections: he began to see a route in.

He turned to Tara and pointed up. She shook her head a second time. Then she grabbed him by the right bicep and drew him away from the castle. She slid down a grassy slope into a depression that shielded them from view.

'What is it?' he murmured.

'We're doing this all wrong,' she hissed. 'Climbing in. The castle's their territory. They're all in there. All their guns are in there. They know the layout. You're acting like we've got superior numbers, but it's just us two.'

'What are you suggesting? We go and knock on the front gate and ask them, politely to come out?'

'Yes. Exactly.'

'Are you crazy?'

'Listen. Out here we have the advantage, OK? They don't know where we are. They don't know what weapons we've got. It's dark. There's cover,' she murmured. 'Let's draw them out and pick them off one by one or at least a few at a time. We can cut them down until there's just a handful inside. *Then* we go in.'

'How do we draw them out?'

'Simple,' she said, grinning, so that her teeth gleamed from her mud-smeared face. 'Give them what they want.'

Gabriel began to see her intent. 'Meaning?'

'You, BB. They want you.'

'So I just march up to the gate and fire a burst into the wood until they come and capture me? How do you know they won't just shoot me on the spot?'

'They won't. Trust me. Ponting will want whoever captures you to bring you to him. He's a gang boss. I know these people,' she said. 'There's a way they like to do things. They want people to know why they're going to die and they like their guys to see it. It keeps them in line.'

'Was that how Fang ran the White Koi?'

Tara shrugged. 'It's how *I* ran it.'

Gabriel pondered her plan. After a few minutes of serious thought he had to concede it beat his hands down. But he had a couple of suggestions to make.

52

Tara took up her position fifty yards back from the castle wall. She brought the Kalashnikov up to her shoulder and fired a single shot into the wooden gate. The report was deafeningly loud in the still of the night. Somewhere away to her right she caught a flurry of white wings: a barn owl startled by the noise had abandoned its hunt.

She slung the rifle over her back and raised the improvised white flag they'd made from a tree branch and Gabriel's T-shirt.

In under a minute the sound of the iron bolts on the inside of the gate broke the silence for a second time. They swung inwards and light flooded out as torch beams swept the ground.

Tara remained motionless until the beams picked her out. The two men sent out to investigate carried Kalashnikovs. They were shouting, both at the same time. Their meaning was clear. *Drop the weapon! Get down! On the ground!* The usual mixture of orders and threats one might expect from nervous security anywhere in the world.

She was relieved they weren't shooting. Gang psychology was her specialist subject, but she'd based her plan on what she knew of triads and the occasional *interactions* she'd had with Colombian drug cartels. There had always been the chance that Serbians did things differently.

Happily for her and Gabriel, it turned out that henchmen were the same in Hong Kong, Bogotá and wherever the fuck this part of Serbia was.

Instead of complying, she raised her hands still higher, letting the flag fall forwards so it flapped a yard or so in front of her head. A nice little distraction.

Then, in a gap as the men briefly stopped their yelling, she called out to them, shouting the phrase Gabriel had got her to learn phonetically.

'Imam informacije za Ratko Popović.' *I have information for Ratko Popović.*

She and Gabriel had debated the precise wording. Would 'your boss' be better than the man's name itself? They'd decided not. 'Boss' was generic, and whilst it might reinforce the idea of the hierarchy, using Popović's name would make it sound more like she knew the man. Now she yelled the second phrase.

'Želeće da čuje.' *He will want to hear it.*

Gratifyingly, her words had the precise effect she'd predicted. The men, while not lowering their weapons, conferred hastily. What happened next was key. They had to approach her.

They were shouting again. Serbian phrases she had no way of translating. She stood her ground, hands upraised. Waiting.

The men were beckoning her, waving their arms and shouting. She ignored them. Finally, judging the moment to be right, she lowered the flag of truce and, turning her back on them, unshouldered the Kalashnikov and lowered it to the ground.

She turned back to face them and raised her arms again. Reassured, they advanced on her, leaving the gate and the security of the castle.

She watched them coming on. The rifle barrels had dropped. They were sauntering, not striding. They were already thinking ahead to their triumphant presentation of the prisoner to Popović. They had already lost the battle. They just didn't know it yet.

The leading man was close enough that she could see the

stubble on his cheeks. Behind him, the second man was pulling a pack of cigarettes out of a pocket. So careless. If they'd been WK soldiers, she'd have whipped them for their indiscipline.

A whistling hiss sliced through the silence.

The man in front gasped. He clapped a hand to his neck, which had sprouted an object like a black pencil. A gout of blood rushed from his mouth and he collapsed sideways. Behind him, cigarette-man was fumbling his rifle up and whirling round, looking for the silent attacker.

Tara was already closing the distance between them as he searched for a target. He was too panicked even to shout, though his lips were working as he tried. When the knife entered his heart, he lost the ability as well as the intention.

She grabbed both torches and switched them off. Shouts were coming from the castle courtyard. Carrying the dead men's Kalashnikovs, she sprinted over to Gabriel, who had just cocked the crossbow.

Three men burst out of the gate. One fell immediately, a bolt sticking out his chest. This close, the power of the crossbow turned each razor-tipped bolt into a killing blow. Tara waited for the men to start firing, which they did, wildly and on full auto. Their bullets whined over her head, disappearing harmlessly into the scrub. She was more economical. The noise of her shots was masked by the barrage coming from the gate. One round each for the two remaining Golden Bough men. The AK kicked satisfyingly into her shoulder.

She looked left at Gabriel and they nodded at each other. In a crouch, she ran back the way they'd come, rounding the rear of the castle and taking up position on the opposite side.

The next group came out shooting. Wild bursts in every direction. Once they'd burnt through their magazines, Tara and Gabriel opened up. Two Kalashnikovs, from two positions, firing fully automatic. The noise was insanely loud and the acrid smell of gun smoke mixed with hot brass filled the air.

Four of the men fell, torn to pieces by the 7.62mm rounds. One, hit in the leg, staggered back towards the gate and tried to close it.

Tara got to her feet, picked up her second Kalashnikov and resumed firing. She strode forwards, her finger clamped on the trigger. In the corner of her eye she saw Gabriel mirroring her actions.

Hot lead poured through the gate, killing the last man from the group and throwing him backwards to land like an action figure discarded by a child tired of playing soldiers.

No way would they send more men out. This had just changed to an infiltration. But if Gabriel's reckoning was correct, and Tara prayed it was, Ponting was down to just a handful of men.

Inside the gate, the courtyard was empty. She saw the same vehicles parked where they'd been before. Someone had fixed the tyres on one of them, but the others were still canted over. A good sign. That meant Ponting hadn't summoned reinforcements, or, if he had, they'd yet to arrive. And he hadn't left, either.

A bullet whined off the stonework to her right, sending a chip of rock flying out that smacked into her cheekbone, narrowly missing her eye. She ran for cover behind the vehicles.

* * *

Gabriel peered over the bonnet of the 4x4. The shot had come from an upper-storey window. It was easy to see which one. The others all reflected the sky in their panes of ancient glass. This one was a solid black rectangle. He aimed at the sill and waited.

The long barrel of a hunting rifle slid forth, emerging like a snake from its lair. He aimed above the point where it intersected with the window frame and fired a single shot, imagining the marksman's head bent to the sight. The barrel tipped up and slid back inside with a crash.

'Now!' he hissed to Tara. Together they dashed across the twenty yards of open courtyard to the imposing wooden front door of the building.

He glanced at the timber from which the door was constructed. Kicking it in wasn't an option. Even the burliest of paras with enough Benzedrine in his system to turn him into a

336

Terminator would only get a bootful of shattered bones for his troubles.

Instead he raised his AK and fired a burst at the black iron lock. Bright splinters flew out and Gabriel flinched as they stung his face.

He shoulder-charged the door, which swung inwards. Tucking into a roll he fell forwards and scrabbled for any available cover.

A burst of automatic fire issued from the darkness, smashing into the wall just above his head. He found himself beneath a rustic-styled table on which a huge glass vase of flowers stood. He heaved it over, sending the floral display smashing to the ground. Water flowed backwards on the sloping floors, soaking his knees.

Tara had slipped into the hallway and darted right. He could see her behind a stone pillar wide enough to completely obscure her from the shooter.

Shots slammed into the table. Gabriel raised his own rifle over the top and answered with a short burst. No attempt at aiming, just a quick spray to encourage the defender to get his head down. He ran out from behind the table to a stone archway. Now he was safe.

He looked across the hall at Tara and signalled for her to join him. He counted down from three with upraised fingers. On 'one', he squeezed the trigger and fired a continuous burst up towards the stairs while Tara, firing from the hip, sprinted across the open ground to join him.

'There's nobody left down here,' she said as she arrived. 'They'd have come out by now. Listen, you were right. I killed five before I left. You got another five. That makes ten. We got ten outside.'

'I hit a sniper at the upper window, too.'

'OK, so that's twenty-one. There's the shooter upstairs and maybe one or two more in reserve, but then that's it.'

'You ready?'

She nodded, wiping sweat from her forehead and further smearing the mud.

'Ponting's up there. It's nearly over.'

He nodded, offered her a tight smile.

'Let's get the bastard.'

She dropped the empty magazine out of her Kalashnikov and

slapped in a fresh one. Gabriel followed suit. Then she turned, heading for the stairs.

'No!' he hissed. 'Not that way.'

She stopped.

'Why not?'

'There'll be a back way up. There has to be. For servants.'

She smiled. 'Good idea.'

And then Gabriel heard a fast, hard sound coming from the wooden stairs – *clunk, clunk, clunk* – followed by an uneven rattle: metal on wood. He struggled to place it.

Then the air seemed to fracture. A blinding flash dazzled him and the noise of a cannon firing shattered the silence. Someone had lobbed a grenade over the balcony.

Beside him Tara was slumped against the wall, her eyes closed. Blood was flowing from under her jacket. Her T-shirt was soaked with blood on the right side, low beneath her ribcage. Christ! Not now. Not when they were so close. She couldn't die on him. She *mustn't!*

He lifted the sopping fabric and got his first good look at the wound. It was a mess. A chunk of metal from the fragmentation grenade had torn through her flesh and opened a three-inch long trough that pulsed with blood and twitching muscles. But she was alive.

He heard footsteps coming from the hall and grabbed his rifle. Lurching forwards he sprayed a burst out from behind the stonework of the arch. A man screamed and toppled over, his dying hand spasming on the trigger, emptying the magazine into the ceiling and bringing wood chips, plaster and tapestry fragments down on his own corpse.

Gabriel rushed back to Tara. She was still unconscious. He struggled out of his jacket and ripped off both sleeves. He wadded up the remains to make a pillow. And scooped her head up before letting it rest gently on the pad of cloth.

He rolled and folded one sleeve into a field dressing and clamped it over the ugly wound in her side. He split the other in half and knotted the two strips together. He threaded the improvised bandage under Tara's ribcage and tied it in place over the wound pad.

It would stop the bleeding, which was fast-flowing but not the powerful jets of arterial spray. So it wouldn't kill her. But the shock might, or infection if he couldn't get her to a hospital soon.

He ran down the corridor, searching for somewhere safe to leave her while he went in search of Ponting. The first door led to a storage cupboard. He swore and ran on. He was luckier with the second.

It opened onto a sitting room, furnished comfortably with leather sofas and, incongruously, a huge flat-screen TV on the wall. He started as he caught sight of a naked blonde lolling in a chair. On closer inspection it turned out to be the sort of joke sex doll men bought for their friends' stag nights.

Back at Tara's side, he lifted her eyelids but the eyes behind were rolled up into her skull. Her breathing was shallow and fast and her pulse was fluttery. Fighting down feelings of panic, he got his hands under her and lifted her inert form. He carried her into the sitting room and laid her on the leather sofa. He curled her fingers around the butt of her pistol and laid it along her right side.

Torn between the need to find Ponting and the desire to stay with his sister, who he prayed wasn't dying, he hesitated, just for a second. Then, clenching his jaw, he left her.

53

Gabriel found what he was looking for after a ten-minute search of the ground floor. A narrow passage led off a stone-flagged scullery.

At the end of the passage, a door opened onto a flight of bare wooden steps. He checked his weapons. The Tokarev was unused. The AK had half a magazine, plus two spares. He should have been cold without a T-shirt or jacket, but adrenaline had a way of shutting down the body's normal responses.

Holding the AK ready across his body, he ascended the staircase. The thought of Tara lying close to death on the ground floor caused him such wrenching pain he could hardly bear to continue.

But what other option did he have? He must kill Ponting now or possibly miss his chance for ever. And if Tara was dead? He would return with enough dynamite to turn the castle, and the remains of those within its walls, to dust.

At the top of the stairs he paused and listened. The hallway was silent. He looked along its length, peering into the gloom, trying to spot a sliver of light escaping from under a door. But all was dark.

He crept along, senses heightened, ready to engage the enemy at the merest mouse scratch of sound.

At each door, he stopped, took a breath, stretched out a hand for the door handle and eased it down until he could toe the door open. The Kalashnikov's barrel went in first, while his index finger remained curled around the trigger. And in each room thus entered he found the same thing. Emptiness. Just the cold, musty smell of old furnishings and unaired spaces.

The hallway jinked left then right in a dogleg and he found himself on a wide landing. A vast Persian rug covered the floor. In the gloom, Gabriel picked out an intricate geometric pattern in which, as he stared closer, he could discern stylised representations of the very rifle he was holding. That placed the weaver in Afghanistan, where ancient traditions and modern warfare had collided to sometimes surprising effect.

He scanned the perimeter of the landing. His pulse jumped upwards as he saw a wide strip of light at the foot of the only closed door.

His mind screamed a warning. TRAP!

So instead of heading straight for the light source, he methodically and silently checked all the other rooms. Each was as empty as the previous set he'd investigated. When he reached the room next to the spot where he was sure he'd find Ponting, he crossed to the shared wall and pressed his ear against the paper.

What he heard convinced him that this was truly the endgame.

The unmistakable double-click of a charging lever being yanked back and released.

He looked down at his own AK. Had he been in a modern building – an office block, perhaps, or a suburban house – he might have sprayed a burst at the wall, aiming at waist-height. A reasonable chance of disabling his enemy without exposing himself to return fire. But the material separating him from Ponting was stronger stuff than plywood or drywall panels.

That left just one option. Going in through the door.

But that was suicide. Ponting would be waiting on the other side, probably behind cover. As soon as he saw the handle move he'd open fire and that would be it. Or he could relax, let Gabriel get inside, and *then* emerge. Either way, it was a sure win at minimal risk.

Gabriel scanned the room, frantic for something, anything, he could use that might give him an edge. A demo block of C4 would have been nice. Or an RPG like the one they'd used against the Lamborghini. But the armoury was elsewhere.

Then his gaze fell on a pair of heavy, floor-length curtains. And a wild idea began to form in his head. Risky? Of course. But his options were narrowing fast. He opened the curtains, feeling shock at the texture of velvet when so much around him was steel, stone and splintered wood.

He lifted the wooden sash and peered out, up and to the left. Yes. This would work. The stonework here was as dilapidated as it had been when he and Tara were considering climbing the outer wall. Mortar was missing from large gaps between the blocks; wind, rain and frost had dug their claws into the stones themselves, producing fissures, lumps and fist-sized holes.

Eight feet to his left was another window. Behind that window sat his nemesis.

Gabriel looked down. A fifty foot drop onto concrete. Unsurvivable. Even the SAS training leap across from the Scottish mainland to the sea stack known locally as Old Tom ended in water.

He tightened his lips. *Better not fall then.*

First, he slung the Kalashnikov over his back. The Tokarev, he stuck into his waistband. He slid his right leg over the sill, tilted his torso until his arms could follow, then levered himself out, and up into a standing position on the narrow stone ledge outside.

A breeze was blowing across the hills towards the front of the castle. He felt it cooling the sweat on his back. Looking to his right, he picked out his first handhold and a couple of deep fissures in between the stones for his toes. He reached out and dug his fingertips deep into the gap, tensing the muscles until the first and second joints were wedged. Then, the moment of truth.

He stretched his right leg out sideways, jammed his toe into another crack and leaned on it to take his weight off the window ledge. Everything held. And so began an agonising, crab-wise climb from the security of the window ledge, out over the drop to the concrete courtyard.

All he could hear was the rushing of blood in his ears and the tiny scuffs as a hand or foot released its grip on the stonework and slid across the face of a block to the next safe harbour. The blocks were rough to the touch, and with each manoeuvre the gritty surface scraped across his chest.

At the halfway point, he went to pull his left toe free prior to moving it to the next foothold. It didn't move. Without thinking, he jerked his leg. The toe of his boot came free and his whole leg swung outwards, unbalancing him.

He felt the fingers of his left hand sliding out of their hold. He glanced up desperately at where his right hand was wedged into a deep crack between two blocks and made as if to force his hand into a fist. With a searing flash of pain, the skin on all four knuckles split as the force of the muscular contraction drove them harder against the enclosing rock.

Now all that held him in place were the top two joints of the fingers of his right hand and an inch or so of boot sole. The momentum as his left leg swung out twisted him around until the Kalashnikov jammed against the wall. He swung back round again until his right cheek was shoved hard up against the stone and his left hand was scrabbling for a hold.

He heaved a sigh of relief as his questing fingertips found a crack in the stonework he was able to exploit and he curled them into it and dug deep for enough strength to arrest his fall.

Breathing heavily from the effort of clinging to the wall, he scraped his left toe up and down, searching for a crack big enough to take it, not daring to look down.

The muscles in his right forearm were screaming as he moved his left knee up and down, circling his foot around for a decent toe-hold.

His ring and little fingers popped out of the crack. What a stupid way to go! After everything he'd been through, to die in a stupid fall. No! This was not happening. This could *not* happen. Not now.

He risked a glance down through the thin space between his chest and the wall. How had he missed it? Just a few inches to the right, a lump of stone protruded from the wall. He lifted his knee and his foot came to rest naturally on its sloped upper surface.

He reinserted his two loose fingers into the handhold and, heart pounding, began inching rightwards.

Finally, he was within striking distance of the window ledge outside Ponting's room. One more move and he'd be able to put his right boot down on the carved block of sandstone.

The sash offered plenty of grips, and its wooden frame and single-glazed panes meant getting through it would be a simple case of kicking it in or shooting straight through it.

Gabriel reached across to his right and curled his outstretched fingers around the edge of the window aperture. Some long-dead stonemason had added a little sculptural flourish to the surround in the form of a twisted barley-sugar decoration.

Offering silent thanks to the man, Gabriel gripped the spiralling grooves and drew the rest of his bodyweight over his right foot until he could step directly onto the window ledge.

He looked in through the multiple panes of glass and there he was, sitting with his back to the window. Ponting.

54

From the back, he could have been any guy in late middle-age. The hair, what was left of it, was bone-white and cut short. At this angle, Gabriel couldn't see Ponting's face except for the line of his cheek and jaw, which were furred with a close-cropped silver beard. He was sitting behind a large wooden desk, a pistol by his right hand, staring at the door on the far side of the room.

The light changed outside. Gabriel glanced up. The moon had emerged from an elliptical gap in the clouds, as if a giant knife had carved a slit in a swatch of dark silk. Gabriel saw his own ghostly face reflected back at him in the glass, overlaid on Ponting's back.

Reaching down, he curled his fingers around the Tokarev's butt and drew the pistol up until it was pointing through the glass at a spot between Ponting's shoulder blades.

Should he just shoot Ponting dead through the glass? It was the safer option. Then he could simply climb in, collect Tara and leave. Gabriel tightened his finger on the trigger.

Then he released it again. No. Because it could never happen like that, could it?

Ponting had to know who was pulling the trigger. He had to know why, as well. To be made aware of the enormity of his crimes.

Ponting had begun his criminal career as a bent cop. A greedy, dishonourable man. But in the years since, he had metamorphosed into a monster.

Men such as he did not deserve to leave the world of the living without a reckoning being made. Bolt-from-the-blue deaths? He-never-even-saw-it-coming deaths? They were for those who lived with honour, or tried to.

So Gabriel shifted his aim by half a foot or so, pushed the Tokarev's muzzle hard against the pane, and pulled the trigger.

As the glass shattered, Gabriel swung himself through, ignoring the scratches and cuts as he burst through the splintered wood and the remaining unbroken panes.

His bullet took Ponting in the right shoulder, ripping through his deltoid muscle and releasing a spray of blood that spattered the desk. He lurched forward, the arm swinging out wide, releasing arcs of blood that hit the walls and ceiling.

Gabriel crashed down into the space behind Ponting in a shower of glass fragments. He was up and diving for the pistol on the desk before Ponting had recovered from the impact.

Yelling in agony and wide-eyed defiance, Ponting made a clumsy left-handed grab for the pistol, but only succeeded in knocking it to the floor. Gabriel raced round the desk and dived onto the fallen weapon.

'That's enough, Ponting!' he roared, getting to his feet with both pistols pointed at Ponting's face.

Using Ponting's own gun, he fired again, hitting Ponting in the left bicep and drawing forth another scream.

'Move again and it's your knees,' Gabriel said as he faced the hated enemy across the desk.

Ponting's eyes were rolling in their sockets. The normal reaction to so much pain would be to cradle the wounded limb, but with both arms out of action he could only sit there with them dangling uselessly by his sides.

His lips parted as if to speak and Gabriel, seized with an overwhelming desire not to hear a single word this monstrous man had to say, jumped over the desk and swiped him across the mouth with the pistol. Teeth flew. Blood followed, dripping in slimy strings into Ponting's lap.

'You killed them all, you bastard,' he hissed. 'Our father. Our mother. Our brother. For that, you're going to die.' He pulled the trigger, hitting Ponting in the stomach. 'For what you and your men did at Srebrenica, you're going to die'. He fired again, to the right side of the chest. 'And for Ali Ibrahimović, you are going to die.'

At these final two words, Gabriel emptied the magazine into Ponting's chest. Foamy scarlet blood erupted from the man's lips and coated his chin as it bubbled down onto his shirt. His head lolled forward on his chest.

It was over.

Gabriel lowered his gun arm and dropped the pistol to the carpet.

He walked around the desk and pushed the dead man's head back. He stared at him, trying to see in the slack features the man Sarah Chow had unearthed in that grainy old newspaper photograph. The ice-blue eyes, unclouded by the passage of time or the burden of any guilt. The mouth, a thin, lipless line.

As he straightened, he heard a click. Without thinking, he dived sideways as a gunshot filled the room with noise. The bullet that would have burst his head like a balloon passed harmlessly to his right and embedded itself in the wall. He scrambled to his right, seeking cover behind the desk. Two more deafening reports shivered the air. Whatever it was, it was big and firing high-powered rounds.

He still had the Tokarev. And if he could get the Kalashnikov free, he could take out the new gunman. If.

Three more rounds slammed into the desk, breaking off chunks and setting the papers inside on fire. Smoke rose from the shattered drawers. Gabriel wondered if there'd be enough to provide cover.

Another two shots followed and at the second, he felt something wrench his right shoulder. What the hell had just happened? He couldn't work it out. It felt as though someone had grabbed the Kalashnikov and tried to pull it off his back.

He slipped the sling off and then all became clear. The shooter had got lucky. Their last shot had hit the barrel just below the foresight, turning a serviceable if inelegant automatic weapon into a club. That left the Tokarev.

How many rounds his assailant had left he didn't want to guess. Or wait for. He crawled over to the other end of the desk, ignoring the pool of blood under the chair in which Ponting slumped.

He rolled out sideways, found his target through the smoke, aimed and squeezed the trigger. The pistol emitted a dry click. The hazy figure turned at the noise. And then a woman spoke.

'Come out, Gabriel Wolfe. Come out now and I will spare your sister. She is downstairs in games room.'

He didn't even have to think. He just stood up and came out from behind the desk, tossing the empty pistol aside. She'd no more refrain from killing Tara than he had from killing her husband. But every second he could delay her was a second when Tara might come out of her coma.

The woman pointing an absurdly large pistol at him – *Desert Eagle*, he had time to think – looked to be about fifty. She had brassy blonde hair worn loose around her shoulders and was wearing a tactical vest over all-black combat gear.

'You know who I am?' she asked.

He realised he did.

'Milena Popović.'

'Very same. Mother to Andrej, who is lying dead with his head blown off from your bullet.' *The sniper at the upper storey window,* Gabriel thought. 'Also Vlado. He is safe in Belgrade. And wife to Ratko Popović, true hero of Serbia.'

'I'm sorry about your son,' Gabriel said. 'He wasn't part of this. But your husband's greed caused the deaths of my parents and my brother. This was my vengeance. Maybe you can understand.' He held his hands wide. 'As his widow, will you swear to keep your word about my sister?'

She held him in a gaze so full of hatred he felt it as a physical force. The pistol hadn't wavered.

'I said I am his wife,' she said slowly. 'Not widow. You make big mistake. But you still kill my baby and for that you pay with your life.'

Something about the appearance of the dead man behind him was clanging in Gabriel's subconscious. Had he made the same mistake twice? First at the house and now here? What was it?

Playing for time, he asked Milena herself.

'Isn't that your husband behind me?'

'Look for yourself,' she said, gesturing with the Desert Eagle's barrel.

Gabriel reversed until the backs of his thighs hit the edge of the desk. Keeping his eyes on Milena, he moved around until he was beside the dead man. He squatted beside him.

Head buzzing, Gabriel frowned. The eyes looked right. The heavy brow, too. And the mouth. Even after all the intervening decades, there was something about the lips that looked right. Why hadn't he looked at the nose? Nothing to see, was there? So why look? But that was the whole point, wasn't it? Nothing to see. But there should have been plenty.

He closed his eyes and the black and white image from the SCMP swam into view. He concentrated, imagining bringing it closer to his eyes. He stared at the burly Special Branch officer standing behind his father. And at the pronounced lump on the bridge of his nose where it had been broken.

He opened his eyes and scrutinised the dead man's face. The nose was smooth, even, regular, and ruler-straight.

No. This *had* to be Ponting. He must have had plastic surgery. Gabriel bent closer, searching for a faint silver line that would indicate a decades-old repair job.

The skin, through flecked with blood, was unblemished. So it was a good plastic surgeon. One of those dodgy operators on the Costa del Sol giving bank robbers new faces for cash under the table.

He swivelled round, keeping low, so that his left side moved into the lee of the heavy wooden desk. He glanced down where one of

Milena's shots had blown the front off a drawer. And there, lying not a foot from his right hand, was a pistol. Unmistakable, even from a quick glance: a second Desert Eagle, this one chrome-plated. The sort of showy, over-compensating gun a gangster might keep within reach during 'friendly' business meetings. Just in case.

'The nose,' he said. 'That's it, isn't it? It's not broken.'

She laughed, a sardonic sound betraying cruelty rather than humour.

'Ratko is handsome man. But his nose? That is ugly. Man called Tomkins break it in fight. Boxing match. Nineteen seventy-seven.'

Gabriel inched his hand into the cavity of the busted-open drawer. The move, when he made it, would have to be fast, precise and perfect. If the gun snagged as he pulled it free, Milena would unload one of those monstrous rounds into his skull or his chest and he'd be dead before he hit the ground. And he'd have to rack the slide just to be sure a round was chambered.

'So who is he, then?' he asked, letting his hand drift half an inch closer to the pistol butt.

'That is Predrag. Most loyal of all our men. He always said he would lay down life for Ratko. Now he has.'

Gabriel closed his hand around the pistol's grip.

'So where is your husband now?'

'He is in 4x4. We kill you then leave before police arrive.'

Gabriel looked up at Milena, picking his spot. It had to be certain and fast. Even in her death throes she could squeeze off a round. It had to be a head shot. He had to cock the gun, straighten his arm, aim, fire and keep firing as she went down.

As he brought his pistol up, and yanked back on the slide, Milena was already turning sideways onto him. Time slowed down. Milena closed one eye. He saw the blood leave her knuckle as she tightened her grip on the trigger.

A man shouted and Milena turned towards the door. The man was carrying a long-barrelled weapon. She fired at him just as he discharged his own weapon. The massive double-boom shattered the silence and the room filled with gun smoke once more. Both had missed. Gabriel didn't.

His shot took Milena in the side of the head. He watched as she fell sideways, arterial blood jetting up to hit the ceiling. Her right hand was still tightly curled around the butt of her pistol as she fell and Gabriel heard the impact as its heavy barrel hit the floor.

55

Beyond her, the man in the hallway stepped into the room. As the smoke cleared, his features resolved into a recognisable face. Danilo. He lowered the shotgun, an over-and-under, and stepped over Milena's corpse.

'Did you tell him?' he asked, jerking his chin at the body behind the desk.

Gabriel shook his head. 'It's not him, Danilo. He's outside. He's waiting for her,' he said, gesturing at the dead woman.

Reality flooded back. Tara! He raced for the stairs, leaving Danilo to catch him up.

He found her in the same position as when he'd left her. Her eyes were closed and when he checked, still rolled up in her head.

He placed his ear to her chest and caught the faint but regular bump of her heartbeat. He checked beneath the dressing. The bleeding had slowed, but she'd need surgery and a blood transfusion before long.

Danilo arrived. 'Your sister?'

'Yes.'

'She is alive?'

'Yes. But she got hit by shrapnel when someone threw a grenade. She's been out cold since.'

Danilo handed the shotgun over. 'Here. Take this,' he said. 'She is a good gun. A Browning. She has never let me down. Go after Popović. I will stay here with your sister.'

Gabriel accepted the gun and the spare cartridges Danilo handed him. He raced off, heading for the main door. It stood ajar. From the other side, Gabriel could hear an engine idling. Light crept under the door. So the 4x4 was facing the castle. Ponting was waiting for Milena to emerge, maybe clutching a bloody souvenir of her encounter with the man Ponting had been avoiding for so long.

He looked around for the light switches and found a bank of them beside a window. He turned them all off, plunging the hall into darkness, then headed towards the door. But he stopped short.

Ponting would be expecting his wife to be the next person to emerge from the door. The sign of a shirtless man wielding a shotgun would produce one of two reactions. Shots. Or a rapid escape. Gabriel wanted neither.

He thought back to the games room. Maybe if Ponting was expecting his wife, he should *see* his wife. Gabriel ran down the hall, back to where Danilo was bending over Tara's supine form. He'd brought a bowl of water and some cloths and was gently dabbing her face clean of the mud that still besmirched it. He looked up as Gabriel arrived.

'Is everything OK?'

'No. But it will be,' Gabriel said, walking past the sofa to the corner and the partially deflated sex doll.

'How is she?' he asked, as he snatched the blonde wig off the doll's head.

'A little stronger. Her eyes are moving now. Under the, ah, the…'

'Lids.'

'Yes, the lids. I think she is no longer unconscious, but asleep. Go, go. I will take care of her.'

'I need your jacket,' Gabriel said.

Wordlessly, Danilo stood and shucked off his dark hunting jacket. He handed it to Gabriel, who buttoned it right up to his throat. Under close inspection it would bear little resemblance to Milena's tactical gear, but it would give Gabriel a couple of seconds. And that was all he needed.

At the front door, Gabriel rested the shotgun against the wall while he pulled the wig on. He was ready.

He pulled the door wide open, keeping behind it as it swung inwards. Then, as if keeping a pursuer at bay, he backed out fast, the shotgun up at his shoulder. Clear of the doorway, he fell sideways, rolled and was up on his feet again next to the 4x4. He smashed the drop glass with the shotgun's muzzle and aimed in through the aperture at the side of Ponting's head.

Ponting jerked his head round, open-mouthed, still trying to process what had just happened. He didn't even have a gun in his lap. Clearly he'd not been expecting any survivors.

'She's dead, Ponting.'

'What?'

'Your wife. Milena. She's dead. Now it's your turn.'

Ponting shook his head. 'You don't have to do this. Just tell me what you want. It's yours.'

'Can you bring my parents back?'

'What? No, but I can—'

'How about my brother? He was five when he died.'

'Look, Gabriel, please, just listen. I screwed up, OK? I know that. But you have to understand, they paid us nothing out there. Not really. Not for what we were doing. We were risking our lives for peanuts.'

Gabriel shook his head, disgusted.

'Don't kill me!' Ponting whined, holding his hands out to Gabriel in supplication. 'Please let me live.'

Gabriel scowled. Was this really how his search for vengeance ended? He'd been expecting a battle-scarred warlord and all he'd found was a pathetic coward pleading for his own life.

Then the shotgun's barrel jerked forwards. He almost lost his grip as Ponting grabbed the barrel with both hands and yanked it in towards him.

'Fuck you, Wolfe!' he screamed. 'You killed my son. You killed my wife! Fuck you! F—'

Gabriel hooked his finger round the trigger and pulled back.

Amplified by the cabin, the shotgun blast was enormous, temporarily deafening Gabriel. The pellets blew a ragged hole in the roof.

Ponting had managed to lift the barrel just as Gabriel squeezed the trigger. He screamed and fell back against the seat, grasping the bloody stump of his right wrist with his left hand. It was the only hand left to him: the other had been blocking the muzzle as Gabriel fired.

Gabriel yanked back on the shotgun and pulled the trigger. Nothing happened. He cursed himself for his inattention. This wasn't an AK with a thirty-round magazine. It was a break-action shotgun. Danilo had used the first shell to shoot at Milena. The second round, Gabriel had just discharged.

Wild-eyed, Ponting gaped at Gabriel. Then he spun round in his seat and opened the driver's door, tumbling out on the concrete. Gabriel raced round the front of the 4x4, but Ponting was already running towards the castle gate, clutching his ruined wrist to his chest.

The gate was open, ready for Ponting and Milena to drive through and escape justice.

Gabriel caught up with him a few feet beyond the threshold. The bodies of the men he and Tara had killed lay scattered about. Ponting dived to the ground and let go of his wrist to scrabble at a dead man's hip, trying to release the pistol from its holster.

Blood sprayed out from the uncapped arteries, hitting Ponting in the face. He swiped at his eyes with his left hand, temporarily abandoning his tussle with the holster. And then Gabriel was on him.

He wrenched Ponting's torso up and away from the dead man and smashed a fist into his blood-spattered face. Ponting tried to roll away but Gabriel stamped down on his right forearm, drawing forth a howl from Ponting's stretched lips.

Then Ponting did something strange. Pinioned by Gabriel's

boot, he jack-knifed sideways, bending his whole body into a 'C'. His left hand shot down towards his ankle.

Gabriel realised what was happening too late to prevent it. Ponting's hand came away from his boot clutching a knife. It arced around and the point buried itself in Gabriel's calf muscle. The sharp burst of agony lanced upwards, through Gabriel's knee and into his groin. He yelled out and jumped back, but not before Ponting had twisted the knife in an attempt to widen the wound he'd inflicted.

'Thought I was finished?' Ponting grunted, staggering to his feet.

White teeth grinning from his bloody mask of a face, he waved his stump at Gabriel. The blood was no longer spurting. The arteries had snapped back up inside the arm and contracted, choking off the flow of blood: the body's natural reflex to the injury.

The knife wove from side to side as Ponting held it out in front of him.

'Maybe I'll go for the full set, eh, boy?' he said, feinting left then jabbing the knife towards Gabriel's chest. 'Get you and your sister and that's everyone.'

By now Gabriel was facing back towards the castle. Ponting stood directly between him and the gate, lit by a floodlight that had just snapped on, bathing the pair of them in a fierce white glare. Gabriel looked down. Ponting's shadow stretched between them, its hard edge just missing Gabriel's right foot.

'Goodbye, Ponting,' Gabriel said, standing perfectly still and letting his hands drop to his sides. 'This is for my parents, for my brother…' He paused and looked past Ponting's left shoulder, 'and for Ali Ibrahimović.'

Ponting frowned. 'What?'

A flat crack broke the silence. Ponting's eyes widened and his mouth dropped open. Blood overflowed his lower lip and ran down over his chin, staining his beard red. It hugged the contours of his jaw before splitting into two streams around the broadhead protruding from his throat.

His good hand reached up as if to pluck the arrow from his

flesh. It made it as far as his breastbone before falling back. Eyes wide with dawning comprehension, he took a step towards Gabriel.

Gabriel took the knife from him and plunged it straight into his chest, over the heart. He let go and shoved the dead man away from him to topple back onto the turf.

Standing in the gateway, Danilo lowered the crossbow from his shoulder.

56

Gabriel, Tara and Danilo sat at a scrubbed pine table in the kitchen. Danilo had made coffee and then dressed Gabriel's wound.

'Tara woke up just after you left,' Danilo said. 'I have checked her temperature. She has no fever and I found some strong painkillers in a bathroom. I don't think the wound is infected, but we need to get her to a hospital.'

'We need to clean up a bit first.'

Danilo peered at Gabriel's face. 'You don't look too bad, all things considered.'

Gabriel smiled. 'I meant the bodies,' he said.

It took them almost an hour to drag all the corpses down to the dungeon. Gabriel fetched a couple of jerrycans of petrol and doused them, before emptying the rest of the fuel over the floor. From the top of the stairs, he flicked a lighter and tossed it down. The final step was to drag a floor-to-ceiling cupboard full of video games across to block the door.

He supposed the Serb authorities might find a reason to investigate at some point, but by then, he and Tara would be long gone. He didn't imagine the persecutors would lose too much sleep over a missing gangster and his men.

At the door of the 4x4 with the shotgun-blasted roof, Danilo touched Gabriel on the arm.

'I came on my quad bike,' he said. 'Follow me back to my cottage. I will leave it there. Then I can give you directions to the hospital.'

Gabriel nodded and started the engine.

On the way to the hospital, Gabriel and Danilo came up with a plausible story to explain his and Tara's wounds. A faulty prop on the set of the action film they were shooting up at the castle. It also gave a degree of plausibility to Gabriel's injuries. Danilo, their local guide had volunteered to transport them to hospital while the film crew stayed behind to repair the damage.

One of the nurses in the emergency room knew Danilo, greeting him with a concerned look as she knelt by the injured woman in a wheelchair. A doctor arrived next, dark circles beneath her eyes. As Danilo explained what had happened, Gabriel could see from her nods and relaxed yet alert posture that the story was sticking. She asked a few questions, which Danilo answered confidently, shrugging occasionally and raising his hands in the universal, 'whaddya gonna do?' gesture. Then she knelt in front of Tara.

'I am Doctor Vegri,' she said in English. 'Can I look at your injury?'

Tara nodded.

Gently, the doctor lifted the edge of the improvised field dressing and peered at the torn flesh beneath. She nodded, apparently satisfied, and swivelled around to Gabriel.

'You are also hurt, Danilo said.'

Gabriel rolled up his trouser to reveal the dressed stab wound. She lifted it and considered the state of his leg. She frowned and pursed her lips.

'It is a clean cut. You are lucky. It needs stitches but there does not appear to be any sign of infection.'

She stood, and paused just long enough to say, 'Miss Wong will be fine. But now we must get her into surgery. One of my colleagues will be along to take care of you.'

They wheeled Tara away, the doctor issuing instructions to a couple of juniors who'd appeared as she marched along.

Danilo led Gabriel to a row of hard plastic chairs beside an empty vending machine.

'Don't worry. I am sure the doctors know what they are doing.'

Gabriel nodded. 'Of course. Listen, Danilo, thanks for coming out when you did. You saved my life. But what made you come up to the castle?'

Danilo rubbed a hand over his face. Suddenly he looked exhausted.

'I wasn't going to. Not at first. I thought to myself, well, here is a fit young man. A trained marksman, no less. He is going to kill Ratko Popović. I thought I would leave you to it. But then, no!' He thumped his thigh. 'I said, really, Danilo? You are going to send him off with a borrowed crossbow and a hunting knife. Against that bastard. So I got my gun and mounted my quad bike and came to help.'

'You could have been killed.'

'Yes. I could, couldn't I? But I am eighty-five years old. I have lived a good life, or as good as I could manage. I have nobody left,' he said with a grimace. 'So I said to myself, maybe this is your last day on earth, Danilo Nušić. But then you will be with Svetlana and Nina again.'

Gabriel held out his hand, which Danilo gripped, maybe with a little less force than the first time they'd shaken hands.

'Thank you.'

'You look, pardon me for saying this, Gabriel, like shit. I am going to find a place that will sell an old man a coffee and a sandwich. Try to sleep. Tara will be a while yet and who knows when they will be ready to stitch you up.'

Gabriel watched as the old man walked off, his head switching from side to side at each intersecting corridor as he looked for a cafe.

He felt fatigue envelop him like a heavy blanket from which there was no possibility of escape. Feeling safe for the first time in days, he allowed his eyes to close. He breathed deeply and let the sounds of the hospital quieten. He listened to approaching footsteps without alarm.

'You did well to sell the house,' Master Zhao said, taking the vacant seat beside him and lighting a cigarette. Gabriel turned to him.

'You're not angry?'

'Angry? Why should I be? Listen to me, Wolfe Cub. Our roots are not twined through the fabric of buildings, any more than they're caught around possessions, like those fast cars you're so fond of. Your roots are your family. You have Tara. Spend time with her. Keep in touch with her.'

'I have Eli, too.'

'Yes, of course you do. She is your family in the here and now, and in the years to come. You've spent too much time looking back, Wolfe Cub. Now you must look forward. To the life you build with her.'

'I know, Master. I was scared before. Scared I'd lose her like I lost Britta.'

'So, tell me, what has changed?'

'I realised that there are no guarantees in this life. We could both resign from The Department and train as teachers and then get killed in a car accident, or get cancer.'

'And what do you take from this realisation?'

'That the only thing that matters is living well – I mean living a good life, like Danilo said. I should try to do what I can to make every day as good as I can make it. Act in good faith. Love those I can and do what I must to protect them.'

Master Zhao nodded and smiled. 'And?'

'And accept that I can't control everything.'

'It sounds as though you have finally learned all the lessons I ever wanted to teach you.'

'I feel you told me those things many years ago.'

'I did, Wolfe Cub, I did. You just weren't ready to hear them.'

Master Zhao stood.

'I'll be going now. I think Danilo is coming back.'

Gabriel followed suit, looking at the man who had guided him for his entire adult life and half his childhood, feeling unaccountably anxious.

'Will I see you again, Master?'

'Of course! I am in your heart as well as your head, Wolfe Cub. You won't get rid of me that easily.'

He left, following the strip of red tape stuck to the floor until it turned a corner and he disappeared.

Gabriel opened his eyes and turned to look at the empty chair to his left. He stretched out a hand and placed it, palm-down, on the plastic. It was cold to the touch.

A nurse was walking down the corridor towards him. He searched her face for a clue. His pulse stuttered, unable to find a rhythm. His palms were sweaty.

The nurse arrived at the row of chairs and squatted in front of him.

She smiled. 'You can see her now.'

ACKNOWLEDGMENTS

I want to thank you for buying this book. I hope you enjoyed it. As an author is only part of the team of people who make a book the best it can be, this is my chance to thank the people on *my* team.

For being my first readers, Sarah Hunt and Jo Maslen.

For their brilliant copy-editing and proofreading Nicola Lovick and Liz Ward.

For being a daily inspiration and source of love and laughter, and making it all worthwhile, my family: Jo, Rory and Jacob.

I'd also like to thank the members of my Readers' Group, The Wolfe Pack. Owwoooo!

And Anne Cater for organising the blog tour to launch *Crooked Shadow*, plus all the brilliant book bloggers who do so much to connect readers and writers.

The responsibility for any and all mistakes in this book remains mine. I assure you, they were unintentional.

Andy Maslen
Salisbury, 2021

ABOUT THE AUTHOR

Photo © 2020 Kin Ho

Andy Maslen was born in Nottingham, England. After leaving university with a degree in psychology, he worked in business for thirty years as a copywriter. In his spare time, he plays blues guitar. He lives in Wiltshire.

READ ON FOR AN EXTRACT FROM *SHALLOW GROUND*,
THE FIRST BOOK IN THE DETECTIVE FORD
THRILLERS…

EXTRACT FROM SHALLOW GROUND

Summer | Pembrokeshire Coast, Wales

Ford leans out from the limestone rock face halfway up Pen-y-holt sea stack, shaking his forearms to keep the blood flowing. He and Lou have climbed the established routes before. Today, they're attempting a new line he spotted. She was reluctant at first, but she's also competitive and he really wanted to do the climb.

'I'm not sure. It looks too difficult,' she'd said when he suggested it.

'Don't tell me you've lost your bottle?' he said with a grin.

'No, but . . .'

'Well, then. Let's go. Unless you'd rather climb one of the easy ones again?'

She frowned. 'No. Let's do it.'

They scrambled down a gully, hopping across boulders from the cliff to a shallow ledge just above sea level at the bottom of the route. She stands there now, patiently holding his ropes while he climbs. But the going's much harder than he expected. He's wasted a lot of time attempting to navigate a tricky bulge. Below him, Lou plays out rope through a belay device.

371

He squints against the bright sunshine as a light wind buffets him. Herring gulls wheel around the stack, calling in alarm at this brightly coloured interloper assaulting their territory.

He looks down at Lou and smiles. Her eyes are a piercing blue. He remembers the first time he saw her. He was captivated by those eyes, drawn in, powerless, like an old wooden sailing ship spiralling down into a whirlpool. He paid her a clumsy compliment, which she accepted with more grace than he'd managed.

Lou smiles back up at him now. Even after seven years of marriage, his heart thrills that she should bestow such a radiant expression on him.

Rested, he starts climbing again, trying a different approach to the overhang. He reaches up and to his right for a block. It seems solid enough, but his weight pulls it straight off.

He falls outwards, away from the flat plane of lichen-scabbed limestone, and jerks to a stop at the end of his rope. The force turns him into a human pendulum. He swings inwards, slamming face-first against the rock and gashing his chin. Then out again to dangle above Lou on the ledge.

Ford tries to stay calm as he slowly rotates. His straining fingertips brush the rock face then arc into empty air.

Then he sees two things that frighten him more than the fall.

The rock he dislodged, as large as a microwave, has smashed down on to Lou. She's sitting awkwardly, white-faced, and he can see blood on her leggings. Those sapphire-blue eyes are wide with pain.

And waves are now lapping at the ledge. The tide is on its way in, not out. Somehow, he misread the tide table, or he took too long getting up the first part of the climb. He damns himself for his slowness.

'I can lower you down,' she screams up at him. 'But my leg, I think it's broken.'

She gets him down safely and he kisses her fiercely before crouching by her right leg to assess the damage. There's a sharp lump distending the bloody Lycra, and he knows what it is. Bone.

'It's bad, Lou. I think it's a compound fracture. But if you can stand on your good leg, we can get back the way we came.'

'I can't!' she cries, pain contorting her face. 'Call the coastguard.'

He pulls out his phone, but there's no mobile service down here.

'Shit! There's no signal.'

'You'll have to go for help.'

'I can't leave you, darling.'

A wave crashes over the ledge and douses them both.

Her eyes widen. 'You have to! The tide's coming in.'

He knows she's right. And it's all his fault. He pulled the block off the crag.

'Lou, I—'

She grabs his hand and squeezes so hard it hurts. 'You *have* to.'

Another wave hits. His mouth fills with seawater. He swallows half of it and retches. He looks back the way they came. The boulders they hopped along are awash. There's no way Lou can make it.

He's crying now. He can't do it.

Then she presses the only button she has left. 'If you stay here, we'll *both* die. Then who'll look after Sam?'

Sam is eight and a half. Born two years before they married. He's being entertained by Louisa's parents while they're at Pen-y-holt. Ford knows she's right. He can't leave Sam an orphan. They were meant to be together for all time. But now, time has run out.

'Go!' she screams. 'Before it's too late.'

So he leaves her, checking the gear first so he's sure she can't be swept away. He falls into an eerie calm as he swims across to the cliff and solos out.

At the clifftop, rock gives way to scrubby grass. He pulls out his phone. Four bars. He calls the coastguard, giving them a concise description of the accident, the location and Lou's injury. Then he slumps. The calmness that saved his life has vanished. He is hyperventilating, heaving in great breaths that won't bring enough oxygen to his brain, and sighing them out again.

A wave of nausea rushes through him and sweat flashes out

across his skin. The wind chills it, making him shudder with the sudden cold. He lurches to his right and spews out a thin stream of bile on to the grass.

Then his stomach convulses and his breakfast rushes up and out, spattering the sleeve of his jacket. He retches out another splash of stinking yellow liquid and then dry-heaves until, cramping, his guts settle. His view is blurred through a film of tears.

He falls back and lies there for ten more minutes, looking up into the cloudless sky. Odd how realistic this dream is. He could almost believe he just left his wife to drown.

He sobs, a cracked sound that the wind tears away from his lips and disperses into the air. And the dream blackens and reality is here, and it's ugly and painful and true.

He hears a helicopter. Sees its red-and-white form hovering over Pen-y-holt.

Time ceases to have any meaning as he watches the rescue. How long has passed, he doesn't know.

Now a man in a bright orange flying suit is standing in front of him explaining that his wife, Sam's mother, has drowned.

Later, there are questions from the local police. They treat him with compassion, especially as he's Job, like them.

The coroner rules death by misadventure.

But Ford knows the truth.

He killed her. *He* pushed her into trying the climb. *He* dislodged the block that smashed her leg. And *he* left her to drown while he saved his own skin.

DAY ONE, 5.00 P.M

SIX YEARS LATER | SUMMER | SALISBURY

Angie Halpern trudged up the five gritty stone steps to the front door. The shift on the cancer ward had been a long one. Ten hours. It had ended with a patient vomiting on the back of her head. She'd washed it out at work, crying at the thought that it would make her lifeless brown hair flatter still.

Free from the hospital's clutches, she'd collected Kai from Donna, the childminder, and then gone straight to the food bank – again. Bone-tired, her mood hadn't been improved when an elderly woman on the bus told her she looked like she needed to eat more: 'A pretty girl like you shouldn't be that thin.'

And now, here she was, knackered, hungry and with a three-year-old whining and grizzling and dragging on her free hand. Again.

'Kai!' she snapped. 'Let go, or Mummy can't get her keys out.'

The little boy stopped crying just long enough to cast a shocked look up into his mother's eyes before resuming, at double the volume.

Fearing what she might do if she didn't get inside, Angie half-turned so he couldn't cling back on to her hand, and dug out her keys. She fumbled one of the bags of groceries, but in a dexterous act of juggling righted it before it spilled the tins, packets and jars all over the steps.

She slotted the brass Yale key home and twisted it in the lock. Elbowing the door open, she nudged Kai with her right knee, encouraging him to precede her into the hallway. Their flat occupied the top floor of the converted Victorian townhouse. Ahead, the stairs, with their patched and stained carpet, beckoned.

'Come on, Kai, in we go,' she said, striving to inject into her voice the tone her own mother called 'jollying along'.

'No!' the little boy said, stamping his booted foot and sticking his pudgy hands on his hips. 'I hate Donna. I hate the foobang. And I. Hate. YOU!'

Feeling tears pricking at the back of her eyes, Angie put the bags down and picked her son up under his arms. She squeezed him, burying her nose in the sweet-smelling angle between his neck and shoulder. How was it possible to love somebody so much and also to wish for them just to shut the hell up? Just for one little minute.

She knew she wasn't the only one with problems. Talking to the other nurses, or chatting late at night online, confirmed it. Everyone reckoned the happily married ones with enough money to last from one month to the next were the exception, not the rule.

'Mummy, you're hurting me!'

'Oh, Jesus! Sorry, darling. Look, come on. Let's just get the shopping upstairs and you can watch a *Thomas* video.'

'I hate *Thomas*.'

'*Thunderbirds*, then.'

'I hate them even more.'

Angie closed her eyes, sighing out a breath like the online mindfulness gurus suggested. 'Then you'll just have to stare out of the bloody window, like I used to. Now, come on!'

He sucked in a huge breath. Angie flinched, but the scream never came. Instead, Kai's scrunched-up eyes opened wide and swivelled sideways. She followed his gaze and found herself facing a good-looking man wearing a smart jacket and trousers. He had a kind smile.

'I'm sorry,' the man said in a quiet voice. 'I couldn't help seeing your little boy's . . . he's tired, I suppose. You left the door open and as I was coming to this address anyway . . .' He tailed off, looking embarrassed, eyes downcast.

'You were coming *here*?' she asked.

He looked up at her again. 'Yes,' he said, smiling. 'I was looking for Angela Halpern.'

'That's me.' She paused, frowning, as she tried to place him. 'Do I know you?'

'Mummee!' Kai hissed from her waist, where he was clutching her.

'Quiet, darling, please.'

The man smiled. 'Would you like a hand with your bags? I see you have your hands full with the little fellow there.' Then he squatted down, so that his face was at the same level as Kai's. 'Hello. My name's Harvey. What's yours?'

'Kai. Are you a policeman?'

Harvey laughed, a warm, soft-edged sound. 'No. I'm not a policeman.'

'Mummy's a nurse. At the hospital. Do you work there?'

'Me? Funnily enough, I do.'

'Are you a nurse?'

'No. But I do help people. Which I think is a bit of a coincidence. Do you know that word?'

The little boy shook his head.

'It's just a word grown-ups use when two things happen that are the same. Kai,' he said, dropping his voice to a conspiratorial whisper, 'do you want to know a secret?'

Kai nodded, smiling and wiping his nose on his sleeve.

'There's a big hospital in London called Bart's. And I think it rhymes with' – he paused and looked left and right – 'farts.'

Kai squawked with laughter.

Harvey stood, knees popping. 'I hope that was OK. The naughty word. It usually seems to make them laugh.'

Angie smiled. She felt relief that this helpful stranger hadn't seen fit to judge her. To tut, roll his eyes or give any of the dozens of subtle signals the free-and-easy brigade found to diminish her. 'It's fine, really. You said you'd come to see me?'

'Oh, yes, of course, sorry. I'm from the food bank. The Purcell Foundation?' he said. 'They've asked me to visit a few of our customers, to find out what they think about the quality of the service. I was hoping you'd have ten minutes for a chat. If it's not a good time, I can come back.'

Angie sighed. Then she shook her head. 'No, it's fine . . . Harvey, did you say your name was?'

He nodded.

'Give me a hand with the bags and I'll put the kettle on. I picked up some teabags this afternoon, so we can christen the packet.'

'Let me take those,' he said, bending down and snaking his fingers through the loops in the carrier-bag handles. 'Where to, madam?' he added in a jokey tone.

'We're on the third floor, I'm afraid.'

Harvey smiled. 'Not to worry, I'm in good shape.'

Reaching the top of the stairs, Angie elbowed the light switch and then unlocked the door, while Harvey kept up a string of tall tales for Kai.

'And then the chief doctor said' – he adopted a deep voice – '"No, no, that's never going to work. You need to use a hosepipe!"'

Kai's laughter echoed off the bare, painted walls of the stairwell.

'Here we are,' Angie said, pushing the door open. 'The kitchen's at the end of the hall.'

She stood aside, watching Harvey negotiate the cluttered hallway and deposit the shopping bags on her pine kitchen table. She followed him, noticing the scuff marks on the walls, the sticky fat spatters behind the hob, and feeling a lump in her throat.

'Kai, why don't you go and watch telly?' she asked her son, steering him out of the kitchen and towards the sitting room.

'A film?' he asked.

She glanced up at the clock. Five to six. 'It's almost teatime.'

'Pleeease?'

378

She smiled. 'OK. But you come when I call you for tea. Pasta and red sauce, your favourite.'

'Yummy.'

She turned back to Harvey, who was unloading the groceries on to the table. A sob swelled in her throat. She choked it back.

He frowned. 'Is everything all right, Angela?'

The noise from the TV was loud, even from the other room. She turned away so this stranger wouldn't see her crying. It didn't matter that he was a colleague, of sorts. He could see what she'd been reduced to, and that was enough.

'Yes, yes, sorry. It's just, you know, the food bank. I never thought my life would turn out like this. Then I lost my husband and things just got on top of me.'

'Mmm,' he said. 'That was careless of you.'

'What?' She turned round, uncertain of what she'd heard.

He was lifting a tin of baked beans out of the bag. 'I said, it was careless of you. To lose your husband.'

She frowned. Trying to make sense of his remark. The cruel tone. The staring, suddenly dead eyes.

'Look, I don't know what you—'

The tin swung round in a half-circle and crashed against her left temple.

'Oh,' she moaned, grabbing the side of her head and staggering backwards.

Her palm was wet. Her blood was hot. She was half-blind with the pain. Her back met the cooker and she slumped to the ground. He was there in front of her, crouching down, just like he'd done with Kai. Only he wasn't telling jokes any more. And he wasn't smiling.

'Please keep quiet,' he murmured, 'or I'll have to kill Kai as well. Are you expecting anyone?'

'N-nobody,' she whispered, shaking. She could feel the blood running inside the collar of her shirt. And the pain, oh, the pain. It felt as though her brain was pushing her eyes out of their sockets.

He nodded. 'Good.'

Then he encircled her neck with his hands, looked into her eyes and squeezed.

I'm so sorry, Kai. I hope Auntie Cherry looks after you properly when I'm gone. I hope . . .

* * *

Casting a quick glance towards the kitchen door and the hallway beyond, and reassured by the blaring noise from the TV, Harvey crouched by Angie's inert body and increased the pressure.

Her eyes bulged, and her tongue, darkening already from that natural rosy pink to the colour of raw liver, protruded from between her teeth.

From his jacket he withdrew an empty blood bag. He connected the outlet tube and inserted a razor-tipped trocar into the other end. He placed them to one side and dragged her jeans over her hips, tugging them down past her knees. With the joints free to move, he pushed his hands between her thighs and shoved them apart.

He inserted the needle into her thigh so that it met and travelled a few centimetres up into the right femoral artery. Then he laid the blood bag on the floor and watched as the scarlet blood shot into the clear plastic tube and surged along it.

With a precious litre of blood distending the bag, he capped it off and removed the tube and the trocar. With Angie's heart pumping her remaining blood on to the kitchen floor tiles, he stood and placed the bag inside his jacket. He could feel it through his shirt, warm against his skin. He took her purse out of her bag, found the card he wanted and removed it.

He wandered down the hall and poked his head round the door frame of the sitting room. The boy was sitting cross-legged, two feet from the TV, engrossed in the adventures of a blue cartoon dog.

'Tea's ready, Kai,' he said, in a sing-song tone.

Protesting, but clambering to his feet, the little boy extended a pudgy hand holding the remote and froze the action, then dropped the control to the carpet.

Harvey held out his hand and the boy took it, absently, still staring at the screen.

DAY TWO, 8.15 A.M.

Arriving at Bourne Hill Police Station, Detective Inspector Ford sighed, fingering the scar on his chin. *What better way to start the sixth anniversary of your wife's death than with a shouting match over breakfast with your fifteen-year-old son?*

The row had ended in an explosive exchange that was fast, raw and brutal:

'I hate you! I wish you'd died instead of Mum.'

'Yeah? Guess what? So do I!'

All the time they'd been arguing, he'd seen Lou's face, battered by submerged rocks in the sea off the Pembrokeshire coast.

Pushing the memory of the argument aside, he ran a hand over the top of his head, trying to flatten down the spikes of dark, grey-flecked hair.

He pushed through the double glass doors. Straight into the middle of a ruckus.

A scrawny man in faded black denim and a raggy T-shirt was swearing at a young woman in a dark suit. Eyes wide, she had backed against an orange wall. He could see a Wiltshire police ID on a lanyard round her neck, but he didn't recognise her.

The two female civilian staff behind the desk were on their feet, one with a phone clamped to her ear.

The architects who'd designed the interior of the new station at Bourne Hill had persuaded senior management that the traditional thick glass screen wasn't 'welcoming'. Now any arsehole could decide to lean across the three feet of white-surfaced MDF and abuse, spit on or otherwise ruin the day of the hardworking receptionists. He saw the other woman reach under the desk for the panic button.

'Why are you ignoring me, eh? I just asked where the toilets are, you bitch!' the man yelled at the woman backed against the wall.

Ford registered the can of strong lager in the man's left hand and strode over. The woman was pale, and her mouth had tightened to a lipless line.

'I asked you a question. What's wrong with you?' the drunk shouted.

Ford shot out his right hand and grabbed him by the back of his T-shirt. He yanked him backwards, sticking out a booted foot and rolling him over his knee to send him flailing to the floor.

Ford followed him down and drove a knee in between his shoulder blades. The man gasped out a loud 'Oof!' as his lungs emptied. Ford gripped his wrist and jerked his arm up in a tight angle, then turned round and called over his shoulder, 'Could someone get some cuffs, please? This . . . gentleman . . . will be cooling off in a cell.'

A pink-cheeked uniform raced over and snapped a pair of rigid Quik-Cuffs on to the man's wrists.

'Thanks, Mark,' Ford said, getting to his feet. 'Get him over to Custody.'

'Charge, sir?'

'Drunk and disorderly? Common assault? Being a jerk in a built-up area? Just get him booked in.'

The PC hustled the drunk to his feet, reciting the formal arrest and caution script while walking him off in an armlock to see the custody sergeant.

Ford turned to the woman who'd been the focus of his newest collar's unwelcome attentions. 'I'm sorry about that. Are you OK?'

She answered as if she were analysing an incident she'd witnessed on CCTV. 'I think so. He didn't hit me, and swearing doesn't cause physical harm. Although I am feeling quite anxious as a result.'

'I'm not surprised.' Ford gestured at her ID. 'Are you here to meet someone? I haven't seen you round here before.'

She nodded. 'I'm starting work here today. And my new boss is . . . hold on . . .' She fished a sheet of paper from a brown canvas messenger bag slung over her left shoulder. 'Alec Reid.'

Now Ford understood. She was the new senior crime scene investigator. Her predecessor had transferred up to Thames Valley Police to move with her husband's new job. Alec managed the small forensics team at Salisbury and had been crowing about his new hire for weeks now.

'My new deputy has a PhD, Ford,' he'd said over a pint in the Wyndham Arms one evening. 'We're going up in the world.'

Ford stuck his hand out. 'DI Ford.'

'Pleased to meet you,' she said, taking his hand and pumping it up and down three times before releasing it. 'My name is Dr Hannah Fellowes. I was about to get my ID sorted when that man started shouting at me.'

'I doubt it was anything about you in particular. Just wrong place, wrong time.'

She nodded, frowning up at him. 'Although, technically, this *is* the right place. As I'm going to be working here.' She checked her watch, a multifunction Casio with more dials and buttons than the dash of Ford's ageing Land Rover Discovery. 'It's also 8.15, so it's the right time as well.'

Ford smiled. 'Let's get your ID sorted, then I'll take you up to Alec. He arrives early most days.'

He led her over to the long, low reception desk.

'This is—'

'Dr Hannah Fellowes,' she said to the receptionist. 'I'm pleased to meet you.'

She thrust her right hand out across the counter. The receptionist took it and received the same three stiff shakes as Ford.

The receptionist smiled up at her new colleague, but Ford could see the concern in her eyes. 'I'm Paula. Nice to meet you, too, Hannah. Are you all right? I'm so sorry you had to deal with that on your first day.'

'It was a shock. But it won't last. I don't let things like that get to me.'

Paula smiled. 'Good for you!'

While Paula converted a blank rectangle of plastic into a functioning station ID, Hannah turned to Ford.

'Should I ask her to call me Dr Fellowes, or is it usual here to use first names?' she whispered.

'We mainly use Christian names, but if you'd like to be known as Dr Fellowes, now would be the time.'

Hannah nodded and turned back to Paula, who handed her the swipe card in a clear case.

'There you go, Hannah. Welcome aboard.'

'Thank you.' A beat. 'Paula.'

'Do you know where you're going?'

'I'll take her,' Ford said.

At the lift, he showed her how to swipe her card before pressing the floor button.

'If you don't do that, you just stand in the lift not going anywhere. It's mainly the PTBs who do it.'

'PTBs?' she repeated, as the lift door closed in front of them.

'Powers That Be. Management?'

'Oh. Yes. That's funny. PTBs. Powers That Be.'

She didn't laugh, though, and Ford had the odd sensation that he was talking to a foreigner, despite her southern English accent. She stared straight ahead as the lift ascended. Ford took a moment to assess her appearance. She was shorter than him by a good half-foot, no more than five-five or six. Slim, but not skinny. Blonde hair woven into plaits, a style Ford had always associated with children.

He'd noticed her eyes downstairs; it was hard not to, they'd been so wide when the drunk had had her backed against the wall. But even relaxed, they were large, and coloured the blue of old china.

The lift pinged and a computerised female voice announced, 'Third floor.'

'You're down here,' Ford said, turning right and leading Hannah along the edge of an open-plan office. He gestured left. 'General CID. I'm Major Crimes on the fourth floor.'

She took a couple of rapid, skipping steps to catch up with him. 'Is Forensics open plan as well? I was told it was a quiet office.'

'I think it's safe to say it's quiet. Come on. Let's get you a tea first. Or coffee. Which do you like best?'

'That's a hard question. I haven't really tried enough types to know.' She shook her head, like a dog trying to dislodge a flea from its ear. 'No. What I meant to say was, I'd like to have a tea, please. Thank you.'

There it was again. The foreigner-in-England vibe he'd picked up downstairs.

While he boiled a kettle and fussed around with a teabag and the jar of instant coffee, he glanced at Hannah. She was staring at him, but smiled when he caught her eye. The expression popped dimples into her cheeks.

'Something puzzling you?' he asked.

'You didn't tell me your name,' she said.

'I think I did. It's Ford.'

'No. I meant your first name. You said, "We mainly use Christian names," when the receptionist, Paula, was doing my building ID. And you called me Hannah. But you didn't tell me yours.'

Ford pressed the teabag against the side of the mug before scooping it out and dropping it into a swing-topped bin. He handed the mug to Hannah. 'Careful, it's hot.'

'Thank you. But your name?'

'Ford's fine. Really. Or DI Ford, if we're being formal.'

'OK.' She smiled. Deeper dimples this time, like little curved cuts. 'You're Ford. I'm Hannah. If we're being formal, maybe you *should* call me Dr Fellowes.'

Ford couldn't tell if she was joking. He took a swig of his coffee. 'Let's go and find Alec. He's talked of little else since you accepted his job offer.'

'It's probably because I'm extremely well qualified. After earning my doctorate, which I started at Oxford and finished at Harvard, I worked in America for a while. I consulted to city, state and federal law enforcement agencies. I also lectured at Quantico for the FBI.'

Ford blinked, struggling to process this hyper-concentrated CV. It sounded like that of someone ten or twenty years older than the slender young woman sipping tea from a Spire FM promotional mug.

'That's pretty impressive. Sorry, you're how old?'

'Don't be sorry. We only met twenty minutes ago. I'm thirty-three.'

Ford reflected that at her age he had just been completing his sergeant's exams. His promotion to inspector had come through a month ago and he was still feeling, if not out of his depth, then at least under the microscope. Now, he was in conversation with some sort of crime-fighting wunderkind.

'So, how come you're working as a CSI in Salisbury? No offence, but isn't it a bit of a step down from teaching at the FBI?'

She looked away. He watched as she fidgeted with a ring on her right middle finger, twisting it round and round.

'I don't want to share that with you,' she said, finally.

In that moment he saw it. Behind her eyes. An assault? A bad one. Not sexual, but violent. Who did the FBI go after? The really bad ones. The ones who didn't confine their evildoing to a single state. It was her secret. Ford knew all about keeping secrets. He felt for her.

'OK, sorry. Look, we're just glad to have you. Come on. Let's find Alec.'

He took Hannah round the rest of CID and out through a set of grey-painted double doors with a well-kicked steel plate at the foot. The corridor to Forensics was papered with health and safety posters and noticeboards advertising sports clubs, social events and training courses.

Inside, the chatter and buzz of coppers at full pelt was replaced by a sepulchral quiet. Five people were hard at work, staring at computer monitors or into microscopes. Much of the 'hard science' end of forensics had been outsourced to private labs in 2012. But Wiltshire Police had, in Ford's mind, made the sensible decision to preserve as much of an in-house scientific capacity as it could afford.

He pointed to a glassed-in office in the far corner of the room.

'That's Alec's den. He doesn't appear to be in yet.'

'*Au contraire*, Henry!'

The owner of the deep, amused-sounding voice tapped Ford on the shoulder. He turned to greet the forensic team manager, a short, round man wearing wire-framed glasses.

'Morning, Alec.'

Alec clocked the new CSI, but then leaned closer to Ford. 'You OK, Henry?' he murmured, his brows knitted together. 'What with the date, and everything.'

'I'm fine. Let's leave it.'

Alec shrugged. Then his gaze moved to Hannah. 'Dr Fellowes, you're here at last! Welcome, welcome.'

'Thank you, Alec. It's been quite an interesting start to the day.'

Ford said, 'Some idiot was making a nuisance of himself in reception as Hannah was arriving. He's cooling off in one of Ian's capsule hotel rooms in the basement.'

The joviality vanished, replaced by an expression of real concern. 'Oh, my dear young woman. I am so sorry. And on your first day with us, too,' Alec said. 'Why don't you come with me? I'll introduce you to the team and we'll get you set up with a nice quiet desk in the corner. Thanks, Henry. I'll take it from here.'

Ford nodded, eager to get back to his own office and see what the day held. He prayed someone might have been up to no good overnight. Anything to save him from the mountains of forms and reports that he had to either read, write or edit.

'DI Ford? Before you go,' Hannah said.

'Yes?'

'You said I should call you Ford. But Alec just called you Henry.'

'It's a nickname. I got it on my first day here.'

'A nickname. What does it mean?'

'You know. Henry. As in Henry Ford?'

She looked at him, eyebrows raised.

He tried again. 'The car? Model T?'

She smiled at last. A wide grin that showed her teeth, though it didn't reach her eyes. The effect was disconcerting. 'Ha! Yes. That's funny.'

'Right. I have to go. I'm sure we'll bump into each other again.'

'I'm sure, too. I hope there won't be a drunk trying to hit me.'

She smiled, and after a split second he realised it was supposed to be a joke. As he left, he could hear her telling Alec, 'Call me Hannah.'

DAY TWO, 8.59 A.M.

The 999 call had come in just ten minutes earlier: a Cat A G28 – suspected homicide. Having told the whole of Response and Patrol B shift to 'blat' over to the address, Sergeant Natalie Hewitt arrived first at 75 Wyvern Road.

She jumped from her car and spoke into her Airwave radio. 'Sierra Bravo Three-Five, Control.'

'Go ahead, Sierra Bravo Three-Five.'

'Is the ambulance towards?'

'Be about three minutes.'

She ran up the stairs and approached the young couple standing guard at the door to Flat 3.

'Mr and Mrs Gregory, you should go back to your own flat now,' she said, panting. 'I'll have more of my colleagues joining me shortly. Please don't leave the house. We'll be wanting to take your statements.'

'But I've got aerobics at nine thirty,' the woman protested.

Natalie sighed. The public were fantastic at calling in crimes, and occasionally made half-decent witnesses. But it never failed to amaze her how they could also be such *innocents* when it came to the aftermath. This one didn't even seem concerned that her upstairs neighbour and young son had been murdered. Maybe she was in shock. Maybe the husband had kept her out of the flat. Wise bloke.

'I'm afraid you may have to cancel it, just this once,' she said. *You look like you to could afford to. Maybe go and get a fry-up, too, when we're done with you. Put some flesh on your bones.*

The woman retreated to the staircase. Her husband delayed leaving, just for a few seconds.

'We're just shocked,' he said. 'The blood came through our ceiling. That's why I went upstairs to investigate.'

Natalie nodded, eager now to enter the death room and deal with the latest chapter in the Big Book of Bad Things People Do to Each Other.

She swatted at the flies that buzzed towards her. They all came from the room at the end of the dark, narrow hallway. Keeping her eyes on the threadbare red-and-cream runner, alert to anything Forensics might be able to use, she made her way to the kitchen. She supported herself against the opposite wall with her left hand so she could walk, one foot in line with the other, along the right-hand edge of the hall.

The buzzing intensified. And then she caught it: the aroma of death. Sweet-sour top notes overlaying a deeper, darker, rotting-meat stink as body tissues broke down and emitted their gases.

And blood. Or 'claret', in the parlance of the job. She reckoned she'd smelled more of it than a wine expert. This was present in quantity. The husband – what was his name? Rob, that was it. He'd said on the phone it was bad. 'A slaughterhouse' – his exact words.

'Let's find out, then, shall we?' she murmured as she reached the door and entered the kitchen.

As the scene imprinted itself on her retinas, she didn't swear, or invoke the deity, or his son. She used to, in the early days of her career. There'd been enough blasphemy and bad language to have had her churchgoing mum rolling her eyes and pleading with her to 'Watch your language, please, Nat. There's no need.'

She'd become hardened to it over the previous fifteen years. She hoped she still felt a normal human's reaction when she encountered murder scenes, or the remains of those who'd reached the end of their tether and done themselves in. But she left the amateur dramatics to the new kids. She was a sergeant, a rank she'd worked bloody hard for, and she felt a certain restraint went with the territory. So, no swearing.

She did, however, shake her head and swallow hard as she took in the scene in front of her. She'd been a keen photographer in her twenties and found it helpful to see crime scenes as if through a lens: her way of putting some distance between her and whatever horrors the job required her to confront.

In wide-shot, an obscene parody of a Madonna and child. A woman – early thirties, to judge by her face, which was waxy-pale – and a little boy cradled in her lap.

They'd been posed at the edge of a wall-to-wall blood pool, dried and darkened to a deep plum red.

She'd clearly bled out. He wasn't as pale as his mum, but the pink in his smooth little cheeks was gone, replaced by a greenish tinge.

The puddle of blood had spread right across the kitchen floor and under the table, on which half-emptied bags of shopping sagged. The dead woman was slumped with her back against the cooker, legs canted open yet held together at the ankle by her pulled-down jeans.

And the little boy.

Looking for all the world as though he had climbed on to his mother's lap for a cuddle, eyes closed, hands together at his throat as if in prayer. Fair hair. Long and wavy, down to his shoulders, in a girlish style Natalie had noticed some of her friends choose for their sons.

Even in midwinter, flies would find a corpse within the hour. In the middle of a scorching summer like the one southern England was enjoying now, they'd arrived in minutes, laid their eggs and begun feasting in quantity. Maggots crawled and wriggled all over the pair.

As she got closer, Natalie revised her opinion about the cause of death; now, she could see bruises around the throat that screamed strangulation.

There were protocols to be followed. And the first of these was the preservation of life. She was sure the little boy was dead. The skin discolouration and maggots told her that. But there was no way she was going to go down as the sergeant who left a still-living toddler to die in the centre of a murder scene.

Reaching him meant stepping into that lake of congealed blood. Never mind the sneers from CID about the 'woodentops' walking through crime scenes in their size twelves; this was about checking if a little boy had a chance of life.

She pulled out her phone and took half a dozen shots of the bodies. Then she took two long strides towards them, wincing as her boot soles crackled and slid in the coagulated blood.

She crouched and extended her right index and middle fingers, pressing under the little boy's jaw into the soft flesh where the carotid artery ran. She closed her eyes and prayed for a pulse, trying to ignore the smell, and the noise of the writhing maggots and their soft, squishy little bodies as they roiled together in the mess.

After staying there long enough for the muscles in her legs to start complaining, and for her to be certain the little lad was dead, she straightened and reversed out of the blood. She took care to place her feet back in the first set of footprints.

She turned away, looking for some kitchen roll to wipe the blood off her soles, and stared in horror at the wall facing the cooker.

'Oh, shit.'

KEEP READING

Printed in Great Britain
by Amazon